TORONTO
SHORT
STORIES

TORONTO SHORT STORIES

Morris Wolfe and
Douglas Daymond, Editors

Doubleday Canada Limited / Toronto, Canada
Doubleday & Company, Inc. / Garden City, New York
1977

Library of Congress Catalog Card No.: 76-52898
ISBN: 0-385-12848-7 Hardcover
ISBN: 0-385-12848-5 Paperback

FIRST EDITION

Printed and bound in Canada. T.H. Best Printing Company Limited

Design by Robert Garbutt Productions

We are grateful to a number of people for their assistance. Eugene Benson suggested the idea of this book to Douglas Daymond. Barbara Fineberg gathered a great many Toronto Stories for us to read. Michele Ducet helped with the research. Leslie Monkman and Carla Wolfe offered helpful comments about the Introduction. Carla Wolfe also proofread the galleys. Betty Corson and Rick Archbold of Doubleday Canada gave us encouragement and valuable advice throughout.

Contents

Introduction

*The typical Torontonian is about five feet,
nine inches high, with fairly wide shoulders
and a dolichocephalic head with an ear on
each side of it.*

STEPHEN LEACOCK

1

Toronto. The name still arouses feelings of deep resentment among many Canadians who live elsewhere in Canada. The word and the place Toronto continue to unify other Canadians as few things can.

Because Toronto looms so large in the consciousness of so many Canadians, one would assume that it occupies a similarly prominent place in our literature, in our mythology. But that's not the case. Apart from a handful of novels by such writers as Morley Callaghan, Hugh Garner, Graeme Gibson, Richard Wright, and Hugh Hood, and some poetry—especially that of Raymond Souster and Dennis Lee—there's not as much there as one might expect. And most of what is there has appeared in the past ten years.

The comparative lack of "Toronto" literature until now can probably best be explained by the fact that until very recently Canadian society was rural. And, as short story writer Alistair MacLeod has written, even now Canadians find themselves most "recognizable, not in Toronto or Vancouver, but in the dusty streets of Margaret Laurence's Manawaka or in Alice Munro's Jubilee." Most Canadians, he says, "are relative newcomers to the urban experience and this reflects itself in the art produced. [Canadians] are not [yet] 'masters' of the city nor do they feel . . . particularly at ease there as far as the development of their artistic perceptions is concerned." In fact, the only Canadian city that has produced a significant body of literature is Montreal.

We define a "Toronto" short story as one that reflects the character, the texture, the setting, of Toronto in some way. But the fact that a story says something about Toronto hasn't, of course, been sufficient justification for its selection. We have included nothing here either merely for historical reasons or because it supported some preconceived notion of what a collection such as this should contain. Each story had to work first of all as literature: it had to offer some fresh insight or perception; most of all, it had to provide enjoyable reading. Some of the twenty stories we've included are familiar; some are new. Eight are appearing in book form for the first time. Some of the writers included are from Toronto; some aren't. The arrangement of these stories has been determined by length, tone, mood, and pace rather than by the dates when they were written.

Before the 1920s few stories made use of Toronto as a setting. There are some mysteries by writers like John Charles Dent (*The Gerrard Street Mystery and Other Tales*, 1888). And there are some sentimental romances by writers such as *Saturday Night* editor Edmund E. Sheppard in the 1890s and Mazo de la Roche in the years following the First World War. But there's nothing very good before Morley Callaghan. For us, the Toronto short story begins with Callaghan in the 1920s and Patrick Slater in the 1930s—the years when Canada began its transition from a rural to an urban society. Seven of the stories in this book were written between 1923 and 1968; all the rest are more recent.

2

The writers of the stories in this anthology obviously didn't set out to write *Toronto* short stories. They set out to write stories about people who happen to live in, and about events that happen to take place in, Toronto. It's we who've chosen to yoke their stories together under this somewhat artificial title. We've done so because, although it's true that individual stories included here might have taken place in other Canadian, or perhaps even American, cities, collectively the stories do reveal something of the distinctive flavour of Toronto.

For instance, almost all the characters in these stories come from somewhere else—either from another country or from a small town elsewhere in Canada. Those who were born in Toronto usually have parents who were born elsewhere. The narrator in Margaret Atwood's "Rape Fantasies" is a young woman from Leamington. The deaf-mute in David Helwig's "Something for Olivia's Scrapbook I Guess" has hitchhiked to Toronto from a small town in Muskoka after murdering her mother. The girl in Don Bailey's "The Walrus and the Carpenter" is from Orillia. The woman in Irena Friedman's "The Neilson Chocolate Factory" is a divorcée from Montreal. Alex in Robert Fulford's "The Good Wife" is a Hungarian refugee. Sagaboy and his friends in Austin Clarke's "They Heard a Ringing of Bells" are West Indians.

From a distance Toronto looks like a magical place to these people. It's a place where people whose roots and pasts are elsewhere believe they can make new beginnings; it's a place where people believe they can make things right or whole. Up close, however, it becomes just another failed dream. For some—Eagle in Gwendolyn MacEwen's "House of the Whale," for example—it becomes a nightmare. And what life in Toronto comes down to is, not making it, but getting by. The narrator in Matt Cohen's "Death of a Friend" says that, when he first came to the city twelve years earlier, "...Toronto was everything to me: the huge and anonymous arena where I would find myself, remake myself, succeed or fail according to the terms of my most obscure and central dreams. Now . . . it's different. The invisible inner gleam has worn off and Toronto is only the place where I live—a big paunchy complex city where I have somehow put down roots and am satisfied to play out my existence."

Other stories reveal a similar pattern. The young woman

in Margaret Gibson's "The Butterfly Ward" is sent to a Toronto neurological ward from Kitchener in search of a cure for her severe psychological problems. The cure involves her undergoing an excruciatingly painful procedure which results in nothing more than her learning to endure the pain of the tests. Raymond Fraser's "Cookie" describes two Maritimers who have gone down the road to Toronto because they assumed they could earn and save enough money there to finance a trip around the world. But they leave Toronto with less than they had when they arrived. In Gwendolyn Mac-Ewen's "House of the Whale" a young Indian describes his experiences after leaving his tribe in British Columbia to come east to Toronto. He is swallowed Jonah-like by the prejudices and confusion of the big city.

Many of the characters in these stories live in downtown rooming houses or apartments. Almost all of them are single and unattached; the only married couples in the book—Alex and Sylvia in Robert Fulford's "The Good Wife," Olivia and the narrator in David Helwig's "Something for Olivia's Scrapbook I Guess," for example—have unsatisfactory relationships. Few of the stories have families in them, and it's significant that two that do, Shirley Faessler's "Henye" and David Lewis Stein's "The Old Lady's Money," are about the Toronto Jewish community. First-generation Jewish immigrants replaced the ghettoes of Eastern Europe from which they'd fled with new self-imposed ghettoes in which they recreated a kind of *shtetl* experience. At the heart of that ghetto experience is the family. Later immigrant groups have also found it necessary to establish ghettoes. "A sort of small town," as Alistair MacLeod puts it, "containing hundreds of recognizable faces, familiar shops and sounds, and boundaries that are recognizably real and which tend to contain as well as to exclude."

David Lewis Stein's "The Old Lady's Money" concerns Aaron's struggle to break free of these boundaries. His ambition, like that of so many educated second-generation Torontonians of that period—the early sixties—is to graduate to the Toronto of England (London) or to the Toronto of the United States (New York). It's that latter ambition that Jim Christy so delightfully parodies in "How I Became Champ."

3

Setting is economically used in these stories. It's not that setting isn't important so much as that the writer of a short story often makes limited references to the physical landscape or geography of the place he or she is writing about. In Margaret Atwood's "Rape Fantasies" it's the CN Tower. In Morley Callaghan's "The Wedding Dress" it's a rooming house on Wellesley. In Hugh Garner's "The Premeditated Death of Samuel Glover" it's a busy corner on Adelaide Street. However, by the end of the book one has encountered many of Toronto's most familiar landmarks. There are references to the island ferry, the city's ravines, Honest Ed's, Casa Loma, the Ontario Hospital on Queen Street, Rosedale, the U of T campus, the Parliament Buildings, and many of Toronto's streets.

The anthology also offers us a sense of Toronto in transition. The gallows at the foot of Berkeley Street, which are described in Patrick Slater's "Adrift," are long gone. So are fine watering places like the Babloor and the old Batts Club at the corner of Huron and Willcocks. Sunnyside is gone, and the McCaul Street Synagogue. In stories like Michael Smith's "Town and Country" and Irena Friedman's "The Neilson Chocolate Factory" one becomes aware of various ethnic groups in the city leapfrogging over one another in an upwardly mobile dash to the suburbs—suburbs that originally began as WASP preserves. Kensington is in one story a Jewish market, in a later story a Portuguese market. The Jews have moved out and up in the world. The reverse of this pattern occurs in Alice Munro's "Dance of the Happy Shades," where we meet the downwardly mobile Rosedale spinster, Miss Marsalles.

There's also a lot about Toronto that's missing from these stories. Suburban life, for instance, is present only in a passing way in a story like "Town and Country." We have no sense of a child's perspective on the city. There's no feeling of what it's like from the inside to be Greek or Italian or Portuguese or East Indian. At least nothing to compare with the *first-hand* view we get of what it's like to be black or Jewish or an Indian in Toronto. Undoubtedly there will be stories that reflect these immigrants' experiences, too, once their children—like the David Lewis Steins and Shirley Faesslers—have grown up writing in English. Missing, too, is a clear picture of Toronto as the centre of English-Canadian cultural life. The view of that life we get in stories such as Matt Cohen's "Death of a Friend" and Robert Fulford's "The Good Wife" is one of intellectual and emotional pretension and sterility. It's a world of artists and writers who are incapable of getting in touch with themselves, let alone with one another, and whose imaginative energy is largely devoted to the erection of barriers to protect themselves.

4

The mood, the tone, of many of these stories is melancholy; the thoughts and comments of characters are frequently tinged with regret. Regret for what they've left behind. Regret that things in the present are at best merely tolerable. Sagaboy in Austin Clarke's "They Heard a Ringing of Bells" tells his friends how lost he sometimes feels in the "blasted five-dollars-a-week rat-trap [he] lives in, on Spadina...." "You know something?" he says. "I have never seen *one* blasted bird in this place yet, and I now remember that, for the first time! Back home, the birds chirping nice songs and then they run off to sleep. And the trees, trees all round where we was sitting down, trees dress up in a more greener coat o' green that this grass."

It seems fitting that all but five of the stories in this anthology should have a first-person narrator. Somehow the world, perhaps especially the world of the large city, has become too complicated for omniscient narrators—narrators who know and understand and can explain the meaning of things. Instead what we get is a kind of fictional autobiography—first-person narrators groping to make some sense of their own small worlds.

Stories such as Marilyn Powell's Toronto Gothic piece, "Home Grown in the East End," and Jim Christy's fantasy, "How I Became Champ," provide a nice change of pace and mood from the documentary feel of many of the other stories. And even though they *are* documentaries, so do Patrick Slater's "Adrift" and Hugh Hood's "Recollections of the Works Department." Although "Adrift," which was written in the 1930s, is about hangings, fire, and death by plague in nineteenth-century Toronto, it has a nostalgic tone that reflects our wish to believe that Toronto then was a simpler and happier place. Hugh Hood's "Recollections of the Works Department," set in a Toronto of only twenty-five years ago, has an even more pleasantly nostalgic quality.

5

These stories do not offer a complete picture of life in Toronto; no collection of stories could. What they do offer is an opportunity to observe the city as reflected by the literary imaginations of twenty short story riters. Life in their Toronto is anything but dull. It's difficult. (Indeed it's almost as difficult as those who resent Toronto could wish it to be.) It's often sad and painful. But it isn't dull.

Until fifteen years ago there were really only two *Toronto* writers—Morley Callaghan and Hugh Garner. More recently—partly because of cultural nationalism, partly because Canadian society has become increasingly urbanized, and perhaps mainly because Toronto has emerged as a cosmopolitan centre—there has been an explosion of writing in and about this city. This is an exciting time in the literary life of Toronto. *Toronto Short Stories* is proof of that.

Morris Wolfe   Douglas Daymond
Toronto
January, 1977

Rape Fantasies

Margaret Atwood

THE WAY THEY'RE going on about it in the magazines you'd think it was just invented, and not only that but it's something terrific, like a vaccine for cancer. They put it in capital letters on the front cover and inside they have these questionnaires like the ones they used to have about whether you were a good enough wife or an endomorph or an ectomorph, remember that? with the scoring upside down on page 73, and then these numbered do-it-yourself dealies, you know? RAPE, TEN THINGS TO DO ABOUT IT, like it was ten new hairdos or something. I mean, what's so new about it?

So at work they all have to talk about it because no matter what magazine you open, there it is, staring you right between the eyes, and they're beginning to have it on the television too. Personally I'd prefer a June Allyson movie anytime but they don't make them any more and they don't even have them that much on the Late Show. For instance, day before yesterday, that would be Wednesday, thank god it's Friday as they say, we were sitting around in the women's lunch room —the *lunch* room, I mean you'd think you could get some peace

1

and quiet in there—and Chrissy closes up the magazine she's been reading and says, "How about it, girls, do you have rape fantasies?"

The four of us were having our game of bridge the way we always do, and I had a bare twelve points counting the singleton with not that much of a bid in anything. So I said one club, hoping Sondra would remember about the one club convention, because the time before when I used that she thought I really meant clubs and she bid us up to three, and all I had was four little ones with nothing higher than a six, and we went down two and on top of that we were vulnerable. She is not the world's best bridge player. I mean, neither am I but there's a limit.

Darlene passed but the damage was done. Sondra's head went round like it was on ball bearings and she said, "*What* fantasies?"

"Rape fantasies," Chrissy said. She's a receptionist and she looks like one, she's pretty but cool as a cucumber, like she's been painted all over with nail polish if you know what I mean. Varnished. "It says here all women have rape fantasies."

"For Chrissake, I'm eating an egg sandwich," I said, "and I bid one club and Darlene passed."

"You mean, like some guy jumping you in an alley or something," Sondra said. She was eating her lunch, we all eat our lunches during the game, and she bit into a piece of that celery she always brings and started to chew away on it with this thoughtful expression in her eyes and I knew we might as well pack it in as far as the game was concerned.

"Yeah, sort of like that," Chrissy said. She was blushing a little, you could see it even under her makeup.

"I don't think you should go out alone at night," Darlene said, "you put yourself in a position," and I may have been mistaken but she was looking at me. She's the oldest, she's forty-one though you wouldn't know it and neither does she, but I looked it up in the employees' file. I like to guess a person's age and then look it up to see if I'm right, I let myself have an extra pack of cigarettes if I am, though I'm trying to cut down. I figure it's harmless as long as you don't tell.

I mean, not everyone has access to that file, it's more or less confidential. But it's all right if I tell you, I don't expect you'll ever meet her, though you never know, it's a small world. Anyway.

"For *heaven's* sake, it's only *Toronto*," Greta said. She worked in Detroit for three years and she never lets you forget it, it's like she thinks she's a war hero or something, we should all admire her just for the fact that she's still walking this earth, though she was really living in Windsor the whole time, she just worked in Detroit. Which for me doesn't really count. It's where you sleep, right?

"Well, do you?" Chrissy said. She was obviously dying to tell us about hers but she wasn't about to go first, she's cautious, that one.

"I certainly don't," Darlene said, and she wrinkled up her nose, like this, and I had to laugh. "I think it's disgusting." She's divorced, I read that in the file too, she never talks about it. It must've been years ago anyway. She got up and went over to the coffee machine and turned her back on us as though she wasn't going to have anything more to do with it.

"Well," Greta said. I could see it was going to be between her and Chrissy. They're both blondes, I don't mean that in a bitchy way but they do try to outdress each other. Greta would like to get out of Filing, she'd like to be a receptionist too so she could meet more people. You don't meet much of anyone in Filing except other people in Filing. Me, I don't mind it so much. I have outside interests.

"Well," Greta said, "I sometimes think about, you know my apartment? It's got this little balcony. I like to sit out there in the summer and I have a few plants out there. I never bother that much about locking the door to the balcony, it's one of those sliding glass ones, I'm on the eighteenth floor for heaven's sake, I've got a good view of the lake and the CN Tower and all. But I'm sitting around one night in my house-coat, watching TV with my shoes off, you know how you do, and I see this guy's feet coming down past the window, and the next thing you know he's standing on the balcony, he's let himself down by a rope with a hook on the end of it from the floor above, that's the nineteenth, and before I can even get up off the chesterfield he's inside the apartment. He's all dressed in black with black gloves on"—I knew right away what show she got the black gloves off because I saw the same one—"and then he, well, you know."

"You know what?" Chrissy said, but Greta said, "And afterwards he tells me that he goes all over the outside of the apartment building like that, from one floor to another, with his rope and his hook . . . and then he goes out to the balcony and tosses his rope, and he climbs up it and disappears."

"Just like Tarzan," I said, but nobody laughed. "Is that all?" Chrissy said. "Don't you ever think about, well, I think about being in the bathtub, with no clothes on . . ."

"So who takes a bath in their clothes?" I said, you have to admit it's stupid when you come to think of it, but she just went on, ". . . . with lots of bubbles, what I use is Vitabath, it's more expensive but it's so relaxing, and my hair pinned up, and the door opens and this fellow's standing there . . ."

"How'd he get in?" Greta said.

"Oh, I don't know, through a window or something. Well, I can't very well get out of the bathtub, the bathroom's too small and besides he's blocking the doorway, so I just *lie* there, and he starts to very slowly take his own clothes off, and then he gets into the bathtub with me."

"Don't you scream or anything?" said Darlene. She'd come back with her cup of coffee, she was getting really interested. "I'd scream like bloody murder."

"Who'd hear me?" Chrissy said. "Beides, all the articles say it's better not to resist, that way you don't get hurt."

"Anyway you might get bubbles up your nose," I said, "from the deep breathing," and I swear all four of them looked at me like I was in bad taste, like I'd insulted the Virgin Mary or something. I mean, I don't see what's wrong with a little joke now and then. Life's too short, right?

"Listen," I said, "those aren't *rape* fantasies. I mean, you aren't getting *raped,* it's just some guy you haven't met formally who happens to be more attractive than Derek Cummins"—he's the Assistant Manager, he wears elevator shoes or at any rate they have these thick soles and he has this funny way of talking, we call him Derek Duck—"and you have a good time. Rape is when they've got a knife or something and you don't want to."

"So what about you, Estelle," Chrissy said, she was miffed because I laughed at her fantasy, she thought I was putting her down. Sondra was miffed too, by this time she'd finished her celery and she wanted to tell about hers, but she hadn't got in fast enough.

"All right, let me tell you one," I said. "I'm walking down this dark street at night and this fellow comes up and grabs my arm. Now it so happens that I have a plastic lemon in my purse, you know how it always says you should carry a plastic lemon in your purse? I don't really do it. I tried it once but the darn thing leaked all over my chequebook, but in this fantasy I have one, and I say to him, "You're intending to rape me, right?" and he nods, so I open my purse to get the plastic lemon, and I can't find it! My purse is full of all this junk, Kleenex and cigarettes and my change purse and my lipstick and my driver's license, you know the kind of stuff; so I ask him to hold out his hands, like this, and I pile all this junk into them and down at the bottom there's the plastic lemon, and I can't get the top off. So I hand it to him and he's very obliging, he twists the top off and hands it back to me, and I squirt him in the eye."

I hope you don't think that's too vicious. Come to think of it, it is a bit mean, especially when he was so polite and all.

"*That's* your rape fantasy?" Chrissy says. "I don't believe it."

"She's a card," Darlene says, she and I are the ones that've been here the longest and she never will forget the time I got drunk at the office party and insisted I was going to dance under the table instead of on top of it, I did a sort of Cossack number but then I hit my head on the bottom of the table— actually it was a desk—when I went to get up, and I knocked myself out cold. She's decided that's the mark of an original mind and she tells everyone new about it and I'm not sure that's fair. Though I did do it.

"I'm being totally honest," I say, I always am and they know it. There's no point in being anything else, is the way I look at it, and sooner or later the truth will out so you might as well not waste the time, right? "You should hear the one about the Easy-Off Oven Cleaner."

But that was the end of the lunch hour, with one bridge game shot to hell, and the next day we spent most of the time arguing over whether to start a new game or play out the hands we had left over from the day before, so Sondra never did get a chance to tell about her rape fantasy.

It started me thinking though, about my own rape fantasies. Maybe I'm abnormal or something, I mean I have fantasies about handsome strangers coming in through the window too, like Mr. Clean, I wish one would, please god somebody without flat feet and big sweat marks on his shirt, and over five feet five, believe me being tall is a handicap though it's getting better, tall guys are starting to like someone whose nose reaches higher than their belly button. But if you're being totally honest you can't count those as rape fantasies. In a real rape fantasy, what you should feel is this anxiety, like when you think about your apartment building catching on fire and whether you should use the elevator or the stairs or maybe just stick your head under a wet towel, and you try to remember everything you've read about what to do but you can't decide.

For instance, I'm walking along this dark street at night and this short, ugly fellow comes up and grabs my arm, and not only is he ugly, you know, with a sort of puffy nothing face, like those fellows you have to talk to in the bank when your account's overdrawn—of course I don't mean they're all like that—but he's absolutely covered in pimples. So he gets me pinned against the wall, he's short but he's heavy, and he starts to undo himself and the zipper gets stuck. I mean, one of the most significant moments in a girl's life, it's almost like getting married or having a baby or something, and he sticks the zipper.

So I say, kind of disgusted, "Oh for Chrissake," and he starts to cry. He tells me he's never been able to get anything right in his entire life, and this is the last straw, he's going to go jump off a bridge.

"Look," I say, I feel so sorry for him, in my rape fantasies I always end up feeling sorry for the guy, I mean there has to be something *wrong* with them, if it was Clint Eastwood it'd be different but worse luck it never is. I was the kind of little girl who buried dead robins, know what I mean? It used to drive my mother nuts, she didn't like me touching them, because of the germs I guess. So I say, "Listen, I know how you feel. You really should do something about those pimples, if you got rid of them you'd be quite good looking, honest; then you wouldn't have to go around doing stuff like this. I had them myself once," I say, to comfort him, but in fact I did, and it ends up I give him the name of my old dermatologist, the one I had in high school, that was back in Leamington, except I used to go to St. Catherines for the dermatologist. I'm telling you, I was really lonely when I first came here; I thought it was going to be such a big adventure and all, but it's a lot harder to meet people in a city. But I guess it's different for a guy.

Or I'm lying in bed with this terrible cold, my face is all swollen up, my eyes are red and my nose is dripping like a leaky tap, and this fellow comes in through the window and *he* has a terrible cold too, it's a new kind of flu that's been going around. So he says, "I'b goig do rabe you"—I hope you don't mind me holding my nose like this but that's the way I imagine it—and he lets out this terrific sneeze, which slows him down a bit, also I'm no object of beauty myself, you'd have to be some kind of pervert to want to rape someone with a cold like mine, it'd be like raping a bottle of LePage's Mucilage the way my nose is running. He's looking wildly around the room, and I realize it's because he doesn't have a piece of Kleenex! "Id's ride here," I say, and I pass him the Kleenex, god knows why he even bothered to get out of bed, you'd think if you were going to go around climbing in windows you'd wait till you were healthier, right? I mean, that takes a certain amount of energy. So I ask him why doesn't he let me fix him a Neo-Citran and scotch, that's what I always take, you still have the cold but you don't feel it, so I do and we end up watching the Late Show together. I mean, they aren't all sex maniacs, the rest of the time they must lead a normal life. I figure they enjoy watching the Late Show just like anybody else.

I do have a scarier one though ... where the fellow says he's hearing angel voices that're telling him he's got to kill me, you know, you read about things like that all the time in the papers. In this one I'm not in the apartment where I live now, I'm back in my mother's house in Leamington and the fellow's been hiding in the cellar, he grabs my arm when I go down-stairs to get a jar of jam and he's got hold of the axe too, out of the garage, that one is really scary. I mean, what do you say to a nut like that?

So I start to shake but after a minute I get control of myself and I say, is he sure the angel voices have got the right person, because I hear the same angel voices and they've been telling me for some time that I'm going to give birth to the reincarna-tion of St. Anne who in turn has the Virgin Mary and right after that comes Jesus Christ and the end of the world, and he wouldn't want to interfere with that, would he?· So he gets confused and listens some more, and then he asks for a sign and I show him my vaccination mark, you can see it's sort of an odd-shaped one, it got infected because I scratched the top off, and that does it, he apologizes and climbs out of the coal chute again, which is how he got in in the first place, and I say to myself there's some advantage in having been brought up a Catholic even though I haven't been to church since they changed the service into English, it just isn't the same, you might as well be a Protestant. I must write to Mother and tell her to nail up that coal chute, it always has bothered me. Funny, I couldn't tell you at all what this man looks like but I know exactly what kind of shoes he's wearing, because that's the last I see of him, his shoes going up the coal chute, and they're the old-fashioned kind that lace up the ankles, even though he's a young fellow. That's strange, isn't it?

Let me tell you though I really sweat until I see him safely out of there and I go upstairs right away and make myself a cup of tea. I don't think about that one much. My mother always said you shouldn't dwell on unpleasant things and I generally agree with that, I mean, dwelling on them doesn't make them go away. Though not dwelling on them doesn't make them go away either, when you come to think of it.

Sometimes I have these short ones where the fellow grabs my arm but I'm really a Kung-Fu expert, can you believe it, in real life I'm sure it would just be a conk on the head and that's that, like getting your tonsils out, you'd wake up and it would be all over except for the sore places, and you'd be lucky if your neck wasn't broken or something, I could never even hit the volleyball in gym and a volleyball is fairly large, you know?—and I just go *zap* with my fingers into his eyes and that's it, he falls over, or I flip him against a wall or something. But I could never really stick my fingers in anyone's eyes, could you? It would feel like hot Jello and I don't even like cold Jello, just thinking about it gives me the creeps. I feel a bit guilty about that one, I mean how would you like walking around knowing someone's been blinded for life because of you?

But maybe it's different for a guy.

The most touching one I have is when the fellow grabs my arm and I say, sad and kind of dignified, "You'd be raping a corpse." That pulls him up short and I explain that I've just found out I have leukemia and the doctors have only given me a few months to live. That's why I'm out pacing the streets alone at night, I need to think, you know, come to terms with myself. I don't really have leukemia but in the fantasy I do, I guess I chose that particular disease because a girl in my grade four class died of it, the whole class sent her flowers when she was in the hospital. I didn't understand then that she was going to die and I wanted to have leukemia too so I could get flowers. Kids are funny, aren't they? Well, it turns out that he has leukemia himself, and *he* only has a few months to live, that's why he's going around raping people, he's very bitter because he's so young and his life is being taken from him before he's really lived it. So we walk along gently under the street lights, it's spring and sort of misty, and we end up going for coffee, we're happy we've found the only other person in the world who can understand what we're going through, it's almost like fate, and after a while we just sort of look at each other and our hands touch, and he comes back with me and moves into my apartment and we spend our last months together before we die, we just sort of don't wake up in the morning, though I've never decided which one of us gets to die first. If it's him I have to go on and fantasize about the funeral, if it's me I don't have to worry about that, so it just about depends on how tired I am at the time. You may not believe this but sometimes I even start crying. I cry at the ends of movies, even the ones that aren't all that sad, so I guess it's the same thing. My mother's like that too.

The funny thing about these fantasies is that the man is always someone I don't know, and the statistics in the magazines, well, most of them anyway, they say it's often someone you do know, at least a little bit, like your boss or something—I mean, it wouldn't be *my* boss, he's over sixty and I'm sure he couldn't rape his way out of a paper bag, poor old thing, but it might be someone like Derek Duck, in his elevator shoes, perish the thought—or someone you just met, who invites you up for a drink, it's getting so you can hardly be sociable any more, and how are you supposed to meet people if you can't trust them even that basic amount? You can't spend your whole life in the Filing Department or cooped up in your own apartment with all the doors and windows locked and the shades down. I'm not what you would call a drinker but I like to get out now and then for a drink or two in a nice place, even if I am by myself, I'm with Women's Lib on that even though I can't agree with a lot of other things they say. Like here for instance, the waiters all know me and if anyone you know, bothers me.... I don't know why I'm telling you all this, except I think it helps you get to know a person, especially at first, hearing some of the things they think about. At work they call me the office worry wart, but it isn't so much like worrying, it's more like figuring out what you should do in an emergency, like I said before.

Anyway, another thing about it is that there's a lot of conversation, in fact I spend most of my time, in the fantasy that is, wondering what I'm going to say and what he's going to say. I think it would be better if you could get a conversation going. Like, how could a fellow do that to a person he's just had a long conversation with, once you let them know you're human, you have a life too, I don't see how they could go ahead with it, right? I mean, I know it happens but I just don't understand it. That's the part I really don't understand.

1975

The Premeditated Death of Samuel Glover

Hugh Garner

IT'S BEEN NOTHING but questions all day at the office. Every few minutes one of the other draftsmen would come over to my board and ask me about Sam's death. "What happened last night? Were you with him? Did it knock him down? Run over him? How'd he look? Was there much blood?"

They have no idea what it's like seeing a friend get killed like that, and having to answer all the questions by the police, the taxi company lawyer, and then by the fellows at work the next day. I'm going to tell it once more, the whole thing, and then I'm through.

Every night at five o'clock for the last seven or eight years Sam Glover and I have taken the elevator together, going home. Sam would buy his evening paper in the lobby, and then we'd walk up the street as far as Queen where we separated, Sam to take a west-bound streetcar, and me to take one going east.

It got to be a habit, this three-block walk, and I enjoyed it because Sam was an interesting old fellow to talk to. He was a bachelor who lived with a married sister away out in the west end of town. From some of the things he told me on these short walks I learned that he was a believer in things like fate and premeditation. It was his favorite subject, and sometimes he'd point to people who passed us on the street and say, "There goes a man hurrying to his fate," or "He wants to reach his rendezvous, that one."

When I'd laugh, he'd say, "You'll find out some day that it's no joke. I've seen it happen. Every man is predestined to meet his death at a time and place already chosen, my boy."

I'd laugh and shake my head.

It was about three years ago that Sam told me where he was going to die. We were waiting for the lights to change at the intersection of Adelaide Street, when Sam said, "This is the place where fate is going to catch up to me."

I looked down at him and laughed, thinking he was joking. He was the type of mousy little guy who would joke like that—or dismember a corpse.

"You may laugh, son, but it's true," he asserted in the good-natured, yet serious, way he had.

"Do you mean to tell me that you're going to be killed on this corner?" I asked.

"That's right," he answered soberly.

When the lights changed, we crossed the street. I said to Sam, "If you know that you're going to be killed here, why do you take this way home? You could walk a block east or west and take the streetcar from there."

"It wouldn't be much use trying to avoid it," he answered. "Some day I'd forget, or have some business to transact down here ——"

"Well, suppose you decided not to die at all. You could move to another town and live forever."

"Nobody lives forever," he answered patiently. "You can't avoid your fate. This is where it will happen, and nothing I can do will prevent it. I'm just hoping that it won't be for some time yet." He looked up at me and smiled apologetically, but I could see that he meant every word.

After that I brought the subject up occasionally as we were

crossing Adelaide Street, kidding him about being short-sighted, and about getting killed before his time if he wasn't careful. He would only smile at me and say, "You wait and see."

Last night we left the office as usual, about two minutes to five, in order to beat the rush to the elevators. Sam bought his paper in the lobby, and we went out into the street.

As we brushed through the five-o'clock crowd I asked Sam how his dyke drawings for the Mountview Refinery were coming along, and he told me he expected to finish them in a week; he was only waiting for some new tank specifications from McGuire, one of the engineers.

Looking up into the blue sky above the buildings I said, "It's going to be a nice evening. A change from the rain we've been having."

"Yes, it is. I'm going to do a little lawn bowling tonight," he answered. "It'll be my first chance this year. The greens have been a mess up to now."

When we reached the corner of Adelaide the lights were in our favor and we began to cross with the crowd. They changed from green to amber when we were halfway across, but we still had plenty of time. He stuck close to me as he always did. I saw this taxi cut around the traffic and begin to cross the intersection as soon as it got the green light, so I shouted to Sam and ran the last few yards to the sidewalk.

I looked around and saw the taxi pick him up and throw him with a sickening plop against a hydrant about twenty feet from the corner. There was the scream of the taxi's brakes and a lot of yelling from the crowd.

By the time I got there two men had laid Sam out on the sidewalk. Everybody was crowding around to get a better look at him. He was dead, of course. One side of his head was squashed like the soft spot in an orange.

A policeman butted his way through the crowd and asked what had happened. The hack driver came over from his car and told the policeman that he hadn't had a chance, this old man ran right in front of his cab. He seemed to be a nice young fellow, and he wanted us all to believe him. I told the policeman I was a friend of Sam's, and that I'd seen the accident. I assured the driver that it wasn't his fault.

The taxi company lawyer came to my place later in the evening and questioned me about the accident. "I can't understand why he'd turn around and run the other way," he kept on saying.

"I've told you it wasn't your driver's fault, so why do you keep asking me questions like that?"

"O.K. I'm only trying to dope this thing out in case they have an inquest," he said.

If they have an inquest, I'm going to tell the truth. I've been thinking it over and I feel sure that Sam would have wanted it that way.

I had nothing against the old fellow, but after listening for so long to him bragging about knowing where he was going to die, it seemed I had to find out whether he was right or not. When I shouted at him to turn back, it wasn't me talking at all. Call it fate or predestination, or what you like, but that's what killed Sam Glover.

1952

Recollections of the Works Department

Hugh Hood

IN THE SPRING of 1952, six weeks after I finished my M.A. courses and involved myself in further graduate studies, I decided that I'd have to find a better summer job.

I had been working for the English publisher, Thomas Nelson and Sons, as a stockroom boy. The pay was low, and the work remarkably hard. I had only been on the job ten days, but after an afternoon stacking cases of *The Highroads Dictionary* (familiar to every Ontario school child) ninety-six copies to the case, in piles ten cases high, I saw that this state of affairs could not go on. These packing cases were made of heavy cardboard, strongly stapled and bound; they weighed seventy-five pounds each and they had to be piled carefully in a complicated stacking system. You had to fling the top row of cases into the air, much as you'd launch a basketball. I started to look for something less strenuous.

At length an official of the National Employment Service who handled summer placements at Hart House, a Mr. Halse, a man remembered by generations of Varsity types suggested that I try to get on the city. I took an after-noon off from Thomas Nelson's and went up to the City Hall, to Room 302, a big room on the west side with a pleasant high ceiling. I was received with courtesy and attention, and after filling out some forms I got a job as a labourer in the Works Department, Roadways Division, payday on Wednesdays, hours eight to five, report to Foreman Brown at Number Two Yard on College Street tomorrow morning, thank you! I stood at the counter a little out of breath at the speed with which I'd got what I came for.

"You're not very big," said the clerk at the counter. "Are you sure you can handle a pick and shovel?" As the wages were twice what I'd been getting, I thought I'd try it and see.

"I can handle it," I said. I've never seen anybody killing him-self at the pick-and-shovel dodge. I asked the clerk for the address on College Street and, oddly enough, he didn't know it.

"But you can't miss it," he said. "It's next to the Fire Hall, three blocks west of Spadina. Ask to see Mr. Brown. And you'd better get on the job on time, the first day at least."

I thanked him and strolled back to Thomas Nelson's where I explained that I'd found something that paid better, and would they mind letting me go at the end of the day. They didn't seem surprised.

"You've got three days' money coming," said the stockroom superintendent dolefully. He sighed. "I don't know how it is. We can't keep anybody in that job." I said nothing about the cases of dictionaries.

Although it was the middle of May, the next morning was brisk, a bright sunny day with the promise of warmth in the afternoon. I was glad that I'd worn a couple of sweaters as I came along College Street looking for Number Two Yard. It wasn't hard to find. It stood and still stands just west of the Fire Hall halfway between Spadina and Bathurst, on the south side of College. It's the main downtown service centre for roads and sidewalks, responsible for the area bounded by Bathurst, Jarvis, Bloor, and the waterfront. Any holes or cuts in the roadway, any broken sidewalks, or any new sidewalks not provided by contractors, are tended by workmen from this Yard. It also serves as a reception desk for calls connected with trees, sewers, and drains from all over town. There's always a watchman on duty to attend to such matters, day or night.

I walked into the office and stood next to a washbasin in the corner, feeling a little nervous. Most of the other men on the crew were ten years older than I, although I spotted a couple my own age. None of them looked like students, even the young ones; they were all heavily tanned and they all discussed their mysterious affairs in hilarious shouts. There was a counter in front of me, and behind it some office space with three desks, a space heater, some bundles of engineers' plans of the streets hanging in rolls above the windows. It was the kind of room in which no woman had ever been, but it was very clean.

Outside a green International quarter-ton pickup with the Works Department plate on the door came smartly into the Yard. A one-armed man got out and began to shout abusively at the windows of the Fire Hall. This was the foreman, Charlie Brown, who conducted a running war against the firemen because they persisted in parking their cars, of which they had a great many, in his Yard. He bawled a few more curses at the face of the Fire Captain which was glued to a third-storey window, and came inside, immediately fixing his eyes, which were brown, small, and very sharp, on me.

"Goddam-college-kids-no-bloody-good," he shouted irritably, running it all together into a single word; it was a stock phrase. He glared at me pityingly. "Where the hell are your boots?" I was wearing a pair of low canvas shoes of the type then known disparagingly as 'fruit boots.'

"Cut 'em to bits in five minutes!" he exclaimed, quite rightly. I wore them to work one day later on, and the edge of the shovel took the soles of them in under five minutes.

"Go across the street to the Cut-Rate Store. Tell them Charlie sent you. Get them to give you sweat socks and boots. You can pay for them when you draw some money." I tried to say something but he cut me off abruptly and as I went out

I could hear him mumbling, "Goddam-college-kids-no-bloody-good."

I had a good look at him as he banged noisily around the office when I came back wearing my stiff new boots. He was a burly man, about five-eleven, with a weathered face, a short stump of a right arm—the crew called him 'One Punch Brown' —a pipe usually in his mouth. He was the kindest boss I ever had on one of those summer jobs; there was no reason for him to care about my shoes. The workmen cursed him behind his back but they knew that he didn't push them too hard. And yet he managed to get the necessary minimum of work out of them. I found out, purely by accident, that the way to make him like you was to say as little as possible. It was fear that made me answer him in monosyllables but it suited him.

Charlie had four men in the office with him and three gangs of labourers out on various jobs, widely separated in the midtown district he was responsible for. In the office were an assistant foreman named George—I can't remember his last name—and a clerk named Eddie Doucette who sometimes chauffeured Charlie around town. Usually Charlie drove himself, and how he could spin that little International, stump and all; he used the stump to help steer, along with the good arm.

Then there were two patrolmen who kept checking the streets and alleys in our district, reporting any damage to the roads and sidewalks, and the condition of any recently accomplished repairs. Johnny Pawlak was one of them, a slope-shouldered rangy guy of thirty-three or -four, a bowler and softball player, the organizer of all the baseball pools. The other was called Bill Tennyson, a lean, wiry, chronically dissatisfied griper, always in trouble over his non-support of his family, and half-disliked and suspected by the rest of the men in the office for vague reasons. Finally there were the three gangs out on the job: Wall's gang, Mitch's gang, and Harris's gang. Wall ran a taut ship, Harris an unhappy ship, and Mitch a happy one. I never worked for Wall, but I did the others, and the difference was wonderful.

When I got back from the Cut-Rate Store it was already

half-past eight. "What are we going to do with this kid?" I heard Charlie Brown ask rhetorically as I came into the office.

"Aimé's still off," said George softly. "You could send him out with Bill and Danny." They stared at me together.

"Ever handled a shovel?"

"Yes."

"Go and help with the coal-ass."

"Coal-ass?"

"Do you see those men and that truck?" They pointed out the windows. Across the Yard beside a couple of piles of sand and gravel a stubby old guy and a man my own age were sitting, smoking idly, on the running-board of a city dump-truck.

"Go out with them today. And take it easy with the shovel or you'll hurt your hands."

I left the office and walked over to tell the two men, Bill Eagleson and Danny Foster, that I was coming with them.

"What's your name?"

"Hood."

"All right, Hoody," said the older man, Bill, "grab a shovel." After a moment he and Danny stood off and studied my style.

"Do much shovelling?"

"Not a hell of a lot, no."

"Swing it like this, look!" They taught me how, and there really was an easy way to do it, one of the most useful things I've ever learned, a natural arc through which to swing the weight without straining the muscles. It was the same with a pick or a sledge; the thing was to let the head of the instrument supply the power, just like a smooth golf swing.

When we had enough sand and gravel, we yanked two planks out of a pile and made a ramp up to the tailgate.

"We'll put on the coal-ass," said Bill Eagleson.

"What's that?"

"Cold asphalt. It's liquid in the barrel and dries in the air. We use it for temporary patches."

Danny and I rolled an oil drum of this stuff around to the bottom of the ramp. Then we worked it up to the tailgate and into a wooden cradle so that one end of the drum was flush with the end of the truck. Bill screwed a spigot into the end of the drum and we were all set.

"You're the smallest, you sit in the middle," they said flatly.

Apparently Danny and the absent Aimé fought over this every day. When we had squeezed into the front seat, Bill checked over the list of breaks in the roadway and we set out. It was already nine o'clock.

As we drove slowly along, the barrel bouncing and clanging in the back, they told me that our job was to apply temporary patches where damage had been reported by the patrolmen or a citizen, to save the city money on lawsuits. The idea was to get the patch down as soon as possible. They weren't meant to be permanent but they had to last for a while.

We stopped first behind some railway sidings on the Esplanade, next to the Saint Lawrence Market, to fix some shallow potholes. Bill filled a large tin watering-can with coal-ass and spread the black tarry liquid in the hole. Then Danny and I filled it with gravel. Then more coal-ass, then a layer of sand, and finally a third coat of the cold asphalt to top off.

"It dries in the air," said Danny with satisfaction, "and tomorrow you'd need a pick to get it out of there." He was quite right. It was an amazingly good way to make quick repairs that would last indefinitely. From the Esplanade we headed uptown to Gerrard Street between Bay and Yonge where we filled a small cut in the sidewalk. Then Bill parked the truck in the lot behind the old Kresge's store on Yonge.

"Time for coffee," we all said at once. We sat at the lunch counter in Kresge's for half an hour, kidding the waitresses, and I began to realize that we had no boss, that Charlie wasn't checking on us in any way and that Bill had only the nominal authority that went with his years and his drivership. Nobody ever bothered you. Nobody seemed to care how long you spent over a given piece of work, and yet the work all got done, sooner or later, and not badly either. If you go to the corner of St. Joseph and Bay, on the east side, you can see patches that we put in nine years ago, as sound as the day they were laid down. By and large, the taxpayers got their money's worth, although it certainly wasn't done with maximum expedition or efficiency.

When we'd finished our coffee it was obviously much too late to start anything before lunch, so Bill and I waited in the truck while Danny shopped around in Kresge's for a cap. He came back with something that looked like a cross between a railwayman's hat and a housepainter's, a cotton affair that oddly suited him. We drove back to the yard, arriving about eleven forty-five, in comfortable time for lunch. We were allowed an hour for lunch but it always ran to considerably more. The three big gangs didn't come into the Yard except on payday, unless they were working close by. It seemed to be a point of protocol to stay away from the Yard as long as possible. Each gang had a small portable shed on wheels, in which the tools, lamps, and so forth could be locked overnight, and these sheds are to be seen all over the downtown area.

After lunch we fixed a few more holes. About two-thirty or three we parked the truck in the middle of Fleet Street with cars whizzing past on both sides. Danny handed me a red rag on a stick. "Go back there and wave them around us," he said. "We'll fix the hole."

I stood in the middle of Fleet Street, that heavily travelled artery, and innocently waved my flag, fascinated to see how obediently the cars coming at me divided and passed to either side of the truck. Now and then a driver spotted me late, and one man didn't see the flag at all until the last second. I had to leap out of his way, shouting, and he pulled way out to his left into the face of the oncoming traffic and went around the truck at sixty-five.

Pretty soon Bill and Danny were finished and we got into the truck and drove off. "Payday tomorrow," said Danny thoughtfully. "You won't draw anything this week, Hoody. They pay on Wednesday up till the previous Saturday."

"We'll buy you a beer," said Bill generously. He began to tell me about himself. He was an old ballplayer who had bounced around the lower minors for years, without ever going above Class B. Afterwards he came back to Toronto and played Industrial League ball until the Depression killed it. Then he

had come on the city, and had now been with the Roadways
Division for fifteen years.

"Just stick with us, Hoody, and keep your mouth shut," he
said, repeating it with conviction several times.

"You'll be with us at least until Aimé gets back," said Danny.

I asked what had happened to Aimé. It appeared that he'd
been found sitting in a car that didn't belong to him, in a place
where the car wasn't supposed to be. He got thirty days and it
was taken for granted that he'd be back on the job, same as
ever, when he got out. Many of the men had had minor
brushes with the law. A few weeks later Danny got caught,
with two of his friends and a truck, loading lengths of drain-
pipe which they planned to sell for scrap, at a City Mainte-
nance Station south of Adelaide Street. They just drove the
truck into the station after supper and spent six hours loading
pipe. They might have got twenty-five dollars for it, dividing
that sum between them. It didn't seem very good pay for six
hours' work; when I suggested this to Danny he shrugged it
off. He hadn't figured out that his time was worth more than
he could possibly have made on that job.

Bill Tennyson, the sulky patrolman, had often been charged
with non-support by his wife, and with assault by his father-
in-law. He passed his nights alternately at his nominal place
of abode, where his wife and children lived, and at a bachelor
friend's apartment in the Warwick Hotel. An unsettled life,
and an irregular, whose disagreeable circumstances he used
to deplore to me in private lunch-hour chat. Charlie disliked
him, and used to ride him quite a lot; he was the only man in
the whole crew to whom Charlie was consistently unfair. He
had that irritating goof-off manner which always infuriates
the man who is trying to get the job done. Yet he had no vices,
drank little, didn't gamble. No one knew how he spent his
money and no one liked him.

He had his eyes on Eddie Doucette's desk job. But Eddie
could type after a fashion, and had some sort of connection
at the Hall which everybody knew about and never mentioned
—he might have been a nephew of the City Clerk or the
Assistant Assessment Commissioner—I never found out for

sure. But nobody was going to get his job away from him.

Eddie wore a cardigan and a tie, and rode around in the truck with Charlie and George, while Tennyson wore sports shirts and walked his beat. The rest of us wore work-clothes of an astonishing variety. My regular costume, after Aimé came back and I had to get off the coal-ass crew, was an old Fordham sweatshirt which my brother in New York had given me and which by protocol was never laundered, jeans, work-boots, and the same pair of sweat socks every day, and they too were never laundered; they were full of concrete dust at the end of the day and by September were nearly solid. I could stand them in the corner, and they never bothered my feet at all as long as I washed off the concrete as soon as I came home.

That first day we got back to the Yard about four. We walked into the office, clumping our boots loudly and officiously on the floor. Charlie and George had gone out somewhere in the truck and wouldn't be back that day. Apart from Eddie, the only person in the office was a man who was sitting in Charlie's swivel chair, bandaged to the eyes. He seemed to be suffering from broken ribs, collar-bone and arm, shock, cuts, abrasions, sprains, and perhaps other things. He was having trouble speaking clearly and his hands shook violently. He and Eddie were conspiring over a report to the Workmen's Compensation Board.

This man became a culture-hero in the Works Department because he was on Compensation longer than anyone had ever been before. Everyone felt obscurely that he had it made, that he had a claim against the city and the province for life. He would come back to work now and then, and after a day on the gang would be laid up six weeks more. They spoke of him at the Yard in awed lowered voices.

"How do you feel, Sambo?" asked Bill solicitously.

"Not good, Bill, not good."

"You'll be all right," said Bill.

The injured man turned back to Eddie who was licking the end of his pencil and puzzling over the complicated instructions on the report. "It says 'wife and dependents,'" he said uncertainly. "We'll put them down anyway. If it's wrong we'll hear about it."

"I want to get my money," said Sambo.

"You'll get it soon enough."

I couldn't think where anybody could pick up that many lumps all at once. "What happened to him?" I asked.

"He was Aime's replacement till yesterday," said Bill unconcernedly, "but some guy on Fleet Street didn't see the red flag. He was our last safety-man before you."

I thought this over most of the night, deciding finally that I would have to be luckier and more agile than Sambo. The next day was a payday, and in the press of events I forgot my fears and decided to stick with the job as long as I could. At lunchtime, the second day, most of the men expressed commiseration at the fact that I would draw no money until next week.

Bill Tennyson came out of the office with his cheque in his hand and an air of relief written all over him.

"Nobody got any of it this time," he said, as nearly happy as he ever was; his salary cheque was almost always diminished by the judgments of his creditors. "How about you, Hood, you draw anything?" I told him that I wouldn't get paid for a week and he stared at me dubiously for a minute, coming as near as he could to a spontaneous generous gesture. Then all at once he recollected himself and turned away.

Charlie Brown told me that if I was short he could let me have five dollars. I could have used it, but it seemed wiser to say "no thanks" and stretch my credit at my rooming house for one more week. He seemed surprised at my refusal, though not annoyed.

"You're on the truck with Bill and Danny, aren't you?"

"Yes."

"Stay out of trouble," he said cryptically and went out and got into the quarter-ton, holding a roll of plans under his stump and stuffing tobacco into his pipe with his good hand. All over the Yard men were standing in clumps, sharing a peculiar air of expectancy. Some went off hastily, after eating their sandwiches, to the nearest bank. Danny Foster let his cheque fly out of his hand and had to climb over the roofs of several low buildings on College Street in order to retrieve it. A quiet hum of talk came from the tool-shed behind the office where the gang-bosses ate whenever they came into the Yard. There they sat in isolated state, old Wall, ulcerated Harris, and the cheerful Mitch, the best-liked man at the Yard, sharing their rank, its privileges and its loneliness.

The undertone of expectation sensibly intensified as the lunch-hour passed; payday was different from other days. The whole business of the gang-bosses on paydays was to ensure that their crews should be on a job proximate to a Beverage Room. One of the reasons that Harris was so unpopular was that he was a poor planner of work schedules; his men often had to walk six or even eight blocks from the job to the hotel. Mitch, on the other hand, seemed to have a positive flair for working into position Tuesday night or Wednesday morning, so that one of our favourite places, the Brunswick perhaps or the Babloor, was just up an alley from the job. I don't understand quite how he managed it, but if you worked on Mitch's gang you never had to appear on a public thoroughfare as you oozed off the job and into the hotel; there was always a convenient alley.

Bill and Danny and I left the Yard sharp at one o'clock bound for some pressing minor repairs on Huron Street behind the Borden's plant. When we got there we couldn't find anything that looked at all pressing, except possibly a small crack beside a drain. We filled it with coal-ass, Bill laughing all the while in a kind of sly way. I asked him what was so funny.

"Johnny must have reported this one," he said. "He knows where we go."

"Go?"

"Oh, come on!" he said.

"Should we stick the truck up the alley?" asked Danny.

"Leave it where it is," said Bill. "Nobody's going to bother it." He was perfectly right. The truck sat innocently beside the drain we'd been tinkering with for the rest of the afternoon, with CITY OF TORONTO WORKS DEPARTMENT written all over it in various places. A casual passerby, unless he knew the customs of the Department, would assume that the truck's occupants were somewhere close by, hard at work. Everything looked—I don't quite know how to put this—sort of *official*. Danny leaned a shovel artistically against a rear wheel, giving the impression more force than ever.

We walked up Huron Street towards Willcocks.

"Where are we going?" I asked, although by now I had a pretty good idea. Anybody who knows the neighbourhood will have guessed our destination already. I'm talking about that little island of peace in the hustle and bustle of the great city, the Twentieth Battalion Club, Canadian Legion, at the corner of Huron and Willcocks. This was the first time that I was ever in one of the Legion halls. I had always innocently supposed that you had to have some kind of membership. Nothing could be further from the truth, and the knowledge-able drinkers of my time at the university would never be caught dead in a public place like the King Cole Room or Lundy's Lane.

It was a custom hallowed by years of usage that Charlie Brown, George, and Eddie Doucette should spend Wednesday afternoon in the Forty-Eighth Highlanders Legion Hall over on Church Street. It gave one a feeling of comfort and deep security to know this.

We went into the Twentieth and took a table by a big bay window. The houses on the four corners of Huron and Willcocks were then perhaps eighty-five years old, beautifully proportioned old brick houses with verandas at the front and side, and a lovely grey weathered tone to the walls. Like many of the original university buildings, these houses had origi-nally been yellow brick, which the passage of nearly a century had turned to a soft sheen of grey. It was one of those beauti-ful days in the third week of May without a trace of a cloud in the sky, the trees on Willcocks Street a deep dusty green, and now that most of the students had left town the whole district seemed to be asleep. That was one of the finest afternoons of my life.

"Are we gonna go back to the Yard?" said Bill to Danny, really putting the question of whether they would take the truck home with them or not. They were deciding how much they meant to drink. And the nicest thing of all from my point of view was that they took completely for granted that they would take turns buying me beers. I was always glad that I had frequent opportunities to reciprocate.

There was an unspoken decision to make an afternoon of it.

Over in the opposite corner, fast asleep with a glass in front of him, sat the inevitable old Sapper who would revive later on to give us a detailed account of his exploits at Passchendaele. Next to him were two Contemptibles with identical drooping wet moustaches engaged in another of their interminable games of cribbage. All afternoon their soft murmur of "fifteen-two, fifteen-four" droned away peacefully in the background. It was a place where a man could stretch out and take his time. In all the time I was in the Twentieth after that, though I saw plenty of men thoroughly drunk, I never saw one really troublesome or nasty.

At a big round table in the middle of the room, all by himself, shifting a pair of small eyes in a head of heroic proportions, drinking mightily, sat a young man whom I vaguely remembered having seen around the university. This was the tenor, Alan Crofoot, now a favourite of Toronto audiences but in those days dabbling in the graduate department of Psychology a block away. We grew to be good friends later on and I often reminded Al that this was the first place I'd seen him close to, though we didn't speak. Once or twice that afternoon he glanced across at our table, plainly wondering why I had FORDHAM lettered on the front of my sweatshirt. I let him work on it.

There wasn't a waiter; you had to go to the window. In a minute Danny came back with three ice-cold Molson's Blue and glasses on a tin tray. As a matter of fact we had had a fairly busy morning, we were sweaty, we had just had a heavy lunch —nothing ever tasted any better than a cold beer on a beautiful afternoon with nothing to look forward to but more of the same.

In those days I had a small local reputation as a better than fair beer drinker with plenty of early foot, though with nothing like the stamina or capacity of Al Crofoot, say, or any of half a dozen other redoubtable faculty members and graduate assistants of my time. But I couldn't even stay close to Bill and Danny, who drank two to my one, never appearing to feel it and never becoming obstreperous or downright disagreeable as I regularly did myself, and as my usual drinking companions often did. It was a great pleasure to pass the afternoon with them. And when five o'clock came they both pressed money on me, in the unspoken recognition that I would naturally go on to another Beverage Room after dinner. We parted on the best of terms.

Soon this comfortable alliance was dissolved by circumstance, when Aimé arrived back at the Yard after doing his thirty days. He flatly refused to go out with one of the gangs; he had earned his place on the coal-ass crew, he felt, and no goddam college kid was going to get it away from him. Bill and Danny were indifferent in the matter, as was natural, and at length, about a quarter to nine the first morning Aime was back, Charlie called me in from where I was sitting smoking to ask me how I felt about it. You see, he respected the prescriptive right that I'd already acquired in the job. There was an unspoken but very strong sentiment at the Yard that once a man got his hands on a soft spot he acquired a kind of generally sanctioned right to it. Charlie peered at me sidewise as I came into the office and leaned casually, as I'd already learned to do, on the counter.

"What about this, Hood?" he asked sharply but, I sensed, half-apologetically. "Aimé wants his job back."

"Fine," I said. He looked at me with relief, palpably surprised that I hadn't made more of a fuss.

"You'll have to go out with Harris," he said warningly.

"Okay."

Aimé looked at me. "No hard feelings, kid, you understand."

"No," I said, smiling. He went outside and picked up a shovel. Soon I could hear him wrangling with Danny over who was to sit in the middle.

"Goddam French-Canadian bastard!"

"Shut your fat mouth, Foster!"

The three of them got in the truck and drove off.

I sat in the office wondering how things would be on Harris's gang. He had the reputation of being a driver, a tough man to please. He hadn't been a boss long and the responsibility bothered him, mostly in the stomach. He had a lean hatchet face and sunken cheeks, the face of an ulcerated man, with hysterical eyes and a marked Birmingham accent. Like many of the men at the Yard he had a lot of trouble with his wife.

He and his boys had been piddling around with a tiny sidewalk installation on Bloor Street, between the Chez Paree and Palmer's, for several days. They couldn't seem to get the camber shaped right and the rain lay in puddles instead of draining off into the curb. Twice now they had had to come back to the job to rip out recently installed bays of concrete. Bloor Street, you understand, was the street of all streets about which we had to be most careful—Toronto's Fifth Avenue—our display street as far as Charlie's professional reputation was concerned. He hadn't wanted to let Harris handle the job, but Wall's gang was tied up elsewhere and the work had to be done immediately.

As a finisher, Harris lacked confidence in himself and the resulting sureness. A concrete finisher has to be able to coax the water in the concrete to the surface, together with as many air-bubbles as possible, smoothing the surface and shaping the sidewalk—sculpting it—so that it curves almost invisibly from a high point in the centre down to either side. This is all done by the eye and the hand, sometimes with the aid of a level and a piece of two-by-four, but always pretty crudely, and Harris didn't have a good enough eye. Concrete is an interesting medium, plastic enough to allow some correction but quick-drying enough to require a firm decisive trowel-stroke and what a draughtsman would call a good line.

Driving me over to Bloor Street, Charlie said little, but I knew he was embarrassed about taking me off the coal-ass truck. I didn't really mind because I'd expected to get a little light exercise on this job, but you'd have thought he was sending me to Siberia.

"Here's another man for you, Harris," he said when we got out of the quarter-ton in front of the Laing Galleries.

Harris eyed me with a great sourness; like everyone else at the Yard he knew that while I wasn't exactly weak, I was damned clumsy. I knew what he was thinking but he couldn't very well say anything; he'd been after Charlie for an extra man for weeks.

"Can you use a sledge?" he asked me doubtfully.

"Sure."

"Go and help them throw the broken stuff in the truck."

I said nothing and walked along the street to where the rest of the gang were cleaning out some bays.

"Got you working now, Hoody," said Freddy Lismore as I wandered up.

"Don't let Harris throw you, kid!" said Wally Butt, the assistant finisher. I grinned and, bending over, began to pick up pieces of broken sidewalk, the largest weighing not much more than thirty-five or forty pounds. Some of them had sharp edges though, and could cut your fingers badly if you weren't careful. Fortunately I had a pair of cotton work gloves in my hip pocket. I wasn't killing myself, but as I lofted a chunk of concrete into the truck Charlie came over and spoke to me.

"You're out of shape," he said briefly. "Work into it slowly."

"All right," I said, "and thanks." He disappeared in his little truck and Harris came back, giving me a highly critical stare. I took it easy all right, but everybody in the gang took it even easier. And as is always the case with any gang of workmen, there was one guy who pottered around between the toolbox and the job, doing absolutely nothing. On Harris's gang that would be "Gummy" Brown, always called "Gummy" to distinguish him from Charlie "One-Punch" Brown, the foreman. Gummy had a single black tooth on the left side of his upper jaw—all the rest was a great void, justifying the nickname. He had been drunk, it was held universally, since the world began.

If you counted Gummy, Harris had seven men under him, and the use of a truck owned by its driver and rented by the city. This truck-driver went back and forth from the asphalt-plant on the waterfront, bringing loads of ready-mixed concrete—we almost never had to mix by hand—and the art of managing the gang largely consisted in exhausting the last load for the day at about ten to four, leaving plenty of time to clean off the shovels and put up barricades and lights, moving at a sober and godly pace, before quitting time. At ten to five Gummy Brown would get the keys to the tool-box from Harris and we'd stick the shovels, picks, crowbars, and trowels in the box. Gummy would lock it with enormous satisfaction and we'd all walk off the job, meeting there by prearrangement the next day. While we were on that Bloor Street job, I had a two-minute walk around the corner to where I lived and I used to be home washing my feet before five o'clock. And this comfortable situation lasted through the early part of the summer.

I stayed with Harris for about six weeks that first summer, all through the ill-fated Bloor Street job, then on Robert Street fixing householders' sidewalks a bay at a time, insignificant jobs, and finally around the Art Gallery and Hashmall's Pharmacy on Dundas Street. I broke out concrete, used the sledge, floated off—the works. The only thing I would never risk was swinging the sledge at a spike. I could never hit the damn thing—poor timing and eyesight, I suppose—and it was dangerous for the man holding the spike.

It might be of interest to the reader to follow a simple job from start to finish. First came the problem of getting the old cement up and out, which could be managed in several ways, depending on its age and hardness. If there happened to be grass or mud at the edge of the sidewalk, we took a long bevelled bar and worked it under the concrete, placing a rock under the bar for leverage. Then a couple of us would rock up and down on the bar to see if we could lift the slab; usually we could. When it was a foot or two off the ground, one of us would hit it in the middle with the sledge, splitting the whole slab into small chunks which could then be thrown into the truck to be disposed of at the waterfront as fill. We would clear out eight or ten bays at a time, shovelling out the rubble underneath and levelling the ground in readiness for the fresh mix.

There could be complications. At a ramp behind the bus terminal on Elizabeth Street we found that the old concrete was over three feet thick, to take the weight of the buses. Worse still, it was criss-crossed by heavy reinforcing wire which resisted pliers and had to be cut, strand by strand, by driving a spike through it with a sledge. This reinforcing wire had to be watched carefully for it was rusted and the broken ends were dangerously sharp; that small job lasted nearly two weeks.

When we had prepared the ground we would send the truck for a load of concrete. This always meant an hour's wait, either around ten-thirty or about two in the afternoon. It made a nice break. We would take things easy, cleaning off the shovels or sneaking a bit of left-over concrete to a home-owner to be used for a patio. The great thing was to melt inconspicuously into the landscape so as not to attract the attention of the ratepayer.

When the truck appeared, we either dumped the concrete into the road and shovelled it into wheelbarrows for delivery to Harris and Wally Butt, on their knees together at the edge of the new installation, or if we were only fixing scattered single bays, two of us would climb into the well of the truck and throw down shovelsful from on high. There was a certain amount of horseplay involved in this; more than once some-body down below caught a great lump of wet concrete in the pit of his stomach.

One morning in late June I was standing in the back of the truck about eleven o'clock, shovelling the stuff into a bay, sweating and feeling pretty loose, when Charlie Brown's head appeared out of nowhere at the side of the truck. The edge of my shovel just missed him and an enormous gout of wet concrete went whizzing past his ear.

"Watch what you're doing!" he said. That's only a rough transcription of what he actually said. In fact he was speaking the dialect that Alastair MacCrimmon and I used to call "cityese," an exotic English, rhythmic, heavily cadenced, comically obscene, with an unmistakable structure. If I were blindfolded in Rangoon and heard two men speaking "cityese," I'd be able to spot them instantly; there's something unique about the scansion.

Charlie got down off the truck and spoke to Harris.

"I need Hood in the Yard," he said.

"Why don't you take 'Gummy'?" asked Harris protestingly. I felt proud.

"I want somebody who's alive," said Charlie disgustedly, motioning to me to join him in the truck. I looked at Harris inquiringly but he shook his head. He didn't know what was up.

On the way back to the Yard Charlie told me about the watchmen. There had to be somebody in the office from around four in the afternoon until eight the next morning, as well as all day and all night on the weekend, which worked out to sixteen eight-hour shifts weekly.

Three old men approaching retirement split fifteen shifts amongst themselves, leaving an extra one to be filled in by one of the workmen. And each of these watchmen was entitled to three weeks' holidays a year for a total of nine weeks to be filled in through the summer. Charlie had decided that my combination of supposititious book-learning and puny physique made me the ideal replacement.

"You can put in the next nine weeks on this job," he said encouragingly. "That'll take you down through August, and then I'll find something else for you to do." I was due to leave towards the end of September.

Now the thing was, I'd been getting used to the work on the gang and enjoying it. On the other hand, every man at the Yard would have given his eye-teeth to acquire this sinecure. I didn't want to turn down what was obviously meant as a kindness, so I said nothing.

Charlie looked at me curiously. "What's the matter? Don't you want to do it?"

"Sure," I said, "it's fine, Charlie." And it turned out to be an interesting job, each shift presenting novel problems. The four to twelve, and the daytime shifts on Saturday and Sunday, brought the most service calls. The twelve to eight was mainly a matter of arranging seat cushions from the swivel chairs on top of the desks, or on the floor, and trying to sleep. Once in a great while you might get a call in the middle of the night, usually from the Traffic Squad, to report that the barricades were down or the lights missing on a hole in the road. Then you had to call out an emergency truck from one of the Yards—there was only one truck available, each Yard providing a stand-by driver in turn—and direct the driver to the danger spot. The time of the call, the trouble, the location, the remedial action, and the precise time that the driver called back to say that the repair was in effect—all these things had to be noted down in a Daily Journal and initialled by the watchman. These books were sometimes produced as evidence in damage suits by City lawyers, and so had to be kept up carefully.

But most of the twelve to eight I spent sleeping, or talking to policemen who came in for a smoke and to warm themselves or to nap for an hour or to hide from the Sergeant. These men patrolled one of the toughest parts of town and were as eager to stay out of trouble as the rest of us. They hated the corner of Bathurst and Queen, for example, because of the half-dozen enormous taverns located there, which meant that Friday and Saturday nights on that corner were real hellers. I'd often seen eight policemen standing in pairs on the corners of that intersection and wondered why. The answer, I was told, was that they just didn't want to come alone.

Many of these fellows were English immigrants, bewildered by the Toronto attitude to the police. They were always complaining about times when they'd been losing a fight and hoping in vain that a citizen might give them a hand. I remember one Englishman in particular who was leaving the force and taking his family back to England because of this kind of thing. He felt alone and threatened in a country where incivility and disrespect for the law seemed accepted and regular.

None of these constables knew much law; none had a clear idea of his powers, and these were constantly exceeded in some circumstances and allowed to lapse in others. They hated and feared all lawyers, and were easily cowed by them. I know one drunken lawyer, a driver of spectacular incompetence, drunk or sober, who despite his erratic behaviour awheel, and despite the dozens of times he's been stopped by traffic officers, has never been fined nor even summoned to court. He bounces aggressively out of his car, announces that he's a lawyer, and the policeman, unsure of his ground, backs off.

On the other hand, when the officer feels that he has the upper hand he is perfectly ready to exceed the limits of his mandate, and is apt to be quite cynical about it. One young constable admitted to me that he always bulled the College Street crowds around, pushing people and threatening them with arrest to persuade them to move on, when there was no conceivable charge he could bring. Most of the people in the crowds, Jews and DP's, had no notion of their rights and legal safeguards and were easily intimidated.

But most of the younger policemen were decent unassuming men, not too happy with their rates of pay and promotion considering the nature of the work, but proud of what they were doing and even of the opinion that it was a dignified public service. I asked them about favouritism on the force and they all agreed that there was very little, and that a man would normally be judged on his merits. Their testimony carries some weight too, because they were all in junior positions and there was nothing in my questions to put them on their guard.

Another instructive aspect of the watchman's job was our emergency sewer service. When there is a very heavy rain the Toronto sewers cause trouble; they are not equipped to carry off the excess water, being designed for normal conditions of flow. If there is an extremely heavy rain they back up, and the water begins to rise in cellars all over town, especially on low ground, in hollows and valleys, and on the lower slopes of hills. And the only real cure for this abnormal state is the end of the storm.

Understandably enough, few householders are aware of this. When they observe the flood rising in the cellar, with its sometimes dismal and offensive accompaniment, they become alarmed, and the result is a flood of calls at the Yard, none of which distinguish between a genuinely blocked and defective sewer—with a tree root in it, say—and one which is in perfect shape but which is just too small for downpour conditions.

I remember afternoons, almost always on the weekend, when the phone rang as soon as I put it back in its cradle, for hours on end. I'd get panicky elderly ladies, people who raved in exotic foreign tongues, frightened children, Bohemians with basement apartments in which their folksong records floated soggily round and round—every imaginable stripe of complaint. There was simply nothing to be done until the storm was over. I tried telling them so but it did no good and at length I learned simply to note the call, and imply, without actually making a commitment, that a service truck would be along. Of course no such service call was ever made unless there was a clear indication in the complaint of some genuine blockage or break. But I never told anybody that.

I channeled and re-routed calls of this and other kinds until the end of August, when the three elderly watchmen had all enjoyed leisurely vacations. By that time I was pretty much regarded as one of the office staff, and Charlie was visibly reluctant to send me back to Harris—it might create a dangerous precedent. The day after the last of the watchmen came back I ambled into the Yard wondering how he'd work it out. He had, you see, a kind of problem in status, or prestige, to resolve. But he was equal and rather more than equal to it.

It was the Tuesday after Labour Day. The Scotch guy (a man never known by any other name, always "the Scotch guy," with a thick burr and a great genius for killing time) was sitting outside the tool-shed when I meandered in. He said nothing but grinned cheerily. When I went into the office Charlie handed me a small can of black paint, a small can of white, two brushes, a box of cleaning rags, and a set of stencils from zero through nine which could be fitted together to form any number up to 9999. He told us where to find a little ladder and the Scotch guy ran to get it. We threw the things in the back of Charlie's pick-up truck and he drove us to the foot of Jarvis Street, where we got out. I was still quite in the dark.

"I want you to re-paint the numbers on the lamp-posts," he said. I'm not joking, that's what he said. "When you get to Bloor Street, come into the Yard and I'll give you a list of other streets." He got into the truck and sped off along Queen's Quay while we looked at each other scarcely able to credit our luck.

We painted our way up Jarvis Street at a snail's pace—boy, did we take it slow! I'd go ahead and slap on a background of black paint. Then I'd walk back—we only had one ladder—and we'd work along, putting on the fresh numbers in a creamy off-white, a kind of eggshell or buff tint. We got up to Bloor Street on Friday afternoon, a matter of four days. When we appeared at the Yard Charlie glared at us in extreme vexation.

"What the hell are you doing here?"

It would not have been possible to go slower.

"We finished Jarvis Street," I said apologetically.

"What, the west side too?"

"I'm afraid so."

He began to root around in his desk and finally drew out a few dog-eared sheets of foolscap with a list of street names on them. He flourished it in the air and then handed it to the Scotch guy.

"Do these!" he said. He looked at us and began to smile and at last to laugh. "There's fifteen hundred dollars in the Estimates to be spent on this job," he growled. "Now get out and don't let me see you around here for at least three weeks."

So I finished out my first summer without any strain.

When I came back to the Yard the next year, I had only two more years' work to do in the Graduate School. I had held a good fellowship which took care of most of my expenses, I'd had a highly remunerative job at the C.N. Express, where you could log seven or eight hours' overtime if you had the nerve and could evade the foreman, so I wasn't hurting for funds quite as much as before.

I went back because I liked it and I even persuaded a friend of mine, Alastair MacCrimmon, to apply for a similar job. He was then an intermittent student at the University and is now a film technician at CBC. Every night in the Chez Paree from eleven till two, he and I would sit around that summer exchanging our observations of life on the city. He was working at Number Six Yard and apparently things were managed there much as they were under Charlie. We used to amuse ourselves by playing a game which we called "Translate into Cityese." Alastair would feed me a line in ordinary spoken English, or I would feed him one, and the idea was to render it with the peculiar diction, cadence, and rhythm of the men on the gangs, getting the feeling as authentic as possible.

"Goodness me," I might say, "we filled that hole in the road yesterday, and there it is again." Alastair would translate this flawlessly.

"The men at the Hall have not sent up our cheques," he would come back straight-faced, "and here it is nearly noon." This would stand a lot of translation.

"Someone has stolen all the lights off the barricades," or possibly, "Itchy-Koo has been drinking and cannot work."

Or most enigmatic, even gnomic, of all: "The truck has stopped and will not go."

It was Alastair who created the legend, on the city, of what Itchy-Koo said when he hit his foot with the sledge, crushing the metatarsal forever. He said: "That hurt!"

It was understood that I would get back my night-watchman's job when the holiday time came; but I put in most of May and June on Mitch's gang. When you remember poor old Harris's anxiety-ridden behaviour, it was a revelation to see the difference in Mitch's methods. He was very relaxed and so was his gang. Everybody had a good time; we were always close to a Beverage Room. And though it was the smallest of the three gangs, we could handle a moderate-sized job much faster than Harris, and nearly as professionally as Wall. The first thing we did that spring, as I remember, was a major installation of double sidewalk on Spadina Avenue just north of College outside the Tip Top Tailors branch store. We were right across from the Waverley Hotel and that branch of †he Canadian Bank of Commerce of which my father had been manager fifteen years before.

In those days Dad used to do a lot of loan business in the district with furriers and garment-trade people during the season, and with independent sales agent, small jobbers and importers, smallwares and novelties salesmen with tiny agencies, and the like. One of these free-lance salesmen, a man called Earl Darlington, came to Dad one day with a peculiar request for a short-term note. Earl could sell anything— he could charm the monkeys off the trees—but he never handled the same line two weeks in a row and so had no established line of credit. However, Dad listened to the story, which was colourful and involved. He had a chance to buy the refrigerator in the Waverley for next to nothing because they meant to replace it. This was not what you and I think of as a refrigerator, but an enormous thing the size of an apartment living-room, with walls in which the cooling devices were intricately cemented. The whole room had to be removed, walls and all. It was like transporting a small house.

Darlington told Dad that he had a buyer for this monstrosity, the old Hunt's Confectionery on Yonge Street, next to Loew's Uptown. All he needed was the money to put a deposit on the refrigerator and to hire a truck with a flat-bed trailer, and a gang of men, to move the thing. Dad listened to this beguiling tale and thought it over, talked to the manager of the Waverley, and in short concluded that it was a chance for Earl to make a dollar, so he let him have the money.

After surmounting fantastic obstacles they got the refrigerator out of the hotel in one piece and onto the trailer. They had the necessary permit from the police to move it, after business hours, and they hauled it up to a lane behind Stollery's on the corner of Bloor and Yonge. In went the trailer and down the lane, but before they got to Hunt's rear door the refrigerator got jammed between the walls of two buildings abutting on the lane. They couldn't back up; they couldn't go forward though they tried their damnedest. They were stuck fast. In desperation Darlington told the driver of the trailer and the gang of labourers to go home and get some sleep—he could see his quick profit being eaten up by overtime—and they'd try again next day. Then he went home himself, leaving about four tons of refrigerator immovable in the lane.

When they came back next morning the trailer was parked where they'd left it but the refrigerator was gone, vanished. Stolen, by God! And it was never traced.

Eventually Dad wrote off the loan.

Watching the men on the gang slide across the street and into the Waverley reminded me of this story and I told it to Mitch, who got a big chuckle out of it. He was then, I should say, about thirty-two or -three, which seemed middle-age to me, though it doesn't any more. Everybody liked Mitch, even Bill Tennyson who came out with us for a day once in a while, moody, difficult, but after a couple of hours' joking with Mitch he would loosen up a bit and tell us about his latest scrap with his father-in-law, an ex-bantam-weight who liked to mix it with him now and then.

Then there was Frank Hughes, another nice fellow—Mitch had all the easy-going types out with him—a hockey player who had spent the previous winter in the Eastern League. He was going to the Detroit camp in the fall and was putting in the summer with us to stay in shape. I don't know how much good the work on the gang did him as far as staying in shape went; but at least, like the rest of us, he got a good tan. Frank used to play fastball with Sherrin's down at the beach and he was enjoying a very good year at the plate, which made him even easier to get along with. Like all ballplayers, he loved those base hits. He weighed around one-ninety and had one of the most powerful builds I've ever seen. He wasn't broad-shouldered; he had low sloping shoulders and a cavernous chest and magnificent legs. He was a defenceman and though I never saw him play, they tell me he could really dig. I weighed around a hundred and forty, but the odd thing was, I had about an inch of reach on him. We used to spar around comically for the amusement of the gang and the passing girls who always had an eye on Frank—he was a very handsome man.

"You look like a pretty good light-weight, Hoody," he'd say. This always convulsed Mitch.

"Try and hit me," I'd say, dancing around jabbing or pretending to tie him up inside. Like most students, I had terrible co-ordination.

"Going to get in shape on the city," we'd sing absurdly, and this was also good for laughs. Then we'd swing our shovels for a minute as though our lives depended on it. A girl would go by and we'd straighten up and inflate our chests, holding ourselves immobile.

"Who's she looking at, Mitch," Frank would say, "me or Hoody?"

The poor girl would blush and we'd gurgle happily and foolishly to ourselves. We never tried to offend or embarrass a passing girl, but they never could resist a peek at Frank, and if we caught them at it, why then the joke was legitimate.

But life on Mitch's gang was too good to last, at least for me, though it went on and on for them and still does. When vacation-time came I went back on the night-watch at the Yard, guarding the piles of sand and gravel and the tools in the shed, feuding with the firemen or throwing a football with them, depending on the state of our relations.

Early in June in the summer of 1953 there occurred the most momentous event of my career as a fill-in watchman—the Coronation of Queen Elizabeth II. There were weeks of preparation of one kind or another in case of crowds, but somehow the most weighty arrangements of the whole affair went untouched until seven-thirty on the morning of that eventful day.

It was a fit day for a Coronation, the sky an absolute crystalline blue, the air dry and soft, and College Street slumbrous and deserted at seven o'clock in the morning. I had promised Jimmy Baird, whom I was to relieve, that I would come on early so he could go home and get dressed up with his medals on for the parade. The bagel shops were silent—you could hear birdsong on College Street!

I was whistling "Land of Hope and Glory" softly to myself as I came into the office. The sound woke Jimmy who stared at me with infantine sleepy eyes, hardly recognizing me—the emergency calls never woke Jimmy—as he rolled off the top of the desk where he'd been lying, straightened his collar and tie, and prepared to leave.

"Anything doing?" I asked.

"Not a thing." There was never anything in the book after Jimmy had worked a shift. I suppose the sight of his lifeless body was enough to frighten marauders away, though; he looked quite dead when he slept.

"Tommy Cowdrey's the driver," said Jimmy as he left. "If anything comes in, call him." He slunk out the door. I stood in the gateway to the Yard for a while, looking east and west along College Street, and there wasn't a sound, nothing stirred. Then, a long long way off, perhaps as far away as Sherbourne Street, I could hear a streetcar, the clicking of the points as the trucks passed over them and then the rumble along the street; it was coming fast and I could predict exactly from the sound when it would come in sight away along to the east about St. George Street. A car with an Alabama plate went slowly past with a tired driver slumped over the wheel. They must have driven all night. A single policeman idled in front of the Mars Grill.

Inside the office the phone rang suddenly, urgently. I caught it on the third ring. It was seven-thirty. "Number Two Yard," I carolled into the mouthpiece, and then I got a shock.

"This is the Commissioner," said a tense voice. "Is Foreman Brown there?"

"No, Mr. Chambers."

"Then you'll have to get hold of him. This is an emergency." The hair stood up on my head; there was real urgency, even fright, in the Commissioner's voice. "We've got to erect a temporary Comfort Station in Queen's Park," he said. "The bandstand facilities won't be nearly enough. I've just had the Parade Marshal on the phone and he's furious." He began to give me explicit instructions.

"We'll use the same model we used on V-E Day. Twentyfour

compartments, twelve of each. Brown has the plans. He'll need workmen, lumber, paint or stain, buckets, chloride of lime, and the appropriate signs. Get him into the Yard and call the crew. Then call me back."

"Yes, sir."

"Very good. Who's speaking?"

"Hood. Fill-in watchman."

"All right, Hood, I'm counting on you. Get busy!"

I called Charlie at once and he was galvanized into action. "You'll find the plans for the model in my desk. Do you know where the key is?"

"Yes."

"Call Eddie and tell him to pick me up. Then get out the plans. Then call Wall and tell him to call six of his best men and have them meet me at the Yard. They'll draw double time, tell him, but they've got to come in. I don't know how we forgot about this." He hung up in great distress of mind and I began to carry out his instructions.

By eight-fifteen Eddie and Wall and six labourers were standing uncertainly in the Yard. Charlie was inside on the phone like some great captain adjusting his tactics after a military disaster. "My right flank is crushed, my centre in full retreat, my left wing collapsing. Very good, I shall attack!"

"Send the partitions to the bandstand," he was shouting, "and some green stain, and don't forget the signs like last time." At eight-thirty he and the men departed for the site of the proposed Comfort Station.

As you remember there was an enormous parade that day which was to assemble on the university front campus, the back campus, and in Queen's Park, and which was to move off at one-thirty. Besides the marchers and police and civil dignitaries, there would be great crowds of spectators, hot-dog and ice-cream vendors, flag and souvenir salesmen—altogether about seventy-five thousand people. I wondered if twenty-four compartments, even adding on the bandstand facilities, would be enough.

Soon there came an anguished call from a pay-phone at

Hart House. It was Charlie. "No buckets!" he wailed.

"No buckets?" I echoed, thunderstruck.

"They're out of them at the Supply Department. Now look, Hood, we've got to have those buckets. There are ten thousand people here already and they all want to use the facilities. Call the Commissioner and ask him to get them from Eaton's Mail Order. They're sure to have some."

I called the Commissioner and he was aghast. "There won't be anybody there today. Maybe I'd better have it broadcast."

"Don't you know anybody at Eaton's?"

"I know Lady Eaton, of course," he said doubtfully. "I've met her at civic functions. But I can't call her."

"We've got to have them, sir."

"All right," he said, "I'll get the buckets. What size?"

"The largest," I said, "galvanized iron." He hung up and in a matter of seconds Charlie was back on the line. "What about those buckets?"

"Chambers is calling Lady Eaton," I said, and he seemed reassured.

At eleven the buckets arrived on the site and instantly the crowds swarmed around the workmen demanding access to them. But the walls and roof weren't complete yet, and Charlie was afraid of offending public decency; he held the besiegers off until the partitions were up and the roof decorously in place while the swarms of bandsmen, hot-dog vendors, and children with balloons grew thicker. At length the last nail was driven home, the last plank solidly in place, the buckets in a glittering phalanx.

The Parade Marshal blew his whistle, the drums rolled; it was one-thirty. The parade moved off and the crowds began to disperse, streaming down University Avenue towards the reviewing stand. In fifteen minutes Queen's Park was deserted except for a child chasing a floating balloon. The Comfort Station went unused.

Away off down on Front Street bagpipes skirled.

Muttering curses, Charlie ascended to the roof-tree, and taking a hammer ripped out the first of the planks. For him, for all of us, the holiday had been a magnificent fiasco.

'*C'est magnifique, mais ce n'est pas la guerre.*' For weeks a pall of meditative, reflective gloom hung about the Yard.

Nothing in my second summer exceeded the high adventure of that day. There were a few memorable happenings, but the glory seemed dimmed. There was the time that Charlie incautiously named Gummy Brown to fill in the extra watchman's shift. I had been on the job for eight hours prior to his arrival and had spent the evening watching the fights on television, on the third floor of the Fire Hall. After the fight was over I had a couple of cups of tea and a chat with the Fire Captain which was interrupted by a hail from the ground floor, which drifted up through the holes in the floors through which the brass pole descended.

"Gummy's here," shouted one of the hook-and-ladder men.

"Tell him to come on up for tea."

"I don't think he can make it."

The hook-and-ladder man was wrong because in a minute a red and black face hove into view on the stairs. It was Gummy, drunker than usual, if that were possible, and making heavy weather of the ascent.

"Chrissakes, Hoody!" he got out. "Whyncha in the office?"

"The fights," I said.

He began a disconnected tirade to the effect that one should never leave his post, seizing a stalk of celery as he eased along the table towards the teapot and inserting it in his mouth.

"Can't chew it," I heard him say before he slumped over.

"Come on, man," said the Fire Captain, "on your feet!" This Captain was a bit of a puritan who disapproved of the free-and-easy manners which obtained under Charlie's aegis. "On your feet!" he said again.

Gummy lifted his head and squinted at him and then, discerning the voice of authority, he rose and lurched backwards out of the door of the lunchroom.

"Watch it there, Gummy!" I cried, but too late. He disappeared soundlessly, magically, through the hole which circumscribed the brass pole, falling freely three storeys to the cement floor of the garage and breaking both legs. Fortunately he was completely anaesthetized against the pain, which otherwise might have been very great. He lay there, the celery stalk between his lips, quietly gumming it like a cow with a cud, while we eased him onto a stretcher and waited for the ambulance.

"Take my shift, Hoody," he said as they carried him off. "Double time."

I saw the Compensation reports on that one, and you'd have supposed that Brown, Norman, 37, married, was the very model of sobriety and conscientiousness. It was at length established that as Gummy's shift hadn't actually begun he was not entitled to compensation. The case was appealed on the grounds that he had been travelling to work, though how a fall through a hole could be construed as "travel to work" rather eludes me. The last I heard, the appeal was pending.

The damned old snake of a Fire Captain was a troublemaker. One evening when I was doing a four to twelve, a Friday night as I recall, four friends of mine appeared with a case of beer and an old car. One of these was later to become a reverend and dignified professor of law at a hoary academic institution and I won't embarrass him by mentioning any names. It was his idea that we should consume the case of beer during my shift and then hasten to the Chez Paree in the car to get in another couple of hours. There were two men and two girls besides me, and the girls drank perhaps a pint each, giving the rest of us a good start.

There was a good deal of singing and noise, and though I had drawn the blinds, a policeman friend of mine twice entreated us to be more quiet, not for his sake but because some people on Nassau Street, two blocks away, had lodged a complaint. And at that he drank a pint of our beer, carefully rinsing off his mouth and hands afterwards.

Now while we were enjoying ourselves in this innocent and peaceable fashion, that spy of a Fire Captain crept across the Yard, peeked around the drawn blinds, and noted carefully what was going on. Having satisfied himself with what he considered enough evidence to obtain my discharge, he withdrew unnoticed. Next day he went to Charlie and told all, but without realizing it he had played into Charlie's hands. It was perhaps true that I was treated with coolness, even severity, for a day or two. There was even some talk of sending me out with a gang again. But Charlie knew, and I knew, and finally the Captain knew too, that the folkways were too strong. The affair was passed over and, in fact, when one of the watchmen suffered a heart attack in September, Charlie kept me on till Armistice Day, a wholesome object lesson to the Fire Captain. I carried on my graduate work during the days.

My last few weeks on the job, the nights were getting pretty chilly, and I had instructions from Charlie to keep the space-heater on all night. "I'm always cold when I come in at eight o'clock," he said, "so keep things good and warm for me, Hood." I promised him that I would. When I went off the job for the last time, on the cold morning of November the 11th, Charlie nodded to me curtly.

"We'll be seeing you, Hood," he said, his sharp little eyes looking all around the office to see that things were in good order. And then, amazingly, "Take care of yourself." I nodded silently and, leaving the Yard behind me, I started for home.

I only ever saw them once more. Four years later I was on Richmond Street on Midsummer's Day, going in to be interviewed by Jack Kent Cooke for the editorship of *Saturday Night*, a job which I had no business applying for and didn't expect to get. As I came abreast of the Consolidated Press Building, my throat constricted and I stopped in my tracks.

For there they all were, Mitch's gang, lounging around a dozen open bays, waiting for the truck. There was Mitch, grinning as cheerfully as ever, Gummy hobbling idly around on a cane, Bill Tennyson, who recognized me and came over to say hello. And there, parked across the street, was a new green International quarter-ton and in it, gripping a pipe between his teeth and puzzling out a roll of plans, sat Charlie. Everything was just the same; they were all the same and would always be the same. I said a word or two, jokingly, to Tennyson, and then he went away.

I glanced at the sky; it was a hard blue and there wasn't a cloud to be seen. I squared my shoulders and went inside to my doomed-to-be-mutually-unsatisfactory interview. And it struck me after it was over, that silly interview on which Jack Cooke wasted half an hour of his time and his indubitable charm, that I'd be wiser not to try for impossibilities but to set down records of things possible, matters like these, tales of the way one man paid for his education in the bad old, good old days before the creation of that warm featherbed for talent, the Canada Council.

1962

Henye

Shirley Faessler

FRIDAYS AFTER SCHOOL I used to get a nickel
from Henye for going with her to the Out Patients Clinic at
the Grace Street Hospital to speak English for her. I was ten
years old and it was a terrible embarrassment for me to be
seen on the street with her, she was so ugly.

Henye was a skinny little woman, all bone, no flesh to her.
Her hair which she wore in two braids around her head was
the same colour as her skin, pallid. Her nose was long, her
voice was hoarse, and on top of everything else she was bent
over in the back.

She would hang on to my arm all the way to the clinic,
pinching it now and then when she felt my attention was
wandering from the recap she was giving me of her ailments,
things to tell the doctor. We would take our place on the
bench, Henye hunched forward with feet dangling free of the
floor, her black stockings twisted and spiralled at the spindle-
leg ankles, and wait for our number to be called. Our turn
would come and I would give the doctor a rundown of her
troubles, she all the while prompting me in Yiddish: *'Zog im,*

Soreh, zog im.' She wanted me to tell him she had not moved her bowels in three days. I would sooner have died. 'I told him!' I would say to her in English. It was bad enough I was obliged to acknowledge before the gentile doctor that I understood the Yiddish she was speaking, let alone speak it in front of him.

Before the nickel was yielded up to me I would have to accompany her back to her house, even though she knew the way home. Not till we were in the house did she take from her pocket the knotted handkerchief in which she kept her change. Her husband, Yankev, who was my stepmother's uncle, would be home from his day's business when I returned his wife from the Out Patients. (Being Friday, Yankev saw to it that the day's business which consisted mainly of deliveries —he was a bootlegger—was done with and finished before *Erev Shabbus.*) 'Well?' he would say to me as Henye was unknotting the handkerchief. 'Did she get a little pinch from the doctor? A tickle, a little feel? She likes that, the old devil.'

Yankev, at that time in his late fifties, was a tall thickset handsome man with a bushy head of hair beginning to grey. He was a vigorous illiterate coarse-natured man with a ribald sense of humour. He loved a bit of mischief, a practical joke. Henye, a year younger than her husband but who looked old enough to be his mother, was a sobersides. Yankev and Henye made a striking pair; the contrast between husband and wife was something to see.

Yankev had a twin. His brother Yudah, whom (it was said) Yankev loved more than he did his own children. The twin brothers Yankev and Yudah were identical. In build, in countenance and voice they were one and the same. I never learned to tell them apart, nor could neighbours or friends distinguish between them. But my stepmother, who was their niece, could tell one from the other. And so could my father, who had no use for either of them, tell them apart. . . .

My mother died when my brother, my sister, and I were very young and a year or so after her death my father, in search of a wife to make a home for his motherless children, met through the offices of a matchmaker the brothers Yankev and Yudah who were seeking a husband for their niece

Chayele, whom they had brought over from the old country. The brothers, after the meeting took place, were not too keen on the match. They thought my father, a Rumanian immigrant who could speak English and could read and write, gave himself too many airs—for a poor man. On the other hand here was Chayele an old maid of thirty-five and altogether without prospects, so they gave in. But they never took to my father. Nor did he to my stepmother's family of Russian immigrants.

Yankev and Yudah were born in Chileshea, a village somewhere in the depths of Russia, Yankev the older of the pair by fifteen minutes. When the time came, they were married to wives picked for them by their father. Yankev in his twenty-first year and older than his brother by fifteen minutes, was the first to be betrothed. The father's choice for Yankev fell to the daughter of a landowner in Propoiske, a village a few miles from theirs. Yankev was informed by his father of the business and a week later he set out with his father by horse and cart for the seven-mile journey to Propoiske to meet his wife-to-be, Henye.

The following, as was told (again and again) by Yankev himself, is an account of the meeting:

There was a bitter frost that night. It was black as pitch when we started out, not even a dog was to be seen on the road. We came to my beloved's house cold as stones. The landowner opened the door to us and we were conducted to a big room with a round table in it, a davenport, a carpet on the floor— very fine. He invited me to the stove to warm myself, giving me several glances. Then to my father he gave a nod. Satisfied.

Satisfied. Why would he not be satisfied? Warming himself at the stove stood a stunning youth—you should have seen me at twenty-one, I was like a tree. Tall, straight, a head of hair like a lion, a neck like a bull.

He took a few steps to the hall, my future father-in-law, and called for his wife. Right away a scrap of a woman came hurrying in. So fast I thought she was on wheels. A nothing of a woman, the size of a sitting dog. She gave me a dried hand, looking me up and down. 'Well, mamushka,' her husband said to her, 'are you pleased with your future son-in-law?' Her voice when it came out, was a croak. 'It is not for me to say. It's for Henyechke to say. If she is pleased with him I will be content.'

A second time the landowner went to the hall. 'Come, Henyechke,' he called to his daughter. 'We're waiting for you.'

The door opened and my beloved came to the room. One look and every-thing went black before my eyes. A duplicate of the mother! A chill fell on me. One minute I was cold, the next minute hot. She gave me her hand. 'Welcome to our house,' she said. The voice even was like the mother's. We were bidden to table and my sweetheart pouring out the tea did not take her eyes from me. Devouring me with her eyes. Meantime the mother—and this is something you would have to see with your own eyes to believe—was doling out the sugar. Breaking it off piece by piece from the sugar bowl which she kept in her lap between a pair of bony knees. Heed yourself, Yankev, an inner voice warned me. Heed yourself.

We drank a second glass of tea, we ate a stingy piece of cake, a spoonful of cherry jam, and it was time to go. My father took my hand and placed it in the hand of my future bride, and the pact was made. Unhappy ill-fated Yankev was now betrothed. It seemed to me I heard a howling of wolves. That witches were coupling, I knew for sure.

I whipped up the horse and we started for home. He talked and he talked and he talked, my father, so pleased was he with this night's business. The handsome dowry he had negotiated for his son, pitting his wits against the landowner's. I would not have to work like a horse to earn a bitter piece of bread as he at my age had done. I could go into business, or buy a piece of land. In a year or two I would be looked up to, respected. He kept on and on. Words piling up, every one of them a stone in my heart. The business of the dowry had not been as easy as I might think, he told me. I was not the only suitor. There was another candidate—'Who?' I said, speaking for the first time. 'The Devil?' 'Enough, Yankev!' he hollered. 'Enough!'

We were late getting home. My mother had gone to her bed, but not my brother Yudah to his. He was waiting to hear my news, I had left with such high hopes. I was a lusty youth at twenty-one—vital! One look at my face and he did not have to ask how I had fared. He signed to me behind my father's back and I followed him to the room we slept in together. I fell on his neck and poured out to him my bitter heart. He rocked me in his arms and hushed me like a baby, 'Shah, shah, shah.' He bade me to com-pose myself. He had a plan. 'Tomorrow in a quiet moment I will propose it to my father,' he said. What plan? I tried to worry it out of him but all I could get from him was, 'Rest easy, Yankev. Leave everything to me.' And as a condemned man with his head already in the noose clings foolishly *to the hope of a reprieve, I was calmed by his words.*

His plan? I heard it next morning. Keeping myself out of sight behind the kitchen door I heard the plan as he put it to my father.

'I beg you, father, let me stand in my brother's place under the canopy. No one can tell us apart. Even you and my mother sometimes have to take a second look to make sure.' (True. The pranks we had played on shiksas in the fields—and even on respectable Jewish girls in our village.)

'Who put you up to this?' my father asked him. 'Your brother?'

'On my word, my brother knows nothing of this plan.'

'Why do you do it then?'

My brother returned no answer.

I jumped from my hiding place. 'For pity!' I shouted. 'For pity, do you hear!'

My father lifted his hand as if to strike me. Which I deserved, raising my voice to my father.

'There will be no trickery,' he said. 'I gave my hand to the landowner, and Yankev gave his hand to the daugher. . . .'

In a month's time Yankev and Henye were man and wife.

The first child of the marriage, a boy, was born sickly. He lived only two weeks. The second child, again a boy, was a compact healthy child. He sickened and in six weeks was dead.

Henye, brooding, mourning the loss of her children, took a strange notion into her head. Two children one after the other had been snatched from her. A punishment, surely. A judgement. She had sinned, wronged, and was now being repaid. . . .

The night of the betrothal when Yankev's father on the way home from Propoiske told his son there was another candidate for the hand of the landowner's daughter, he was speaking the truth. Not the Devil, as Yankev conjectured, but a young man from Samatevitz who, prior to Yankev by a week or two, had been viewed and sent on his way after tea, a piece of cake, and cherry jam with a half-promise (which he took to be a firm commitment) that the dowry together with the land-owner's daughter was as good as his. A week or two later when Henye clapped eyes on Yankev, all was up with the suitor from Samatevitz. The jilted suitor made a fuss. He demanded compensation. In rubles. The landowner peaced him off with soft words. The rejected suitor left in a dudgeon. Making an ominous pronouncement. 'God will repay me,' he said.

God will repay me . . .

These words came back to Henye, chilling her heart. Pregnant again and determined not to let this one slip away from her, she conceived a plan for holding on to her third child. To ensure the continuance of the child about to be born to her, she must solicit the pardon of her rejected lover. She was resolved that unless she petitioned his forgiveness no issue of hers would live to see the light of day.

Her third son was born and Henye, to ward off the Evil Eye, gave him the name Alter (Old One). Then as soon after the birth as she was able to, she put her plan into operation. She clothed the infant in old swaddling clothes, tatters, and journeyed with him by foot to the cemetery where her rejected suitor (who in the interim had died) lay buried. There, by his grave, she pleaded for pardon. Holding in her arms a ragamuffin whom no one on earth, or under, could conceivably covet, she begged forgiveness for the wrong she had done him.

Alter survived and thrived. At sixteen he was almost as tall as his father Yankev. Five more were born after him. The last born of the five, a girl. All persevered and held fast. Henye became shrunken and humped over in the back.

Yudah too had married and was fathering a family.

A few months after Yankev's marriage to Henye the father negotiated for Yudah a marriage with a girl called Lippa, a pretty girl from a nearby village. Yudah, as was the custom, brought his wife home after the marriage and lodged her under the parental roof. With Lippa, the family consisted of seven. The old people, the twins, their wives, and Chayele, orphaned grandchild of the old people. (The child's mother, sister of the twins and older by a few years, was widowed early in marriage and died shortly after, leaving Chayele orphaned.)

Lippa over the years gave birth to four children; the first born a boy, and the other three, girls.

The old people died and the twin brothers in their forty-third year decided to emigrate to the new world. Yankev taking with him Alter, and Yudah taking his firstborn, the brothers set out. Their wives and remaining children to be sent for when they were settled. They set sail for the new world, all four, not a word of English among them. Their language was Yiddish. To their work people and to the peasants in the field, they spoke Russian. Not one had been a greater distance than fifty miles (if that) from Chileshea. They brought food on board ship, not knowing for sure if they would be fed. They docked in Halifax, thinking they were in America.

They entrained for Toronto and were met at the station by a gang of people: *landsmen*, relatives, a junto of compatriots who had emigrated years before. The first few weeks were given over to conviviality. Parties were given for them, dinners, suppers; days and nights were spent in nostalgic reminiscence. Their cousin Haskele (called behind his back Haskele the Shikker) toured the twins with their sons around the city in his car. He showed them Eaton's, Simpsons, the City Hall, Sunnyside, the Parliament Buildings, Casa Loma, the Jewish market on Kensington, and the McCaul Street synagogue.

Finally the business to hand—how to make a living—came up for consideration. The brothers were counselled, warned what to watch out for. Toronto was not Chileshea. Plenty of crooks on the lookout for a pair of greenhorns with money in their pocket. It was decided after a succession of councils and advisements that the best plan would be to start small. The name Chaim the *Schnorrer* (gone to his rest a few months since) came up at one of these sessions. He had started small and was rich as Croesus when he died. His investment? A few dollars for a peddler's licence, a few dollars for a pushcart— and the wealth he accumulated in six years!

'Who knew how rich he was getting, the fish-peddling miser. He lived in a garret and slept on two chairs put together and ate *dreck*. We took pity on him. Only when he was dying in the Western Hospital from dried up guts that it came out how much money he had. He grabbed a hold of every doctor who put a nose even in the public ward, and begged them to save him. "Save me," he told them, "I've got money I can pay." He showed them bankbooks. A thousand in this bank, two thousand in another bank. In his shoes alone they found over four hundred dollars.'

The brothers obtained a fish-peddling licence each, equipped themselves with carts and taking over Chaim the *Schnorrer's* circuit peddled their fish in the Jewish district, the area bounded by College and Spadina, Dundas and Bathurst streets, and beyond. And made a good thing of it. In less than three years they were able to provide passage for their families.

Henye arrived with their four sons, their daughter, and their niece Chayele. Yudah, his wife Lippa having died a year after his departure, had only his three daughters to greet.

All this happened years before I was born. . . .

When Chayele came to us as stepmother I was six years old. We lived in rooms over the synagogue on Bellevue Avenue, and Yankev with his wife Henye and their daughter Malke, who was a dipper at Willard's Chocolates and engaged to be married to a druggist, lived around the corner from us on Augusta Avenue. Their youngest son, Pesach, lived with his wife, Lily, in the upstairs flat of his father's house. Their other four sons were domiciled with their wives and children around and about the city.

Yudah lived with a married daughter a few blocks from his brother's place.

Yankev was a social man. He loved company and almost every night of the week friends and relatives would gather at his house on Augusta Avenue. My stepmother too went there almost every night, and I used to tag along with her. I loved going to Yankev's, what a hullabaloo! No one spoke, everyone shouted, Yankev's voice rising above the hurly-burly. 'Henye!' he would call out when the full number was assembled. 'Where is she, my beauty?'

Henye would be sitting in a corner of the kitchen apart from the hubbub, and Yankev who knew exactly where she was located would make a great play of searching her out. Looking to the right of him, to the left of him, behind him, he would lift his head finally and craning it over the assembled company would direct his glance to her station.

'Ah there she is, my picture. What are you sitting there like a stump? People are in the house. Bring something to table. Fruit, a piece of cake. Make tea.'

Henye would rise to fill the kettle while Yankev, his eye on her, might mutter sotto voce: 'Crooked Back.'

Night after night they sat at Henye's table, friends and relatives, eating her food and laughing at Yankev's abuse of her. Now and then, not out of loyalty to her or compassion, but for the sake of mischief, for the sake of quickening the action, Henye would be prodded by one of the company to defend herself, to make some reply to her husband. 'Say something to him, Henye!'

Hunched over in a corner chair and blowing on her tea which she drank from a saucer, Henye would lift her shoulder in a shrug. 'Let him talk,' she would say, making her standard reply, her voice grating, harsh. 'As a dog howls so Yankev speaks. Does one dispute with a howling dog? Let him talk.'

One time I saw her go into a frenzied tantrum at Yankev's Crooked Back remark. Crooked Back was a commonplace in his vocabulary of insult. He had worse names for her. Old Devil, Witch, Scarecrow—these names went unheeded by Henye. Were passed over with a shrug from her, a spit on the floor. But this night for some unanswerable reason she was stung, inflamed by Yankev's 'Crooked Back' as she was filling the kettle. She went berserk. She stamped her feet like Rumpelstiltskin. Slammed the kettle, spilling water from the spout. With head thrust forward and bony arms bent at the elbow she busied herself with the back of her dress, unfastening it at the neck. Pulling at her undergarments till she had them far down enough to expose and lay bare her disfigurement, she turned her back to the company and displayed to them her dorsal hump.

'In his service,' she said in her rasp of a voice. 'In his service I have become crooked and bent. In my father's house my back was straight. In Yankev's service it became bent.

Yankev has a right to insult me, I've earned it from him.'

She exhibited her twisted back, making sure everyone at her table had a good look. Like a mannequin displaying to a roomful of buyers some latter feature in haute couture, so Henye pirouetted and spun before them, pointing to the hump on her back.

The collection was titillated by this turnabout in the evening's advancement. They applauded her. She was given a handclap. 'Good for you, Henye! Give it to him!'

Yankev was stunned. Dumbfounded. But only momentarily. Quickly his surprise gave way to anger.

'Cover yourself!' he bellowed. 'Cover yourself, you shameless old Jezebel! In my service!' he thundered. 'The gall of the woman——'

He rose to his feet and with shoulders back and handsome head lifted high he strutted a few steps in his kitchen like a cock. He squared himself against the wall, facing the company.

'I was a stunning youth! You should have seen me at twenty-one, I was like a tree! Tall, straight, a head of hair like a lion, a neck like a bull.' He pointed an accusing finger at Henye who was hooking herself up at the back. 'She became bent in my service? A lie! In her father's house she was straight? A lie! As you see her now so she was when I beheld her the first time. On my word my friends, no different. One look at this picture my father had picked for me and I was taken with the ague. One minute I was cold, the next minute hot——'

'Enough!' came Yudah's voice from the assembly. 'Enough, Yankev.'

Yankev turned an astonished face to his brother. 'You turn on me too? Is this Yudah, my second self, who speaks? Is this Yudah who volunteered out of pity for Yankev to stand in his place under the canopy?' Without another word, Yankev took his place again at the head of his table.

Henye, her own effrontery having gone to her head like wine, was not through with him yet. (Social ascendancy over Yankev was a potent draught.) Buttoned up now but unmindful of the kettle, she spoke up again.

'No need,' she said. 'There was no need for Yudah to step into Yankev's place, and there was no need for Yankev himself if I was so unpleasing to him, to take me for his wife. There were others,' she said, preening almost. 'One of my suitors died after I married Yankev, and left his curse on me for disappointment. I lost two children. I went to his grave after Alter was born, to beg his pardon——'

Yankev leapt to his feet, revivified. 'True! She went to beg his pardon. It's my pardon she should have begged, not his. He was lying undisturbed, unplagued—and she went to beg his pardon. He was liberated, *I* was in bondage—it's Yankev's pardon she should have asked. Yankev!' he cried, bringing his fist to his chest and thumping himself like Tarzan.

Henye had had her brief moment. Now it was over and the company was restored to Yankev's sway.

When I knew the brothers, their fish-peddling days were behind them. It was during Prohibition and they were making an easier dollar peddling illicit booze. The fish cart however was still in use. For deliveries. The topmost tray, concealing the bootleg booze in the interior of the cart, contained for the sake of camouflage a few scattered pickerel, a bit of pike, a piece of whitefish packed in ice. Yankev, to accommodate expanding trade, had a phone installed in the hall of his house and it rang at all hours, a customer at the other end asking for Jack. Their customers, for the most part gentile, could not get their tongues around Yankev so they called him Jack. Yudah was called Joe.

The brothers had acquired a bit of English, enough to see them through their business. Their inventory and records were kept in a lined exercise book, in Yiddish. Customers were designated by descriptive terms, nicknames: The Gimpy One on Bathurst, Long Nose on Lippincott. Using their fish carts mocked up with a scattering of moribund fish in the topmost tray, they made their deliveries to Big Belly, Short Ass, The Murderer, Big Tits, The Pale One, The Goneff, The Twister, The Tank.

They operated a long time without running afoul of the

law. But were apprehended eventually on a delivery run, and took a pinch. Which resulted in a fine. A sobering experience this, their first skirmish with the law, and despite loss of revenue and the clamouring of customers, the brothers lay low for a while. Then started up again. The fish cart, now that the cops were on to them, was held to be unserviceable, so the brothers bought a car and Yankev learned to drive it. Yudah, of a more nervous disposition than his brother, never learned to drive.

Again they went a good time unmolested by the law, and suddenly were fallen upon, nabbed by a pair of plainclothes-men as they were loading the car. The load was confiscated and the brothers, in full view of neighbours who had come out to watch, were hustled into the squad car.

Henye was petrified. Frightened that she'd be hauled up too she scurried for a hiding place, hollering, '*Gevald!*'

On the books a second time, the brothers drew a stiffer fine. Further, Yankev was prohibited from keeping so much as a single bottle of whisky on his premises, with a warning from the bench that a third offence would result in a jail sentence.

This gave the brothers a jolt. They were really shaken up. But it didn't stop them from selling. They kept to their course—but with more caution than before. Yudah with a few bottles stashed on his person would by foot or by streetcar, depending on his landing-place, make a discreet delivery. Yankev, equipped likewise, would take Henye for a ride in the car. Which she loved. 'In a car I could ride to Moskva,' she used to say. Yankev made a few stops en route, explaining he had to collect some money owing him, and with the motor running she sat quite content waiting for him. An unwitting shill, and terrified of the law, Henye accompanied her husband on his deliveries and never tumbled that she was fronting for him.

And so things went till one Friday with the brothers at Shul, and Henye at her pots, two plainclothesmen without a search warrant or even a knock on the door, came directly in and began taking the place apart, looking for booze. Henye hollered, '*Gevald!* A pogrom!' and fainted. Her daughter-in-law Lily, screaming, came running down the stairs with Pesach

close on her heels. The cops continued their search. Unearth-
ing a couple of cases which they stored in their car, they sat
themselves on the verandah awaiting the brothers' return.

The shame of it! People coming from synagogue and police
on the verandah as if waiting for a pair of bandits. Henye
banged her head on the wall. 'Let them wait inside!' she cried,
and as Pesach went to fetch them she hid herself in the toilet.
The brothers came in and before the law could put an arm on
either of them, Pesach, youngest of the sons and quickest in
the head, made a verbal deposition to the cops. He claimed
the whisky was his. Which flummoxed the cops. Briefly. All
three were taken to the station, all three booked, and Monday
when the case came before the bench Pesach stepped forward
and taking his oath on the Bible swore the whisky was his.
And with the help of a lawyer, made the story stick. Pesach
drew a fine for keeping on convicted premises declared by the
law to be out of bounds.

The same night, and at Henye's behest, a family conclave
made up of Yankev's five sons with their wives, Malke with
her boyfriend the druggist, Yudah's four children with their
partners, all talking at once exhorted the brothers to put an
end to the business. Now that they were known to the law it
was too risky. Both were well fixed with money in the bank,
they were getting a good income from the two pieces of
property they had bought, Yudah had only himself to provide
for, Yankev with a paid-up house was getting rent from
Pesach, Malke was paying board. The brothers were reminded they were sick men, both. (They had become asthmatic in the last few years, with an advancing seriousness of
chest congestion. A fright, a scare, the least bit of physical
exertion brought on a fit of coughing, a whooping strangling
seizure alarming to behold.)

The brothers gave up the booze. They were together all
day as before, but now there was no occupation for them,
nothing to do with their time. They played checkers by the
hour, casino, and went oftener to the synagogue than before.
In the spring of that year they sat on Yankev's verandah
drinking a glass of tea sweetened with slices of peeled apple.

I used to bring my homework to Yankev's verandah and would hear them talking nostalgically of the bootlegging days. They missed the action. 'The day is like a year,' said Yankev. 'But for that old devil of mine we'd still be in business.'

Augusta Avenue was a busy street and the brothers, to invent a bit of diversion for themselves, sat on the verandah making asides to each other about the passersby going to and coming from the market. Their eye one day was caught by a new nose in the neighbourhood, a big woman with an excessive bosom, her breasts under a cotton dress swinging free and unleashed. The brothers gawked. Yankev nudged Yudah: 'If one of those should fall on your foot God forbid—every bone would be crushed.' They fell over themselves, winded, short of breath from laughing. 'Och toch toch,' they gasped, gulping for breath, pummelling themselves on the chest. 'Och toch toch.'

Unperceived by the brothers, Henye had come out with a pot of fresh tea. In one wink she took in the scene. 'Shame on you. A pair of old men. Shame on you both,' she said, and spat.

Slowly, Yankev turned his head in her direction. 'To *look*, you old devil—is that forbidden too?' He snatched the tea pot from her hands. 'Get back in the house, I'll pour out myself.'

In the summer of that year, Yudah fell sick. Painfully congested and unable to speak, he lived only nine days. People came to the house of Shiva to comfort Yudah's children, the bereaved brother, and it was remarked by them that Yankev overnight had become an old man. When Shiva was over Yankev came every morning to the synagogue above which we had rooms to say Kaddish for his brother, and fell into the habit of coming upstairs after prayers to while away some time with his niece Chayele. He used the side door of the synagogue which gave secondary access to our place, a short climb, eighteen steps in all, but for Yankev a laborious ascent. You'd hear his 'och toch' as he paused every few steps.

One morning before sitting down to his tea he extracted from the inside pockets of his coat three bottles of whisky. 'A little favour, Chayele,' he said to my stepmother, 'to put away for a couple of days these few bottles.'

'With pleasure,' she responded, and hid them in the far end of the dark hall in an unused bunker filled with junk. He thanked his niece, and to me he gave ten cents not to say anything to my Pa.

Next morning he came as usual for his glass of tea and before leaving took a bottle from the bunker and put it in his pocket. In a few days the bunker, denuded of booze, was replenished. With six bottles. In a short while (the bunker unable to accommodate the increasing supply) whisky was being stored in the room my sister, my brother, and I slept in. A few bottles under the bed I shared with my sister, a few bottles under my brother's bed.

Two or three times a day, except on the Sabbath or a Jewish holiday—and never when my father was home—Yankev made his sorties to and from our place.

People remarked on the change in Yankev. They said he was becoming his old self again.

One day in the late Fall on a Jewish holiday with the synagogue packed out and a few members of the congregation standing out front in their prayer shawls taking a breather, a squad car drew up and two cops emerged, making straight for the outside door abutting the synagogue, which was the primary entrance to the stairs leading to our place. A quick inspection uncovered bottles in the bunker and bottles under the beds. They began querying my stepmother, who didn't understand a word they were saying.

'Ask her what's all this whisky doing here,' they instructed me. 'Ask her who it belongs to.'

I put the question to my stepmother, then gave them her reply. 'She says she can't give you a straight answer because her head is spinning with fright. She wants you to take the whisky and go before my father comes home.'

They told me to ask her this, to ask her that, and as I was saying for the twentieth time, 'She would like you to take the whisky and go before my father comes home,' we heard his step on the stairs.

Without preamble, my father was taken over the hurdles.

They told him right off they knew the whisky was not his. They knew who it belonged to, but that didn't absolve him from guilt. His place was being used as a drop. 'What do you get paid for keeping?' they asked him.

'I am not in a court of law,' said my father (showing off his English). 'In my own house I don't have to answer any questions.'

'Okay let's go,' they said, and my father, before going submissively downstairs with the cops, gave hell to my stepmother in Yiddish.

Doing my stepmother's bidding I ran to Yankev's house with the intelligence. Yankev and Henye with their daughter Malke and her boyfriend the druggist were at supper.

Yankev clapped a hand to his forehead. 'A *klog!*' he wailed, 'a *klog!*'

Henye set up a holler. 'He's been selling again! He wants to bury me, that *Poshe Yisroel*.'

Yankev beating his hands together lamented his fate. He was certain my father would open up, sell him down the river. A third conviction meant jail. Asthmatic as he was he would never survive even a short term in jail. He would die there like a dog. His life was in the hands of the Rumanian Beast (his name for my father behind his back). 'A frightening contemplation,' he moaned. 'Frightenino.'

My stepmother came running. Pa had called from the station. From what she understood he never told on anybody. He took the blame on himself—but somebody had to go right away to the station with five hundred dollars. 'Bail,' she said. The word had been dinned into her head.

'Thank God!' said Yankev. 'The Almighty One has not forsaken me after all.'

And with my father cooling his heels in the pokey, Yankev sat down to finish his supper. 'Now another problem comes up,' he said, drinking his second glass of tea. Who was to go to the station? He didn't dare put a nose in there. And neither did Pesach with a conviction against him. Malke's fiancé rose from his place. 'I'll go,' he said.

'Finish first,' said Yankev, pointing to the druggist's dish of compote. 'The jail isn't on fire. He's not sitting there in a holocaust.'

My father was tried and because of the inside door of the synagogue giving secondary access to our rooms was convicted and fined for keeping whisky in a place held by the law to be public.

Yankev put up the money for the fine, and the same evening his four sons came to their father's house to upbraid and lecture him. They said they were surprised that their father, a man of principle, would go back on his word. And Yankev listened acquiescently, attended their words without demur. 'A mistake,' he conceded, 'a mistake.' Henye snorted. Next day friends and relatives came in their numbers and Yankev, constrained to give an ear to them too, acknowledged he was ashamed of having gone back on his word. Henye, filling the kettle, gave out a short derisive laugh. Except for a muttered *Gazlan!* as she set her husband's glass of tea before him, she had nothing to say.

In the following months Yankev became soft as butter. Henye's days became easier; he had stopped belabouring her. He let up on her altogether. When company came she still kept to her corner chair, but she could open her mouth now without being jumped on.

In January Yankev fell ill and was taken by ambulance to hospital. First day, he was allowed no visitors. Second day only his wife was permitted in the sick-room. Henye sat by his bed peering at him through the oxygen tent and crying

'Don't mourn me, I'm still alive,' said Yankev, and signed to her to go.

His third day in hospital his children were allowed in two at a time, and on the fourth day (Saturday) it was given out to them by the doctor that their father was very low. Saturday noon we had a hysterical call from Pesach. His father was dying, he said, and requested of my stepmother that I be sent right away to fetch Henye. Yankev was asking for her.

When I came to Henye with my tidings she was sitting at the kitchen table drinking tea from a saucer. I told her I had come to take her to the hospital. 'Yankev wants to see you,' I said. She put her saucer down and with hands clasped loosely in her lap studied my face. 'Yankev sent for me?' she said in her harsh voice. I waited for her to get ready but she continued at table rocking back and forth and muttering to herself. I caught the words *'mechilah betten.'** She rose abruptly from her chair and a minute later returned in her coat and shawl.

We trudged through the snow, Henye with shawled head thrust forward holding on to my arm and keeping up a hoarse monologue on our way to the hospital.

'So the time of reckoning has come and Yankev sends for his wife. *Mechilah betten,'* she said, nodding her bent head. 'What is there to forgive? Everything—and nothing. Without Yankev I'll be alone. Alone like a stone. I have children—God give them health—but children are one thing and a husband is another. A husband is a friend, my dear. So Yankev hollered at me, called me names—that's nothing, it's soon forgotten. Like last year's snow. I had my faults too. Yankev was an open-handed man and I was a—' she gave me a sideways glance—'I know people called me a stingy,' she said, using one of the few English words in her vocabulary. 'And also other faults. Sinful faults nobody knows about except Henye. Jealous, jealous, jealous. All my life jealous,' she said with a rueful shake of her head. 'People liked Yankev, I was jealous. My sister-in-law Lippa was pretty, I was jealous. People said Lippa is like a little doll, I ate my heart out. Least little thing, I laid the blame on Lippa. Yankev loved his brother Yudah, again jealous. I tried many times to come between them——'

She stopped to kick snow from her shoes, then passed under her dripping nose the handkerchief she used on the Sabbath bound around her wrist like a bandage, and we continued.

'People said Yankev doesn't like his wife—what do people know? You're a young child so you won't understand,' she said (I was fourteen), 'but if a woman is disliked by her husband, uninviting to him, she cannot give him even one child—let alone eight children. I was very sick when Malke was born and who looked after me? Not my sister and not my mother.

*To beg forgiveness.

Yankev. Who fed me from a spoon like a baby? Yankev. He went two miles by foot to buy me an orange.'

We came in sight of the hospital; she stopped to take a dab at her eyes with the back of her handkerchief-bandaged wrist. Being the Sabbath Henye would not ride the elevator so we walked the four flights to Yankev's room. She searched the faces of her children who were standing in the corridor, then opened the door to her husband's room. She stood by his bed looking at him; he appeared to be asleep.

He opened his eyes, and motioned her to sit down. 'Henye,' he said, 'I have a request——'

Henye leaned forward. 'No need, Yankev. All is forgiven——'

'Good,' he said, nodding his head. 'Good.'

'And I beg your forgiveness,' she continued. 'I beg your forgiveness for——'

'What is this?' he said, looking at her in puzzlement. 'I'm not dying yet. You'll have plenty of time to ask for my forgiveness.'

'The children said you sent for me? I thought, God forbid——'

He laughed. 'Och toch toch,' he gasped, pummelling his chest. Henye handed him his glass of water. 'Don't worry I'll climb out. My time isn't up yet,' he said, sipping water from his glass. 'I sent for you to tell you something—but I don't want the children to know, you hear?' He paused to summon breath. 'The last few weeks I took a little order here, a little order there——'

Henye gaped.

'In the summer kitchen behind the new bag of potatoes,' he continued, 'you'll find a few bottles—'he paused for breath—'so if a customer phones——'

Henye didn't wait to hear the rest. With Yankev still talking she rose to her feet and the next minute she was out of the room.

'Come,' she said, taking hold of my arm. And to her children clustered outside their father's door, 'He'll live,' she said.

Holding on to my arm Henye sped along the snow-covered

streets, I had to run to keep pace with her. She opened the door to her house and beckoned me to follow. Speeding through hall, through kitchen, she proceeded to the back of the house lean-to, which they called the summer kitchen. This small area used as a store-house contained the Passover pots and pans and dishes, jars of preserves, bushel baskets of apples, onions, carrots, and in a corner of the summer kitchen two burlap bags of potatoes; the one in use easy of access, the unopened one wedged in the corner and barricaded behind several earthenware crocks containing pickled cucumbers, beet borscht, and kvass.

Seizing hold of it by its neck, Henye lifted the foremost bag of potatoes, thrust it aside, then stooped to the earthenware crocks (which had to be shifted in order to gain access to the hindmost bag of potatoes). I watched Henye, a little gnome with black shawl sweeping the floor, grappling with the unwieldy crocks.

'You try,' she said. 'Young hands are stronger.'

Tilting the crocks and rolling them on their rims I managed, with Henye clearing space for them, to open a passage wide enough to admit a burlap bag of potatoes. Together, we pulled the bag from its lodging and there, as Yankev said she would, Henye found a few bottles. Four. She took two bottles and bade me to take the other two. 'Come,' she said, and I followed her to the kitchen.

She pulled the shawl from her head and took off her coat. 'Open up a bottle,' she directed me. She took the bottle to the sink. 'Here's a customer for you, Yankev,' she said, and emptied it down the drain. She told me to uncap another one. 'Here's another customer,' she said, and that too went down the drain. A third bottle was emptied. Draining the last one down the sink, she turned her head to me. 'When it comes to whisky Henye is not a stingy,' she said slyly.

'I would give you something,' she said, thanking me, 'but Shabbus I don't carry money.' Then as I made to go, she called me back. She pulled open a drawer in which she kept odds and ends, her pills, her medicines, and the knotted handkerchief with its nickels and dimes. 'Take ten cents,' she said, pointing

to the knotted handkerchief. I took hold of the knot and applying the technique I had seen her use so many times—a tug,
a twist, a pull, a pluck—went to work on it. I couldn't even
loosen the knot, let alone untie it. I returned the handkerchief
to the drawer. 'You'll pay me tomorrow.'

Three days later Yankev came home.
    Company came the same night to welcome him home.
Henye bustled and scurried about. Unbidden, she brought
fruit to table, cake, and made tea. 'What an escape,' said
Yankev, shaking his head. 'To scramble out of their hands—a
deliverance, my friends,' he said solemnly. 'A deliverance.'
    With Yankev home, the phone began ringing again. One
night at supper the phone rang, and Henye went to it. The
call for Jack. 'Jeck?' she said. 'Jeck not home. In Hallyefacks,'
she said and hung up.
    For the first time since coming home, Yankev showed
anger. 'Don't make a fool of me, Henye!' he said as she
resumed her place. 'Attend to your business and leave my
business to me——'
    '*His* business,' she said. 'It's my business too. You took me
in for a partner, you forgot? Last Saturday in the hospital
when you sent for me—you don't remember? You told me
where the whisky was, you told me to attend—and I did.
When I came home a customer was waiting so I gave him
the whisky.'
    Yankev stared. 'A customer was here? In the house?'
    Henye pointed to the sink. 'That customer.'
    Yankev rose and made his way to the summer kitchen.
He returned and without a word took his place at table.
Henye, undisturbed, continued with her food. She poured
him a glass of tea and dropped into it a heaping spoonful of
cherry conserve. 'You saw for yourself there's no more
whisky?' she said. He made no reply. She poured some tea
from her glass into her saucer. 'We're out of business, Mister
Jeck,' she said, bringing her saucer to her lips—and Yankev
despite himself began to laugh. 'Och toch toch,' he gasped, and
signaled her to get him some water. 'You old devil,' he said,

his breath restored, 'you'll be the death of me yet.'

'Don't worry, Yankev,' she returned, 'you'll bury me.'

Henye's words were prophetic; two months later she died in her sleep.

I went with my stepmother to Henye's funeral. With the service at the open grave concluded, Yankev took hold of the shovel. 'So swift, Henye, so fast,' he said, shovelling earth on the coffin. 'You left in such a hurry there was no time for me to ask your forgiveness. I ask it now. Intercede for me, Henye,' he said, then handed the shovel to his oldest son Alter.

People came all week to the house of Shiva to comfort Henye's children and her bereaved husband. Henye was lauded, praised to the skies. Her children, concurring, wept at every mention of their mother's name while Yankev, obsessed with the speed of Henye's departure, talked of it without beginning and without end.

'So fast,' he said. 'Like a whirlwind. We ate supper, we talked of Malke's wedding next month, how much will it cost for the hall, how much for the music—' Malke began to cry. Her father gave her a baleful look and continued. 'All of a sudden she said "I feel like to go to bed." Henye to go to bed before twelve, one o'clock? Henye to leave dishes on the table? I went up myself to bed an hour later, maybe two hours later—who can remember—and she was asleep. Of *that* I'm sure. She turned around when I put on the light. In the morning she was cold.' He struck his forehead with the palm of his hand. 'When did she die? Of what? And without a word!'

Six months after Henye's death Malke was married to her druggist. With Malke gone, Yankev sat at Pesach's table Friday after Shul for the Sabbath meal. Now and then Lily's mother, an active widow, a big woman who drove her own car, spoke English, and lived in an apartment, made a fourth at Pesach's table for Friday night supper—and it was observed by Pesach that his father seemed more animated the nights the widow came for supper.

Before long it was put about that Yankev was going to remarry.

One afternoon we heard the familiar 'och toch toch' on the stairs giving notice of Yankev's approach. Without any waste of time he told my stepmother what was on his mind. 'The truth, Chayele, will I be making a fool of myself?'

'Why a fool?' my stepmother replied.

'People will laugh,' he said. 'Yankev a *chossin* in his old age——'

'Let them laugh,' said my stepmother. 'What kind of life is it to be alone?'

In March, a year to the month of Henye's death, Yankev was married and went to live with his new wife in her apartment. Three months went by, and not a word from Yankev. My stepmother began to worry. She handed me a scrap of paper with Yankev's new phone number. 'Phone,' she said. His wife answered the phone. 'Yankev went for a stroll,' she said in English. 'Tell your mother I'll be going to the market tomorrow and I'll drop him off at your place.'

Next morning we heard Yankev making his ascent. He came to the kitchen spruced up in a navy blue suit. 'Och toch toch,' he gasped, fanning himself with a panama hat. 'I'm not used any more to steps—in the building we have an elevator.'

My stepmother fussed over him. She made tea, complimented him on his attire, his looks—'You lost a little weight, Yankev?'

'Lost a little weight,' he repeated. 'She put me on a diet. Gives me grass to eat.' (His word for lettuce.) He pointed to his glass, indicating it was to be filled again. 'It's good to drink tea again from a glass,' he said. 'She gives me tea in a cup. What taste is there to a glass of tea in a cup? Chayele, Chayele, Chayele,' he said, shaking his head and sighing.

My stepmother was disturbed. 'You're not happy?'

'Happy,' he echoed. 'It's like you said—what kind of life is it to be alone?'

All at once he was his old self again. He smiled at my stepmother, a look of mischief coming to his face. 'She bought me a pair of pyjamas,' he said. 'Yankev sleeps now in pyjamas, and his missus like a man sleeps also in pyjamas. First thing in the morning she opens up a window, and makes exercises. First of all she stretches,' he said, demonstrating with his arms aloft. 'Then she bends down and puts her ass in the air. And that's some ass to put in the air, believe me. And all day, busy. Busy, busy, busy. With what? To make supper takes five minutes. Soup from a can, compote from a can—it has my *boba*'s flavour. A piece of herring? This you never see on the table, she doesn't like the smell. A woman comes in to clean— with what is she busy, you'll ask? With gin rummy. True, gin rummy. They come in three or four times a week her friends, to play gin rummy. They cackle like geese, they smoke like men. Dear, my wife says to me, bring some ginger ale from the frige, the girls are thirsty—she hasn't got time to leave the cards. Girls, she calls them. Widows! Not one of them without a husband buried in the ground,' he said with sudden indignation. 'Dear, she calls me, nu? Before me there was another Dear and she buried *him*. Once in a while without thinking, I call her Henye. She gets so mad, oh ho ho. So I make a mistake sometimes, it's natural? How does a man live with a woman all his life and blot out from his memory her name——'

He rose suddenly from his chair, took a handkerchief from his pocket and blowing his nose in it went to the mirror over the sink and peered in it, dabbing at his eyes. 'Cholera take it,' he said, 'there's something in my eye.' My stepmother looked away; next minute we heard the sound of a horn. Yankev went to the window. 'There she is, my prima donna.' He embraced his niece. 'Drives a car like a man,' he muttered, and took his leave.

1971

They
Heard a Ringing
of Bells

Austin Clarke

"WHAT IS THEM I hearing?" Estelle asked, looking up at the skies.

"Them is bells, darling," Ironhorse said.

"It is a man up there playing pon them bells," Sagaboy explainmd. "They is bells that you and me and Ironhorse Henry hearing play so nice."

"Bells playing hymns? God bless my eyesight! Boy, this Canada is a damn great country, in truth!" she exclaimed.

"It don't have nothing like this back in them islands, eh, old man?" Ironhorse said, really teasing Sagaboy, who was a Trinidadian.

"Well, let the three o' we sit down right here pon this piece o' grass, and listen to that man up there in thm skies playing them bells." And they did what Sagaboy suggested. They sat on the grass, in front of the tower which seemed to become more powerful and mysterious with each ring of the bells that resounded in the hearts of these three West Indians. Estelle spread her dress around her like an umbrella. Sagaboy and Ironhorse Henry took off their jackets, and without offering her one of them they sat down. Estelle was sitting on the bare grass. But the grass wasn't cold.

The bells were ringing hymns. And the voice of the bells swept a tide of freshness through Estelle's heart, and washed out the heaviness of deportation that had been lingering there. The immigration department had given her one week to leave the country.

Looking up at the bells, she said, "I am too glad the Lord open up this door, boy! Imagine me, nuh, imagine me up in this big-able country. I can't imagine it is really me, Estelle, sitting down here! I sitting down here, this bright Sunday afternoon, listening to some damn man up there, sayino he playing hymns on bells! Well well well, what the hell's next? Who would have think that I would ever live to see a thing so nice? I can't believe my ears at all, at all. It is the wonders o' God, boy, the wonders of the good God, cause I poor as a bird's arse and I am still up here in Canada. And I *know* that a good time can't happen to any and every man, saving that man stand in possession of money. If he have a piece of change in his pockets, he could get in a plane, God! and he could be taken to the ends of this earth, *swoosh!* in the twinkling of an eye! Man, I barely had time to swallow a mouth-ful o' hot-water tea back in Barbados, before, bram! I wasn't in a different place. And now, look me! . . . I am up in this big-able Canada. From a little little village somewhere behind God back I come up here, and now enjoying a little goodness o' life. Little good living that only the white people and the rich black people back home does enjoy. And now, ha-dai! the thing turn round, boy! It turn round as good as a cent. This is what I calls *living*. This is the way *every* black person should live! Look, I putting my hand pon a blade of grass . . . look, Henry, look Saga, man, this blade of grass is the selfsame grass as what I left back in Barbados. The said grass that I now sitting down pon, the same grass, man; but only *different*. And it is different only becausing it situated in a different place. A different, but a more better, more advance place than where I come from; and because o' this I am telling you now, this blessed Sunday afternoon, that I glad glad as hell that life still circulating through this body o' mine."

Neither Ironhorse Henry nor Sagaboy could find words of comment for this waterfall of feeling. Ironhorse had not heard anything like it since he left Barbados, more years ago than he cared to remember. But as Estelle talked he had watched her; and, with her, he had listened to the bells singing in his heart. And there he found a deep love for her. A love so great that he could not find words to express it. But he knew he had to remain silent; that he might never get the opportunity to tell it to her. She was Sagaboy's woman. And she was going to be deported next week. There she was, so near to him now; in a few days, so far away; and he could do nothing, nothing except wish that something would happen to his good friend Sagaboy, that he would cough his guts through his mouth, that he would die from the tuberculosis that rackled in his chest like stones in a can.

And Sagaboy, sitting on the other side of Estelle, remained very quiet as if he was in a dream. Then, it seemed, the bubble of his dream burst, and he tugged at a blade of grass near his feet, and exploded, "It ain't no wonders of no blasted God, woman! You have just start to live like you should have been living from the day you born. But instead, you been spending your lifetime down in Barbados, the same way as your forefathers and foremothers been spending it . . . in the kiss-me-arse canefield, and in slavery. Down there you didn't have food to eat, nor proper clothes to put on your back, and you didn't comprehend the piece o' histries involve in that kinda life, till one morning, bright and early, Satan get in your behind, and you look round, and bram! your eyes see that topsy-turvy world down there, and you turned round and look at yourself, and you didn't see nothing but rags and lice and filth and misery and the blasted British. And what happen? Revolutions run up inside your head, child, and you start to put two and two together. And you say, be-Christ, it ain't true, pardner, that is not true, at all! So what happen next? You pull up stakes and run abroad. You come up here in a more progressive country, but you still going exist in a worser life than what you was accustomed to back home. Look, every one o' we, you, me, Ironhorse here, we get so

damn tired, we get so damn vexed . . . you down there in
Barbados, and I in Trinidad, and brisk-brisk! it is pulling out,
for so! Setting sail. Pawning things that we never own and
possess, borrowing and thiefing, and we sail for Canada. It
have millions o' men and women from the islands who set
sail already for Britain. And that situation is a funny funny
piece o' histries, too. I sits down in my bed over on Spadina
Avenue, and I laugh hard hard as hell, hee-hee-hee! at all them
people who say we shouldn't make Great Britain more blacker
than she is or was, in the first Elizabethan era. And all the time
I does be laughing, I does be thinking of long long ago when
the Queen o' Britain send all them convicts and whores and
swivilitic men and women overseas, to *fluck-up* and populate
the islands! Well, darling, now the tables turn round, because
this is the *second* Elizabethan era! And it is the islands who
sending black people, *all kinds,* the good and the bad, the godly
and the ungodly, and we intend to fuck-up the good old
Mother Country like rass, as my Jamaican friend would say.
Man, I hear if you look round in Britain this afternoon you
swear to God that you ain't in Britain no longer, but that you
back in the islands. Black people? Oh rass!" And straightway,
he broke into the popular calypso, *Yankees Gone and Sparrow
Take Over Now.*

"God, that boy does talk as if he have a mouthful o' honey
inside his mouth," Ironhorse said appreciatively.

"Sagaboy, you talking the truth. You have just talk a piece
o' truth . . . you call it histries, but I haven't heard nobody talk
it that way, yet!" Estelle said, agreeing.

And then they stopped talking and listened. The bells were
ringing. You could see how the bells changed the tense expression on Estelle's face, an expression which emigration had
placed there; and how they brought fear, a fear for the
wondrous works of God, in its place. And looking more
closely, you could see a primitive beauty painted on the sharp
cheekbones and on the large mouth which gave her the
haughtiness of a black princess.

"What hymn that is, what hymn he playing there?" she
asked. "Ain't that hymn name *The Day Thou Gavest Lord Is*

Ending? Ain't it that said hymn? The selfsame tune, Henry, the same tune, Sagaboy. And that is the very-same song they took my father, God rest his soul, to the grave with! You should have seen him when they pull him outta the sea, drown, and with the water in his body, making him big like a whale, and still looking powerful and strong as he use to be when he was living and in the flesh. Lord! and when they come and tell me that my father *dead,* oh God, Henry, Sagaboy, I cry and I cry till I couldn't find water to cry with no more. And the people in the neighbourhood come and look in at the oval hole in the top o' the mahogany coffin when the undertaker-man had bring him home. And the whole village bow down their heads in respects o' the dead, in Pappy behalfs, cause my father was a man who had lots o' respects in the whole entire village and in the districts round our village. And the old women in our village bow down their heads low low low, and say, Thank God that at least He make a good dead outta Nathan. Nathan look nice as a dead. God go with thee, son, they say. And when they say that, all the men with their big bass voices start up singing this very hymn that you and me hearing coming outta that tall tower-thing. And Lord! water come to everybody's eye. The weeping and the crying and the singing. When they was weeping all that weeping, I had a funny feeling that they wasn't weeping only for my father, but for all the fathers that was ever killed by the cruel hands of the waves in the sea. And then they start filing past the coffin, singing; and the women were wringing their hands, like they was wringing out clothes, earlier that very-same day . . . God! I think I seeing it now, clear clear before my two eyes, as I listen to the magic and poetry coming outta that bell up there, this Sunday after-noon. And to think, just think that the first time I going to call back all this to mind is now that I have escape from that blasted past-tense village in Barbados to come up here, in Canada. Man, it is a long long time ago now, cause my father dead, when he dead, he left me a little girl in pigtails."

The bells were ringing still, ringing loud and clear in the quiet Toronto afternoon. Estelle's voice broke down, and she started to hum along with the carilloneur. It was a clear voice, a soft voice. A voice like a stream of crystal water fighting to reach the sea.

"A lot o' salt water separating me from the place where my father drown. And I still remember it to this day," she went on. "I even remember the dress I wear, which was the said white dress that my half-sister Bernice wore when she got baptise in the Church o' the Nazarene. A white shark skin piece o' material that Mammy had bought at a sale. And when we reach Westbury Cemetery, shadows was walking through the evergreen trees, round the graveyard. And a man come, a big, fat, ugly black man dressed down in black, come and put dirt on top o' the coffin, and then he pull off the silver things that was screwed-on to the coffin, and as quick as a fly he push them inside his pocket; and then sudden so, like how you see dusk does fall outta the skies and nobody don't know, sudden so, that same man drop my father contained in that coffin-box in the hole, and Lord! I couldn't see my father's face no more. Such a mighty screeling went up, such a terrible crying escape from the women that you would have thought the heavens was collapsing, and it weren't just a poor fisherman that was taken to his resting place under a sandbox tree. And I remember that the people in the village was so poor, most of them, that only a handful could afford to rent a motor car from Johnson's Stables to follow my father in. Most of the men had was to follow on bicycles, and some even had to carry their women and their wives on the bicycle bars."

She paused for a while, it seemed, to permit the bells to return the sadness of the funeral to her mind, and stir up the memories lurking there. She went on, "I can see his face now. I can see Pappy face before my two eyes right now. And I swear then, as I take the oath now, I swear blind that he wasn't dead in truth, cause I thought I could see his lips move, or did want to move and open, and whisper something to me from the grave. And I sorry sorry that up till now I don't know, and I can't imagine what the hell it was Pappy wanted to leave with me in the way of wisdom or advice, as he parted from me in the quick. I am the onliest living soul who see the dead attempt to talk. The only one who see that happen. And because o' that, I swear blind that they put my father to rest before his time was up. You understand what I mean? What I mean to affirm and state is this: down there in that damn island, the people don't have no lot o' respect, and a undertaker-man could make a mistake like nothing and put a person in a coffin and nail up that coffin and lower him in a grave be-Christ, before that dead-man is really a dead-man, before he stop breathing. Because them undertakers is really sharks and barracudas. Once they *suspect* that you will soon be a dead-man, that you are in a poor state o' health, that you are passing away, and they know they stand to get a few coppers for burying you, well, boy, they rushes like bloody-hell and they would *kill* you and turn you into a dead person if they think you ain't deading fast enough. Some stupid old women say it is a good thing, because God did love Pappy, and that is why He take my only father to His grave. But·I don't believe that. Even now, at my age, I still don't think that God could say He is in love with a man, and then turn round and put His hand pon that man, strangulate him, and drop him dead, and in the quick, and still say He *love* him? Standing up by that grave that evening I hold up my two hands, high high in the air, and I screamed so bloody hard that they get frightened and they had was to drag me, still screaming and twirling pon the ground, mind you, to a motor car, and administer smelling salts to my nose to revive me and pacify me. Cause, don't matter how rough and cruel a father treats you, boy, a father is a father. That happen long long ago. Long ago, the Good Lord lift up my poor father up in the heavens with Him. And that is my testimony to the two o' you, as I sitting down here betwixt the two o' you, this bright Sunday evening in Toronto Canada, hearing this hymn, this selfsame tune that carried Nathan Sobers, my father, to his grave in Westbury Cemetery. Ain't you hearing that same hymn,*The Day Thou Gavest?*"

"I hearing it, Estelle, darling, I hearing it like anything," Sagaboy said, in a whisper, as if his voice had left his body and was now distant, far off, lost in the sea of time. Estelle's words had taken him back to his family and his home, tucked away

out of memory in Trinidad; and they had made him think of
the recent death of his Karen, his wife from Germany.

"Ain't it strange, ain't it wondrous strange how a person
remembers things that happen so long ago? And ain't it
strange too, how a simple thing like a bell in a tower could
cause that same person to travel miles and miles in
memory . . ."

"Strange!" Sagaboy told her. Still, his voice was far away
across the ocean, miles away from the grass and the tower
and the university campus where they were sitting and from
the invisible hand of the carilloneur playing hymns on his
bells. And then the bells stopped ringing; and then the three
of them became bored with time resting so heavily on them,
for they could think of nothing to do, or say, now that the bells
had stopped ringing.

All you can hear now is the heavy breathing from Sagaboy,
as he chews on a match stick. Henry begins to chew a match
stick too. Suddenly he stops chewing, and offers a cigarette
to Sagaboy, and to Estelle.

"Back home, I won't be seen dead with one o' these in my
mouth, and on a Sunday, to boot!" she said. "What is one
man's medicine is a next man's poison."

"You in Canada now, darling, you not back home," Ironhorse Henry reminded her. And with that, the conversation
died; and the stillness and the sterility of a Toronto Sunday
returned. Estelle blew smoke through her nostrils and her
mouth at the same time, looking at the cigarette as if it was a
bomb, and shaking her head, and muttering again about one
man's medicine being another man's poison. Sagaboy started
to cough. Ironhorse Henry looked up at the tower to avoid
looking into Estelle's eyes. Sagaboy got up from them, and
went aside to cough freely, and to spit. He could hardly control his breathing as the coughing racked his body in two, like
a hairpin. A lump came up in his throat. The lump tickled him
so much that he almost laughed, that he had to shut his eyes.
Water began to spring from his eyes as the lump came nearer
to his mouth. Then, as if playing a game with him, it went back
down deeper. Sagaboy coughed and coughed, and when he

did manage to spit . . ."*Blood!* Is blood I see?" But he wiped his feet on it, and hid the evidence from himself, and from Iron-horse Henry and from Estelle, who did not even look behind them while he was coughing.

Estelle broke the heaviness of the evening with a rasp-like noise of her teeth, and emphasized it by shaking her head from side to side, in despair. "Ain't no fairness in this damn world, you know that?" And when Ironhorse Henry had no comment, she added, "Now, look at me. I been here now, how much weeks? Four weeks going pon five, waiting and waiting pon them bastards at the immigration office, to give me a chance so's I could make a better woman outta myself. And you think they would give me a chance?"

"Your chance going come, love," Sagaboy said, returning to join them, and knowing, of course, that her chance would never come.

"I been hearing that tune since I was a little girl in pigtails. I know a man who waited his chance cause everybody was always telling him his chance going come. And you know how old that man was when his chance come?" She paused for effect; and then she said, "On his blasted death-bed!" And they burst out laughing. It was a tense, joyless, clench-teeth laugh. "I am getting more and more older every day, sweet-heart. I don't have time to wait. That is old slave talk. Wait, wait, wait. If the greedy wait, hot going cool! If you patient, God going bring you through in the name o' the Lord. If a enemy hit you in your face, on the right hand side, you must then turn round and present him with the other side o' your fisiogomy, and let him lick-in that too. Christ Almighty, I telling you now that if I could just get one *little* chance, one little opportunity to work as a domestic servant in this place, be-Jesus Christ, I not waiting. I not waiting, nor praying, nor faltering. Not Estelle."

"This is a white man country, woman," Sagaboy teased her. "You want to cause a race riot?"

"I see eye-to-eye with Estelle," Ironhorse Henry said, in a manner which he hoped Estelle would understand, and in a tone of voice which implied more than was said. "Me and you view this situation in the same fashion. It is a shame that only a certain class o' individual could get through the doors o' immigration, and a next class o' people can't even squeeze through, at all!" He cleared his throat while they pondered on his words. He spat, neatly and accurately, on a cigarette box about ten feet away. "Now, you take them Eyetalians. *Them* is people!"

"How they get into this discussion?" Sagaboy wanted to know.

"Now, take them Eyetalians," Ironhorse continued, "them Eyetalians, man, you does see them Eyetalians coming into this country be-Christ, as if Canada is in Rome and not in Northamerica, and . . ."

"And why the hell you don't turn into a Neyetalian, then? Why you don't learn to talk in the Eyetalian tongue, and become a Neyetalian?"

"I not arguing nor affirming that it have anything particularly wrong with not being a Neyetalian," Ironhorse Henry explained, "and I not saying that as a Westindian man, I am better off or worse off. All I affirming is that every day you look round in this city . . . now, you take the corner o' College and Spadina where you live! Man, when I first land up in Toronto, you didn't see ten Eyetalians at that corner. Now? All you seeing is Eyetalians Eyetalians and be-Christ, more Eyetalians. You in *Italy* now, old man, you aren't no longer in Toronto."

"God, but I like them Eyetalians too bad, though!" Estelle said. "I like to see them talking and holding up their two hand up in the air, and laughing and crying and shouting for blue-murder as they talks . . . brabba-rabba-brabba-rabba-seenioreeta! God have given that tribe a very pretty tongue and a real sweet language. And I like to see how the women does dress-down in black, from head to toenail, and still manage to look so womanish, in a positive kind o' way, as if a woman was create to always look that way, and in that manner and fashion o' dressing, in order to be a lady. I am only a part-time citizen o' Canada, but I have never see *one* Canadian woman look as if she was glad to be a woman. She want to be a *man!*

You understand what I mean? Them Canadian women, particularly the old ones, with their false hair and their false teet' and rimless glasses, Jesus Christ, they don't look as if they is really women at all. And they certainly don't behave as if they is mothers, neither! Everybody always looking as if she come outta a fashion book that gone outta print in the last century."

"Child, don't let nobody hear you say these things! Shut up your mouth tight tight, cause you not born here. Don't criticize the same people that going put bread in your mouth. Keep your tail betwixt thy legs, and live and let the blasted white people live, too. That is my philosophy of the histries o' man." It was Sagaboy cautioning her, with great excitement in his manner. And this brought out a tiny rackling in his chest. It became louder and noisier until he had to cough. But the more he coughed, the more the rackling in his chest continued. He got up from them again, and went behind the small building where he could be at ease to untie the knots in his chest, until the bulldozers there smashed up the eruption inside him. And as the cough was about to break and calm down, a lump wormed its way up to his mouth. Afraid to spit it out, he closed his eyes and swallowed hard. But the moment it hit bottom, the coughing and rackling blew up again, like a storm. The lump returned to his mouth, and he closed his eyes and spat. He moved swiftly away from the spot because he did not want to look at it. Once he did turn, and try to look down, but the memory of the previous shock made him move away fast; and he rejoined his friends. But before he could return, and while his guts were erupting, Ironhorse Henry had placed his hand on the fat of Estelle's legs, soft as a feather in a breeze; and he had looked into her eyes, and for a moment, one moment, had expressed the pain that was in his heart.

"I love you bad as arse," he told her, from the bottom of his heart.

"Look, man, behave yourself, do," she said, and then laughed away his profession of love. All this happened while Sagaboy was coughing; and all the time, Ironhorse Henry wished he would drop down dead.

"You find it getting chilly here?" Sagaboy asked them.

"You have consumption, or TB, or something?" Ironhorse asked. He glanced at Estelle to see if she was as revolted as he. And when he saw that she was not, he added, "You gotta be careful with that fresh-cold, man."

"Oh, little coughing can't harm him," she said, putting a pin in Ironhorse's balloon of love.

And then they heard the bells again, loud this time, as if the man in the tower wanted to drown out their voices. They did not recognize the tune that the bells were playing now. And for a long time they sat, silently, arguing in their minds that they did know the tune, but listening all the time to the magic in the hands that tolled the bells so beautifully. They listened, wondering how a man could receive such power of beauty, such sweetness, such purity from his hands, and put them into bells . . . bells that were made to call people to church, to toll them to the sides of graves, to drop flowers on the coffin of a friend, or a lover, or a father.

"Jesus Christ, listen. Listen to the poetry in that damn bell, though!" Ironhorse said, raising his head to catch the smallest note, the softest ting. "That man playing that bell like how great Gort used to caress his tenor pan in the steel band, back in the old days. Too blasted sweet. Man, listen to that damn bell."

"What you say this place name?" Estelle asked.

"The campus," Sagaboy told her.

"I got to come back here, again, some time soon, and hear some more o' these white people bell-music."

"You know something? I just realize that Sunday evening is the same all over the blasted world. We sitting down here in Canada, pon the grass, and it is the same thing as when we was little boys back home, sitting down in a place we used to call The Hill," Ironhorse said. Poetry also was coming with his reminiscences. "Every man should sit down on a hill at least once in his lifetime, on a Sunday afternoon or evening, preferably alone, and look at the sea, and think about the past and the present and the future, and learn how to know himself. You gotta be yourself, alone, sitting down pon that hill of time, with the sun sinking behind your back and the moon rising in your face, both at one and the same time, before you is man enough to come to me and affirm that you really know yourself."

"I remember that feeling, old man," Sagaboy said, as if he was really experiencing it again, right in their presence. "I remember that emotion. I remember how every Sunday night back home, we used to sit down on a hill called Brittons Hill. Me and the rest o' the boys, sitting down pon that damn hill, like if we was in a upstairs house looking down in the sea. And the same feeling, like I was lost, you know, like I wasn't worth nothing like how sometimes the same feeling does overpower me in that blasted five-dollars-a-week rat-trap I lives in, on Spadina, right here in this kiss-me-arse advance country . . ."

He took a beaten-up, half-smoked cigarette from his pocket and put a match to its black tip. ". . . and the birds chirping. You know something? I have never see *one* blasted bird in this place yet, and I now remember that, for the first time! Back home, the birds chirping nice songs and then they run off to sleep. And the trees, trees all round where we was sitting down, trees dress-up in a more greener coat o' green than this grass. And then a funny thing would happen. Just at that moment before shadow and darkness take them up in their hands as if they was little children put to bed, be-Christ, they would turn *more greener* still! We would be sitting down in the midst of the evening dusk and shadows, thinking bout what and what we was going to be when we grow up to be big strong men. And if on that particular Sunday we did have a nice feed, like split-pea rice and fry pork, or something nice and heavy in the bowels, well, pardner, everybody want to be something, or somebody great and powerful. Like a doctor, or a police commissioner, or even a plantation manager. And you don't know that one evening, I must have been so blasted full o' black-eye peas and rice that I say I wanted to be the *governor o' the whole blasted West Indies*. Be-Christ, if that ain't dreaming, tell me what is? But one boy, Lester Theophillis Bynoe, all he wanted to be, with a full-belly or no full-belly, was a hangman. And you know something? Be-Christ, that is what he turned out to be! He is the biggest, the blackest, and the best hangman in the whole Caribbean! But if things wasn't so great, kitchen-wise or food-wise, or if our mothers had give us a regular stiff cut-arse with a window stick or with a piece o' bamboo, well, everybody want to jump on a boat and become sailors and buccaneers. And always, after we finish wishing and dreaming, you could hear the church bells from St. Barnabas Church, miles and miles of sugar canes away, over the fields, coming right up to your two earholes. Church bells, old man, *ding-dong-ding-dong!* . . ." His coughing aborted his reverie, and it shook him like a huckster shaking a coconut to see if there is any water inside. Ironhorse Henry rushed to him, and held him around the waist; and Estelle became very alarmed, as Ironhorse Henry beat the coughing man's chest to dislodge the thorns of pain that were inside him. And Ironhorse took out his own handkerchief, and gave it to Sagaboy to put to his mouth. "Let we go home," he said when the heaving permitted him to form a word. "That damn bell ring till it give me a headache. And it chilly as hell here, too."

And they walked hurriedly away from the campus. Shadows were running slow races across the front lawns, and across the large circle of green grass in front of a large grey building. The bells kept ringing for a while, and then they stopped. And then Estelle pushed her arms through both their arms, through Sagaboy's, on her left, and Iron-horse Henry's, on her right, and like this they walked on in the darkness of the bells.

1971

How
I Became Champ

Jim Christy

ALL THIS HAPPENED back in the late Sixties, a long time ago, before I was what I am now. I was not only unknown, I was a bum. I woke up around noon one day in the Spring after a roaring drunk. First thing I did was check my wallet to see if everything was gone. It wasn't, strange to say. I still had four bucks. I had worked two days pushing a wheelbarrow and blown my pay check, all except for the four bucks, on wine and a shot of coke, cocaine. Anyway, I hit the streets with a vicious hangover. The bums were muttering on the corner. I drifted over to Yonge Street and who should I espy but none other than J. R. Topolabumbo, or just plain Bumbo, as he was called. Not that I knew any of the literary crowd back then, understand, only Topolabumbo and I only met him because, drunk, I once drove a girl friend's car smack into his front porch. Topolabumbo usually ran the other way when he saw me but today he didn't see me in time. Being urbane, Bumbo tried to make the best of the situation. "Still writing ah . . . ah . . ."

"Christy."

"Yes, yes, of course. Still writing, Christy?"

"Yeah. I wrote another novel last month."

"Really? Splendid." Bumbo reeled off some bits of gossip intended to titillate me and when a polite couple of minutes had elapsed, he excused himself saying he had to run out to the airport to meet some Russian poet. As he turned to go he said, "Oh, by the way. Here's something you might be interested in. Norman Mailer's up here. At a training camp for pugilists. Sully's Gym. Just your milieu, isn't it? Hmmmm. Yes, I'd go myself but for this Russian. Bye now."

I hadn't seen Mailer since the Pentagon back in '67 at which time I got a rifle butt in the ribs and he got all the glory. He was there with Robert Lowell. I was there with a waitress from Alexandria. I knew the training camp so I figured I'd go on over and have a look. Besides, I owed Mailer one.

I went back to the room first to get my bag, just an army surplus shoulder thing, in which I kept three or four of my latest novels. I always took the bag and the novels whenever I thought there was a chance I'd meet somebody important who could give me a break.

Sure enough the gym was surrounded by cars with New York as well as local license plates. Inside, the place was packed with a lot of well-dressed people. Women who all looked like Gloria Steinem and men of two types, sharpie types that Mailer had picked up somewhere and literary types. The air was thick with cigar smoke, gauloise, and pot. Also there were some writers from the tough guy school who certainly didn't look like tough guys.

Mailer was in the ring going through the paces with his sparring partners. He didn't look bad. He didn't look so good either. I wasn't impressed. He boxed like a guy who's had a lot of lessons but at heart is a bum. Real flashy. He bobbed, he weaved, he kept moving, tossing the left, looking for an opening. Once you have all that down and you practice you at least can make an impression. You'll knock out a lot of bums but you'll never go all the way.

I watched him for awhile. Then I got bored and walked over near the tables they had set out with drinks and sandwiches.

People eyed me suspiciously and subtly nudged me from the table. I was dressed in my patched jeans, army boots, flannel shirt, and a flower scarf around my neck. My hair was greasy and it fell onto my shoulders. I needed a drink badly. I circled around, approached the table from all angles but I was always rebuffed. Finally I gave up and remembered I had most of a pint left in my bag. I kept taking nips from it and walkino around the gym looking up at Mailer every once and awhile but mainly digging the leg that was everywhere. Plenty of class broads. Some luscious leg. Some heavenly ass. I hadn't had any for two weeks, not since I picked up a hippy chick with acne who was tripping on acid in High Park. I was thinking of what I'd do to each one when the announcer moved into the ring and shouted that the champ Norman Mailer was going to defend against the choice of the local talent, if there was any. Mailer had already, I heard, knocked out Dave Godfrey earlier in the afternoon. Godfrey had been seated at ringside and when Norman looked over the ropes at him, Godfrey fainted.

Mailer hadn't had occasion to come North for years, not since *Naked And The Dead* anyway, at which time he came up to deal with a particular thorn in his side. He hit town to dispose of the man known as The Man Who Knocked Down Papa. Norman couldn't stand that kind of challenge. He won handily and was heard to say, "I never believed it anyway."

The man was announcing the challenger, Mordecai Richler. Somebody beside me said in a gravelly voice, "What a fucking mismatch!" It was a little guy with a cigar, no more than five foot four.

"This guy Richler is going to get creamed," said Shorty.

"Yeah, he doesn't have a chance," I said. "Never did."

I took a drink of the bourbon. "Hey, let me have a taste of that," said the guy. I let him.

Richler was dancing around holding his fists over his head. He had flashy trunks on with Maple Leafs all over them.

The bell rang. Richler came out with that mincing style of his and Mailer charged low like a bull and hit him a left cross, got the right ready, but before he could deliver Richler crumpled to the canvas. Even Mailer was surprised. Richler was out cold.

"I knew it," muttered the little guy. "What a joke. Why, if I was younger I think I could give him a go. He's overrated after all. What does he know. He went to Harvard. I matriculated on boxcars for Christ's sake. These guys are all alike, bunch of phoneys."

"Who are you anyway?"

"Hugh Garner."

"Oh yeah? I read your books."

"Is that a fact?"

"Yeah."

"Well, that and fifteen cents will get me a cup of coffee."

"My name's Jim Christy."

"Never heard of you."

"Just wait."

They managed to lift Richler off the floor and onto a stretcher. The announcer asked whether there were any more challengers to the Champ. Marquis of Queensbury rules. There were no answers because there weren't any contenders or so everybody thought. They hadn't counted on me. I raised my hand and called out, "I can take the bum! Let me at him!"

There was a collective gasp and a look of surprise on all the faces. I made my way towards the ring and I noticed some guys smirking, some women giggling, asking each other, "Who is this funny young man?" Fuck 'em. I was the new thing, baby. James Dean, Jack London, John Garfield, Arthur Rimbaud, all rolled into one. A bad mother whose time had come.

I got to ringside passing Mailer's corner on the way. He laughed at me. José Torres was in his corner. Torres shook his head. "Wowee! They's gone be some ass-kicking soon!"

"Yeah, bum," I hollered. "And I'm going to be doing it. Shut your mouth or you're next."

Somebody had taken the sneakers off of Richler's corpse. I put them on. Somebody gave me some shorts. I noticed a tall brunette looking at me. She had nice legs in a midi-skirt slit up the front. I eyed the slit. I got an erection. She was braless under a Paris Review T-shirt. Dark nipples. I changed into the shorts. She noticed even more.

"Who are you?" she asked.

"Christy. Jim Christy."

"Never heard of you."

"Just wait."

"You a writer?"

"I'm a writer."

"What do you write?"

"Everything. Mostly novels."

"Anything published?"

"Poem a couple years back."

"That all?"

"Yeah."

"Well, my name's Dawn. I'm the best agent in New York. If you show well against Norman, I'll take a look at some of your stuff, honey."

"What if I win?"

"Don't be silly."

"I'm not."

I climbed into the ring, danced around. There was no one in my corner. The ref put the gloves on me. He called me and Mailer to the center of the ring and gave the instructions. Mailer tried to psyche me with his tough guy Irish accent. It didn't work. We came out at the bell, touched gloves and Mailer charged in swinging like a bull. I danced away. He thought he'd end it quick. I'd already outlasted Richler.

I didn't throw anything but a couple of jabs the first round. I let Mailer do all the work. He fought from a crouch, hands up by his eyes, elbows tucked in at his sides, chin in. He thought he looked like Marciano. Actually he looked like Seymour Krim. He had some style, I must admit, but no real power. He got by on other people's sloppiness. He was all ego. He taunted me switching to his Italian street fighter accent. I didn't scare.

I dropped my right to see what he'd do. He reacted predictably, coming in on me. I took a shot. It stung. He got carried away, smelt the kill, got careless. I just danced away. He'd shown himself. His round.

At the bell he came on slugging. Hitting with everything. For a second I became intimidated by his reputation. Just a second. He nailed me with a combination and I went down. Got right up. The ref held me off for the mandatory eight count. I looked at Norman. There was anxiety in his eyes. He hadn't expected me to get up. Nobody else would have. He came in fast but careful. I let him have a few stiff jabs. I backed him to the ropes, landed a right to the midsection. He was flabby. It buckled him. I right-crossed him to the canvas. The bell rang. Round even.

This is it, I thought. The crowd was looking at me with new eyes. They knew Norman was in trouble. The first challenge in years, I was. Norman was slumped on his stool. I was standing. I was fast as a welter, hit like a heavy.

Norman came out gamely and caught me with a solid right. It hurt but I backed away and shook it off. I floated around him like a butterfly. I was everywhere at once, hitting him at will. He went down on one knee. Got up at four. This was it for Norman. Papa had taught him a lot of things but he'd never learned to go the distance.

I dropped my hands, danced, showed my style. Dropped him with a long jab. The crowd roared. It was a new era beginning. Mailer managed to get up at nine. I came in with a right upper cut and it was all over.

They mobbed me. They loved me. There was suddenly a blonde on my arm. I saw the brunette trying to get near. I made my way to the dressing room. Mailer was still on the canvas getting the salts. I locked the crowd out except for the blonde. We made it quick on the rub-down table. Then I let the others in. A guy from McGraw-Hill asked me whether I had any novels to show him. I gave him a couple. There was another guy from New Directions. I gave him two. The brunette rushed to my side, put her arms around me, stroked my hip.

"I'll be your agent," she said breathlessly.

"Yeah, okay, baby."

"I'll make you a million dollars."

"Fine, baby."

"Let's get out of here."

"Okay, baby."

Everybody wanted to know where they could get hold of me. I started to tell them my Shuter Street address but Dawn said, "He'll be with me at Sutton Place. Call there."

"Tomorrow," I added.

"Yes, tomorrow," she said.

We went out to her car. An E-type Jag. She drove like a maniac. The doorman smiled at Dawn. He looked at me and sniffed. I tapped some cigar ash—Havana—on his shoes. Somebody had given me a cigar.

"Nice places you stay in," I told her in the elevator.

"I always stay here when I'm in town. You should see my place in New York. Why don't you come down and live with me for a while?"

"Sure, baby, why not."

When we got to her room there was a drunk lying in front of the door, a few cans of Colt .45 Malt Liquor, a bottle of cream sherry, and a pint of bourbon lying around him. I thought he was some conventioner. She said, "What are *you* doing here?"

"You know this bum?" I asked. He was dressed almost as bad as me. He had on a flannel shirt just like me only his had even more wine stains. He tried to focus his eyes and he slurred. "I came all the way up from Lowell in a taxi. Wild ride. Just to see you."

"I can't see you, Jack. Take a walk."

"Who is this guy anyway?" I wanted to know.

"That's Jack Kerouac."

"Oh."

"Hi!" he muttered. "You know. . ." he burped. "I was the world's best writer. I wrote with *feeling*, for God's sake."

"Yeah," I said. "Well, step aside, Jack baby. I'm here to stay."

He said something as we stepped over him. Something about creating a generation. I couldn't make it out.

Dawn and I stayed in bed, fucking until Dawn came. Ha, ha.

A few hours later the publishers' men, the girls from the magazines, the TV people were all there. McGraw-Hill and New Directions both bought my books. McClelland and Stewart arranged an emergency government grant to meet my agent's demands for an advance on a book of travel pieces.

Dawn and I split. We went over to my room to get the rest of my stuff to take to New York. I had fourteen novels, enough poetry for three books, and a few dozen short stories. When we got there Mrs. Sikorsky, the landlady, an old snaggle-tooth hag with sticks for legs and knots for knees, was waiting on the front steps.

"Ay youa Chriss-ut-tee. You lousy goot for nossink. You paying me da rent or I calling da poe-leases!"

I peeled off a crisp ten and a crisp five and handed them to her. "Here ya are, creep. Keep the change. I'm moving out."

I went in, got my stuff, came out. I got in the car, lit a joint, uncapped a new bottle of scotch, leaned back and looked at Dawn's long classy legs. "Yeah," I mused out loud. "So this is the good life!"

Dawn smiled and started the car and we took off. For New York and glory.

1974

The Walrus
and the Carpenter

Don Bailey

MY MOTHER TOLD me once that my father
named me Jake Barnes when I was born. My real name is Gus
though. He named me in the hospital. He was drunk and on
his way to war. I haven't seen him since but the name has
stuck in my mind. I always wonder what he meant.

I'm sure my father is alive. My mother claims he wasn't a
bad man, just careless about little things. She always had to
remind him to get a haircut.

He's like a photograph in my mind, one of those brown-
tinted old-fashioned ones, and I see him standing in the open
doorway of an old farmhouse in Sicily. He's still wearing his
brown uniform but it's faded and floppy now and he's bare-
headed. Instead of a rifle he holds a shovel and beside him is a
heavy woman, her arms folded and her head turned toward
the brightness in the picture that's probably the sun. Also
there are two small children playing at my father's feet and
their faces too are turned toward the sun. Only my father's
face stares out beyond the black marks that are his eyes.

The photograph is the imagining of a young boy. It's easily

96

explained. My mother still keeps their wedding picture promi-
nently displayed and in the real one the figures are something
the same, my mother is a short, heavy woman and there are at
least two flower-girls who preceded the procession from the
church where the photographer waited patiently on the steps
for the ceremony to be over.

Only the details have been altered to suit the occasion. At
funerals I've noticed there are no photographers.

When I was young, on special occasions like Christmas or
Easter I have half expected many times for my father to enter
the room pointing mutely at his watch and shrugging his
shoulders. His voice will be gone, a throat wound perhaps, and
he'll be unable to give explanations. The main thing is he'll be
close enough for me to see his eyes and in my mind I see
them smiling.

I like to daydream. It's more fun to make up your own
history than it is to just let things happen around you that
someday you have to remember. And what you remember
you know is what the record shows.

I guess I don't like being judged by outsiders. That's why I
quit selling cars a couple of weeks ago. As the temperature got
higher and more people wanted to take off to the lakes and
beaches so did the prices on our cars. And I just got sick of it.
I tried to tell guys with a couple of kids that the bus was more
practical. They got mad. The manager heard about it and he
got mad. I didn't get mad, just tired, and I left it for a little
while and wandered around the city, walking along Bloor in
the heat, thinking of my old man and curious if he too was
feeling the warm somewhere and maybe reading a book on
the porch of one of the boarding houses for old men on
Sherbourne Street.

During the second week I met Bill.

He hadn't altered much in the three years. Still just as thin
and grinning like a tall snake. He wasn't doing anything
either. He never did. The welfare department was supporting
his family. It gave him more time to think, he said. He still
hadn't decided what to do with his life. After all he's still
only 23. Not like me, almost 27. And because the summer was

dying so beautifully we decided to take the ferry to the island and sort of see it off.

The bus was crowded, but gradually as we progressed south the people thinned out. Dry old ladies with wrinkled Honest Ed's shopping bags stepped out as careful as chickens scratching in a new yard. Hordes of grasshopper kids springing in the air off the top step and diving out as soon as the doors opened. And mothers chasing after them like they wanted to put them in jars. And Bill and I smiling, free from everything in the scene except enjoying it.

And then this kid I hadn't noticed popped up in front of us from the next seat. Strange looking. Short and squat, almost like a toad standing on its hind legs. No neck and goggly eyes. A butterfly nose. I've never seen a butterfly nose and that's what it was like; as if she had none, just a top lip that ended at her forehead.

"Hiya," she said. "I betcha I know what you're doin'."

Bill spoke. "Oh yeah?"

"Yup, I know. But I'm not gonna tell ya."

"How come?"

"'Cause it's a secret."

"Sure," he said, and she bounced from her seat and stood in front of us wearing tiny red shorts and a white crisp blouse; neat and waiting. And the blouse had humps in it like maybe one of those magic fairies had tried to convert her to a princess, but his wand had a short circuit. Or maybe a prince came along when she was sitting on a log somewhere catching flies and he kissed her but she had bad breath and the job only got half done.

Anyway the bumps on her blouse meant she was more than a kid, and for sure a female. Maybe even a woman. But she carried a tin pail, one of those kind with Jack and Jill painted on the side, and she had a yellow plastic shovel. She was staring at us and waiting like we were all going to get together and build sand-castles.

Bill didn't say anything.

"You're going to the island on the boat!" she said finally. It came out like the proud answer to an important question.

"Right!" Bill said. "Give the kid a cigar, Gus."

I kept my mouth shut though.

"I knew," she said, and then after a pause, "I'm goin' too." And she smiled. It was a great smile. A huge, wide, deep smile that swallowed her face and left only bright teeth and those goggly eyes. Her voice belonged to a bull frog and I wondered again about her origin. As if someone had dreamed her up.

She didn't seem to notice how loud she was. Or maybe she didn't care. There are too many whispers around anyway. But it embarrassed me, her loudness. I think I'd be a lousy soldier, I'd never be able to kill a man with something as loud as a gun.

She jumped back into her seat and turned to face us.

"I'm goin' for the whole day!" she bellowed. "An' all by myself too. Except I gotta be back in time. They're real strict about that."

"Who is?" Bill asked.

"At the hospital!" she said, like he was an idiot.

"Oh yeah. Sure, the hospital. Humane Society or what?"

"What?"

"What hospital are ya talkin' about?"

"The Ontario one. The big place on Queen Street. It's real huge," she said proudly, like it was her own private castle. "See, I got this paper to show where it is." She pulled a folded sheet of paper from her pocket and showed us a pencil-drawn map.

"Yeah," Bill said. "I know where you're talkin' about now."

Great, I thought. Just what we needed, a loose nut from the looney bin.

The girl was talking now. Spewing out words like a stream being fed by melting ice in the spring.

"I was there in Orillia for a long time, but I've been in this hospital only a little time an' they're gonna get a job for me. . . . I'm gonna do housework. I'm good at that."

"Geez that's real great, eh Gus?"

"Swell," I said.

"My name's Mary," she said, sticking out her small hand. Bill shook it and I wondered if inside he was laughing. Then she thrust it at me. It wasn't webbed, only cold and roughened.

Bill introduced us. "I'm Bill and this is Gus."

"I'm glad I metcha," she said, and I knew she wasn't kidding. "Are youse gonna stay all day too?" she asked.

"Sure am," Bill said. "Gonna swim and soak up some of that sun."

"I brought sandwiches," she said, tilting the pail up to show us the brown bag inside. "Did youse bring some?"

"We're going to grab a hamburg when we get over there," I said, hoping to stop the development before the picture became clear and we were trapped inside it. I worry about my own daydreams like that sometimes, that I'll crack up and end up inside one of them.

"Oh, but youse shouldn't waste your money! You're supposed to save your money.... Youse could have some a mine if ya want. I got lotsa them. Cheese-and-ham ones."

"You hang onto them," Bill said. "You'll get pretty hungry over there."

"But I got lots ta share."

Jesus, I thought, wouldn't the bus ever reach the end of the line? It felt like the whole day was crumbling apart. Her and her lousy sandwiches. But the end was still four or five stops and she continued her ticker-tape talk. She was asking about our non-existent jobs. I didn't particularly want her to know. It wouldn't make any difference but she seemed so interested, as if it really mattered. It made me want to laugh except her seriousness wasn't funny.

"Do you work?" she asked.

"Well sorta," Bill said. "See, we're in this band . . ."

"A band! Like the Beatles? Like at dances? Like that?"

"Sure, we play everything. Go to dances all over. Right now we're takin' a rest 'cause we just finished a tour in the States."

That was it for her. Here was the magic fairy again or the prince. The second time round. It was televised on the screens of her bulging eyes and even her lips seemed to be puckered, ready to receive the message. Waiting for the hovering wand to descend, the kiss of freedom, delivery from one world into another. And Bill, the experienced and accomplished delivery boy, all charm and sweet seriousness.

"Do youse go on the radio sometimes?" she asked.

"Ah . . . well sure. Yeah. Like we made some records, eh Gus?"

I ignored him and looked out the window. We were almost there. I could see the lake.

"Gus's the modest type, but you should hear him sing. He really sings up a storm."

"I wish I could hear him," she said, and I felt like blowing the whole joke by giving her a little sample. But I didn't.

"Ah, well ya see, he's not allowed to sing anywhere but where we're workin'. It's in his contract, see?"

She nodded solemnly.

"Do you sing too?" she asked.

"Oh sure, I sing but mostly I play drums. Last year I got voted second-best drummer around by onea them magazines down the States."

He talked low now, in confidential tones. "I'd show ya, but I'm not allowed to either." He was really enjoying himself, but I wondered why he'd told her second-best, why not first?

"If ya wrote down the name of the band, I could hear youse sometimes on the radio," she said.

"Sure," he said, and wrote something on the folded sheet with the map she handed him.

The bus stopped. The end of the line. We got out and the girl followed us at a distance. Like in India, I thought.

Inside the depot we had to wait for the boat. I walked out of the shade, where the benches were, and stood in the sun on the dock waiting for it. I could see it off in the distance floating in slow. Like a tired dream that you try and make finish itself before you wake up. A tired dream chugging in for more passengers.

In the city a ferry is a big boat. They're like painted pictures. From far off they look so clean and real. Real the way you imagine things to be real. Or the way you want them to be. But up close they look lousy. Dirty and cracked, and the kind of real that makes you feel old and tired. A screwball thought of an Indian summer day but not one with a bad feeling. The word I guess is inevitable. Boats do that to me; I love them.

Like I love old ladies even if they make you think of dying. And daydreams. They all add up to the same thing somehow.

The sun was a distant blowtorch burning the skin of the few people around and in my eyes they began to disappear like paint peeling off a house, or snakes shedding.

My main thought was how to get rid of the girl. Bill and her were a few yards away under the canopy. They sounded like two seagulls clucking over a fish; at least half dead, no longer able to swim on their own, beginning to rot and no longer real.

"Hey Bill!"

He came over. The girl remained. I wasn't the one who was casting spells that day. The kind she wanted. I could only break them, which sometimes isn't a bad position to be in. I hoped the girl understood that.

"What're you doing?" I asked.

"Just havin' a few laughs," he said. "Hey, she really believes all that jazz about the band. Says she's gonna save her dough so she can get a radio of her own to listen for our songs. Is that too much or what! We got ourselves a fan, Gus!"

He grinned and our lives were timeless. We had never been close friends. We'd shared mutual things like girls and drinking, playing and laughing as he laughed now. He was always more pleased with himself than I was, but for a moment I felt suspended inside his freedom and overhead the seagulls and harbour kites dipped and soared as if to say they too had no strings attached. And I thought of my father and wondered if he had chosen not to have a son, if he had intended to leave behind a ghost, if something had interfered with his plans.

The boat had become more than a picture now.

"Aw com'on, Gus, it's only a laugh. What the hell. Cheer up."

"Yeah, I guess so. The thing is, I don't want us getting tangled up with that kid. It'll end up us having to drag her all over the island. You know. I mean, she wants company."

"Don't be nuts," he said. "We're gonna dump her soon's we get there. I'm just havin' a few laughs. Anyhow, she's 24. She told me."

"Sure," I said, as if that made everything okay.

The boat docked and we boarded with the others, who lugged on their blankets and baskets with radios blaring and dogs barking at each other as if their outings would be incomplete without it.

Mary ran back and forth across the deck on her awkward legs; the pail swinging in one hand and the yellow shovel in the other.

"Isn't it big!" she yelled. "It's really big!"

And people smiled at her excitement. Bill laughed and suddenly she was right, the boat was big. As big as her smile. And it made me feel good.

"I betcha this boat could go anywhere," she said.

We began to move, the huge propellers churning up the water.

"Even . . . even in the ocean, I betcha."

"Sure," I said, caught up in the mood. I knew how Bill had felt earlier. Peter Pan and Wendy. We'd all fly away on our boat to never-never land.

"What's the pail for?" I asked.

She was slow answering. And then:

"One time I learned this story about this man an' a walrus. Did ya ever see a walrus?"

"Sure, he's seen 'em. He's got an uncle who's a walrus, eh Gus?"

"I don't mean like that," she said. "I mean a real live one. Like in the zoo."

"No, I never have," I said.

"Me neither, but I seen a picture once. They look awful scary . . . an' this story, the walrus ate a whole bunch of clams. He tricked them. Him an' the man."

"I remember that," I said. "It's a poem. I had to learn that in school." And I remembered: the walrus and the carpenter/ were walking close at hand/ they wept like anything/ to see such quantities of sand. Yes I remembered that.

"So you're gonna go over there and fill your pail with clams for supper, eh?" Bill said.

"No, I wouldn't do that," she said. "The walrus was mean. I just wanna . . . just wanna have them."

"But whaddaya gonna do with them?" Bill persisted.

"Just keep them. They could live in the pail if I put lots of sand in it. They could, couldn't they?"

"Sure," I said. "They'd love it." I felt like a sentimental jerk but figured the lake was polluted so there wouldn't be any clams anyway.

She smiled. "I hope I find some."

Bill was laughing and it was like loud lappings of the waves against the boat as we squashed down the water. We were close to the other shore now.

"Collecting clams!" he said. "Hey Gus, that's too much, eh? For pets."

"I think it's a great idea," and I meant it, though I didn't know why except that Mary was right, the walrus was mean, a mean bastard and the world was full of walruses. Carpenters too. And there's lots of oysters around. Or clams. Anyway, what's the difference?

"Com'on," I said. "We'd better get downstairs. We're going to dock in a minute."

We walked down from the top deck and waited in front of the metal grille. The boat shivered to a stop and as the grille slid open Bill began to run. He split off down the ramp like a kicked dog. I followed like another dog intent upon retrieving a thrown ball. I heard Mary yelling behind us as we both barreled along.

"Wait up! Wait up for me!"

And part of me wanted to but I continued my pursuit of Bill and caught up at the small river that winds its way through the island. Bill was panting; like a large happy dog after his master's given him a good run. And laughing too. It seemed to be his day to laugh.

"Well, we're clear of her anyway," he said.

Clear of her, I thought. Clear of her? Do you suppose the walrus said, that they could get it clear? I doubt it, said the carpenter and shed a bitter tear.

Clear of her.

If seven maids with seven mops swept for half a year . . .

Clear of her.

"Yeah, it looks that way," I said, and thought, probably my father crossed the ocean on a boat. Did that explain anything? Was that the reason I couldn't swim, for example, or were there other motives in his leaving?

We walked over to the south beach. We bought hot dogs and containers of honey dew, but I kept thinking of the Jack and Jill pail with its ham-and-cheese sandwiches. Bill had a grand time sending out eye signals to all the young girls we passed. It wasn't my day for girls. I thought of juicy oysters and clams.

The water was freezing and after one quick plunge I waited on the beach while Bill floundered around for a few minutes. I started to build a sand-castle with my toes.

Bill came back, blue and chattering. "Let's go for a walk."

So, still in our bathing-suits, carrying our clothes, we wandered.

Something had happened to Bill in the water. As if the glow he'd worn had been washed away. He began to talk and I thought: the time has come, the walrus said, to talk of many things: of shoes and ships and sealing wax, of cabbages and kings and why the sea is boiling hot and whether pigs have wings.

"I've gotta get a job," he said.

"How come?"

"I've just gotta, Gus. It's drivin' me nuts, this sittin' around. Louise always bitchin'. It didn't use to be so bad but now the kid's always sick and cryin' and there's already another one on the way. You never seen the kid, did ya?"

"No," I said.

"I'm just sick of the whole thing. It used to be fun but now. . . . Sometimes I feel like an old man," he said jokingly, but he sounded worried or maybe scared.

"There's lots of things you can do," I said.

"Naw, I'm just a clown."

I didn't have an answer for that one and he seemed content not to get one. We walked in silence and our walk took us in a circle so that sometime in the late afternoon we approached the same dock we had disembarked from. We were dressed now.

"Might as well head back on the next boat," Bill said. "An' Gus. . . ."

"Yeah."

"Forget that stuff I was saying. Sometimes things just seem that way. You know what I mean?"

"Sure," I said, because it was the only sensible thing to say. I hadn't understood much of what he'd actually said, only that he'd needed to say something to someone, like spitting phlegm out of your throat and then you forget it. It's only embarrassing if someone sees you.

We sat on the bench to wait.

And then I saw her. The girl, Mary. About a hundred yards across from us was a small lagoon with a strip of sand that hardly anyone used for a beach because it faced the city and people considered the water there to be more polluted than at the south end. But there she was. Probably latched onto the first piece of sand she saw after we ran away from her, I thought. I saw the flash of her red shorts, but it was her voice alerted me. A bullfrog's troubled croak. She was surrounded by four or five guys and I saw they were laughing.

Bill saw and heard too.

"Com'on," I said and began to run.

We had to cross a little bridge and the first thing I noticed was the Jack and Jill pail lying on the ground, mashed flat. Beside it, the yellow shovel in two pieces. She was in the middle of a circle they had formed, crying. Sobbing really, her breath coming in great gulps as if she was swallowing flies. And she waved a folded piece of paper in front of her like a flag. But not of truce or surrender. More like a victory banner.

"It's true! It's true! He wrote it right here if youse don't believe me," she insisted.

And then she saw us and her face split and swallowed itself in that great smile.

"That's him!" she said, pointing at Bill.

"What's happening?" I asked.

"Aw nothin' really, man, we were just passin' and all of a sudden she comes on to us about these clams she's diggin' for. And like she wants us to help her," one of the group said.

His friends laughed.

"Then," he continued, "she starts to strap it on us about how she met this guy on the bus who plays drums in a big group and he's her buddy. Ya know, the whole thing. The broad's a nut."

He didn't look like a mean guy. Not walrus mean. He was sort of like the guy who if he came to buy a car from me and I warned him he was getting a rotten deal, would get mad because he figured I was pulling a fast one on him. A kind of dumb person who probably meant no harm.

"But he's the one!" Mary said, excited now and waving her banner of paper at Bill. "He's the one that plays the drums. He wrote down the name."

Her eyes waited for confirmation from his lips. And the group of young men waited too. And me. All of us, waiting.

"I don't know what she's talking' about!" Bill said. "I never wrote down anything."

He looked frightened. "All I know about her is she comes from a nut-house. I've got nothing to do with her." And he turned and began to walk away.

Her face sagged and folded back into its flatness. Like a suitcase quietly closing, or a clam winking shut. She didn't cry any longer. Or smile.

"Just a loose bug from the bug-house," one of the men said.

"Aw, leave her alone," I said. It was all I could manage.

"Sure. Sure. Who wants to waste their time on a nut anyway?" And they shuffled away.

I stood there wondering what to say. She spoke.

"I never found no clams."

And that seemed to be the saddest thing of all. And I thought: and this was scarcely odd; because they'd eaten every one.

I ran back to the dock where the boat was pulling in. I didn't look for Bill in the crowd and I never saw him. Our meeting, the day, everything faded and all I wanted to do was sleep, sleep. And dream a new dream. A new day.

Funny though how things haunt you. Last night I was drinking, got a little high and went walking along Queen

Street, thinking about my old man, wondering if he was walking somewhere and if we ever walked in time, like we were in a parade, marching together with one of us carrying a flag. And all of a sudden I thought of Mary. I wanted to know about her. I walked over to the hospital and people kept shuffling me around but finally some guy knew who I was talking about.

"Mary? No, she's not here anymore," he said, smiling. "Went out on her own . . . oh, about two weeks ago. Getting along very well. She's living with a family, doing housework. I could give you the address if I can have your name. I'm sure they wouldn't mind her having a friend drop by. I'm sure she'd . . ."

"No, no," I said. "That's okay. I hardly know her. I was just interested."

I half ran from the place and outside I kept thinking, good, she's doing housework. Good. Christ, isn't that good! And lucky too. And I knew if right then my old man had stepped out of the photograph in my mind and met me walking along that street, I wouldn't have told him about her. It was just one of those things. I was happy to have it for myself. It was like the name he'd given me. If I'd had the chance to tell him, he wouldn't have known what I meant anyway.

1973

Adrift

Patrick Slater

JACK TRUEMAN'S DOG was a black and tan collie with a bob-tail. His was the general-purpose breed of a drover's tyke; and he was all dog. Jack claimed to own the sharp-eyed, self-reliant fellow—but that was a matter of opinion, merely. In the dog's way of looking at things, Rover owned Jack Trueman; and Trueman—he owned me. When a smart, clever dog has something of his very own, you understand—say a smelly bone or an unruly boy—naturally he thinks highly of his own property. And he puts up with the smell of his own bone and the kicks of his own boy as one of the inconveniences of proprietorship, just the same as you and I put up with taxes.

Rover liked, at times, to have his boy throw sticks for him; and, of course, sticks can not be thrown if they are not fetched. But he only fancied that sort of thing in moderation. When the sport ceased to amuse him, he would cock his leg against a post, and then run away on business of his own. This was clear evidence, you will agree, that Rover was the chief executive.

Jack Trueman had not bought the dog; nor had he been given the dog. One day, Rover had left the drover's team he was looking after, and had dropped in, casual-like, to inspect the alley at the side and the stable in the rear of the Tavern Tyrone. He fancied the look of the place and the smell of the slop-bucket. Off-hand, he decided he would like to own a boy who lived round an interesting place like that. So the two of them struck up a bargain on the spot—at least they thought they did. There was a mutual misunderstanding so complete that things worked out all right.

Rover was old enough to have sense, but young enough to be full of devilment. He was a regular fellow. He never got into any squabbles with girl dogs; but the body-odours of any gent of his own kind who strayed within a block of the Tavern Tyrone seemed very displeasing to him. And, when he fought another dog, Rover stuck right at the job till he gave a thrashing to the son of a bitch, or enough silly humans ran together to make it a draw. Jack and his collie got into street fights daily. I was their partisan and did a lot of grunting for them. The three of us skylarked that spring about the streets of Toronto.

One June day, we were down to the foot of Berkeley Street to see a double hanging; and that surely was one glorious, well-filled day. There was a high stone wall clear around the prison which stood close to the bay-shore; and the Fair Grounds lay open to the west. Two men, Turney and Hamilton, were to be hanged on a Tuesday morning. To give the public a tidy view of the drops, both before and after taking, a double gallows had been built facing the Fair Grounds and high on top of the prison wall.

Before the early-risers were abroad, hundreds of heavy farm carts and lumbering wains came creaking into town with their loads of merry, holiday-making country folk from far and near. Along the muddy roads came also bands of stalky farm lads, faring stoutly on foot, with stick in hand and bag on back, stepping down thirty miles or so to see the doings. Two men were to be killed by the law in the morning as an example to the public; and the schools throughout the district were closed that the children might benefit by so valuable a lesson in morals and good living. That day the taverns of Toronto did a stirring business.

'Your soul to the devil!' said young Jack to me. 'Let us hooray down and see the necks stretched.'

The hangings had been set for ten o'clock in the morning; but an hour ahead of time there was a good-natured throng of thousands jostling one another before the grim prison walls. It was the sort of crowd one sees nowadays at a big country fall fair. Neighbours were greeting neighbours, and joshing over local affairs. Men carried their liquor well in those days; and, of course, mothers had brought the young children in their arms. What else could the poor dears do?

A stir among the men on the prison walls told us the death procession was coming. A hush of awed expectancy fell upon the great throng. And this gaping crowd, stirred with thoughts of human slaughter, was standing in the most humane and tolerant colony Europe ever established beyond the seas! New England had been developed by the labour of convicts transported to be sold as serfs on an auction-block. We are often told of the *Mayflower* landing the Pilgrim Fathers on the Plymouth Rock. Oh yes! But we hear little of the fact that for a century every other merchant ship touching a New England port landed a cargo of convicts on the Pilgrim Fathers. The outposts of those colonies were pushed westward by rough frontiersmen who murdered as they went on frolics of their own. The southern colonies were developed by slave labour, and the full wages of that slavery have not yet been paid. One of the first laws passed in Upper Canada, in 1793, provided for the abolition of slavery; and, in dealing with another human, there has never been a time or place in Canada, save in her wretched prisons, that any man could with impunity make his will a law to itself.

You ask what brought thousands of people together to see such a terrible sight as a double hanging; and I answer you that fifty thousand of the likes of you would turn out any morning to view a well-bungled hanging today. A murderer is a celebrity; and people run open-mouthed to see a celebrity, to hear him speak and see him decorated—or hanged—as the case may be. Every crowd hungers for excitement and is looking for a thrill. Every mob is by nature cruel and bloodthirsty. With all his clothing and culture, man remains a savage, a fact that becomes obvious when a few of them run together.

The breath going out of thousands of throats made a low murmur as the murderer, William Turney, in his grave clothes and pinioned, came into public view and stoutly mounted the stairs of the scaffold platform. A priest walked beside him. Behind them strode a hangman, who was closely masked.

It was a matter of good form—and decently expected in those days—that a murderer make a speech and exhort the public. A lusty cheer went up as William Turney stepped smartly forward to make his speech from the gallows. His was an Irish brogue; and his voice was loud and clear.

'Die—like—a—man!' shouted loud-voiced Michael, the smuggler.

Turney had been working the fall before as a journeyman tailor at Markham Village. He dropped into a local store one dark night to get a jug of whisky to take to an apple-paring bee. As the clerk, McPhillips, was bending over the liquor-barrel, Turney stove the man's skull in with a hammer, and then rifled the till. He turned off the spigot, blew out the candles, closed the wooden shutters, and quietly went home to bed. The dead body was not found till the morning after. No one had seen Turney abroad the night before. He came under suspicion the next day because he rode to Toronto on a borrowed horse, and bought himself for cash money a pair of boots and a leather jacket. But that, you'll agree, was not hanging evidence.

Turney, however, needed money for his defence; and while lying in gaol at Toronto he got a letter smuggled out to his wife. The poor simple woman was no scholar; and she asked a neighbour to read it for her. The letter told her the sack of money was hidden under a loose board in the floor of their back-house at Markham Village. He bade her get the money and give it to the lawyer-man. So the damaging evidence leaked out. How much wiser to have let the solicitor's clerk visit the privy!

On the scaffold, Turney made a rousing speech. He shouted to us that he had been a British soldier in his day, and was not afeared of death. Turney thanked us all kindly for the compliment of coming to his hanging. It was sorry he was for killing the poor man, McPhillips, who had never hurted him and had treated him as a friend. The crime, he told us, had not been planned, but was done on the spur of the moment. The devil had tempted him, and he fell. He had run home that dark night in a terrible fear. The wind in the trees sounded in his ears like the groans of poor tortured souls in hell. Hanging, he told us, was what he deserved. Let it be a lesson to us all.

Turney's feelings then got the better of him. He broke down and wailed loudly, praying that God would prove a guardian to his poor wife and fatherless child. The crowd did not like the tears. The high-pitched cries of women jeering at the miserable creature mixed with the heavy voices of men urging him to keep his spirits up.

'Doo—ye—loo—ike—a—maa-hun!' boomed Michael, the leather-lunged.

In the pause, Turney got a fresh holt on his discourse. He went on to tell us he had been a terrible character in his day. He had started serving the devil by robbing his mother of a shilling; and, in after years, while plundering a castle, he had helped wipe out an entire family in Spain. He explained that a full account of his high crimes was in the printer's hands. He beseeched everyone to buy a copy for the benefit of his poor wife and child. In the hope of getting a few shillings for them, Turney stepped back to his death with these great lies ringing in our ears.

At the foot of the scaffold stairs, the other felon requested the Protestant minister who walked beside him to kneel and have a session in prayer. The murderer seemed in no hurry to be up to finish his journey. The clergyman tried the stairs carefully, stepping up and down to prove them solid and sound. But it is hard to convince a man against his will. The hangman waited a tidy space, and then spit on his fist. He took the victim by the scuff of his neck and the waist-band and hoisted him up the stairs, the clergyman lending a helping hand. The crowd jeered loudly; but, once up in open public view, the felon's courage revived. Hamilton came forward with stiff, jerky little steps; and, in a high-pitched voice, he admonished us all to avoid taverns, particularly on the Sabbath.

Then the serious business began. The executioners hurried around, strapping the legs of their victims and adjusting the caps and halters. The culprits assumed a kneeling position over the traps and prayed to God for mercy.

A loud murmur went up from the thousands of throats— 'Aw!'—as the bolts were shot. The two bodies tumbled down to dangle on the ropes and pitch about. It took Turney quite a while to choke to death. The other body seemed to drop limp.

This business of hanging folk should be intensely interesting to every Canadian of old-country British stock. The blood strain of every one of us leads back to the hangman's noose. Many a man was smuggled out of Ireland to save his neck from stretching for the stealing of a sheep.

And public hanging had something to justify it. In the olden days, human life was of little more account than it is today; and hoisting bodies in the air, and leaving them to rot on gibbets, was thought to be a rough-and-ready warning to evildoers. What a pity public hangings were ever done away with! Had they continued a few years longer, the horrible practice of hanging men would have passed away under the pressure of public opinion.

At any rate, Jack Trueman and I profited greatly as a result of William Turney's speech from the gallows. We ran off at once for copies of his 'confessions' to the office of the *British Colonist*, a paper printed on King Street; and we spent the rest of the day crying our wares on the streets and in the taverns of Toronto. We refreshed ourselves with peppermint bull's-eyes made by Sugar John, who combined a tavern with a candy shop on the east side of Church Street.

To make it a perfect day, a fire broke out that evening in a row of frame dwellings at the north-west corner of Richmond and Yonge streets. The flames shot up quickly, cutting into heavy clouds of smoke. Away everyone ran to the scene of the fire. The city had a paid fire marshal and several volunteer fire companies; but fires were frequent that summer, and only heaps of smouldering ashes usually marked their battle-scenes.

The engagement opened that evening with a wild charge of one-horse carts. Drunken drivers whipped their old horses into action hell-split, wheeling batteries of water-barrels. The first carter with a civic licence arriving at a scene of a fire with a puncheon of water got a municipal grant of £3, Halifax currency. Subsequent hauling was done, however, on a time basis; and the second fillings arrived in a more leisurely fashion.

After a time, the municipal fire-pump came on the scene. The hose was reeled off in lively fashion, and attached to a fire-plug on the water-main at Yonge Street. The volunteers rushed to man the pumps. They speedily discovered what everyone else already knew—that there was no pressure in the water-mains after nightfall. A meeting of excited rate-payers was held on the spot to protest against the wickedness of Mr. Furniss of the gas and water company. But he was there himself to tell them, good and plenty, he gave the town all that £250 had paid for. There was a great running together of newspaper editors and a deputation was finally dispatched to measure the depth of water in the company's tank. Meanwhile the flames licked up frame buildings at their pleasure; and things got so hot that the municipal pumping equipment itself caught fire. An enthusiastic detail of volunteers were busy pitching furniture out of upstairs windows, and smashing and rifling the contents of dwellings in and near the general direction of the blaze. People grabbed small things and ran home with them to save them from the fire.

I was watching a tipsy carter in a dispute with an open-headed barrel of water, when the scene closed so far as I was concerned. Something had apparently lost its balance in the two-wheeled cart. The puncheon upset and won the argument. The carter disappeared in an avalanche of water. He emerged spluttering and talking to God. At that moment a flying bed-mattress caught me fair on, and I went to earth beneath its enfolding arms. I wiggled out, only to dodge a flying jerry mug. I have not crossed the briny ocean, thought I, to have my head cracked with a dirty old thing like that. So I went off home and called it a day.

A large number of negro families were living in Toronto at that time; and their shining black faces and rolling white eye-balls startled my young Irish mind and held me in a pop-eyed fascination. For years previously, fugitive slaves had been drifting northward by undercover routes; and many of the more resourceful and enterprising of them reached the British line and settled in southern Ontario. Public opinion was such in Canada, at that time, that negroes were permitted to cross the border freely, and, while slavery continued to exist on the continent, it remained practically impossible to extradite a black man out of Canada on any charge whatever. Among the cabins in the southern plantations, there had grown up a tradition that far away under the North Star could be found a paradise of freedom over which a great queen reigned. On first setting foot on Canadian soil, the fugitive slave kneeled to kiss the bosom of a kindly mother; and all would be well with her soul had every other immigrant to Canada had within him the spirit to do likewise.

Just across the way from Mr. O'Hogan's, there was a col-oured tavern run by Jim Henderson, a big, black, deep-voiced negro who told thrilling tales of slavery in the south. Jim had a weakness for fatty fried meats, and, to regulate his system, he made a practice, every Friday night, of gurgling down the full of a big bottle of castor oil, to the delight of sundry urchins who assembled for the occasion. Rolling his eyes and smack-ing his lips, Henderson would then shuffle off back for a glass of gin to cut oil out of his gullet. The negroes in Toronto were a harmless, law-abiding body of simple-minded people. These ex-slaves worked as labourers and teamsters; and a few of them were already property-holders, and took part in the stormy elections of the day. Some of their descendants have risen to important positions in Canada; but the climate has proven too rigorous for the majority of them.

Everything is relative in this life, and especially so the

element of time. A summer takes longer to pass in the inquir-
ing days of childhood than does an entire decade further along
life's journey. As that long summer dragged on, the plague
came and hung over the town like the dread, intangible wraith
that chokes one in a nightmare. There was fear and dread in
everyone's heart; and it was the deep, smothering fear of
utter helplessness. We all wore little bags of camphor about
the neck. The angel of death seemed to mark at random the
door-lintels of the chosen ones. Perhaps the death toll of 1847
has been exaggerated; but, in a literal sense, the poor died by
the hundred. In the summer and early fall of 1847, 863 poor
Irish died in Toronto, and, of the 97,933 emigrants who sailed
from Irish ports for Canada in the spring and summer of that
year, 18,625 souls did not live to feel the frosts of a Canadian
winter.

The plague was a terrible thing, but kindly in its way because it was swift about its business. One afternoon my poor
young mother fell ill. She was lying on an old straw tick in the
corner of the room upstairs. When I found her, she was cold
and clammy and in frightful distress. I threw her old shawl
over her and ran for water. Within five minutes every other
occupant of the house had cleared out. Mr. O'Hogan set off
post-haste to bespeak the death-cart to take her body away. I
ran around to get Mistress Kitty O'Shea. I knew she would
help me, because she was out night and day nursing the sick.
She came right over, and stayed till my mother's body stiff-
ened with the rigor. Poor Kitty O'Shea! She died herself the
day the plague struck down Michael Power, the first Catholic
bishop of Toronto; and they both laid down their lives minis-
tering to the sick on the streets of Toronto. Perhaps He
that sitteth in the heavens has found a place among His many
mansions for the soul of Kitty O'Shea!

My mother begged for the priest. He put the holy oil on her,
and her mind was comforted.

'Sit over by the window,' Mistress O'Shea said to me. 'Your
mother doesn't want you to be looking at her, Paddy. She
doesn't want you to remember the look of her face in the
sickness.'

The dip-candle stuck in a bottle guttered and spent itself during the watches of that terrible night. The agonies of the destroying disease were distressing.

As the sky began to brighten with the dawn, the stiffening collapse of the disease overcame my mother's body. Mistress O'Shea crossed herself as she covered the rigid face.

I hoisted the window to let the soul get out.

Two rough-looking men with a one-horse cart came in the forenoon to take my mother's body away. They were gathering bodies of the Catholic poor for burial in a potter's field at the east side of the city. They had started off with a load of empty board coffins, and Mr. O'Hogan's place was the final call on that trip. They placed an empty coffin on the street. They came upstairs with a heavy bag made of ducking.

I knew my mother as not yet dead because only one eye was closed. But they shoved her stiff body into their bag and tied the mouth of it with a stout cord. One of the men shouldered the burden and bore it to the street. The lid of the coffin was hammered on. It was hoisted up into its place on the cart. The cart trundled off up York Street. And I followed after.

As we rounded the corner of Richmond Street, Dick Crispin was opening the bar-room door of his yellow tavern. Mr. Crispin had been in service with Sir John Colborne, the governor; and his public house was much frequented by official gentry from below stairs. The carter hollered to him for a drink. Coachman Dick brought out a generous flask of whisky, and set it on the roadway. The body-gatherers drank to the souls of the departed, and emptied the bottle. Of course, they had been tight already. But they were brave men, doing a necessary and dangerous duty. Drinking heavily was the only precaution they knew.

It was a curious funeral procession that wended its way along Richmond Street, up Church, and east on Queen Street —an old cart full of corpses, two drunken carters, a dirty, ragged little urchin with tear-stained face, and a bob-tailed collie that did not understand. The road cleared in front of us; and people closed doors and ducked up alleys as we passed along.

Anyway, there was one sincere mourner present, which is more than some great funeral processions have. The whole affair had been sudden, and it seemed terrible to me. I felt sick. There was a strange co-rumbling in my belly. The essence of true sorrow is always self-pity. I was not so much sorry for my poor mother. I felt helpless and utterly lonely; and I was sorry for myself because they were taking her away from me.

I followed along after the cart, blubbering and poking my grimy knuckles into my eyes. Rover knew I was in distress, and he wanted to help me.

I was bothered that the old cart made so much noise. They might be hurting her.

I got to thinking that prayers should be said for her. I sobbed out what I could:

> *Hail, Mary, full of grace!*
> *The Lord is with thee;*
> *Blessed art thou among women,*
> *And blessed is the fruit of thy womb, Jesus.*

The cart rattled on to Queen Street.

> *Holy Mary, Mother of God,*
> *Pray for us sinners, now and*
> *At the hour of our death. Amen.*
>
> . . . .
> *May the souls of the departed*
> *Repose in peace. Amen.*

They put the load of bodies into one great hole. The cold of the grave was in my heart.

When I got back home, they were fumigating the house and Mr. O'Hogan told me to clear out—I was not wanted there. I asked for my mother's things. They had all been burnt—so he said; but I didn't believe him.

'And there,' I accused him, 'you liar, you have my father's own stick in your hand!'

Mr. O'Hogan chased me out onto the street and threw the stick after me.

I faulted him roundly in Irish as I ran to pick it up; and the man crossed himself.

'What were you saying to the man, little boy?' an old gentleman inquired of me.

'I was putting a curse on him,' I explained. 'I was blasting his soul to the devil for a dirty, lying thief.'

I still keep that stick by me, for I hold it very dear. It reminds me of the old, unhappy, far-off days when my father died 'evic' and left me as his whole estate his Irish blackthorn stick.

So not a stitch nor token have I to remind me of my mother. But when the sunbeams strike down sudden-like through the storm-clouds, I think of the glint in her fun-loving eyes. And, when the rain-thrush flutes his neat little tune to the clearing sky, I hear again the soft, lovable brogue of that poor little, forgotten, black Irish mother of mine.

When night set in, I slipped down the alley to the east of the Tavern Tyrone. Rover whined a welcome from the stable door. It is a quality of a dog's friendship that he knows all your secret faults, yet remains loving and kind to be sure; and he will never despitefully use you. I was sick and tired as a child is after hysteria of any kind; and I was actually weak, because I had fasted the livelong day, which is sore against the grain of a little boy's belly. I laid me down in the sweet, crisp hay; and Rover snuggled over beside me. In my utter loneliness, the dog's sympathy and loving-kindness refreshed me, and my body felt warmer. Sobbing, I fell asleep.

1933

The
Butterfly Ward

Margaret Gibson

SOMETIMES IT CAN be beautiful inside this
space. Most people, people who can ride on buses and streetcars and eat doughnuts for breakfast if and when they want
and don't have to dial O on their phones to make a call, would
think that statement crazy. Maybe it is a bit crazy. Even phone
calls cannot be simple here, everything twisted into complications, but I am getting used to it now.

I have been here a month now on the neurological ward of a
big hospital in Toronto. The biggest, I am told, with new
wings that gleam and old ones that make me feel like a nun
hiding in a bombed-out convent. I come from Kitchener, that
is my home, but they sent me here. They, whoever *they* may
be, said that the doctor working here on my case, Dr. Carter,
is the best neurologist in Ontario, maybe even all of Canada.
The mysterious and secret *they* who have so neatly pigeon-
holed my life. I wonder if I was supposed to be impressed with
this news as my mother packed my suitcase and told me of all
the wonderful little boutiques in Toronto, slipping in the
famous name among the dried coloured flowers of the

121

boutiques. My father stood in the doorway with his pipe in a reassuring mouth. I was not impressed. I had seen so many doctors for the secrets that dwelt inside my nebula that I was not. If a year or two ago they had told me of the famous Dr. Carter in this huge city hospital in Toronto—then, then I might have been impressed. Not now. I am a cynic, old and tangled in the opal of my mind. I was 21 last April, it is the end of May now. I came to this place—NEUROLOGICAL WARD, it was like that in bold letters—on the 28th of April and it is now May 30th. Yes, sometimes it is quite beautiful. I lie in my bed at night and creep into my nebula and watch fire and white matter like fine mists drifting past, I float with the clouds. There is no fire in there, my imagination has placed it thus so it can drift with the white mists. I have always loved beautiful things.

They have come to poke and pin Mrs. Watson. She moans, no, no she cannot drink another quart of water and no more needles. Now, now, they murmur softly. I am supposed to be asleep but I watch from the fine mists of my nebula, so beautiful and secret in there. I know this game and how to grit your teeth and pretend it doesn't matter that ten times in one night you are pinned with needles like a butterfly to a board or that you must drink a quart of water each time until it is like a poisonous liquid, a gas bloating up your stomach. Now, now, the two nurses murmur softly, only two more to go, with their pins and poisonous liquid. One jabs her in the hip with the long, slender needle, pinned again, the other holds out the quart of water to her in a plastic jug. No, Mrs. Watson whimpers, I feel sick to my stomach. Now, now, they murmur. The pinned butterfly drinks the poisonous liquid, the two collectors of butterfly wings stand beside her board to make sure she drinks it all. They go. The pinned butterfly flutters and gasps and is free for another two hours. I know this game and how to play it. I have been the butterfly three times. The injections keep the liquid from pouring out, from escaping the body, otherwise the doctors could not get a clear picture of the bloated nebula. Brain, to strangers to this place. I know this game.

Mrs. Watson flutters and gasps trying her twisted wings. "It's all right, Mrs. Watson," I murmur now from outside my nebula. I am lying in bed on the neurological ward and I must say to this woman that it is all right. She is 40 but looks nearly 60. I am 21 but look eighteen. I must say to this woman that it is all right. She has never been pinned on the butterfly board before nor drenched inside with the poisonous liquid bloating her stomach. She has only been here five days.

"Is that you, Kira?"

"Yes," I answer softly. My mother is fond of Russian books and her greatest desire is to go to Russia someday and see the Kremlin and its turrets gleaming in the sun in white snow, thus the name Kira, which is Russian. At my conception visions of Russia and bells and snow going on forever and ever and the Kremlin shining in the sun were mingled with the sperm that made me, Kira. They lay in her womb ready for the sperm that would make me a Russian. Waiting, simply waiting unbeknownst to my father. The sperm came and the womb filled with Russia mingled with the sperm and received its new comrade, Kira. I have forgotten what it means but something very lovely I am sure. Mrs. Watson whispers in the darkness, "You are such a nice girl, Kira, so young. What are you doing here? Are you crazy?"

"No," I say.

"They sent me here from a mental hospital. An O.H. I don't belong here, I didn't belong in that other place either. They said I cried all the time and got angry and threw things but I didn't! Liars, all of them! I don't do those things, you can see that for yourself. I thought the mental hospital was bad but this is worse. I'd rather have a shock treatment any time— zzz—burns out the brain. Does that scare you that I'm from a crazy joint?"

I can see her grey hair frizzled in the darkness like the zzz sound. "No," I answer because it doesn't, nothing much does anymore.

"Then why are you here?" Her voice is curious, grasping for a reason she can borrow.

"I have fits sometimes and no-one knows why. The pills for

epilepsy don't work for me. Maybe I'm a new breed of epilep-
tic I don't know."

"They said I had fits and threw things and hurt people but
I never did. Everyone lies, don't you forget it ever, everyone
lies so they can get just what they want from you. They lie."
Her teeth look purple in the dark and tiny night lights.

"What do they want from you?" I ask.

Mrs. Watson leans toward me from her bed, turning her
head closer to me, her breath smells of the poisonous liquid.
"Money," she whispers fiercely, "money! I've written my
lawyers over and over again to let me out of the crazy house,
to tell them how it is all a lie and a sham to get my money, but
I know my lawyers never got those letters, never saw the
truth. Otherwise I'd be out of there, out of here. The doctors
at the crazy house opened them all and laughed and took more
money from my estate, ripping my letters to bits, destroying
vital information. Just take, take from my estate, laughing
while they do it." Mrs. Watson's fierce whispers are filled with
hate. I say nothing. I have never known a crazy person before,
I am not sure of her map. "I heard you been here a month,
right?"

"Yes."

"They . . . the staff, do they do this thing with needles and
water often? I feel like I could throw up all over this bed but
I can't."

"That's because of the needles."

"Well, do they do this often?"

What can I say? I have been pinned on the butterfly board
three times and tomorrow comes the bigger board, the worst
one. I do not want to tell her about what will happen tomorrow morning. They have pinned me to the butterfly
board so often because the famous Dr. Carter can find
nothing. Maybe she will be lucky and they will find something
in her nebula. "No," I finally answer, "not often."

"How often?"

A nurse with a flashlight beams it into our corner of the
small ward. "Kira, let Mrs. Watson get some sleep, her next
injection is in less than two hours. You know we like our

patients to rest, sleep between injections." The flashlight beam is gone and she with it. For a moment we do not speak. In fact I don't want to talk to Mrs. Watson and her secret estate any longer. I have decided that I do not like her with her fierce whisper and teeth showing purple in the dark and her breath and her frizzy-zzz grey hair.

"How often?" she repeats.

Now I am mechanical in my answer but I will not tell her about tomorrow, I have decided that, I will not tell her. If she were my friend I would tell her but she is not. "If they find what they're looking for in the picture of your brain maybe just once, maybe you will be lucky. If they don't find it they will do it again. Maybe three times."

"Ahh God, you had it done three times?"

"Yes."

"Ahhh God!" she moans. "What happens in the morning, they told me I can't have any breakfast, what happens in the morning Kira?"

"They weigh you . . ." I say and let my voice trail off into a pretend sleep. Maybe I will really fall asleep.

"And then?" I do not answer, I breathe deeply as one does in sleep. "And then?" Her hand, thin and veined and wretched-looking is pulling at the sleeve of my nightgown like an old bird's talon. I do not move or speak. "And then?" Her voice is frantic, demanding. I say nothing, I am breathing deeply. She releases the sleeve of my blue cotton nightgown. I hear her whisper hatefully, "Bitch! You little bitch! Let me tell you something, sleeping brat, sleeping little brat, I am the only sane person left in this whole damn world, little brat!" I am glad that I did not tell her what will happen in the morning, she is no friend of mine, she hates me because my veins do not bulge and I have never been to a crazy hospital. I belong to no private club. I am awake for her next injection, I hear the butterfly gasp and flutter and then I am asleep. The pill they gave me at 9 o'clock has finally worked, my nebula turned dark with sleep. Drifting in the mists until morning.

It is a quarter to eight in the morning. Everyone in the small ward is awake, there are six beds in this room counting mine.

Three on one side, three on the other. I am lying on my side waiting for my breakfast, pretending I do not hear Mrs. Watson's demand and question over and over, "And then?" I eat my milky scrambled eggs and cold toast and drink the coffee which is good and hot this morning. I brush my long hair then lean back against the two pillows with a lighted cigarette in one hand, my coffee cup in the other. Today I have no tests, I can smoke and drink coffee and watch the television my parents rented for me. The third day I was here a girl from some other part of the neurological wing in a wheel chair came into this small ward and screamed at me, "Where did you get the TV! Who from?"

"From my parents," I answered.

"Christ, are you stupid!"

A nurse called her by her name, Linda, I think, and she wheeled herself out of the room giving me a hateful glance. I didn't know what she was talking about and I hated Toronto with its huge hospitals and the famous Dr. Carter. I felt like crying. I asked a nurse to tell Dr. Carter that I wanted to go home. The Cogitator came. "This is just because you are unused to hospital routine. You've never been hospitalized before, have you, Kira?"

"Only for a day and a night occasionally."

The Cogitator, a woman called Dr. Wells, patted my hand and told me that I would get used to it. She told me to call her Karen. Dr. Karen Wells. She is in her late thirties and has nice legs and wears eyeshadow. She patted my hand that day and said, "You'll get used to it." She is chief Cogitator for Dr. Carter. One sees Dr. Carter only during the great pinning day or as he flies through the ward, white coat flapping, nodding to his charges, a group of new Dr. Carters trailing behind him from bed to bed. He talks about you at your bedside as if you had merged with the pillow and the new Dr. Carters fumble and ask and answer questions with reddening faces. Perhaps they sense their smallness, know already that they will never be a great and famous Dr. Carter, only small Dr. Carters. There is room for Greatness in only one on this ward.

They have weighed Mrs. Watson. "Gained nine pounds,"

she says aloud to everyone in the small ward. "Feel like I could burst open," she says to Miss Smith who has Parkinson's disease, "What do you think of that? After my money, all of them." Miss Smith does not answer, only the tremors in her arms seem to weigh the related message and respond to it. Her face frozen in rigidity reveals nothing. "Nine pounds on their vile water in one night," she says again. The first time I gained ten pounds. Oh, how my nebula must have showed up clear and bright and bloated on their pictures! I ignore her. She pulls at my sleeve, I will not talk to her. "Brat! Bitch!" she whispers even in daylight to me. I drink my coffee. If she were my friend . . . She is not. At ten o'clock The Pinners with a touch of mania to them come and take Mrs. Watson away. She is going to the big butterfly board but she does not know it. Not yet. "I don't get angry or cry, ask that brat Kira! She knows. Thinks she's too good to talk to me. Ask her, that brat knows the truth!" Truth? She is asking The Pinners as they walk her from the small ward, "What's going to happen? What's going to happen?" Her voice is plaintive. The Pinners do not answer, saying only, "There, there," and they are gone.

She said I knew the truth. I used to think I knew all there was to know about truth. I am slender and pleasant looking with long auburn hair and I graduated from high school with honours, in the top fifteen. That was a truth, the diploma and the cleverness. I went to the graduation dance with Adam, who was tall with husky shoulders and sky-blue eyes and soft brown hair, who had been telling me for the last year how much he loved me and that we should consummate our love. He wore a navy blue suit and pale blue tie and I wore a long pink gown with a scoop neck and we danced all night together and drank a tepid fruit punch from a huge crystal bowl. Our love was never consummated. That was another truth. Adam finally gave up telling me how much he loved me, mouth aching from the word and left me. I didn't care too much.

I went to work in The Home for Retarded Children, that was a different kind of truth. There were mongoloids there and waterhead babies and the simply retarded, retarded beyond grasp or pain. Flies buzzed in the spring and summer in the playground where the children who were mobile went out to play. They constantly fell and cut and bruised themselves, the flies knew this and followed them, a dark buzzing cloud ready to light on the open wounds. The buzzing cloud followed them back into the Home when play period was over. Even after their wounds had been cleaned and bandaged a few flies still hovered with tenacity near the children's beds. Limbs of rubber, the waterheads. Some of them were quite beautiful, limbs of rubber, toes touching forehead. I felt no disgust or pity. I did feel compassion but more than that I felt necessary. That was another truth. "Why do you work in a place that's so depressing and pays so poorly? You're so smart, get a better job," everyone said to me. "Go to university with your fine brain," my mother said. They didn't know that I would simply be a numeral at university, perhaps a clever numeral but a numeral all the same. I could think of no other job that would make me feel as necessary. I tried to discuss this with my mother, this truth. I thought that she of all people having held Russia in her womb would understand. I was being a good proletarian working for the collective for a small amount of money per week. My mother had pointed out to me again and again since childhood the Mennonites when they came into town in their horse-drawn wagons, travelling with ease among cars and buses and pedestrians. "Look how selfless they are." She said it over and over again as we bought fruit and vegetables from the somberly dressed Mennonites. Mother, who should have understood but did not, said, "You should go to university. It's a very fine thing you are doing working at the Home but Kira you can't go on like that forever. Save your money and then you and I and your father, if he wants to, will go and see Russia next year and the next year you will go to university. It would be a shame to waste such a good brain. Study—study child psychology if you want. But don't waste that brain of yours, Kira."

"Russia?"

"Yes, the most beautiful country in the world. People for the people, green forests, all that snow, the Kremlin in the winter. . . ." She did not understand that there in Kitchener,

Ontario, I was being a good proletarian. But I was doing it out of selfish reasons like a spy. It made me feel necessary.

I got a small apartment with a girl who was a beautician when I was nineteen. I filled the apartment with plants and flowers of all colours and sizes and watered them carefully and put plant pills in their soil before going to work at the Home. The beautician sat under the hairdryer each night for at least two hours, filing and polishing her nails as she sat there. Her hair was as brittle as dried twigs and the colour of straw in the sun. I was happy. That was a truth. It was when I was just twenty that I moved into the nebula, or that is to say it moved in on me. I would have a seizure and remember nothing afterwards. "A convulsion, kind of," my roommate with the twig hair told the doctor. I had never thought about the brain, at least not my brain, despite my working in the Home—much less the nebula that had moved in on me. But that realization was only to come later, of the nebula. That was the newest truth, the next truth. I had e.e.g. after e.e.g. and still nothing, minor tests and finally this huge hospital in Toronto with the famous Dr. Carter. "The best in Ontario, maybe in Canada," my mother had said. I was not impressed. My nebula. As I said, it can be beautiful inside this space.

I am dressed in pale blue brushed denim jeans and a blue cotton top. I sit propped up on my bed watching television and drinking coffee, no tests for me today. They came for Mrs. Watson at 10 o'clock, it is now 10.20, I know that for certain because the Phil Donahue Show is just beginning. Mrs. Watson with her secret fortune is now pinned on the biggest butterfly board of them all. There is no anaesthesia for the dying butterfly. Yes, she will feel that this is dying. No anaesthesia, nothing can interfere with the test. She lies on the sterile table, hands clenched by her sides. Dr. Carter will tell her to unclench her hands. Two long needles, one on either side of her face have been driven through her jawbone. Pinned. Dr. Carter will tell her to lie perfectly still, the butterfly will lie pinned like that, still and dead for half an hour. Dr. Carter and others will peer into her bloated brain but only Dr. Carter will matter.

The first time I was the butterfly on the giant board, the pain of it—the sheer, smooth glass covering the butterfly board, from wing tip to wing tip, that first time it took The Pinners three tries before the giant pins settled properly into my jawbone. I thought perhaps my jawbone like my fits was different and unexplainable. The last two times however I was pinned in a neater fashion. I did not move, not the first, second or third time. I did not cry. I threw up afterward each time, ten pounds of poisonous liquid down the toilet. The first time I sat beside the toilet after, sweating and holding my head in my hands, my long hair stank of vomit and my mother waited for me anxiously outside the washroom. We had been sitting in the cafeteria after the pinned butterfly had risen from the board and suddenly I knew I was going to be violently ill. Mother, kind and gentle, wanted to come with me. "No, alone," I managed to say.

"Kira, please." I made it just in time to the washroom. It was there, I think, in that tidy, stinking cubicle that I perceived my brain as a nebula and it was then too that I knew what was in it and what they would never find. At first it was just an idea, a play toy in the long hours of white boredom, but as the tests went on and on, thrice the butterfly, my pain the smooth glass shield, it was no longer a toy. It is my escape. I am not a Mrs. Watson, but when the night comes or I think I cannot bear another commercial for Brillo Pads or Mr. Clean or when I have another e.e.g., I crouch in the mists of my nebula where it is beautiful and everything is calm, safer somehow in that beautiful misty space. "You'll get used to it," and Dr. Karen Wells had patted my hand. It seems so very long ago now. This hospital in the big, shining car city, so many cars here, with streets of sparkling light at night, this city of Toronto where there are no Mennonites, just the famous Dr. Carter who has become the next truth and with him the nebula. Is it the final truth? I am something of a novelty. They probe and pin and stick and pill and nothing changes, nothing works. I was always so ordinary before, simply Kira, a bright comrade born in an alien land but I adjusted, and my life read like a dull book, a simple map.

I think of my mother at home. Is she standing in front of the somberly dressed Mennonites buying their fruit and vegetables and marvelling at their selflessness? Soon I will get a letter from my father and he will write an amusing piece of poetry in it and tell me the latest news of everyone I have known and everyone he knows. He never runs out of words to fill sheets of paper with for my letters, the words brim over the pages like the tears in his eyes when I left. Tall, quiet Father, pipe in his reassuring mouth, gentle, tears in his eyes when I left for this huge monument to science and flesh. Mother finds it difficult to fill a single sheet of paper with words and yet it is she who comes here when I am pinned to the giant board, three times she has come; it is Father who cannot force himself to be witness. To what, I wonder? The Pinning, the aftermath of The Pinning of course. Tears brimmed up in his eyes when I left. Is it because of Russia, the land of the worker, the harsh land, the proletarian land, that my mother can come and bear witness like a good and sturdy comrade and my father cannot?

It is 11 o'clock, the Phil Donahue Show takes a commercial break. The Pinning has been over for ten minutes for Mrs. Watson. Is she vomiting now? Weeping? Cursing the laughing doctors who opened her letters to her lawyers? I only vomited. Dr. Carter himself said I was a very stoic person, Dr. Karen Wells, chief Cogitator, beamed at me and so did the lesser Cogitators at these words for me, all for me, from the famous Dr. Carter. Three times on the butterfly board and I have yet to weep. Is it that I am stoic or simply that I have the secret of my nebula and tell no-one? You see I have deduced what is wrong with my brain. Why don't I tell them? It would all be so simple. Would they think me high-strung giving in to stress? I'm not though, I am a sturdy comrade. I crouch in the mists of the nebula.

Mrs. Watson has to be helped back to her bed, she is weeping and moaning, fingers tentatively exploring her aching, burning jawbone without actually touching it, sketching the pain of it in the air. "I want all my personal belongings! I'm leaving your Dachau!" she screams. The nurses try to calm her down, "There, there," they say. It is their code word. "Nazis!" she screams and begins to tear apart her bed. Pillows fall to the floor, a sheet tears, the night table topples over with a crash and the splinter of the glass ashtray. Pinned again. The slender, efficient needle plunges into her leg muscle. She sleeps. One nurse sighs and then turns to me smiling, "How are you today, Kira?"

"I'm all right, a little bored, I guess."

"You can go down to the cafeteria or to the gift shop and buy some magazines, there's nothing scheduled for you today." She means to be kind to this novelty, Kira-stoic.

"I probably will after lunch," I reply. Two aides are straightening up the mess of Mrs. Watson's bombed-out bed, removing the ripped sheet. Mrs. Watson rolls like a piece of clay as they pull it out from under her, oblivious, her mind in a place of Not. Not anything, darkness is not even there. What strength in those thin bird-claw hands!

The next day is simple. I have another electroencephalograph. The needles are placed all over my scalp, little pin pricks, no pain. Blink. Stop. Deep breath. Stop. Fast shallow breathing. Stop. Deep, slow breathing. Stop. Blink rapidly. Stop. How used to all this I have become. Dr. Wells patted my hand, "You will get used to it." Later after the e.e.g. is over I take a brief walk around the hospital block. It is now June. The June air is sweet and cool, a slight breeze caresses my hair and scalp where minutes ago it was covered with the little pin pricks of needles. I do not stay outside long. Soon I am back in the small ward watching The Mike Douglas Show. I drink a ginger ale and smoke. There is a comedian on and everyone in the TV audience laughs, even I laugh a little. It is June second, the beginning of my second month here. The nurse comes and gives Miss Smith a new pill to try, as if anything on earth could stop the small volcano in her arms and fingertips or smooth out the rigidity of her shoulder and face. I am given new pills to try out, grey with black little dots on them. I swallow the three round pills and soon my mind begins to feel heavy. My nebula fills with fat rain clouds. I sleep.

It is June the fifth. I received a long letter from my father today with an amusing poem in it and he ends by saying that he knows that what the doctors are doing is right and that soon his Kira will be healthy and home.

I am to be pinned to the giant butterfly board again this morning, hands flat on the board, no flutter of wings. I could tell them quite simply that the thing that causes my fits is not a thing that a pill can cure. The amoeba. Yes, that is what it is. I knew that after my first pinning to the great board. It is nourishing itself on what they call my brain, enveloping the minute organisms held there. It floats in my nebula. It does not matter how many quarts of water or needles they give me at night to bloat my brain, everyone knows that an amoeba changes shape and because it is so changeable the famous Dr. Carter will never catch it on his bloated-brain scans. Why do I not tell them this? They would not put me in a crazy house like Mrs. Watson, who now wanders in a daze on a new drug, sometimes bumping into walls and furniture. No, not good stoic Comrade Kira. High strung and nervous under all the strain of it they would say kindly. Dr. Karen Wells would simply pat my hand as she did on my third day here when she first told me I'd get used to it. Why don't I tell them that it is the amoeba eating away that is causing me to faint, have fits and forget? Why not?

I am walking to the elevators with The Pinners now, in a few more minutes I will be the butterfly, wing tip to wing tip pinned on the giant board. They will look and find nothing, the famous Dr. Carter will shake his head in confusion. I feel no shiver in the pit of my stomach as I have on other Pinning Days—this will be my fourth time on the giant board. Yes, I am getting used to it. I will lie pinned there as still as the dead butterflies in a collector's box, lovingly, carefully pinned. I will lie like that for half an hour and then my wing tips will flutter faintly and I will rise, the secret of the amoeba held within my lovely, fluttering wing tips, fluttering softly in the large Pinning Room. Everyone will smile. Poor butterfly. Yes, I am getting used to it. Perhaps that is the final truth of them all, the last.

1976

A Wedding~Dress

Morley Callaghan

FOR FIFTEEN YEARS Miss Lena Schwartz had waited for Sam Hilton to get a good job so they could get married. She lived in a quiet boarding-house on Wellesley Street, the only woman among seven men boarders. The landlady, Mrs. Mary McNab, did not want woman boarders; the house might get a bad reputation in the neighbourhood, but Miss Schwartz had been with her a long time. Miss Schwartz was thirty-two, her hair was straight, her nose turned up a little, and she was thin.

Sam got a good job in Windsor and she was going there to marry him. She was glad to think that Sam still wanted to marry her, because he was a Catholic and went to church every Sunday. Sam liked her so much he wrote a cramped homely letter four times a week.

When Miss Schwartz knew definitely that she was going to Windsor, she read part of a letter to Mrs. McNab, who was a plump, tidy woman. The men heard about the letter at the table and talked as if Lena were an old maid. 'I guess it will really happen to her all right,' they said, nudging one another.

134

'The Lord knows she waited long enough.'

Miss Schwartz quit work in the millinery shop one afternoon in the middle of February. She was to travel by night, arrive in Windsor early next morning, and marry Sam as soon as possible.

That afternoon the down-town streets were slushy and the snow was thick alongside the curb. Miss Schwartz ate a little lunch at a soda fountain, not much because she was excited. She had to do some shopping, buy some flimsy underclothes and a new dress. The dress was important. She wanted it charming enough to be married in and serviceable for wear on Sundays. Sitting on the counter stool she ate slowly and remembered how she had often thought marrying Sam would be a matter of course. His love-making had become casual and good-natured in the long time; she could grow old with him and be respected by other women. But now she had a funny aching feeling inside. Her arms and legs seemed almost strange to her.

Miss Schwartz crossed the road to one of the department stores and was glad she had on her heavy coat with the wide sleeves that made a warm muff. The snow was melting and the sidewalk steaming near the main entrance. She went light-heartedly through the store, buying a little material for a dress on the third floor, a chemise on the fourth floor and curling-tongs in the basement. She decided to take a look at the dresses.

She took an elevator to the main floor and got on an escalator because she liked gliding up and looking over the squares of counters, the people in the aisles, and over the rows of white electric globes hanging from the ceiling. She intended to pay about twenty-five dollars for a dress. To the left of the escalators the dresses were displayed on circular racks in orderly rows. She walked on the carpeted floor to one of the racks and a salesgirl lagged on her heels. The girl was young and fair-haired and saucy-looking; she made Miss Schwartz uncomfortable.

'I want a nice dress, blue or brown,' she said, 'about twenty-five dollars.'

The salesgirl mechanically lifted a brown dress from the rack. 'This is the right shade for you,' she said. 'Will you try it on?'

Miss Schwartz was disappointed. She had no idea such a plain dress would cost twenty-five dollars. She wanted something to keep alive the tempestuous feeling in her body, something to startle Sam. She had never paid so much for a dress, but Sam liked something fancy. 'I don't think I like these,' she said. 'I wanted something special.'

The salesgirl said sarcastically, 'Maybe you were thinking of a French dress. Some on the rack in the French room are marked down.'

Miss Schwartz moved away automatically. The salesgirl did not bother following her. 'Let the old maid look around,' she said to herself, following with her eyes the tall commonplace woman in the dark coat and the oddly shaped purple hat as she went into the gray French room. Miss Schwartz stood on a blue pattern on the gray carpet and guardedly fingered a dress on the rack, a black canton crepe dress with a high collar that folded back, forming petals of burnt orange. From the hem to the collar was a row of buttons, the sleeves were long with a narrow orange trimming at the cuff, and there was a wide corded silk girdle. It was marked seventy-five dollars. She liked the feeling it left in the tips of her fingers. She stood alone at the rack, toying with the material, her mind playing with thoughts she guiltily enjoyed. She imagined herself wantonly attractive in the dress, slyly watched by men with bold thoughts as she walked down the street with Sam, who would be nervously excited when he drew her into some corner and put his hands on her shoulders. Her heart began to beat heavily. She wanted to walk out of the room and over to the escalator but could not think clearly. Her fingers were carelessly drawing the dress into her wide coat sleeve, the dress disappearing steadily and finally slipping easily from the hanger, drawn into her wide sleeve.

She left the French room with a guilty feeling of satisfied exhaustion. The escalator carried her down slowly to the main floor. She hugged the parcels and the sleeve containing the dress tight to her breast. On the street-car she started to cry because Sam seemed to have become something remote, drifting away from her. She would have gone back with the dress but did not know how to go about it.

When she got to the boarding-house she went straight upstairs and put on the dress as fast as she could, to feel that it belonged to her. The black dress with the burnt orange petals on the high collar was short and loose on her thin figure.

And then the landlady knocked at the door and said that a tall man downstairs wanted to see her about something important. Mrs. McNab waited for Miss Schwartz to come out of her room.

Miss Schwartz sat on the bed. She felt that if she did not move at once she would not be able to walk downstairs. She walked downstairs in the French dress, Mrs. McNab watching her closely. Miss Schwartz saw a man with a wide heavy face and his coat collar buttoned high on his neck complacently watching her. She felt that she might just as well be walking downstairs in her underclothes; the dress was like something wicked clinging to her legs and her body. 'How do you do,' she said.

'Put on your hat and coat,' he said steadily.

Miss Schwartz, slightly bewildered, turned stupidly and went upstairs. She came down a minute later in her coat and hat and went out with the tall man. Mrs. McNab got red in the face when Miss Schwartz offered no word of explanation.

On the street he took her arm and said, 'You got the dress on and it won't do any good to talk about it. We'll go over to the station.'

'But I have to go to Windsor,' she said, 'I really have to. It will be all right. You see, I am to be married tomorrow. It's important to Sam.'

He would not take her seriously. The street lights made the slippery sidewalks glassy. It was hard to walk evenly.

At the station the sergeant said to the detective, 'She might be a bad egg. She's an old maid and they get very foxy.'

She tried to explain it clearly and was almost garrulous. The sergeant shrugged his shoulders and said the cells would not hurt her for a night. She started to cry. A policeman led her to a small cell with a plain bed.

Miss Schwartz could not think about being in the cell. Her head, heavy at first, got light and she could not consider the matter. The detective who had arrested her gruffly offered to send a wire to Sam.

The policeman on duty during the night thought she was a stupid silly woman because she kept saying over and over, 'We were going to be married. Sam liked a body to look real nice. He always said so.' The unsatisfied expression in her eyes puzzled the policeman, who said to the sergeant, 'She's a bit of a fool, but I guess she was going to get married all right.'

At half past nine in the morning they took her from the cell to the police car along with a small wiry man who had been quite drunk the night before, a coloured woman who had been keeping a bawdy-house, a dispirited fat man arrested for bigamy, and a Chinaman who had been keeping a betting-house. She sat stiffly, primly, in a corner of the car and could not cry. Snow was falling heavily when the car turned into the city hall courtyard.

Miss Schwartz appeared in the Women's Court before a little Jewish magistrate. Her legs seemed to stiffen and fall away when she saw Sam's closely cropped head and his big lazy body at a long table before the magistrate. A young man was talking rapidly and confidently to him. The magistrate and the Crown attorney were trying to make a joke at each other's expense. The magistrate found the attorney amusing. A court clerk yelled a name, the policeman at the door repeated it and then loudly yelled the name along the hall. The coloured woman who had been keeping the bawdy-house appeared with her lawyer.

Sam moved over to Miss Schwartz. He found it hard not to cry. She knew that a Salvation Army man was talking to a slightly hard-looking woman about her, and she felt strong and resentful. Sam held her hand but said nothing.

The coloured woman went to jail for two months rather than pay a fine of $200.

'Lena Schwartz,' said the clerk. The policeman at the door

shouted the name along the hall. The young lawyer who had been talking to Sam told her to stand up while the clerk read the charge. She was scared and her knees were stiff.

'Where is the dress?' asked the magistrate.

A store detective with a heavy moustache explained that she had it on and told how she had been followed and later on arrested. Everybody looked at her, the dress too short and hanging loosely on her thin body, the burnt orange petals creased and twisted. The magistrate said to himself: 'She's an old maid and it doesn't even look nice on her.'

'She was to be married today,' began the young lawyer affably. 'She was to be married in this dress,' he said and good-humouredly explained that yesterday when she stole it she had become temporarily a kleptomaniac. Mr. Hilton had come up from Windsor and was willing to pay for the dress. It was a case for clemency. 'She waited a long time to be married and was not quite sure of herself,' he said seriously.

He told Sam to stand up. Sam haltingly explained that she was a good woman, a very good woman. The Crown attorney seemed to find Miss Schwartz amusing.

The magistrate scratched away with his pen and then said he would remand Miss Schwartz for sentence if Sam still wanted to marry her and would pay for the dress. Sam could hardly say anything. 'She will leave the city with you,' said the magistrate, 'and keep out of the department stores for a year.' He saw Miss Schwartz wrinkling her nose and blinking her eyes and added, 'Now go out and have a quiet wedding.' The magistrate was quite satisfied with himself.

Miss Schwartz, looking a little older than Sam, stood up in her dress that was to make men slyly watch her and straightened the corded silk girdle. It was to be her wedding-dress, all right. Sam gravely took her arm and they went out to be quietly married.

1927

Home-grown in
the East End

Marilyn Powell

ALIDA STARTED COMING home again on visits. She arrived one day in the east end of Toronto. The cab-driver pulled two large suitcases with stickers out of the trunk, and she settled into the room with the window looking out on the backyard, where the yellow cat on its lead attached to the clothesline walked up and down in an undeviating path below her. It was January.

Next door, Mrs. Elfridge saw the cab arrive and depart because she had been dusting the pictures on top of the old upright piano. First Mr. Elfridge's mother, then Mr. Elfridge, then Carly in the bonnet she knit him when he was a baby— my, wasn't he a peach though? The silver mug he'd won for being so beautigul held pride of place in the china cabinet right now. Beside the birthday bunting that was used on every birthday, including his one-and-twentieth. But her attention was taken away from her dusting by the great display Alida was making there in the street. "She was wearing a fur coat, dad," Mrs. Elfridge observed when the two of them, she and Mr. Elfridge, sat down to supper that evening. "In a neighbourhood of cloth coats she's bound to wear a fur one. Black Persian lamb, mink collar, and the stickers on her suitcase said Detroit, Buffalo. She swung her hips like a horse out of traces, and she was, if you know what I mean!"

The first time Mr. Elfridge saw Alida was the following Friday when he was coming home from work in the fish and chip shop. The strong smell of vinegar mixed with sweat reminded him that Saturday night he was due for his weekly bath, and he was thinking about that when he bumped into her under the streetlamp that stood in front of both their houses. He noticed that her mouth was purple-red, as though it had been eating berries, and he told Mrs. Elfridge so before he went up the stairs on Saturday night with his cake of Lifebuoy and a library book.

It was really what Alida was that frightened Mrs. Elfridge. Too overt, too sexual, too primitive; she raised in Mr. Elfridge a flurry of long-forgotten urges never realized. Alida—Wonder Woman, Sheena of the Jungle, the voluptuous, waistless heroine curved like a cartoon saying "Draw Me"—as an exotic dancer who could be hired at reasonable rates for any club or downtown function. She had cards printed up and distributed, carrying them to beer parlours at the intersections, disappearing through the doors marked "Ladies and Their Escorts," and reappearing emptyhanded. When the taverns closed, long after the rest of the street had gone to bed, Alida's laughter could be heard and the rough sound of male laughter, changing every night at her front door. The old lady she came to see denied any kinship with her. "Thank heavens," murmured Mrs. Elfridge, jolted out of sleep on one occasion, her pink hairnet askew, "that Carly, my joy, my own, is safe from her."

Mrs. Elfridge's joy, winner of baby contests and spelling bees, was at home that January because he'd failed at just about everything he'd tried since adolescence including two years at university which Mrs. Elfridge financed by cleaning offices down on Queen Street. For two years she polished desks, emptied ashtrays and pushed an industrial vacuum up and down.

She kept her work a secret from the neighbourhood of course. And Mr. Elfridge, considering the fact that he didn't like Carly, never had, smothered his rage at the maternal sacrifice and the unnaturalness of a university education for someone, even his son, from that neck of the woods—and planned his own revenge. As for Carly, he didn't care if the entire east end and his mother's church knew she was a cleaning lady. He failed his courses anyway and retreated to the attic at the end of two years, barricaded himself in and played records on a wind-up victrola until he gave them up too. He'd taken the path of least resistance, grown fat from reclusion, confirming the double chin that was forming at puberty, and his skin was pasty and white, deprived of ultraviolet. He'd become a solitary who took his meals on trays and left his laundry like droppings on the stairs at the end of each week when Mrs. Elfridge collected it. The outside world, namely his mother and father, saw only his hand reaching out for necessities then drawing in again. Without explanation he had diminished to signs and traces.

But if the outside world couldn't see him, Carly could see it. By engineering a chink between the door and the frame, chipping at it patiently over the months with a table knife, putting his eye to it when it was done and cocking the other, he could see the comings and goings on the attic stairs. His mother, with her small shoulders hunched and puffing from the weight of the trays, neared and centred in the chink three times a day. "There, my pet," she'd say, "is breakfast—lunch—dinner. Eat it all up. Clean your plate." His father came seldom and then just to repair a loose stairboard or such, and all he gave to the squint was the length of his back as he wielded his tools. No matter. The important thing was neither of them knew he was looking at them. Carly was free to see. Nothing was required of him. He was free.

And free to amuse himself with the view out his narrow, sloping windows, one on the back wall above the backyard from which he studied the yellow cat, and the other on the side wall, looking back and across at the old lady. Her house was shorter than his own. By a stroke of luck and an extension that was his attic room, his window was situated in exactly the right place to give him almost her total domestic drama. Awake at seven, let the cat out on the line at eight, pull him in at six, when she and he shared a meal in the kitchen with the sansevierias.

When Alida arrived, Carly saw her too and gave up watching the old lady. He saw her drink tea in the kitchen, saw her pause on the landing, saw her in her bedroom, framed like a perfect miniature. A tickle, a flicker, a fever devoured him, and he began to resent the hours she spent at the front of the old lady's house. And the daylight because it obscured her indoors. In the evenings she would sit illuminated in the halo of her vanity table lamp, and he would talk to her and about her to himself. "Luscious brushes her hair tonight, brushes it with quick, light strokes. I can see the blue sparks fly and feel the hair crackling. From the bottles on her dresser she selects one, dabs perfume behind her ears and down the cleft, puts colour on her lips." In time it seemed as if the red mouth opened, and she began to talk to him. "Beloved, I've been to Buffalo, Schenectady, Syracuse and New York. Never in all my travels have I seen a boy as fat and delicious as you. If only you were here beside me." He began to think of how he could come to her.

"He wants a telescope, dad."

"A what?" Mr. Elfridge was frying onions in a pot the day of the blizzard. He was frying them in salt, pepper and butter, and he ate them for his health. He was wearing his windbreaker and fedora, the way he invariably did when he felt cold coming on.

"A telescope so he can explore the stars."

A sound like the buzz of a saw issued from the kitchen. Mr. Elfridge was grinding his teeth. They were worn down to short, yellow stubs because for the last two years he had also been grinding them in his sleep. "He's going backwards—you know that. He's playing with toys up there in the attic. He's found his old things, pulled them out of the boxes, and now he plays with them on the floor. Who's he talking to up there anyway? He'll soon be a baby, big and bouncing, better for mumsy than a grownup man."

Mrs. Elfridge wasn't listening. She never did when Mr. Elfridge was working himself up in one of his lathers. Instead, she concentrated on Carly's medals from school, bronze and silver, up to and including grade four, for perfect attendance, standing on the mantel in the parlour. She sighed. What a delectable he'd been, bringing home two candies from school, one for himself, one for her! From the teacher. Wasn't he winning in the fancy he'd had about the ball of silver he made from his father's cigarette-box liners? He'd hold it in the close centre of his hand, and invite her to peek through his fingers at the man inside his hand, inside the silver ball. And when she did, he'd snap his fingers shut together, and she'd see his closed fist, swollen beyond its normal size.

Mr. Elfridge jabbed the onions with a fork. Hadn't she—hadn't she sent Carly to school when he was five without a fly in the pants she made him—snip, snip, out of a pattern? They were green and there were dimples on his knees. But the little boy came home crying and wouldn't go back until she installed a zipper. When he was sixteen, he kept two crayfish in the attic and raced them and pinched ground beef from his mother's larder to feed them. By some half-remembered instinct they repeatedly made their way to the sea down three flights of stairs, ending exhausted in the vestibule, feelers probing the hardwood floor. Once they began their arduous descent when Mrs. Elfridge was entertaining the Presbyterian auxiliary. Scratch, scratch, bump. Scratch, scratch, bump. Slowly, painfully, falling stair by stair onto their backs and up again, they continued down to their defeat in the Presbyterian auxiliary's midst. Humiliated, exposed, Mrs. Elfridge scooped them up and, grasping them behind their pincers, delivered them to Carly and the attic, where they died. And all she would admit was "he's exceptional."

She was out there now in the vestibule, putting on her cloth coat and hat, no doubt intending to set off after the telescope. She was drawing the bundle buggy after her.

"Where are you going?"

Mrs. Elfridge's hat angled rakishly on one side of her head, and he could smell her face powder. "The weather report says we're in for a heavy fall, drifting up to six feet or more, traffic snarls and stops. I'll be back before we're snowed into next week."

"I'm thinking of having the attic closed off," her husband called after her, but she was already on her mission down the front path.

That same afternoon Mrs. Elfridge was seen in the bakery, the butcher's shop, haggling over a roast for Sunday, and the junk shop, from which she emerged carrying a long, cylindrical parcel wrapped in brown paper and tied with string. Mr. Elfridge spent the afternoon working in the fish and chip shop, peeling potatoes and thinking about sawing boards to the same length, five feet, and choosing nails, particularly long and thick. That evening he went off alone to the public house because Mrs. Elfridge wouldn't allow liquor at home, went in the entrance marked "Ladies and Their Escorts" and got into a conversation with a lady about blizzards. "I remember blizzards," he told her, "before I settled down. Out west when I was logging in my twenties, and I had icicles on my nose, it was that cold. But we huddled together, and the night grew warm and moist like the inside of a cow's mouth." He winked at her. That evening a telescope lay on Carly's tray next to his napkin, with a tag, "love, mother."

The frost was curling in fingers up the pane of Carly's side window, and he was breathing excitedly, trying to keep a small oval of territory clear. The day of the blizzard, all day, he had been watching—since the first snow began to fall in soft, bright flakes, then harder, and now since the snow had begun to build a wall below the frost, undulating across his line of vision. It was night outside. Alida was not at home. She had gone out several hours ago he guessed, though he had no watch and couldn't tell. Anyway, her vanity light was still out, and she always turned it on when she was in. In her bedroom.

He was frantic with expectation. Beside him on the floor was the telescope at the ready, fully extended to give absolute magnification. Fumbling for it, he accidentally kicked his supper tray, still there, and the clatter startled him. A shiver went through his immense bulk. He had been sitting for such a long time, dreaming about what it would be like to see her in depth, to penetrate the space his naked eye couldn't reach. Now that he had the means he was afraid. Suddenly he thought about his appearance. There were no mirrors in his attic. He had not seen himself in two years. Not from head to toe, not looking at himself as he looked at his mother and father. He did not even have a distinct idea of his size. He simply grew and evolved, and his mother cut him clothes from larger and larger patterns.

He held his hand up in front of the window. The palm was broad and puffed, the fingers pudgy. He had trouble undoing his buttons or tying his shoes, so he didn't bother anymore. He was lumbering and ponderous in his movements, but, oh, Alida wouldn't mind. He would be her child and lay his head against her breasts, rosy as apples. She would love him, seeing in him the beautiful boy he had been. A flood of recollections in pictures came to him each more real than the present. He was ten and sliding down the "icies" in the park on a bobsled; the hill was frozen glass. He was ten and skating. His britches had leather patches on the knees. He was five and spiralling backwards.

There! He tensed and brought himself shudderingly back. The light went on in her bedroom, and just as suddenly Luscious was there, half in shadow like the moon and laughing with her head thrown back. She crossed to the window, and for a moment he imagined she saw him and was going to speak to him as she always did. In his mind, intimately, affectionately. "Beloved, I am glad to see you!" But tonight was somehow different. She paused, seemed to consider drawing the blind, shutting him out. Then she shrugged, laughed again and turned away. In the glow of her lamp she was starting to undress. Hardly daring, he reached for the telescope and, trembling, put it to his eye. How marvelous! It was as if he travelled the distance between and stood behind her, following the soft material of her dress as it hissed and passed every curve of her body on the way to her feet. Next she was removing her stockings with the black seams, kicking her shoes in front of her, lifting her legs like a dancer, one, the other, peeling the sheer things away. The bed was in front of her, three quarters in the frame. She was turning, pivoting. She was glimmering and dazzling his sight. At last the tender underthings were discarded, falling in successive waves.

He was not aware of the man waiting on the bed until the man bent her to him and her image shattered, the man and she thrown into some kind of hybrid—her hair spread in a black fan around her, his face contorted, middle-aged and wheezing. With a sharp cry Carly sprang back, toppling clumsily. The telescope flew wildly from place to place, lost. Then the lens smashed.

The snow was blowing in drifts around the house, swallowing it up and muffling sounds. On the second floor a clock was ticking and receding. Mrs. Elfridge was asleep under flannel blankets. The place beside her was empty.

On the third floor a sour smell rose from the week's dirty socks piled against the wall, stiff from wearing and heaped like corpses. Books were thrown open, pressed back on their spines, when suddenly a gust of wind animated them, riffling their pages. One of the attic windows was open. The snow was driven inwards. The attic was abandoned.

They found Carly, after a week's desperate search, when the drifts thawed in the backyard. He was frozen stiff, his knees drawn up to his chest, his head bent, hiding his double chin, as though he had simply gone to sleep there, dreaming his liquid, prenatal dreams. He had pushed and squeezed and thrust himself through the narrow space that had been his hold on life, hurtling to the earth in silence and landing with a great mellow thud. The telescope, battered from the descent, lay beside him.

They buried him privately, secretly, in an outsize coffin, lining it with the silver mug he'd won in the contest, the curls his mother had preserved in lavender, and his medals—

erasing all the symbols of his existence. Mr. Elfridge closed off the attic with five foot boards and stout nails. Mrs. Elfridge told the neighbourhood her son had gone to Africa to do missionary work and might never return. The snow melted. The old lady put her yellow cat out on the line. And Alida went to Buffalo, where, it was rumoured, nine months later she gave birth to a baby boy.

1977

The Neilson Chocolate Factory

Irena Friedman

THIS IS A story which starts with the casual unwrapping of a Neilson *Crispy Crunch,* a name which suddenly —far away from Toronto—is as evocative as the warm fragrance of chocolate which forever lingered over the neighbourhood.

"What, a chocolate factory?" my friends would laugh. "In Toronto?"

It's true, the factory made the neighbourhood sound like the world-famous Berne or Haarlem, though in fact it was a rather undistinguished area which some called Little Italy and others Little Portugal. Well, some of *us* called it that. The Italian and Portuguese immigrants who lived there were not likely to think of it as anything resembling their homelands. But though the winters were harsh and inflation kept rising, more and more of them seemed to move into the neighbourhood, planting tomatoes and vine in their backyards and sweeping the dry autumn leaves with a fervour equal only to their longing for the warm regions they had left behind. At four or five in the morning, one could see window after

149

window light up in the houses around the factory as the men would get up to go to work, often labouring for twelve, fifteen hours a day while their wives scrubbed and laundered and waited on tables and the children played football on the icy streets. Only on Sundays, an air of contentment would settle over the neighbourhood and the smell of chocolate would give way to that of home-baked bread or roasting lamb. Only then did those rapidly maturing faces seem to relax as uncles and aunts would arrive and, taking little Giorgio or Rafael on their knee, ask:

"What are you gonna be when you grow up, hey?" while the child, barely able to restrain his pride, would answer: "Me, I'm gonna be a doctor," or—as inevitably—"Me, I'm gonna build chocolate factories!"

Some of the men on my street were employees of the Neilson factory, but the only person I knew was Manuel de Sousa, my landlord. The funny thing was, I could never find out just what he did there. An inscrutable Portuguese immigrant, his English seemed hopelessly inadequate whenever we had a disagreement. Which, I might have known from the start, the two of us—worlds apart—were bound to have our share of.

"Hello, I see you have a flat for rent," I said, that rainy September evening when I finally found him home. Manuel, I remember, glared at me as though I had come to expropriate him.

"How many?" he snapped after a prolonged scrutiny.

"One, only me," I said, smiling, trying not to look overly eager. But, almost at once, he started to close the door in my face.

"Too big, too expensive for you," he said and I wondered whether it would be in my favor to tell him I was a free-lance journalist and needed extra space for an office.

"Hundred and forty dollars, *too much!*"

Hundred and forty dollars, in Toronto, hardly seemed like too much. "How many rooms?" I asked.

"Three and one kitchen, no fridge, no stove."

"Oh I see." Even so, it seemed like a bargain—I could always

pick these up second hand, I decided. "Can I see?" I asked.
And at last, he stepped aside to let me pass.

"You no have husband?" he asked.

"No, I'm . . . not married." To say I was divorced would not,
I suspected, help me get the flat. And I needed no more than
one glance to know that I definitely wanted the place. An
entire floor really, it was surprisingly beautiful—bright and
immaculate, with a sun room and stained-glass windows. I
was much too excited to notice, until the very end, the absence
of one obvious room.

"No bathroom?" I asked, puzzled to have missed it and
wondering why in the world he was acting so indifferent.

"Downstairs," he said, flicking off the lights.

And I, again: "Can I see?"

Well, it turned out the bathroom was in the basement and
that I would have to share it with him. Though it was perfectly clean, I remember thinking it could be a problem, for—
he told me then—he lived right there, across the hall from the
bathroom. Now, it was my turn to feign nonchalance.

"You live alone?" I asked while he, with sudden defiance,
snapped: "You want the flat, yes or no?"

I didn't understand any of it but I could take care of myself.
I said yes, I would take it—quickly, before he could change his
mind. Above all, I was puzzled that a man in his mid-thirties
would own a three-storey house and live, alone, in the musty
basement.

"You sure you can pay the rent?" he asked as I wrote out
the first month's cheque.

"I'm sure," I said and, ignorant as I was, added: "Don't
worry, I earn as much as a man."

Monday must have been the day they mixed the chocolate at
the factory, for on those days the smell was so strong, one
expected those red, home-grown tomatoes to have a cocoa
taste. I moved into the flat the first Monday in October and I
remember wondering whether I would eventually sicken of the
sweet, persistent smell which Manuel, wearing his factory
clothes, seemed to have brought with him right into my flat.

"So much furniture!" he said when I and two friends came back with my possessions from Montreal. "You buy it all?" he asked, looking, I remember, baffled and awed. He hovered around us, eyeing with inexplicable intensity the velvet couch, the Persian rugs. Now and then, he would give us a hand but mostly, he just stood there, pretending to busy himself with a light fixture or cupboard door, but looking the way a man might while handing over a family heirloom to a pawn-broker. He seemed curious too about my friends, Stuart and Jean-Paul.

"That man, the tall one, he your husband, no?" he said when the two of them had gone to return the trailer.

"I'm not married," I repeated. I couldn't understand why he should look so downcast about it. Did he, I wondered, feel uneasy about having a single woman in the house? Did he mind my bringing male friends over?

Stuart and Jean-Paul drove back that night and the next few days assured me Manuel was likely to keep a perfectly respect-ful distance. Both he and the Melos upstairs worked day and night, coming home, it seemed, only to eat and sleep. My desk was in the sun room, overlooking the garden, and each day, I would see him arrive in his chocolate-stained overalls and bend over the crisp, leafy plants, picking a ripe tomato, a green pepper. He pretended not to know I was there, though more than once, he must have heard the typewriter. His daily vege-table picking—slow and self-absorbed—was one of several rituals I was getting to know. Twice or three times a week, he would take out the garbage bins before going to work and, when he came home, carry them back under my windows where he would linger for suspiciously long moments, whis-ling and rattling the lids and, from time to time, glancing furtively into the lit-up living room. Once a week, on Satur-days, he would drive down to Kensington Market and return with heavy sacks of potatoes and newspaper-wrapped fish which he fried every Saturday before going out into the drive-way to wash and polish his '71 Chevy. The car stood locked up in the garage all week, but he washed it faithfully all the same: once a week, after the trip to the market.

It was an unusually mild fall and I was beginning to discover the city—looking for curtain material in cluttered textile shops or for a paper lantern in Chinatown. Toronto seemed supremely organized for shopping purposes: Fabric and hardware stores on Spadina, second-hand furniture on Queen Street. Each day, the radius of familiar territory expanded and each day, the toy-like streetcars would bring me back to the more familiar streets I was beginning to think of as home. That was the fall I wore nothing but black until one day, I perceived the Italian and Portuguese widows smiling at me like unlikely but sympathetic sisters. I could see it so plainly in their eyes: Ah, so young, poor thing, and already in mourning! I didn't mind their silent solicitude. There was something comforting in that feeling of shared bereavement—shared anything, I suppose. But soon after that, my black outfit—skirt, sweater, leotards—began to seem like a parody of their loss and I went back to wearing green corduroy skirts and maroon sweaters—the clothes which, I had to admit, were more properly mine.

Manuel's place was directly under my living room and, judging from the area it occupied, must have consisted of no more than one small room where he slept and cooked his fish and his potatoes. I say *must have* because he seemed as secretive about his place as an adolescent hiding old *Playboys*. When, one evening, I knocked on his door to ask about the fuse box (which turned out to be in his room), he kept the door open a crack, so that all I could see was the pale green corner with its peeling paint. It was not until a day or two later, however, that I fully realized the extent of his shame, his pride.

That afternoon (it was Saturday and Manuel was, as usual, washing his car in the driveway), I found my telephone dead and opening the back door, asked whether I might use his. I would have preferred to ask Ava-Maria upstairs but I had seen her leave with her husband only a short while earlier, on their way to the market and laundry.

Manuel turned off the hose and said yes, he would bring it up in a minute. I noticed, while waiting, that the vine leaves had turned quite yellow and the tomatoes were beginning to rot. I thought, with some surprise, that he must have had a plug phone, but the surprise turned to pained astonishment when he came upstairs carrying an *unwired* telephone which he at once proceeded to connect to an old phone box out in the hall.

"Manuel, I am sorry... I didn't know you were going to——"

"No trouble, no trouble," he kept repeating, crouching on the floor with two screwdrivers.

"I'm sorry, really, I'm sorry."

"Is okay, you no have stove yet?"

"No, I'll probably get one this week."

"Everything costs too much money, no?" he smiled. He told me then about the job he used to have in the Sudbury mines and how, one winter, he slipped on the ice and broke his back.

"Nine months I no work," he said, "But Workmen's Compensation, they no pay me." He told me they paid only for work accidents. "And now," he said, "I wait another year for marry." He looked at my living room wistfully, then turned to face me again.

"I read your name in newspaper last week," he said, "Raoul and Ava-Maria, they want to know why you no have husband, I tell them you write for Toronto *Star*, right?"

"And you, what do you do?" I asked, just then more out of desire to change the subject than real curiosity.

"I work at Neilson Chocolate Factory."

"Yes, I know, but what do you do, exactly?"

"Chocolate, lots and lots of chocolate, mountains of chocolate," he said with a great gesture. "You like chocolate?"

"Yes, I like." I was gradually lapsing into his kind of speech.

"In Portugal, even in holidays, we no have much chocolate and now ... I no like," he finished sadly. I was intrigued by his talk of marriage. He was always alone. He had no visitors, male or female. And he worked about fourteen hours every day.

"Do you have a fiancée?" I asked, dialing the telephone company.

"No," he said, "I no have enough money." He waited while

I talked to the telephone people, watching the squirrels in the garden pluck the rose hips from his bushes and disappear quickly among the yellowing foliage of his vegetable garden. I too had no visitors that first month. I was new in Toronto and was just beginning to meet people.

Those first two weeks, while looking for a stove, I would often eat at Lydia's Roti Shop around the corner. Lydia was a big Jamaican with an enormous bust pressing against the white jersey she wore day in and day out. Her voluptuous, knowing body seemed strangely incongruous with the shy and self-effacing expression on her aging face. She looked like a woman whose adolescence had congealed below the lines and wrinkles of middle age. She was married to a man from Trinidad and her roti shop was a favorite hangout for other islanders. A mother to some and object of sexual fantasies to others, she kept the place open day and night, making excellent, the best, roti. I acquired a great taste for the spicy, cheap stuff and for the Caribbean music the customers played on the juke box. Bent over the oozing pancake, I would eavesdrop on their conversations.

"Listen to me, man, you let that woman have a finger and, I tell you, she'll soon want a hand!"

"Hey, man, you don't know what you talking about, Pearl and me, we——" The voices sharp and urgent and, whatever the subject, as inexplicably optimistic as that relentless music. They knew how to live it up, those islanders and, late at night, it was an especially good place to go to, the hot spice lingering in my mouth for a long time after. Barely five minutes away, Manuel's house—the street—was always a startling surprise after Lydia's shop. Everyone, it seemed, went to bed here by ten. Like Manuel and Raoul, they all had to get up at four or five in the morning and leave for work before it was quite light. I don't know whether Neilson's had a night shift or not, but the chocolate smell continued to hover over the neighbourhood long after the workers had gone to sleep.

Now that I think about it, my problems with Manuel seemed to start when I first hung up my curtains. At the time, I didn't give it a thought, but he seemed to take it as a personal affront that I should want to protect my privacy. Perhaps he thought it was a rebuke for his curiosity, perhaps he saw it as an assertion of immoral intentions (I say *intentions* because, living below me, he must have known my lifestyle was above reproach). In any case, he began greeting me with extreme coldness, looking at once guilty and accusing whenever we met on the stairs and muttering under his breath when I said "How are you?" It is possible, however, that his mood had nothing to do with me, for twice that week, some friend of his arrived at the house and, for a long time, banged on Manuel's door and called his name. It was sometime past nine and Manuel had just arrived from work, but he did not come to the door and I did not let the man in. If there was anything I understood, even then, it was that he would want no one to see his place.

It was the week before Hallowe'en and, every afternoon, some child would ring my bell and ask me to buy a Neilson chocolate bar.

"How much?" I would ask.

"One dollar."

"One dollar!" It seemed like a lot, even for a large bar, but—for some reason—they all pushed the same product and all, somewhat timidly, demanded one dollar. When I asked why it cost so much, they just stared at me with their dark, somber eyes, so that I was never sure whether they had understood me. Only one of them—a fat, red-cheeked boy with energetic gestures—did not lose his bearings. Perhaps someone had already prepared him for the question, for the words were hardly out of my mouth when, meeting my eyes, the boy said: "It's for the poor people, the Greek and Portuguese and Italian people." Something told me he was lying, but I bought the chocolate anyway and ate it all that same night. Only after it was finished did I start to curse the boy. The chocolate bar turned out to be full of almonds and probably worth close to a dollar, but all the same, I was by then quite certain that the boy had lied.

My search for an antique table took me to the outlying suburbs of Toronto where families renovating or selling a home would advertise in the paper, quickly disposing of their possessions for half the price an antique dealer might want. I had no car in those days and used public transit, speculating about a given area on the basis of passengers getting on and off the subway. At Rosedale, for example, there would be elderly, meticulously-dressed women, or bearded men who worked as editors or radio producers; at Davisville, secretaries and hairdressers would get off; at Finch, housewives with small children and businessmen returning home. Sometimes, I would wonder whether Manuel, or the Melos, ever made it to these parts of town, to the ravines and lake, and what they might have thought of the pink faces framed by coiffed hair or fur collars. Far from the city centre, the buses had the blank serenity of people on their way to church and the further away one got, the paler and more homogeneous the faces seemed.

Heading back, on the other hand, the buses and trains would become microcosms of cosmopolitan fervour: The Greek and Jamaican and Chinese returning home from factories and fish shops, chattering in a language they would have identified as English, though no English-speaking person could hope to understand more than the occasional word. Here, a Macedonian tailor might be heard discussing the sign for his shop with an Italian barber, or a black hosiery sorter her child's tonsilitis with a blonde Ukrainian mother. The further south one got, the more weary and uncouth the faces seemed. But the eyes—most often black, but sometimes blue or green—were strangely luminous and, glancing at my sixty-dollar boots or suede coat, bright with patience and hope.

Hallowe'en night brought the children to my door once again, this time in large groups of five or six, dressed as queens and gypsies and cowboys, and repeating their "Trick or treat" over and over, as though I might otherwise fail to understand their lisping command. They came well into the night, the sons and daughters of my weary neighbours who would greet me on the street, but cautiously, making it clear that some time would have to pass before they knew how to treat me. Judging from the quantity of Neilson chocolates in the children's bags, many of them indeed were employed at the factory, but the children—with their feather crowns and painted faces—had not yet lost their enthusiasm.

"Look at all the *Burnt Almonds* I got!" they'd say, or "Pepita's mother gave you more *Rosebuds* than me!"

Ah, how sweet must have been the sleep of those dark-eyed children who lived by the factory and who, night after night, drifted into dreams of luscious, aromatic plenty.

I had meanwhile settled down to a routine of work and relaxation—going out to the theatre, meeting new friends.

"Can you imagine?" my visitors would say, "tons and tons of chocolate processed every day, *yum!*"

I was beginning to have quite a few visitors and could not help but notice that each time a car would park in front of the house, one of my neighbours would be watching from the windows across. In a way, even then, I could appreciate their point of view: why, they must have asked, does she not go to work in the morning? Why does an attractive woman live all alone? And why, yes why, do all these men come to visit—in the morning, at night?

At first, I was amused and joked about it with my visitors, most of whom were in fact professional acquaintances. Soon, however, my life in the house became incomprehensibly difficult.

In the first place, Manuel was developing personal habits which made the bathroom unusually disagreeable. The bathroom, I should point out, had been unpleasant even before that. I couldn't possibly have known this that first day, but the plumbing was so cheap that flushing the toilet brought about a kind of gurgling in the drains of both sink and bath, sometimes so violent that it seemed as though any moment, both would overflow with toilet water. Now—it was the beginning of November—I began to find the yellow sink spattered with chocolate-like stains and strewn with black hair. A week later, Manuel stopped flushing the toilet, going on to make every conceivable effort to offend me. It was an unmistakable protest, but why? What was he trying to tell me? It wasn't long before I was allowed to find out.

All through October, I had lived with no heat whatsoever. Occasionally, at night, it would get rather cold but it had been for the most part a sunny, warm month and, knowing how hard Manuel worked for his money, I had not complained. Right after Hallowe'en, however, fall arrived, with surprisingly low temperatures and gusty winds which blew away the last leaves of vine Manuel had planted. The neighbourhood cats, which used to hide among the swiss chard, were now plainly visible in the balding garden and, every day, I would hear the hissing of their encounters intermingled with the howling of the wind. Still, the heat was not turned on and, reluctant to complain, I began to spend more and more time by the steamed-up windows of Lydia's shop. Going home, the sharp air made the chocolate seem to come from a great distance—as though heralding the approach of snow—and my warm breath would be visible in the chilly night. At last, I decided to speak to him.

"Manuel," I said, hearing him come home one night, "it's very cold now, could you please——"

He did not let me finish my sentence. "Yes," he said, "I wanting to speak to you. Today, when I come home for lunch, you have friend in your flat!"

"Yes?" I said, thrown off by his finger which pointed accusingly in my face. What did my friend have to do with the heat?

"All the time," he went on, "you have friends and friends, you make music, laughing—I can no sleep all night!"

"But Manuel," I said, "I've never had a friend later than eleven."

"You lying, you have friend after one last night!"

"Oh no, that was a long-distance call."

"No!"

"Yes!"

It went on like that for a while, Manuel claiming I had men

overnight, I—truthfully—denying; Manuel repeating he couldn't get any sleep, asking when did I do any work anyway; and I, losing my patience, saying it was none of his business, I worked when I wanted to, I didn't have to keep his hours!

Well, that was just what he seemed to be waiting for.

"Yes, you must," he finally said, "From tomorrow, no friends and you go sleeping at ten, like everybody."

I could hardly believe my ears. "Look," I said, "you can't tell me what to do, the flat——"

"You no go to sleep and work, I want new tenant end of December!"

At last, I gave up. I couldn't understand his outrage, the obvious lies. I liked working at night so that, in fact, most of my friends came for lunch or tea and, as I had pointed out, no one had every stayed past eleven, though I certainly did not want to be denied my rights.

What was I to do?

He couldn't evict me, I knew, but he could make life unbearable unless I complied with his wishes. That was clearly out of the question. I was not about to start retiring at ten. I could not possibly live without friends. And I couldn't—I had meanwhile forgotten all about it—go on without heat. It was all very well for Manuel and the Melos—they were out most of the time—but I—was he trying to freeze me out, I wondered; was there someone else he wanted to rent the place to?

I decided to talk to an acquaintance who worked for Legal Aid, making my way downtown through the first snowstorm of the season. Already, I was beginning to think I would probably have to go, but "It's out of the question," the lawyer said; my landlord could do nothing to evict me, unless—he said—unless he had relatives he wanted to rent the flat to. I don't know why, but it was only then that I remembered seeing Manuel go down the week before with two gallons of paint. I had thought nothing of it at the time but there, in the lawyer's office, I had an overwhelming intuition.

"Manuel," I confronted him that very night, "you are planning to move upstairs, aren't you?"

He looked confused as a child, then—all at once— belliger-
ent. "How you know that?" he asked.

I just glared, looking—I hoped—confident and wilful.

"You speaking to Raoul?"

"No, no—Look," I finally said, "if you wanted the place to
yourself, why didn't you tell me last month?"

He looked down at his feet. "I change my mind," he said,
guiltily, but with a curious sense of pride.

"Are you getting married?"

"No—one, two years maybe."

"Then why do you suddenly want the flat, why?"

He shrugged his shoulders and would not tell me. One
thing I did know: If he wanted the place for himself, there
was nothing I could do. Like it or not, I would have to start
looking for a new place. It was damn annoying and I wanted
to insist that he owed me an explanation, at the very least.
Yet, with some part of me I must have understood something
because, despite it all, I could feel no hostility toward him.

"I'll be out end of the month," I said, turning to climb the
stairs, but stopped by the offended look on his face.

"No!" he said, leaving his door unguarded for once, "you
no have to go before end of December, I give you one month,
two."

"Well, I don't want to stay any longer than I have to."

"But please," he begged, "you no understand, I . . . you
Canadian, I Portuguese, you can no understand."

"Maybe not," I said and went up the stairs to my flat. I could
hear him pacing downstairs for a long time after, well past
eleven, anyway.

The colder it got, the more powerful the chocolate smell
seemed to grow. By mid-November, the factory seemed to be
stepping up its production toward Christmas and I hardly saw
Manuel in the next two weeks. The day after our confronta-
tion, the heat was turned on and, for the rest of that month,
the bathroom was kept as immaculate as it had been at the
start. The utter desolation of the garden, however, made it
difficult to believe that I had lived in that house for less than
two months. I had thought, when I learned I'd have to go, that

I would look for a place downtown, away from the immigrants' disapproving eyes and their stifling lifestyle. But in
the following days, as I'd pass Lydia's shop or watch the
children play around the factory, the thought of leaving the
street, of breathing plain winter air devoid of all sweetness,
became as painfully sharp as first frost. There was only one
apartment building on the street and, for days, I had ignored
the red sign: APARTMENT FOR RENT. I wanted to be able to come
and go, to pull up my blinds at ten or eleven without feeling
like the scarlet lady in some small village.

Well, it was a two-bedroom apartment and though it had
nothing special to recommend it, I took it on impulse one
afternoon, on my way from the Italian grocery. I felt curiously
fortunate once I paid the deposit—as though, after all, I had
been permitted to stay close to home.

Manuel was a changed man after our encounter. He had
painted his room downstairs and found a new immigrant to
move in as soon as he moved up to the first floor. Once or
twice, I heard visitors' voices downstairs and he seemed to
have bought himself a radio. One day, he came back from the
market with crated grapes and, over the weekend made, he
later told me, fifty bottles of wine, which left the basement
area sticky with dark, purple stains and attracted innumerable
fruit flies multiplying rapidly, though we sprayed and
sprayed.

When Ava-Maria told him I had fallen and sprained my
ankle, he came up to see me and, shy as a village boy, handed
me a box of Neilson chocolates.

"One day you tell me you like chocolates, remember?"

"I remember," I said. "Thank you very much."

There was an awkward silence between us, then—looking
up at the ceiling—he said: "I gonna help you move, OK?"

"Oh no," I protested, "really, it's not necessary."

But he looked as obstinate as he had that first day. "Yes,"
he said, "I gonna help you."

And that was that. He would not take no for an answer,
saying he knew someone with a truck and that he and Raoul

would help. I don't know why, but I could not bring myself to eat those chocolates, finally packing them with my kitchen stuff.

When the day came, they showed up as agreed, he and Raoul and Ava-Maria, the four of us carrying the bookshelves, the couch, the Tiffany lamp. We were all a little awkward, I think, but Manuel made every effort to help me forget that, all said and done, I was still getting evicted. At one point, Ava-Maria and I stood watching while Manuel and her husband manoeuvered the large secretarial desk which—Manuel insisted, laughing—could not have come through that door. Ava-Maria smiled and moved closer beside me.

"You still mad?" she asked, searching my eyes in the dark.

"I'm not . . . mad," I said, more embarrassed than ever.

"Manuel," she said, "he no like to live in basement after you come here."

"But why, has he told you why?"

She shrugged her shoulders, much as Manuel himself had done—as though, the gesture seemed to say, I could not possibly hope to understand.

"You are a woman and you Canadian," she said at last, "and you make lots of money—he no like that."

"But I'm not rich," I protested, "I have no money in the bank."

She only smiled—the slight, resigned smile an adult might bestow upon a slow child. "You no work in a factory," she said. "You born here."

The men meanwhile had managed to get the desk through the door, though the collapsible typewriter stand kept springing out.

"You gonna write lots of stories for Toronto *Star*, yes?" Manuel said, grinning, and I nodded, smiling back.

As soon as I get settled, I thought, I'm going to contact Neilson's and do a story for *Weekend* Magazine. I did phone their PR man several times that year and told his secretary what I wanted. She had a polished, executive-secretary's voice, but her name was Miss Lopes. She said her boss, Mr. Amado, would call me back as soon as he was free. He never did.

1977

Cookie

Raymond Fraser

WE WERE ON our way around the world that summer, Sully and myself—Toronto, Vancouver, San Francisco, Mexico, Caracas, Dakar, Casablanca, Barcelona, Paris, Rome, Athens, Cairo—but first stopping off at Toronto to save some money to finance the trip. After more than a month there we were so broke that we were surviving on dry toast and tea—that's all we could afford to eat. Our room was on Jarvis Street, on the top floor of an old brick house with weeds in the front yard, the bricks soot-blackened and the windows filmed over with dust. Because of the look of the house our room surprised us, when we first saw it; it was bright, clean and spacious, and the rent was only eight dollars a week. We paid the first two weeks, but not the last four. It was all trust and generosity on the part of our landlord, who was everything landlords aren't supposed to be—while we were the worst examples of tenants. He took us at our word that we'd find work and pay the rent—and in the end let us sneak off in the night. He was an eastern European of some sort, Polish maybe, with a name full of z's and x's and c's, and a profound sadness in his eyes. We never found out anything about him, he lived a few doors down the street from his rooming house, and when we fell behind in our rent we kept clear of him. But when we met him he never said a word about the rent. The sadness in his eyes made me feel guilty, a little.

There was a janitor in our building, a Newfie by the name of Kearns who looked like the Hunchback of Notre Dame without the hump—an apelike cross-eyed character with a crazed scowl on his face. As was typical at that address he was drunk more often than not. He used to get the passions for Cookie, who lived on the second floor in the room directly beneath ours. Different nights we'd hear him lurch up the stairs from his basement room and start hammering on her door. In a thick-tongued voice he'd shout, "Is you in, Cookie? Cookie, is you in? Open the door! I wants to see you! Cookie, is you in? Is you in there, Cookie?"

He'd get no response, but all the same he'd stand there for a good half hour beating on the door and hollering. You could hear his voice thundering through the building.

"Cookie, is you in? I wants to see you! Let me in, Cookie! It's me! Is you in there?"

You'd swear her room was empty—for all the reaction he got—but he knew when she was there. Usually after a time we'd hear her voice call out through the door, "Go away and leave me alone!" That's all she'd say, but the fact she said anything at all encouraged him.

"Is that you, Cookie? I wants to see you! I knows you're in there! Open the door, Cookie, let me in! I only wants to talk to you!"

It got on your nerves. After a long time he'd stomp off, muttering drunkenly, only to return in a few minutes and start all over again. "It's me, Cookie! I'se got something I wants to tell you! Is you there, Cookie? Open the door!"

Just to look at the man in broad daylight was unnerving. Those nights when he was ranting around we kept our door locked and talked in whispers—afraid he'd change course and come up and murder us—to relieve his frustrations—"If that crazy bastard don't kill us we'll starve to death," said Sully. Our hunger made us apprehensive; we talked about making tracks. The landlord had to run out of tolerance, despite his goodheartedness. Luckily he never looked into our room. It was a shambles, a dump, mostly because of the newspapers. We used to get them from the open boxes on the streets, pretending to drop a dime into the slot. Every day we got the *Globe & Mail*, the *Star*, and the *Telegram* and scanned the Help Wanted ads. We knew what we were after:

> *Sailing yacht cruising tomorrow for the Caribbean urgently requires two young deckhands, experience not necessary, New Brunswick natives preferred. Must be able to hold their liquor and willing to entertain millionaire owner's two beautiful and debauched teenaged daughters; excellent salary.*

Once we'd read through the papers they got tossed aside and left where they landed, so that after five weeks there were more than a hundred of them scattered from wall to wall. It got to be like a carpet of newspapers a foot deep covering the entire floor. Then there were bottles: wine bottles, rum bottles, gin bottles; and tin cans, and cigarette packages, and bags of garbage. It was a disgusting mess. You could hardly get into the room.

Our finances had shrunk to the point where we had thirty-five cents between us, and we were getting weak and more indolent than usual from our tea-and-toast diet. Aware that we had to make some kind of move we'd been intending for the last four or five days to strike for home, only we hadn't quite got around to it. We found it hard to break our habit of staying up all night—playing cards, drinking tea, eating toast, talking about one thing and another—and then sleeping from dawn until mid-afternoon, at which time it was too late in the day to set out hitchhiking a thousand miles. What we were after was an early morning start, to get away while the landlord was still asleep and when we'd have a full day ahead of us on the road. But when dawn appeared and we'd been awake the whole night all we felt like doing was hitting the sack.

It was nine o'clock in the evening and I'd gone down to the second floor where the building's only toilet was located, and I was just starting up the stairs again when Cookie's door opened and she peered out at me. "Come here, doll. Come here, I want to see you."

We knew Cookie quite well by this time, different occasions she'd asked us in for a drink. She was always at the bottle, every day, never a day off. We used to see her from our window setting out in the afternoon for the wine store, dancing along on her tiptoes, waving her arms and sailing up the street as though there was music in her ears. She was in her late fifties—quite a dilapidated old thing—but she tried to keep up her appearance as best she could. Her hair was bleached, her face thickly powdered, her cheeks rouged and her fingernails polished scarlet.

"Have a drink with me, doll. I don't want to drink alone. I've got some wine. Come into my room, doll." Judging by her glassy eyes and the slur of her voice she'd been doing well enough on her own so far. I said I wouldn't mind a drop.

"Sit down, doll. Where's your friend?" Her room was smaller than ours but with the same essential furniture: bed, small table, chest of drawers with mirror, two chairs, a hot-plate. The bed was low to the floor and unmade and Cookie eased herself carefully onto it and sat there with her hands clasped primly in her lap.

"Where's your friend? Where's Sully? I haven't seen Sully at all today."

"He's upstairs."

"Go and get him, doll. Bring him down and we'll all have a drink together. I like your friend."

"Okay."

I left her and went upstairs and found Sullivan lying on the bed with his nose in a newspaper, going through the used car ads. He was quite the sight, stretched out with his grimy bare feet crossed and his shirt off and his face fuzzied with the beard he was trying to grow, the picture of a holed-up con, a fugitive from the chain gang.

"Cookie's invited us for a drink," I said.

Without taking his eyes off the paper he said, "Yeah? Not again."

"Why—did she already ask you?"

"I can't stand that old whore . . . always trying to drag you into her room. I don't want to have to listen to her."

"Plug your ears. Come on, let's go."

"Naw, I don't want no wine."

"Are you sick?" I stared at him, amazed. "When did you ever turn down a drink before?"

"Listen to this. Fifty-three Pontiac, good condition, only two hundred bucks——"

"Never mind that. Come on."

"We should've bought one when we had the money, when we first come up. We could've got an old heap for a hundred-fifty, two hundred bucks——"

"We should've done a lot of things."

"And got out of this hole, took off for Mexico, we'd be there right now. Just think——"

"Come on, Sully. What're you stalling for?"

"I'm not stalling."

"Well let's go downstairs and get at the grapes. She'll have it all drunk."

"Naw. You go, I don't feel like it."

"She's got smokes. There's a pack open on her table."

When we had money Sullivan was accustomed to smoking two large packs a day. When we started to go broke he switched to rolling his own until the time came when he couldn't even afford to buy a package of tobacco. So then he took to rummaging about in the garbage bags for old butts which he broke apart and used the tobacco to roll further cigarettes out of, and then he made still more cigarettes out of these butts, and so on, until there wasn't a grain of tobacco to be found in the room.

He laid the paper aside, considered a moment, then sat up and said, "Okay, I need a nail real bad. Only I ain't staying long."

When we went downstairs Cookie's door was open but she wasn't in her room. We went in anyway and took a chair.

There were three water glasses full of wine on the table along with a bottle that was half full. On the floor beside the table there was an empty bottle.

"She must be in the can."

Sullivan's eyes immediately lit on the pack of cigarettes. He picked it up, removed two and put them in his shirt pocket and replaced the package.

"She'll never miss those."

A minute or so later Cookie waltzed unsteadily through the door and said in her husky, slightly nasal voice, "Hello my boys, it's so good you came to visit me, I'm always happy when you come to visit me." She smiled, showing her long divided yellow teeth. "Have a drink. I poured you both a drink. And have a cigarette. I'm so happy to see my boys."

With deliberation she moved behind the table and sat on the bed, and we got into the wine. Out of the corner of my eye I saw Sullivan help himself to a cigarette and slip an extra one into his pocket.

"How are you, boys? How are you, Sully? I haven't seen you since . . . when was it you were here——"

"I'm all right, just fine," said Sullivan.

"And you . . ." She didn't remember my name. "How are you?" she said.

"Not too bad."

"And how are you, Sully? You're looking sweet. You were here yesterday, weren't you? We had a party, I think. I have a hard time remembering. Yesterday——"

"Nope, I wasn't here yesterday."

"No? I thought, doll——"

"You must've dreamt it, Cookie."

"Did I, doll?"

"You were probably drunk—imagining things." Sullivan gave me a sidelong look as if to say, "See, I told you she's crazy."

"I wasn't drunk, sweetheart. I've never been drunk in my whole life. I like to have a glass of wine every now and then but I never get drunk." She began to rock slowly back and forth on the bed. Her eyes fell on me. "Was it you? Were you here yesterday? Maybe it was you?"

"It wasn't me."

"No?"

"No, it must've been someone else."

"Yesterday . . . afternoon? Oh, I can't think too well today."

"I was over in the park yesterday afternoon—after I got up, I mean."

"Oh well. I'll figure it out later . . . . How's everything, boys? How's life treating you?"

"Not bad."

"I'm glad to hear it." She paused a second, and said: "You know boys, I get lonely here all alone. You want me to tell you something? Every night I lie in bed and I feel so lonely, and I just lie here waiting for my boys to come home and raise hell. I don't sleep well. No, I don't sleep well at all . . . . I lie here and it's quiet and I think, pretty soon my boys will come home and I won't be alone anymore. I hear you up there, singing and laughing and I know you're having a good time and that makes me feel better. It's like having company, I don't feel so lonely." She reached uncertainly for her glass and took a sip. "Light me a cigarette, doll."

Sullivan lit her one, at the same time slipping another one for himself into his pocket.

"Thank you, love. How's everything? Tell me, how are things going with the two of you?"

"Well . . . to tell you the truth, Cookie, not all that good," I said. "No money and no jobs and we're way behind in our rent."

She nodded understandingly.

"Gord was behind in his rent, him and Nan never paid no rent. Do you know Gord and Nan?"

Gord and Nan were a vagabond couple in their late thirties who had been living in the room next door to Cookie's.

"There're gone now," said Cookie.

"They are?"

"Yes, they left three nights ago. I miss Gord, him and Nan, they were nice to me. They were five weeks behind when they left. They gave the old man a pile of garbage to hold till they came back, they gave him a box of old clothes and broken dishes. It was just garbage. I'll tell you something, boys, they'll never come back, I know their kind. They don't want that garbage they left behind, they wouldn't have taken it with them anyway. That's stuff's a dime a dozen. I know those kind of people, I know them, I've been around. They wait for the right time and before you know it they've run off. They tell the old man they'll pay him next week, every week they tell him that until finally he's glad to be rid of them. He's too soft, the old man. I always pay my rent, every week. I never get behind. But Gord and Nan, they wait till the right moment and then they leave, I've seen their kind before. A dime a dozen. Let me tell you something, Sully." She reached over and tapped him on the knee. The room was that small we were all within arm's reach of each other. "They won't be back. Do you know that?"

"I guess they won't," said Sullivan.

It wasn't long before our glasses were sitting empty on the table beside the wine bottle. Seeing this Cookie said, "Pour yourselves a drink, boys, help yourselves. I've got another quart in the closet."

I felt Sullivan's arm nudge me. He refilled the glasses.

Being half starved the way we were even one glass had quite a strong effect. It went straight to the head. I helped myself to a cigarette, even though at the time I didn't smoke too much.

"I miss Gord," Cookie said, rocking back and forth, her eyes bleary. "He used to come in with a bottle of wine and talk to me. But they won't be back. Nan said she didn't like this place and she wants to travel. When they make their money in Delhi with the tobacco they won't be back. That's where they went, they went up to Delhi to pick tobacco. After that they'll probably go down to the States or out West. If they ever come back to Toronto they'll get another place, they'll never pay the old man his rent. . . . You know something, boys, I miss Gord. When he was here he used to throw that fellow from downstairs out. I hate that man. There's something wrong with him, he's mental."

"You mean the janitor?"

"He's not the janitor. He only thinks he is. He doesn't get paid, the old man gives him his room free for doing some odd jobs, it's only charity. There used to be a woman staying across the hall and he bothered her, he never stopped bothering her, always saying there was something wrong with the lights. Oh, he's sly. She left within a week. He comes to my room too but I put a spoon in the door. There's no lock so I have to put a spoon in it. He came up the other night and I told him I was resting. He tried to get in but he couldn't because I had a spoon in the door. It would take two men to open my door when it's locked like that. He's a dirty son of a bitch. He'd call the police if you ever took anything from one of the rooms."

While she was rambling on my fingers played absently with the tinsel off the wine bottle top. I shaped a little hat out of it and put it on my head and looked in the mirror. Suddenly noticing me Cookie said, "You look cute, doll. It looks good on you. But it wouldn't look good on me, it's not my style. Let Sully try it, see how it looks on him."

"Go way for Jesus sake. Don't be so simple." Sullivan swept my arm away as I tried to put the hat on his head.

"Tell me boys, how's everything? How's it going with my boys?"

"Not so good," I repeated.

"Open that other bottle, Sully. It's in the closet. Do you see it there?"

"Yeah, here it is."

"Open it, doll. This one's almost finished. Have a cigarette. Was I dreaming about yesterday, lover? I can't think clearly today."

Her cigarettes were rapidly disappearing, due mainly to Sullivan pocketing them every chance he got. Before opening the new bottle he poured the remnants of the old one into our glasses. Cookie took hers, which was full to the brim, and with a mechanical, seemingly unconscious movement picked it up and in one long drink drained it dry. For a minute she was still, sitting with her hands in her lap and her eyes distant and entranced. Then she shuddered. "A cigarette, doll," she said.

I gave her one and held a match to it. "You're very kind to me," she said.

Normally Sullivan had a lot to say, but since we entered Cookie's room he'd hardly opened his mouth. Now he leaned towards me. "Why don't we shove off out of here tonight," he said out of the side of his mouth. "Pack our stuff and hit the road."

"What's that, Sully?" said Cookie.

"Nothing. I just said how great it was to have a drink for a change."

"Is that what you said? Have some more if you like. Anything for my boys."

"Tonight? You mean now?" I said to Sullivan.

"Sure, why not? We won't feel any better tomorrow."

He was right. We couldn't put it off forever, and in the glow of the wine the open road even seemed inviting, now that I thought of it. Even in the black of night.

"All right. Let's go," I said.

"In a few minutes."

We spoke in undertones, but it didn't much matter. After that great gulp of wine she'd taken, Cookie despite being only a few feet away was off in a world of her own, talking to herself.

". . . that dirty son of a bitch, he went to the old man and told him we were having a party and the old man came over and told everyone to get out. . . . They were my friends and we were just having a good time but that animal downstairs was jealous. I wouldn't let him in, I didn't want his ugly face around, so he told the landlord and everybody had to leave. . . . They all left except old Joe. I like Joe. He was too stubborn. He lay on the bed and wouldn't move. The landlord left and Joe stayed. . . . But we had a fight later and I haven't seen him since. But I'm going to surprise him. I'm going to get prettied up and visit Joe, he lives just down on Dundas, I know the place . . . that'll surprise him. . . ."

"What're we waiting for?" I said.

"Hold on a minute," said Sullivan.

"I like old Joe, he's a real gentleman when he's around me,

but that filthy bastard downstairs, he should be in a zoo. I know what he's like. He wants to get my boys in trouble, he's jealous of everyone. He's jealous—" Her eyes made an attempt to focus on Sullivan—"he's jealous of you too, doll, he knows you came to see me yesterday, he knows we were drinking together, he knows what we were doing in here together, doll——"

I snorted. Sullivan's face suddenly turned red as a beet. "You're nuts, Cookie, you're out of your goddam mind."

"What's that, honey? Oh . . . I feel dizzy. I feel tired, boys . . ."

She rocked backwards and forwards, like a little girl, then reached for her empty glass and put it to her mouth, tipped it, looked curiously at it and put it back on the table.

"Don't laugh, you asshole," Sullivan said to me. "I told you she's nuts."

". . . there's something I should tell you boys, a lot of people don't know this but I don't have to pay for my room . . . . Did you know that? I'll let you in on a secret . . . I'm an undercover agent for Eaton's. You didn't know that, boys . . . They give me all the money I want . . ."

"Let's get going," I said.

"Hang on, I told you. Don't be so impatient."

"I'll go and pack our stuff."

"No sir, you're not leaving me alone with her."

". . . I'll kill that man downstairs. You can't trust him, he'll get you thrown into the streets, he doesn't deserve to live . . . I'm going to kill him."

Sullivan took the remaining few cigarettes out of the pack and put them in his pocket with the others.

". . . I got a sharp knife hid away and if it's the last thing I do I'll kill him. He's not going to hurt my boys . . . They come to me tired and it's not enough to comfort them, I have to get him. I'll get him with my knife . . . like this." She made a sleepy, half-hearted gesture. "Right in the spinal cord. . . . It's dangerous but I'll do it and they won't catch me . . . You won't tell on me, will you, boys? My boys won't tell on me. He's out to get them but I'll kill him first. May God be with me . . ." Her head was nodding.

"Cookie, you better lie down and rest awhile," said Sullivan.

"Eh? What did you say, doll? Pardon me . . . I didn't hear you."

"Lie down and rest awhile, why don't you?"

"Rest?"

"Sure. We'll stay here, and when you've had a rest we can drink some more."

"That's right, doll. Drink some more . . . you're right . . . all right, love, I'll just have a rest . . . I'm a little tired. . . . Thank you, doll."

She stretched herself out on her back with her legs hanging over the side of the bed. "I'll kill him . . . revenge will be mine, I'll kill that man . . . son of a bitch . . . he won't hurt my boys . . ."

Sullivan looked at me and winked. Putting the cap back on the newly opened bottle of wine he tucked it in his belt and said, "Okay, let's haul arse." As we headed up the stairs to get our things ready he said, "This is just the stuff we need for the road."

1974

Death of a Friend

Matt Cohen

I HEARD THE news shortly after it happened. It was near the end of August, during one of those late summer heat waves that sometimes hold Toronto to ransom, a night I hadn't slept at all but only lain on top of the sheet, trying to persuade myself that the fan was doing something. Even though I was awake, I hesitated to answer the telephone when it rang. When I did, Marion's voice cut through the night with its usual abruptness.

"Gavin's killed himself," she said.

"What?"

"Gavin's dead."

At my age, which is thirty-eight—going on fifty, it sometimes seems—I have learned to be prepared for the death of a friend. But not Gavin, who was more than a friend, who was at the least indestructible. I tried to say something. The noise of the fan's motor filled the room: a giant insect seeking somewhere to land.

"Are you all right?" Marion has a harsh voice that cannot give anything away.

"Sure," I said. "I'm all right." I had pushed myself up and was lighting a cigarette. "Where are you?"

"I'm at the hospital." The fan and her voice were melting together, shivering and buzzing in my skull. Her words blurred, then came into focus. "I'm just standing at a pay phone in the emergency room."

"Do you want me to come down there? Or can you come here?"

"I'll take a taxi. There's nothing left to do."

By the time I was dressed and had coffee on the stove, Marion was at the door. I live in an apartment in one of those increasingly rare Toronto houses—a rambling brick house that sits on a lot big enough for a high-rise. When I moved here, twelve years ago, other houses like this surrounded it. Now when I look out the window past the two oaks that survive in the front yard, I see metal balconies and concrete. But in the old days, when Gavin and Marion and I were close, and our lives mixed in so tight we hardly knew ourselves as separate people, I could sometimes sit here in my living room, looking out at other windows as shaded and baroque as my own, and be completely held by the magic of this place.

I had unlatched the door and Marion, as she used to, came in without knocking. I heard the sharp sounds of her shoes against the hardwood floor and then, suddenly—as if it was ten years ago—she was standing facing me in the kitchen, arms hanging helplessly at her sides.

"Goddamned idiot," she said. "What did he have to do that for?" Anyone else who looked like Marion would have been beautiful; she had thick black hair, long and parted in the middle, small snubbed features, wide-set brown eyes and sensuous lips—all frozen into a determined mask by her amazing and inflexible will. In pictures she looked sensational; in person, as Gavin once said fondly, she looked like a dentist.

"Coffee or a drink?"

"A drink," she said. "I'm already drowning in machine coffee." Automatically she reached for the cupboard above the refrigerator where I kept the whisky—close to the ice— and as if it wasn't several years since she had even been in this apartment she helped herself to what she needed. And, without asking, she made me a drink too—the way I used to like it—two shot glasses of Scotch and two pieces of ice. "Can't trust city water," Gavin would say. He was a purist, and in his most religious moments he even omitted the ice.

We went and sat in the living room, Marion and I, the survivors. We sat side by side on the couch; and if ten years ago we had also been in this place—me insulting her and her yowling at me like an outraged cat—that only drew us closer now.

"Do you want to tell me?"

"I don't know." She found herself a cigarette and lit it carefully, moving her hands and fingers slowly—trying not to shake.

"It's been bad," I suggested. "I heard it had been bad with him lately."

"You know how he was," Marion said.

When I first met Gavin Donnally he was sitting behind his office desk—as old then as I am now. He was one of those men who attract rumours and so I already knew about his legendary bottle a day, and about the novel he was supposed to have been working on for more than a decade: a brilliant, huge novel that seemed never to get finished. In his hand he held a sheaf of papers, my own manuscript. It had taken me almost a year to write, though it was only a section of a projected novel; and I had no doubt that on Gavin's verdict rested my entire future. Although he wasn't yet forty, he looked much older. His face was lined and aristocratic, his grey hair combed back from a widow's peak, and his eyes red-rimmed and shadowed. Somehow this mask of fatigue and dissipation only made him seem more romantic to me, a hero of success and failure.

In comparison, and sitting in his office I couldn't help making the judgement, I felt fat and callow. He must, I thought, see hundreds of hopeful young writers like myself every year, petitioning him with their crazy stories. My own, I now realized to my total embarrassment, must be even worse than most. At the time, Gavin had reached the final position of his career and was the senior editor of a large publishing house. The manuscript I had shown him was a long story, one of three I intended to make up a book that would depict—how can I put it?—my youth in a small town. In addition to having written the first, I was already well into the second, a sentimental rendition of my coming of age. And the third, the triumphant journey from the town to the city, lay glistening hopefully in my mind, needing only the slightest encouragement to be set down in all its splendour. Sitting across from Gavin Donnally, waiting for him to deliver his judgement, I already knew what it was.

"You'll have to excuse me."

"What?" Gavin always liked to say 'what?' in an aggressive way. He later explained that it gave him the edge in conversation—though I must admit I eventually decided he had drunk himself deaf.

"I shouldn't have wasted your time with the story."

"Oh that." With a delicate gesture he set down the offending manuscript, and then flicked his fingers nervously, as if to clean them.

"It's not very good."

"Take off your coat," he said. Then he plugged in a kettle, preparing to make coffee. I measured out the implications of this: the necessary minutes to be consumed.

"I read your story," he said. "It's got something. A way with words. A feel for childhood. Something very touching."

When the water had boiled, we would discuss the contract.

"I understand it's part of a novel," he said. He was referring to my letter, where I had explained the entire plan. As he spoke I was reminding myself to buy another thousand sheets of yellow paper to start the final third.

"It's almost done," I said. "Maybe I should have waited to show you."

"No," Gavin said. He had a very considered and precise way of speaking, each word a neat little knife cutting through the messy world. "I'm glad you showed me now." He sighed unhappily.

"You can write," he said. "You do have a talent." He sighed again. My heart was exploding—this was it: cynical editor takes young novelist under wing. I would have to get a new suit. And a haircut. Maybe even contact lenses.

"You know," he said. His voice dropped. Later on I knew this meant he was moving in for the kill. "God knows you have talent. And a real sentimental feeling for things. And yet. Somehow. It just doesn't make it. There it is."

He leaned across the desk to see how I was taking it. I remember how uncomfortable my mouth felt, frozen in mid-smile. I had hardly heard him—in fact I had been thinking about the size of my advance and only now was absorbing what he'd said.

"Well?" he asked, still aggressive.

"Well," I said. "There it is. But you think there's hope?"

"Oh yes. There's always hope. You never know what some-one might do. Especially someone as young as you. How old did you say you were?"

"Twenty-six."

"Oh. I thought you were younger."

"I see," I mumbled. But I didn't. Gavin smiled graciously at me—as if in fact he had just informed me that his firm would publish this and all my future works, sight unseen. Then he stood up and made us cups of instant coffee.

"I like your dialogue," he said. "Have you ever considered writing for television."

"I never watch it."

"Maybe you should." And that was how we started, Gavin and I. When my first script was sold, I telephoned the news to him.

"Congratulations," he said. "Let me take you out to dinner."

In those days, Toronto was everything to me: the huge and anonymous arena where I would find myself, remake myself, succeed or fail according to the terms of my most obscure and central dreams. Now, of course, it's different. The invisible inner gleam has worn off and Toronto is only the place where I live—a big paunchy complex city where I have somehow put down roots and am satisfied to play out my existence. Even if they tear down this house, I suppose I will stay, living in another apartment, re-writing other people's television scripts, teaching my drama course at the university. In a way I have become like Gavin Donnally: older, thinner, more cynical—readier to fuel the ambitions of others than try my own again.

But then, with my first sale, the dream was at its brightest, and I could believe the future was in my blood. When I went to the restaurant Gavin was there already, red roses at the table, and sitting with Marion, young then too—and if not beautiful, at least striking.

She was wearing a deep cut black dress, looking expensive and sophisticated. Her face was composed, breaking apart only when Gavin said something that was supposed to be witty. For some reason, I don't know why, I concluded she was a poetess—another one of Gavin's discoveries. Sometimes, almost in passing, he would put his hand lightly on her arm. As if to draw her closer. As if—perhaps I was only being jealous—to tell me that when it came to strangers, they belonged to him. And because Marion let him do this, I mistrusted her right away.

But I could hardly blame her because that night—drinking and in favoured company—Gavin was in his best form, talking in that remarkable dry voice of his that swooped and soared like an erratic bird: a gift, he used to say, of his Irish ancestors.

"And you see this young fellow here," Gavin said, pointing me out to Marion in his way—charming and condescending. "He can put words in people's mouths and take them out again, like the devil himself." In his more gregarious moments, Gavin liked to lapse into fake dialect. "You see he's sold a play now for the television, and one day he'll be writing for the stage and screen."

"That's very nice," Marion said.

"Will you listen to her? Who does she think she is?"

"A poetess," I guessed.

Marion laughed, suddenly and abruptly, her open hand

slapping the table as she did, her whole docile pose broken apart in this one gesture.

"Guess again," Gavin shouted happily. "You have to guess again."

I appraised her carefully. I could see there was something I had missed: a plain gold ring on her wedding finger.

"A nun," I said. This time only Gavin laughed—and without enthusiasm.

"You're getting worse," he said. "We're going to have to tell you." He leaned over the table and smiled handsomely, the way he had smiled at me in his office, but with that slight added spark which meant he had been drinking for several hours. And even though he looked old and dangerously close to his own thin edge of drunkenness, there was something attractive about his dissipation, about that part of him still an adolescent searching for a wall. I wondered why he wasn't married—or if, as with his novel, he preferred to make his way slowly through all the possibilities.

"Marion is a producer," he said. "A woman of affairs. She works for a movie company; in fact she owns half of it."

"Gavin tells me you have an idea for a film," Marion said. With her harsh voice she gave the impression of the bank telephoning to announce an overdraft. I looked at Gavin.

"Tell her," he said.

"Well yes," I mumbled. "Though it's nothing spectacular."

Marion laughed again, so hard that she coughed on her drink.

"You have to *pretend* to believe in it," she said. "If you can't, how can I?"

"He's very modest," Gavin offered.

"It's a family habit."

"Tell me about your film."

"Well," I began, "It's about a young man who comes to the city full of dreams—"

"Oh God," Marion groaned.

"He's only joking," Gavin said. "It's his modesty. Give a writer a few drinks and he's absolutely useless."

"Maybe you should work out the details," Marion said,

smiling to tell me she understood what Gavin had done.

"All right," Gavin said. "Next week. Same time, same place. But you have to give us your movie before dinner. No movie, no food." He tipped the bottle and all was forgiven.

"I have to talk about it," Marion said finally. "You don't mind?"

"I want you to."

"I'll need another drink." This time she waited for me to get it. I brought in the bottle of Scotch and the pot of coffee.

"It started a year ago," she said. "He had been having headaches every night and finally I got him to go to the doctor. They did tests, a whole week of tests, and then one day they phoned him up—*over the telephone*—and told him he had a small tumour between his brain and his skull." Her voice shook. She grabbed my arm and then let go. Steady again. *Over the telephone.* So that was how they did it to him. Unfair, because Gavin had more class than that; he always gave the bad news face-to-face, unafraid of the reaction.

"You remember when we went to Florida last spring?"

"Yes."

"Well, we didn't. We went to Boston and he had the operation. They gave him one chance in five to live—and he made it. Then they told him it might grow there again. They couldn't tell if they had got it all."

"How could he have hidden the operation? They must have had to shave his head?"

"He got a hairpiece. He figured it all out beforehand. Gavin was very clever that way, making things seem proper on the surface." Her hand closed over mine. Not tenderly, or even sadly, but hanging on—squeezing until it hurt. "You know what I mean," she said.

"Sometimes." Her hand over mine. Still wearing the plain gold ring Gavin Donnally had given her fifteen years ago, when he first asked her to marry him. She had refused him then, but being attached to him and afraid to hurt him, had at least worn the ring. And then, five years later, took the rest.

"I never loved him," Marion said.

"Of course you did."

"No, I never once loved him, not even for one night."

We were sitting side by side on the couch. After all these years we were the survivors. We had outlived him; even our betrayals had outlived his honesty. And now Gavin's death was starting to find a place in me, breaking a hole in me as easily as a small mushroom breaks apart a concrete floor.

"I've always told you the truth," Marion said.

"Yes."

Our eyes locked together. I remembered how happy Gavin had sounded when he told me they were getting married. His voice then, for once, was neither cynical nor controlled—just happy that finally someone would release him from the contrived pattern of his life. And his eyes, watching mine, already knowing what I was trying to hide.

"He loved you," I said. "He stopped his whole life to let you in."

"I never should have married him."

"Are you sorry?"

Marion's face almost softened. In the months that we were lovers, there were moments when her face looked like this. But now, as then, the look passed quickly. She was learning that with age there is nothing that cannot be hidden. How long was it since she had come here? Minutes, hours—I couldn't tell. I stood up and opened the drapes. Outside the sky was a deep humid blue.

"I had affairs, you know. And twice I left."

"That's all right." I turned around. She had gotten to her feet and was glaring at me—the old Marion, face impassive and eyes spitting anger.

"I don't need you to forgive me. You of all people." And then suddenly she was across the room, pressed against me.

The second dinner did not follow the first exactly as planned. Unfortunately, Marion was busy overseeing the funeral of her bankrupt film company. Then, within a month, she had recovered from this disaster and surfaced again as the producer of a series for educational television. Gavin, with his encyclopaedic knowledge of matters literary and historical,

was made research consultant for the series; and I somehow
became responsible for writing the scripts. Soon the three of
us were meeting several evenings a week: working, drinking,
gossiping, and most of all, listening to Gavin as he talked
about anything and everything under the sun. In those days
I was so completely in his spell that I took everything he said
as gospel. And Marion, too, seemed utterly hypnotized by
him. In his apartment we would sit literally at his feet, taking
notes while Gavin reclined in his arm-chair, retelling the
history of the country to us, making it come alive not only as
a wild and romantic frontier but also, in some peculiar way,
as an enterprise that was *noble* in intent, that took the best of
the European experience and matched it up against a continent that could not be touched by even the most extravagant
of human excesses. Or so it seemed at the time.

It's hard to look back and say *there* it was. But it is true: it
was those few months that made me a writer—the nights
spent absorbing another man's way of looking at things, and
the mornings and afternoons spent at my typewriter—writing, re-writing, trying to hammer out some sort of script that
could mean something to someone else. Of course it was
Gavin's vision that I was trying to give, not my own, but I
didn't care about that; I only wanted to share the excitement
I had started to feel about living in this place, now.

Looking back at myself I can hardly believe I was ever so
unbearably innocent. I thought of myself as an artist, as being
utterly sensitive to the smallest nuance of feeling in others.
And, of course, I was missing everything.

One night, when I was walking Marion home from one of
the marathon sessions at Gavin's, she stopped me as we drew
in front of her apartment building. "How's the script going?"
she asked.

"Fine," I said. This seemed a peculiar question. We had just
been talking about it and dissecting it for the last six hours.

"Do you think this is a good way to go about writing,
spending so much time talking?"

"What do you mean?" There was about her now a calcu-
lating look I hadn't seen since the first night we met. Then I

remembered how easily she had survived the failure of her company, and how easily she seemed to manage all the business details of this series, as if, beyond Gavin's living room and romantic stories, there was a world of real fact and solidity where she was absolutely the master.

"I don't know," she said, as if considering all this for the first time. "I mean, this is supposed to be something *you're* doing, you know."

"Don't you think it's good?"

"It's extremely good," she said. "Really."

"You can hire someone else if you want. You shouldn't be stuck with me just as a favour to Gavin."

Marion laughed, in that brusque way of hers, an unsettling sound in the deserted late-night streets. "I'm not like that," she said. "Don't ever think I'm like that."

"I don't," I said. "But if you want to change your mind, now would be a good time to do it."

"Don't worry," Marion said. She looked at me curiously. "Why don't you come up for coffee. I have to go to sleep soon, but you can stay for a few minutes." Her invitation surprised me. Somehow, despite the fact she usually walked home with me, I assumed she belonged to Gavin.

In those days, everything worth having seemed to be Gavin's. His apartment was filled with books, chairs, paintings, ornate rugs—a collector's cave where a man could keep out the world.

Marion's was the opposite. One white wall was faced by a long walnut desk. Her furniture was all hard-edged and expensive, as if planned by an interior decorator on a spaceship theme. In the middle of Marion's desk were ledgers and an adding machine. One almost expected to see production charts and graphs on the wall. Riding up in the elevator I had thought perhaps she intended to seduce me, but, seated in the moulded plastic chair with my mug of coffee steaming on the parquet floor, I realized that nothing could be less likely.

"I didn't mean to criticize you," Marion said. "I just thought that we might be taking up too much of your time. Have you been working on anything else, besides the scripts?"

"No."

"Most writers secretly want to do a novel, or a book of short stories."

"I tried that," I said. "Gavin told me that television would suit me better." I felt hurt and betrayed. It was, after all, Gavin who had started these meetings, and Gavin who kept arranging new ones. And if Gavin and Marion wanted to spend time alone, she could have stayed at his place after I left.

"I'm sorry," Marion said. There had always been an easy flow of conversation at Gavin's, but now, alone, we seemed to be at cross-purposes. I wanted to leave, and was already thinking about the excuses I would make to Gavin when he telephoned for the next meeting. If we got together once a week it would be enough; then the job would be over and we wouldn't have to see each other again. My coffee wasn't finished but I stood up, glad to be out of her uncomfortable plastic chair.

"I feel tired tonight," Marion said. Her face was impassive as always, but her voice had suddenly changed. Her eyes opened wider. I was standing above her, unsure of what was happening, aware only of the sudden panic that had broken loose in her.

"Please," she whispered. "I'm so tired." She reached out with her hands. I pulled her to her feet, but as soon as she was up she started to lose her balance, and I had to hold onto her to keep her from falling. Half-carrying, half-dragging her, I got her into the bedroom and onto the bed. It was part of the same fantasy as the rest of the apartment—cold and white. But when I started to leave Marion held onto me, her fingers digging into my arms. Even as I lay down on the bed I could feel her drifting into sleep, breathing slowly and deeply, her arms tight around me for warmth.

The first signs of dawn were in the room now; a heavy blue light was growing in the centre, pushing back the shadows, showing us our faces, pale and exhausted. The bottle stood between us, and we drank from it in little sips and swallows, no longer bothering with ice and water now that we had something we could share: this whisky, a communion of Gavin's blood thinned to suit our less human veins—Gavin's blood between us as for this one moment we couldn't help believing we had killed him, his death like a curse on all our betrayals, inconsistencies, the web of misunderstandings and desire that had held us together and now kept us apart.

"Do you remember how it was?"

"Yes, I remember Gavin." I felt a growing blackness inside of me, his death, and leaning forward to tip the whisky into the glass asked myself, for once, who or what had died for him.

"Not Gavin," Marion said. "You and I. Same scene, same place." She looked at me aggressively, the way Gavin had taught her.

"Of course," I said. Of course, that is, I had done everything possible to forget it. On the morning after that first night, when we woke up fully dressed on her bed, we had looked at each other and without hesitation taken our clothes off and made love: our bodies still warm from each other's arms. And then on nights after that, at my place or hers—always guiltily secret from Gavin—we would spend the late hours together. But it was never easy and smooth as it had been that one first time. The more our bodies needed each other, the more our minds and emotions resisted, as if beneath the physical surface we were unable to touch each other. And yet, it was still compelling; despite the endless false starts and reservations, there were times we released whole lifetimes of desire.

Then one day Marion told me she had also taken Gavin as a lover.

"I see," I said.

"No you don't."

"I don't want to own you."

"No. But I won't do it again." This admitted half-crying, half-shouting, enough to bring on more love-making, more of that frantic passion that had first overwhelmed us but now simply pursued us to exhaustion.

We were too much alike, too abrasive. And when we turned in on ourselves, with only our secret to hold us together, we found that it finally wore itself out. Marion arranged to go to England for six months; and I went west. When we came back to Toronto we were both very busy. Our nights together tapered off and the feeling of reunion we should have had never happened. Nor did we ever officially end it. It seemed to just slowly disappear until the time Gavin told me the good news.

"I never forgave you for that last night," Marion said.

"No, I don't suppose you did."

"Maybe we could forget it now, or leave it lie. Gavin was never one for holding grudges."

"No, he wasn't." And now that she had said it, I realized Gavin had never been petty, not Gavin. When he had published his novel—at least Marion had given him the will to overcome that—he dedicated it to both of us, putting us alone, side by side on the same page. As if he knew only he could make a space for us to be together in.

The room was beginning to be light. In another couple of hours the heat would hang over us again, and Gavin's death would start to be incidental to the weather. In the funeral parlour it would be cool enough. They would have his body there by now, and I would have to go to see it.

There is a small porch that leads off my kitchen, suspended twenty feet above the lawn by rotting wooden posts and a few iron braces. We went and leaned precariously over the railing, letting the early morning air breathe its way around us. Some days I hate the city, it smashes up against me—a jungle of smoke and flesh. And then there are other times, like this, when it lives again for me, and its life presses out of the new air, starting again.

"He killed himself with pills," Marion said. "And then he phoned the ambulance. He didn't want me to come home and find his body—just a note, telling me what had happened."

The night before they got married Marion came over to visit me. One last time, she said, though it had been months since we had spent even an hour alone. Just one last time, but I couldn't. I was feeling too self-righteous and relieved, rehearsing my best man's toast and already involved with someone else. We ended up standing in the middle of my kitchen, half-dressed, shouting at each other. The next day at the wedding I felt truly close to both of them, assisting with the rings, the champagne, the toasts: finally we had been defined. It was like being released from a long uncertain purgatory.

"I've missed you," Marion said. "Gavin did too. Last week he asked me why we hardly ever saw each other anymore. He hated that, old friends slipping away. Secretly he was a crazy optimist. He believed in everyone, even me."

Optimists don't kill themselves, I wanted to say. But didn't. Who knows what people do. Marion's shoulders shook against my arms. She was crying again; and my own tears were starting to gather in the blackness.

"I did love him," Marion said. "I did." Our hands touching, sealed together in the early morning heat.

1976

House of the Whale

Gwendolyn MacEwen

OF COURSE I was never a whale; I was an Eagle. This prison is a cage for the biggest bird of all. I'm waiting for them to work their justice, you see, and while I'm waiting I'm writing to you, Aaron, good friend, joker. The hours pass quickly here, strange to say; I have all kinds of diversions. The nice fat guard with the bulbous nose and the starfish wart at the tip often greets me as he makes his rounds. I make a point of waiting at the front of the cell when I know he's coming. And then there's Mario in the next cell who taps out fascinating rhythms at night with his fingernails against the walls.

I don't have an eraser with me, Aaron, so any mistakes I make will have to stay as they are, and when the pencil wears down, that will be that.

I can't help thinking how young I still am—23. Twenty-three. Can I tell you about my life again? It was normal at first. I wrenched my mother's legs apart and tore out of her belly, trailing my sweet house of flesh behind me. I lay on a whale-skin blanket and watched the water; I sucked milk; I cried. I was wrapped up in thick bearskin in winter. I was bathed in

191

the salt water of the sea. My mother was taller than all the mountains from where I lay.

There were the Ravens and the Eagles. You already know which I was. When I was old enough to take notice of things around me, I saw the half-mile line of our houses facing the waters of Hecate Strait. And I saw the severe line of the totems behind them, guarding the village, facing the sea— some of them vertical graves for the dead chiefs of old. Some totems, even then, had fallen, but our Eagle still looked down on us from the top of the highest one, presiding over the angular boats on the beach, the rotting cedar dugouts and black poplar skiffs. (Someone ages before had suggested getting motors for them—the boats, that is—and the old men of the village almost died.)

I was turned over to my uncle's care after I passed infancy, and he spoke to me in the Skittegan tongue and told me tales in the big cedar-plank house. I've long since forgotten the language, you know that, but the stories remain with me, for stories are pictures, not words. I learned about the Raven, the Bear, the Salmon-Eater and the Volcano Woman—just as your children someday will learn all about Moses or Joshua or Christ.

I never knew my father; after planting me in my mother's belly he left to go and work in the Commercial Fisheries on the mainland. He forsook the wooden hooks and cuttlefish for the Canneries—who could blame him? Secretly, I admired him and all those who left the island to seek a fortune else-where, to hook Fate through the gills. But he never came back.

Our numbers had once been in the thousands but had dwindled to hundreds. My grandfather, who was very old, remembered the smallpox that once stripped the islands almost clean. He remembered how the chiefs of the people were made to work in the white man's industries with the other men of the tribe, regardless of their rank; he remembered how the last symbols of authority were taken away from the chiefs and *shamans*. A chief once asked the leader of the white men if he might be taken to *their* island, England, to speak with the great white princess, Victoria—but he was refused.

Sometimes I heard my grandfather cursing under his breath the Canneries and hop fields and apple orchards on the mainland. I think he secretly wished that the Sacred-One-Standing-and-Moving who reclined on a copper box supporting the pillar that held the world up would shift his position and let the whole damn mess fall down.

When I was young some of our people still carved argillite to earn extra money. It was a dying art even then, but the little slate figures always brought something on the commercial market. The Slatechuk quarry up Slatechuk creek was not far from Skidegate; and there was an almost inexhaustible supply of the beautiful black stone, which got shaped into the countless figures of our myths. I remember having seen Louis Collison, the last of the great carvers, when I was still a child. I watched his steady gnarled hands creating figures and animals even I didn't know about, and I used to imagine that there was another Louis Collison, a little man, who lived inside the argillite and worked it from the inside out.

(The fine line, Aaron, between what is living and what is dead . . . what do I mean, exactly? That party you took me to once in that rich lady's house where everyone was admiring her latest artistic acquisition—a *genuine Haida* argillite sculpture. It illustrated the myth of Rhpisunt, the woman who slept with a bear and later on bore cubs, and became the Bear Mother. Well, there were Rhpisunt and the bear screwing away in the black slate; Rhpisunt lay on her back, legs up, straddling the beast, her head thrown back and her jaws wide open with delight—and Mrs. What's-Her-Name kept babbling on and on about the "symbolic" meaning of the carving until I got mad and butted in and told her it was obviously a bear screwing a woman, nothing more, nothing less. She looked upset, and I was a little drunk and couldn't resist adding, "You see, I too am *genuine Haida*." And as the party wore on I kept looking back at the elaborate mantelpiece and the cool little slate sculpture, and it was dead, Aaron, it had *died*—do you see?)

My mother wove baskets sometimes and each twist and knot in the straw was another year toward her death. And she sometimes lit the candlefish, the *oolakan* by night, and we sat around its light, the light of the sea, the light of its living flesh. Sometimes the old *shaman* would join us, with his dyed feathers and rattles, and do magic. I saw souls and spirits rising from his twisted pipe; I saw all he intended me to see, though most of the people left in the village laughed at him, secretly of course.

My grandfather was so well versed in our legends and myths that he was always the man sought out by the myth-hunters—museum researchers and writers from the mainland—to give the Haida version of such-and-such a tale. My last memory of him, in fact, is of him leaning back in his chair and smoking his pipe ecstatically and telling the tale of Gunarh to the little portable tape recorder that whirred beside him. Every researcher went away believing he alone had the authentic version of such-and-such a myth, straight from the Haida's mouth—but what none of them ever knew was that grandfather altered the tales with each re-telling. "It'll give them something to fight about in their books," he said. The older he got, the more he garbled the tales, shaking with wicked laughter in his big denim overalls when the little men with tape recorders and notebooks went away.

Does he think of me now, I wonder? Is he still alive, or is he lying in a little Skidegate grave after a good Christian burial—a picture of an eagle on the marble headstone as a last reminder of the totem of his people? Is he celebrating his last *potlache* before the gates of heaven; and has the *shaman* drummed his long dugout through waves of clouds? Are the *ceremonial* fires burning now, and is my grandfather throwing in his most precious possessions—his blue denim overalls, his pipe?

(Remember, Aaron, how amazed you were when I first told you about the *potlache*? "Why didn't the chiefs just *exhibit* their wealth?" you argued, and I told you they felt they could prove their wealth better by demonstrating how much of it they could *destroy*. Then you laughed, and said you thought the *potlache* had to be the most perfect parody of capitalism and consumer society you'd ever heard of. "What happened," you asked, "if a chief threw away everything he owned and ended up a poor man?" And I explained how there were ways of becoming rich again—for instance, the bankrupt chief could send some sort of gift to a rival chief, knowing that the returned favour had to be greater than the original one. It was always a matter of etiquette among our people to outdo another man's generosity.)

Anyway, I lie here and imagine grandfather celebrating a heavenly *potlache*—(heaven is the only place he'll ever celebrate it, for it was forbidden long ago by the government here on earth)—and the great Christian gates are opening for him now, and behind him the charred remains of his pipe and his blue denims bear witness to the last *potlache* of all.

Some of my childhood playmates were children of the white teacher and doctor of Skidegate, and I taught them how to play *Sin*, where you shuffle marked sticks under a mat and try to guess their positions. They got sunned up in summer until their skins were as copper as mine; we sat beneath the totems and compared our histories; we sat by the boats and argued about God. I read a lot; I think I must have read every book in the Mission School. By the time I was fifteen I'd been to the mainland twice and come back with blankets, potato money, and booze for the old *shaman*.

I began to long for the mainland, to see Vancouver, the forests of Sitka spruce in the north, mountains, railroads, lumber camps where Tsimsyan and Niskae workers felled trees and smashed pulp. My uncle had nothing to say when I announced that I was going to go and work at "the edge of the world"—but my grandfather put up a terrific fight, accusing me of wanting to desert my people for the white man's world, accusing my mother of having given birth to a feeble-spirited fool because on the day of my birth she accepted the white man's pain-killer and lay in "the sleep like death" when I came from her loins. And then he went into a long rambling tale of a day the white doctor invited the *shaman* in to witness his magic, and the *shaman* saw how everything in the doctor's room was magic white, to ward off evil spirits from sick flesh, and he saw many knives and prongs shining like the backs of salmon and laid out in neat rows on a white sheet; from this he understood that the ceremony wouldn't work unless the magical pattern of the instruments was perfect. Then the doctor put the sick man into the death-sleep, and the *shaman* meanwhile tried to slip the sick soul into his bone-box, but he couldn't because the doctor's magic was too powerful to be interfered with. It was only when the doctor laid out exactly four knives and four prongs onto another white sheet, that the *shaman* realized the doctor had stolen the sacred number four from us to work his magic.

I worked north in a lumber camp for a while; we were clearing a patch of forest for an airplane base. In one year I don't know how many trees I killed—too many, and I found myself whispering "Sorry, tree" every time I felled another one. For *that* I should be in prison—wouldn't you think? Wasn't it worse to destroy all those trees than do what I did? Oh well, I can see you're laughing in your beer now, and I don't blame you. Anyway, I really wanted to tell you about Jake and the other guys in the bunkhouse, and what a great bunch they were. I learned a lot about girls and things from them, and since I didn't have any stories of my own like that to tell them, I told them the myth of Gunarh—you know the one; you said the first part of it is a lot like a Greek myth—and all the guys gathered round, and Jake's mouth was hanging open by the time I got to the part about Gunarh's wife eating nothing but the genitals of male seals. . . .

"Then she took a lover," I went on, "and her husband discovered her infidelity and made a plan."

"Yea, yea, go on, he made a *plan*!" gasped Jake.

"He——"

"SHADDUP YOU GUYS, I'M TRYING TO LISTEN!"

"When they were asleep after a hard night, the lover and the wife. . ."

"Hear that, guys—a HARD night!"

"Jake will ya SHADDUP!"

"——Gunarh came in and discovered them together. He killed the lover and cut off his head and his——"

"Jesus CHRIST!"

"Jake will ya SHADDUP!"

"—and put them on the table. . . ."

"Put *what* on the table?"

"It ain't the *head*, boys!"

"Jesus CHRIST!"

"So the next morning his wife found her lover gone, and she went to the table for breakfast—you remember what she usually ate—and instead of . . ."

"O no! I'm sick, you guys, I'm sick!"

"SHADDUP!"

"—well, she ate *them* instead."

"Jake, will ya lie down if you can't take it?"

I never did finish the story, because they went on and on all night about what Gunarh's wife ate for breakfast, and Jake kept waking up and swearing he was never going to listen to one of my stories again, because it was for sure all Indians had pretty dirty minds to think up things like that.

Almost before I knew it, my year was up and I was on a train heading for Vancouver; the raw gash I'd made in the forest fell back behind me.

At first I spent a week in Vancouver watching the people carry the city back and forth in little paper bags; I stayed in a strange room with a shape like a big creamy whale in the cracked plaster on the ceiling, and curtains coloured a kind of boxcar red which hung limply and never moved. I drank a lot and had some women and spent more money than I intended, and after standing three mornings in a row in a line-up in the Unemployment Office, I bumped into you, Aaron, remember, and that was the beginning of our friendship. You had a funny way of looking at a person a little off-centre, so I was always shuffling to the left to place myself in your line of focus. I can't remember exactly what we first talked about; all I know is, within an hour we'd decided to hitch-hike to Toronto, and that was that. At first I hesitated, until you turned to me, staring intently at my left ear, and said, "Lucas George, you don't want to go back to Skidegate, you're coming east." And it was that careless insight of yours that threw me. You always knew me well, my friend. You knew a lot, in fact—and sometimes I was sure you kept about 50% of your brain hidden because it complicated your life. You were always a little ahead of yourself—was that the reason for your nervousness, your impatience? You could always tell me what I was thinking, too. You told me I was naive and you liked me for that. You predicted horrible things for me, and you were right. You said my only destiny was to lose myself, to become neither Indian nor white but a kind of grey nothing, floating between two worlds. Your voice was always sad when you spoke like that. . . .

Hey Aaron, do you still go through doors so quickly that no one remembers seeing you open them first?

My grandfather's tales, if he's still alive, are growing taller in Skidegate. My mother's baskets, if she's still alive, are getting more and more complicated—and the salmon are skinnier every season. My time's running out, and I'd better finish this letter fast.

You were silent in B.C. but you talked all the way through Alberta and Saskatchewan; we slept through Manitoba and woke up in Ontario. The shadows of the totems followed me, growing longer as the days of my life grew longer. The yellow miles we covered were nothing, and time was even less.

"Lucas," you turned to me, "I forgot to tell you something. In B.C. you were still something. Here, you won't even exist. You'll live on the sweet circumference of things, looking into the centre; you'll be less than a shadow or a ghost. Thought you'd like to know."

"Thanks for nothing," I said. "Anyway, how do *you* know?"

"I live there too, on the circumference," you said.

"What do you do, exactly?"

"I'm an intellectual bum," you answered. "I do manual work to keep my body alive. Sometimes I work above the city, sometimes I work below the city, depending on the weather. Skyscrapers, ditches, subways, you name it, I'm there. . . ."

Aaron, I only have a minute left before they turn the lights out for the night. I wanted to ask you. . . .

Too late, they're out.

"Well," you said, the first day we were in the city, "Welcome to the House of the Whale, Lucas George."

"What do you mean?" I said.

"Didn't you tell me about Gunarh and how he went to the bottom of the sea to rescue his wife who was in the House of the Whale?"

"Yes, but—"

"Well, I'm telling you *this* is the House of the Whale, this city, this place. Ask me no questions and I'll tell you no lies. This. This is where you'll find your *psyche*."

"My *what*?"

"This is where you'll find what you're looking for."

"But, Aaron, I'm not looking for anything really!"

"Oh yes you are. . . ."

We stood looking at City Hall with its great curving mothering arms protecting a small concrete bubble between them. Behind us was Bay Street and I turned and let my eyes roll down the narrow canyon toward the lake. "That's the Wall Street of Toronto," you said. "Street of Money, Street of Walls. Don't worry about it; you'll never work there."

"So what's down there?" I asked, and you pointed a finger down the Street of Walls and said, "That's where the whales live, Lucas George. You know all about them, the submerged giants, the supernatural ones. . . ."

"The whales in our stories were gods," I protested. And you laughed.

"I wish I could tell you that this city was just another myth, but it's not. It smacks too much of reality."

"Well *what else*!" I cried, exasperated with you. "First it's a whale house, then you want it to be a myth—couldn't it just be a city, for heaven's sake?"

"Precisely. That's precisely what it is. Let's have coffee."

We walked past the City Hall and I asked you what the little concrete bubble was for.

"Why that's the egg, the seed," you said.

"Of *what*?"

"Why, Lucas George, I'm surprised at you! Of the *whale*, of course! Come on!"

"Looks like a clamshell to me," I said. "Did I ever explain to you where mankind came from, Aaron? A clamshell, half open, with all the little faces peering out. . . ."

"I'll buy that," you said. "It's a clamshell. Come on!"

I got a job in construction, working on the high beams of a bank that was going up downtown. "Heights don't bother you Indians at all, do they?" the foreman asked me. "No," I said. "We like tall things."

He told me they needed some rivetting work done on the top, and some guys that had gone up couldn't take it—it was too high even for them. So I went up, and the cold steel felt strange against my skin and I sensed long tremors in the giant skeleton of the bank, and it was as though the building was alive, shivering, with bones and sinews and tendons, with a life of its own. I didn't trust it, but I went up and up and there was wind all around me. The city seemed to fall away and the voices of the few men who accompanied me sounded strangely hollow and unreal in the high air. There were four of us—a tosser to heat the rivets and throw them to the catcher who caught them in a tin cup and lowered them with tongs into their holds—a riveter who forced them in with his gun, and a bucker to hold a metal plate on one end of the hole. They told me their names as the elevator took us to the top— Joe, Charlie, Amodeo. I was the bucker.

Amodeo offered me a hand when we first stepped out onto a beam, but I couldn't accept it, although the first minute up there was awful. I watched how Amodeo moved; he was small and agile and treated the beams as though they were solid ground. His smile was swift and confident. I *did* take his hand later, but only to shake it after I had crossed the first beam. I kept telling myself that my people were the People of the Eagle so I of all men should have no fear to walk where the eagles fly. Nevertheless when we ate lunch, the sandwich fell down into my stomach a long long way as though my stomach was still on the ground somewhere, and my throat was the elevator that had carried us up.

I found that holding the metal plate over the rivet holes gave me a kind of support and I was feeling confident and almost happy until the rivetter came along and aimed his gun and WHIRR-TA-TA-TAT, WHIRR-TA-TA-TAT! My spine was jangling and every notch in it felt like a metal disc vibrating against another metal disc.

After a while, though, I got the knack of applying all sorts of pressure to the plate to counteract some of the vibration. And when the first day was over I was awed to think I was still alive. The next day I imagined that the bank was a huge totem, or the strong man Aemaelk who holds the world up, and I started to like the work.

I didn't see you much those days for I was tired every night, but once I remember we sat over coffee in a restaurant and there was an odd shaky light in your eyes, and you looked sick. A man at a nearby table was gazing out onto the street, dipping a finger from time to time into his coffee and sucking it. I asked you why he was so sad. "He's not a whale," you answered.

"Then what is he?" I asked.

"He's a little salmon all the whales are going to eat," you said. "Like you, like me."

"Where are you working now, Aaron?"

"In a sewer. You go up, Lucas, and I go down. It fits. Right now I'm a mole and you're the eagle."

Aaron, I've got to finish this letter right now. I don't have time to write all I wanted to, because my trial's coming up and I already know how it's going to turn out. I didn't have time to say much about the three years I spent here, about losing the job, about wandering around the city without money, about drinking, about fooling around, about everything falling round me like the totems falling, about getting into that argument in the tavern, and the fat man who called me a dirty Indian, about how I took him outside into a lane and beat him black and blue and seeing his blood coming out and suddenly he was dead. You know it all anyway, there's no point telling it again. Listen, Aaron, what I want to know now is:

Is my grandfather still telling lies to the history-hunters in Skidegate?

Are the moles and the eagles and the whales coming out of the sewers and subways and buildings now it's spring?

Have all the totems on my island fallen, or do some still stand?

Will they stick my head up high on a cedar tree like they did to Gunarh?

Will the Street of Walls fall down one day like the totems?

What did you say I would find in the House of the Whale, Aaron? Aaron? Aaron?

1971

The Good Wife

Robert Fulford

ALEX WAS AN embarrassment to his friends, a source of amusement to his enemies. His friends were few, but remarkably steadfast. Sylvia never decided whether they stuck to him out of pity or habit, or whether—like herself—they clung blindly to the image he projected on first meeting, that of a serious, arrogant and confident European intellectual. In any case it remained a source of astonishment to Sylvia that after all these years she and Alex still received dinner invitations, even occasionally were asked on weekend trips to the country.

The attitude of Alex's enemies, on the other hand, was altogether clear. They believed him a poseur and an egomaniac. Worst of all, he was condescending to his betters. Sylvia, slipping past a cluster of animated talkers at a party, once overheard a professor of fine art talking about Alex's attitude: "Hradas is impossible. People who condescend out of superiority are bad enough, but to condescend out a mind crammed with nothing but shallow journalistic claptrap—that's ridiculous." Sylvia shrank away. She knew too well what he meant—had known it, in fact, even before she married Alex. He struck her almost from the beginning as a man living beyond his intellectual means. She had no way of being sure, of course—she was a Canadian girl, Rosedale bred, educated modestly enough at Victoria College, Toronto, where she spent four years trying fruitlessly to understand Northrop Frye. Alex, on the other hand, was a Hungarian, a "graduate of the class of '56"—as he liked to put it. Behind him in Hungary there were poems (which she never learned to read and he never translated), a film script or two (he didn't bring copies out with him) and a few published essays "in the style of Lukacs," as he said. Sylvia never quite grasped Alex's pre-1956 politics, but she dimly inferred from his Hungarian friends' not too polite comments that he had been in his youth—he was only twenty-two when he "came out"—rather more willingly Marxist than they considered proper. She was given to understand that in their circle it was acceptable to espouse Marxism, but only if it were done with an ill grace. She imagined the students of Alex's generation to have been rather like the incipient stock brokers and public relations men of her own—people who permitted themselves to benefit from capitalism but not to enjoy or admire it.

She and Alex met when he was giving a lecture to the Victoria College Lit Society and Sylvia, as editor of *Acta Victoriana*, was asked to thank him. Alex was then still in what he later called "my Hungarian period." He spoke on the aesthetics of George Lukacs, and though the members of the Lit Society had read nothing of Lukacs and had barely heard of him they listened carefully, in the solemn and uncomprehending way of dutiful students.

Afterwards, over coffee, in a dusty, ancient room crowded with the remnants of the audience, Sylvia established that Alex had spent three years driving a taxi in Toronto. Now he was finishing an M.A. at the university. He was writing his thesis on John Milton.

"Why?" Sylvia asked.

"Because that's what my professors seem to expect," Alex said.

"Do you always do what people expect?"

"No, only when it seems necessary."

"Do you know what I expect from you now?" Somewhere within herself Sylvia gasped at her audacity. She had never said anything even remotely like that before.

"Yes," he said. "You expect me to take you to your room and make love to you."

As she awoke in the morning she told herself: *now* I'll feel different. Then she became conscious of his thick legs against hers, his arm against her shoulder, his sour breath brushing her face. She felt only marginally different. For years she had preserved her virginity against the onslaughts of young ministers' sons from rural Ontario towns, some of whom persisted for months. Now she felt a rightness in the way she had surrendered it, to a stranger from a country she had never dreamt of visiting. Sexual love, after all, was distant and exotic, something she had never observed in her parents' home or among her friends. How appropriate that it should come to her through a man so aloof and so different from anyone she had ever met. She remembered the conversation of the night before, the curt way he accepted her sherry and removed her clothes, never speaking her name. It was the way a European intellectual should make love. But then, what should happen in the morning?

She slipped out of bed, went silently to the bathroom, returned to find him opening his eyes. In the fresh light, morning-bearded, he was older. She felt something good and thought it might be love.

They were married four months later, by a homosexual professor who was also a clergyman, in the Emmanuel Chapel. Her father and mother, though they never much liked Alex— or any foreigner, for that matter—had greeted him almost joyfully. He was the first boy in whom their only child had ever shown interest and his arrival on the scene meant that they might begin hoping to become grandparents. As Sylvia had often noticed, this was the main goal of their lives.

Sylvia was a shy girl whose determination and concern only occasionally broke through—and then very late. It wasn't until the night of their wedding, as they drank champagne in a room at the Park Plaza, that she asked Alex about his career.

"What do you mean, 'career'?"

"I mean, what will you do—for a living?"

"For a living, I will live." Alex was under the false impression that he could spontaneously compose epigrams in English. Even this early it was beginning to annoy Sylvia.

"No, I mean about money. You know I'm going to teach, and there'll always be lots of jobs for teachers. But that won't be enough money. And you can't go back to the taxi."

That was when Alex finally began to reveal his plans. Sylvia would teach, Alex would write. She would bring in the money until success, as it inevitably would, came his way. They would not think of children—not for a while.

Ten years later Sylvia was indeed a schoolteacher, instructing reluctant but for the most part even-tempered Toronto adolescents in the works of Harper Lee, Gore Vidal, and other authors placed on the curriculum of the Ontario secondary school system. The fact that she had never understood what Frye said about poetry turned out to be of no importance. Poetry, for the most part, had largely disappeared from the schools, to be replaced by old TV plays and Pulitzer-Prize-winning novels.

At school, among her simple and undemanding students, Sylvia was happy. At home with Alex, in their apartment on the third floor of an old downtown house, she was miserable. She lived with a secret she could tell no one. She was ashamed of her husband.

She imagined that someday she might acquire a friend in whom she could confide. "I guess I still love him," she would tell this imaginary person, "and certainly I love him in bed—he's the only man I've ever had, he's the whole of manhood to me. And in his way he's charming, he still seems interested in me, sometimes he's considerate. But he embarrasses me, he makes me feel uncomfortable. He's not really very *smart*, and he's not talented. Everybody knows it except him."

Sylvia never said these things because she was not a talker. Something had taught her, long ago, that confessions of this kind were not to be made except under the most intimate circumstances. She was a listener—"a good listener," as one of the teachers at school had told Sylvia while describing at length the breakdown of her own marriage to a tyrannical and alcoholic salesman. The phrase had been spoken with a certain condescension, as if an actress were speaking of a good audience. There was an implication that some people led dramatic and interesting lives and some people didn't.

Perhaps it was all the listening Sylvia did that prevented her from ever thinking seriously of leaving Alex. She knew some divorced women—the teacher at school, several old university friends—and she could not see that they were now better off alone. She could not imagine how they lived their lives, what it was that made them go home and make dinner for themselves. Alex, she understood, was the purpose to her life, and though she felt the need for a better purpose she couldn't imagine one. Moreover, the idea of divorce offended her sense of order. It was something other people did, messy people.

So she neither spoke nor acted. Sometimes she thought about taking up group therapy. She saw herself sitting in a psychiatrist's office, describing her feelings to a roomful of gravely concerned strangers. But, just as she had no intimate friends, she had no therapy group either. There was nothing wrong with her. One doesn't sign up for group therapy just because one doesn't admire one's husband.

She sometimes wondered if Alex should sign up, but the thought always brought a smile to her face. Of course he wouldn't do anything like that. Alex believed he understood himself, and anyway psychotherapists to him were all "the acolytes of the mad doctor of Vienna."

Alex got that phrase from Nabokov. Most of the things he said were derived from his reading—not from novels or poetry but from literary essays, and interviews in magazines like the *Paris Review*. Alex was not really a writer and not actually much of a reader either. He was, as he liked to put it, *un homme des lettres*.

"A phrase," as one of their friends said, "that covers a multitude of sins." As a man of letters Alex found it necessary occasionally to write poetry. He had brought out three slim volumes, sharing the costs of printing with his publishers. The reviews had been negligible. He himself wrote reviews for the newspapers and occasionally articles for the magazines. He also wrote scripts for Canadian radio—he especially liked doing scripts about explorers who kept voluminous diaries: he would have Sylvia copy out long sections of their descriptions, finding this the easiest way to fill the allotted hours—and a few times he wrote television plays. Each of these things, Alex made clear, was a minor event in his life, definitely not a part of his larger work. His larger work, whatever it was, never appeared.

At parties Alex would patronize poets of clearly greater talent than he. "I think you're improving remarkably," he would say to some established master, unaware of the effect of his words. In his newspaper reviews he would mark down as "promising" some writer who had produced four massive and widely praised novels. Glancing over his Toronto *Star*, Alex would say to Sylvia: "I see old Callaghan's trying to make a comeback" or "Mailer's still stuck in journalism—he'll never get his real work done."

Home from school, Sylvia closed the door of their tiny apartment behind her. As always at this time of day, the living room seemed to her a chaos—Alex's messed piles of books and magazines and manuscripts, the remnants of his lunch, two empty beer bottles.

Alex was on the phone. "They've done it again, the bastards," he was telling someone. His accent thickened when he grew angry. "All right. Goodbye." He hung up.

Sylvia kissed his forehead. "Who've done it again, darling?" She began neatening, nervously, knowing something already of what he was to tell her.

"Who do you think? The Canada Council." He handed her a letter. "That's the third time they've turned me down. God! What a country!"

How could Alex know Sylvia found this outburst absurd? From the beginning she had been taught that she and her people were of no special interest to anyone, and by now she saw Alex, whatever his faults, as one of her own. That there *was* a Canada Council, to whose grants one might aspire, was miracle enough for her. That Alex, with his meagre talent, should demand a grant by right was simply outlandish. And in any case he had received *some* grants—a junior Canada Council a few years ago, then a little Ontario government grant to teach poetry part time in a high school. Secretly she believed this was as much as he deserved, perhaps more. She suppressed her feelings.

She looked down at the letter. "They don't give very clear reasons."

"No. The bastards. As usual they just say there were more bloody people who wanted grants than they had money."

"Alex, I'm sorry."

"Sorry? Is that all you can say? Is that the limit of your compassion, your perception? Sorry! Thanks! Well, it's just one more damn defeat. My God, why did I ever come to this country? I'd have been better off in Budapest."

There was a pause, of a kind Sylvia knew well. Years ago she had begun to think of these pauses as the expression of something that was at the core of their marriage. Between her and Alex, as she imagined it, there was a huge granite boulder. They stood on either side of it, unable to touch each other or the boulder itself. The boulder was Alex's idea of himself, his sense of what he was or might be. She couldn't touch that, couldn't shove it aside; nor could she even acknowledge that its existence caused her anguish. Still, she was certain that Alex knew about the boulder and knew about her feelings. Almost every day he would shout at her in rage and almost every day she would imagine he was on the point of questioning her about her opinions. Any moment now, she would feel, he'll force me to say what I think. But each day, as this moment grew near, he drew back. Then came the pause. This time it lasted a full minute.

"Well. The Turners are coming. I'd better get dinner ready."

She went into the kitchen and began scraping vegetables.

An hour later she heard Alex admitting the Turners. She came out of the kitchen, drying her hands, as Alex kissed Helen Turner. Michael Turner kissed Sylvia, completing the social-sexual ritual with which all their meetings began. Michael, taller than either of the Hradas and much taller than his own wife, leaned over to enter their living room. Alex went to the kitchen to make drinks.

Sylvia had always thought of Michael's height as a symbol of his part in their lives. He bent over them like a tree sheltering small animals from the rain. Of all the well-known writers Alex had courted and then insulted in the last ten years, Michael was almost the only one who remained their friend. He dealt easily and gracefully with Alex's outbursts. Sylvia suspected that Alex, with his combination of mediocrity and eccentricity, was a kind of pet for Michael. Alex was, after all, an immigrant, never really to be accepted in the world Michael was born to. Alex was part of multi-culturalism, an idea Canadians like Michael admired without exactly embracing. Michael would never admit it, even to himself but— Sylvia believed—he was charmed by the "ethnic" quality of people like Alex.

And there were moments, she imagined, when Michael was both pleased and intimidated by Alex's sense of European superiority, his unspoken but clear belief that a tragic accident of history had placed him in a community of barbarians. Sylvia could understand why Michael accepted this because she, too, as a Canadian, often felt ill-educated and faintly uncivilized. Sometimes she believed that she and Michael, for all their differences, shared this one secret.

Michael was the kind of man Sylvia escaped by marrying Alex: a son of the manse, liberal, uncommitted, well adjusted, the sort of Canadian who still thought Lester Pearson the best prime minister Canada ever had. He taught English at York University and wrote short comic novels which were well reviewed in England. He seemed to take his status for granted, as if he had never dreamt that his career might work out otherwise. Just as—in Sylvia's view—he took for granted the calm, well-spoken and not overly educated wife who had given him three children and no trouble at all.

Alex, handing around the drinks, made it clear that he knew just what he wanted to talk about. "I had rather hoped this might be a celebration. Alas, it turns out to be a wake." Sylvia noted the "rather," noted the "alas." Alex was not content to be a Hungarian-Canadian. He wanted also to be an Englishman.

Michael's raised eyebrows simultaneously conveyed curiosity and granted permission to go on.

"The news is not good," Alex said. He drew from his pocket the letter. It had already acquired the worn look of documents that are too often handed around. "They turned me down. *Despite* your letter of support."

Michael smiled the self-deprecating smile his friends knew so well. "Perhaps I've lost my power to persuade. *If* I ever had any."

"No, I don't think it's your fault at all, Michael. Don't blame yourself. My guess is that someone up there has it in for me."

"In what sense?" Michael's question was guarded, as if he knew it must be asked but couldn't bear to put any emotion into the asking.

"Simply this: three times I've been turned down for the senior arts fellowship, despite the highest qualifications, despite support from people like you. And not only that: I've been left off the literary selection board, I've not even been consulted about the book promotion project. Do you see what I mean? It begins to form a pattern."

Michael paused and both of the women stared at him. Now deal calmly with this, Sylvia thought.

Finally Michael spoke. "I don't think you could call it a *pattern*, Alex. I don't think anyone is against you."

Alex leaned forward, his free hand waving towards Michael. "No? Well of course it's very easy for you to say. You aren't on the receiving end. You've got your committees, your novels, your prizes. It's rather different for someone like me."

"Really, Alex," Sylvia began, "really——"

"And don't *you* say it's nothing." Alex turned to her. "I know what's happened. I've gored one of the wrong oxes." His voice was rising. "That's the way it is in this country. As long as you remain a quiet little mouse, agreeable to everyone"—here he glanced at Michael, a combination of temerity and fear in his eyes—"it all goes smoothly. But if you speak out, say what you think, actually *exercise* some of those famous Anglo-Saxon freedoms, then the axe comes down."

Michael sat back and sipped slowly on his martini. Sylvia felt it her duty to intercede again.

"I don't really think that's quite fair, Alex. Michael is as outspoken as anyone."

"Outspoken!" Alex wheeled now on Sylvia, taking in with a gesture both Michael and Helen. "Do you call what he writes outspoken? Those gentlemanly little essays in the *Tamarack,* deploring censorship, worrying endlessly about American influence on television. My God, the man"—now he pointed directly at Michael—"the man wouldn't know censorship if it bit him! I know censorship. I endured it in Hungary. Now I'm enduring it here." Alex said the last sentence with grim satisfaction, as if something he had been chasing had finally fallen into his hands.

Sylvia decided it was time for what her sociology professor had called tension management.

"Well, of course, Alex, you've had difficulties. But that has nothing to do with Michael and——"

"Difficulties!" Alex was not prepared to be managed. "I've had every possible obstacle put in my way. Including a wife who clearly doesn't understand what I'm talking about."

Michael and Helen glanced at each other. They looked down at their glasses for refuge. Their glasses were empty.

"I think I have dinner about ready," Sylvia said, rising.

"Just a minute. Sit down! I haven't finished. What exactly did you mean when you said I wasn't being quite fair?"

"Well, I——"

"I'll *tell* you what you meant. You meant that I'm paranoid, didn't you? That's another thing about this country. Anyone who sees what he's up against is immediately a paranoid."

Michael cleared his throat. Sylvia saw a familiar expression on his face. Michael was about to rescue the situation with a joke. "Well, paranoia is always a relative thing. They said Trotsky was paranoid. He claimed Stalin would send a man to kill him."

"That's beside the point." Now Alex turned to Michael. "What I'm saying is that I can't get *any* support, not even from my wife. She smiles at me all the time, pretends to encourage me, but secretly she thinks I'm nothing. I'm worthless. Isn't that true?" Now he was again facing Sylvia.

Sylvia, inside herself, was staring at the boulder. She had always hated it, but now that she saw it disintegrating she felt nostalgia. A little plea went up from her heart: give me back my lies!

But Michael was back in the discussion again, his lean, earnest face inclined toward Alex. "I hardly think that's quite true, Alex. Sylvia has been as good a wife as any man could ask for, and she always shows the keenest interest in your work."

"A good wife!" Now Alex was standing, waving his arms up and down like a man signalling the start of a race. "A good wife! She's as far from a good wife as anyone I know. She undercuts me whenever she can, she laughs at me behind my back, and"—he paused a moment—"she's barren." He looked at her in triumph, his argument ended. "In some countries she'd be divorced for that alone."

There flashed before Sylvia's mind a picture of her squatting behind the cupboard door in their bedroom, inserting the diaphragm on—how many—a thousand occasions? Another picture: a tearful Sylvia, standing at the foot of the bed, crying, begging Alex to be allowed to conceive. The begging had stopped years ago.

Sylvia tried, but she could not keep herself from looking at Helen Turner. There she saw what she knew she would see: that combination of smugness and guilt which crossed, however fleetingly, the face of every mother when she contemplated the childlessness of another woman. Helen's

expression turned Sylvia's hurt into a rage that rushed up-
ward from her stomach.

"But Alex, it was you who never wanted children." She
stopped, giving all her strength to the struggle to keep
from sobbing.

"That's your story now, of course. But in fact we would
have had children if you'd been the kind of woman I deserved.
I could have had *sons*! And with the support of the right
woman I could have *been* something—instead of this!" His
wave took in the apartment, Sylvia, the Turners, the Canada
Council letter on the table—as if they were all part of his
degradation.

Finally Helen Turner spoke. "I think we've come at a bad
moment. I think we should go." Michael mumbled something,
gestured reassuringly in response to Sylvia's apologies,
unfolded his legs. But Alex wasn't finished.

"The trouble with you Anglo-Saxons"—he now turned his
rage on Helen, to her clear surprise—"is that you can't stand
a little truth. Get right down to the bone and you people
retreat. All right, go. But remember what drove you away:
an honest man speaking the truth at last." He walked to the
kitchen, glass in hand.

They were out the door in a moment. There were no kisses
this time. Sylvia, turning back to the living room, contemplated at once the ruin of their friendship with the Turners
and the waste of her elaborate dinner. One seemed at least
as important as the other. Alex returned and sat in silence.
He bore the look of a man who had done a hard piece of work
exceptionally well.

Since there was nothing she could say to Alex, Sylvia said
the usual things to herself. I'll stay, she said. After all, I'm
all he has. Or, put it another way: he's all I have. And besides,
I never really admitted anything. Perhaps we can learn
to lie again.

1976

Something for Olivia's Scrapbook I Guess

David Helwig

I WAS ALONE in the shop as I watched the two of them coming up the street. Olivia was on television being interviewed with a discovery, Harold Bettmann, 'one of the most exciting young sculptors working in Canada today' (Toronto *Star*). I felt a bit sorry for Olivia over the Harold thing. He is not a nice young man, and to a bystander he seems too obviously to be trying to reach the top of the mountain of success by a route beginning with a tunnel into my wife's private parts. Still, I knew better than to say anything to her. Anyway, they were on television together, and I certainly wasn't going to watch. So I stood in the front window and watched Barrow Man and the girl.

I wasn't really surprised to see her tagging along after Barrow Man as he came up the street. Women can smell it on him, I've often observed that. My wife, for example: when Barrow Man walks into a room she shuts her mouth and sits very still licking her lips now and then. And that's about the only time she stops talking. You wouldn't think there'd be any mystery about him; at least a couple of times I've heard him going out the back door as I came in the front, but still, when he comes into a room, Olivia shuts her gob and sits with that funny look on her face. No one else does that to her, and there are lots better looking than Barrow Man, more charming, more intelligent. But women like him. They look at that bony face, and that thick hair, and they smell whatever it is he has and bingo. So I wasn't surprised to see this young girl following him along the street as he pushed his barrow of tatty flowers.

Our place is just north of Yorkville, where Yorkville is going to expand next, that's what the real estate man says. Anyway Olivia and I have a shop there, full of handicrafts and imported odds and ends that nobody buys. Barrow Man lives next door with a gang of others, upstairs from something that's trying to be a coffee house.

Barrow Man is unscrupulous, have I established that? Suppose not. Well he is, but just about women, just about sex really. I've seen him fill a fifteen-year-old with wine and take her upstairs without even paying much attention to who she is. He thinks it's good for them, that's the secret, and otherwise he's kind and generous. Only for him it's not an otherwise. He thinks that sex is good for any woman at any time and place whether she thinks so or not. Maybe that's what women see in him.

So as I say, I wasn't surprised that afternoon when I saw the girl following Barrow Man up the street. He'd been down at his usual spot on Cumberland selling flowers that he'd picked from parks and gardens the night before or got from florists who were ready to throw them out. Flowers have been getting a lot of publicity this year, and he sold them cheap and made enough to stay alive.

The girl who was following him up the street was dressed in clothes that were worn almost to tatters and were too big for her. Every few feet she would stop. It seemed as though Barrow Man could hear when her feet stopped moving, for he would turn around almost immediately and motion to her with his hand. Gradually she would get up her courage and move forward a few feet. It took them five or ten minutes to cross the distance between the point where I first saw them and the house. Barrow Man's missionary zeal amazed me. To go to all this trouble when he could have half a dozen women in the neighbourhood for the asking. Old Jane, whose room was next to his, was an attractive and universally accommodating girl.

When they reached the front of the house, Barrow Man made an elaborate gesture indicating that he lived there and inviting the girl to sit down at one of the outside tables. It was then I caught on that she must be a deaf mute. From the way she was dressed, you'd think he'd picked her up at the Salvation Army or an orphanage somewhere. She sat down at a table and Barrow Man disappeared inside.

The girl had a strange flat frightened face that looked straight ahead and gave the impression that she was waiting for some kind of blow to fall on her from behind. Call me sentimental, but I didn't much like the idea of Barrow Man seducing this pathetic little deaf mute.

He came out of the house with a lemonade for her and put it on her table. She didn't want to touch it in a way, but she was probably hot and thirsty and needed it. Barrow Man kept after her and she finally took a drink. While she was drinking, Barrow Man went over to the barrow of flowers that he had left at the curb and took out a handful of zinnias that he must have got from somebody's garden. He carried them over to the girl and gave them to her. I had to admire his technique.

I walked out of our shop and along the pavement toward the two of them. Just as I got to the barrow of flowers, I thought of a way to neutralize what he'd done. I took a bunch of chrysanthemums, a little wilted and obviously second-hand, and carried them over to the girl. She was holding the gaudy zinnias in her hand, and she didn't move or object when I began to put the chrysanthemums in her hair. The hair was full of tats so it was easy to find places to stick the flowers. It was soft, too, and reminded me of the days when Olivia's hair was brown.

Two kids about sixteen, a boy and girl who had the room

across from Jane but hardly ever came out, had seen us from the window and appeared from the house. They'd lived there for weeks, but this was only the second time I'd seen them. They joined in the game, running to get flowers and carrying them to the table. They put them on the girl or placed them around her. Jane was looking out the upstairs window and threw me a couple of paper flowers from her room. I wound the wire stems around the girl's wrists. Within a few minutes, the barrow was stripped of all its flowers which now covered the girl, the chair she sat in and the table in front of her. She made a lovely funeral. The four of us and Jane, who had come downstairs, and even Walter, who had come out of the shop, stood and admired her. Barrow Man tried to get her to smile and finally she did. She seemed to relax a little and looked at the flowers, for the first time really.

'Who is she?' It was one of the young kids that asked.

'I don't know who she is,' Barrow Man said. 'She was hanging around near my stand all afternoon.'

'What are you going to do with her?' I said.

'Well, right now,' he said, 'she looks so gorgeous I wouldn't dare touch her.'

'Maybe you should take it easy.'

'What do you think I am? I'm full of loving kindness. I sell flowers and make people happy. I let you crazy people steal every one of my flowers to give her. I just want to make her happy.'

'But not everyone has the same idea of what will make her happy,' Jane said.

'You mean sex,' Barrow Man said. 'You're all against sex. What a lot of nervous people you must be.' He walked over to the girl, picked up her hand, and kissed the back of it.

'I'm hungry,' he said, 'and I suppose she is too. Some of you nervous people who stole my flowers should buy us something to eat.'

'Get them some food, Walter,' I said. 'I'll pay.'

It was after six, so I went home, closed the shop, and made myself a sandwich. I planned to go back next door, but I can't afford to eat at Walter's prices. With my sandwich I had a

couple of stiff drinks of rye and water which didn't do anything very metaphysical to me. I went back over to see what
was happening next door, taking the bottle with me in a paper
bag. What Barrow Man calls the fuzz is very active around
our streets.

The girl was still sitting at her table with Barrow Man and
was still covered with flowers. She had drawn a bit of a crowd
from the houses nearby, and Walter was doing some business
for a change. I paid him for what Barrow Man and the girl had
eaten and sat down at the table with them. I poured out of my
bag into a coffee cup and gave Barrow Man some, too.

I looked at the girl. She seemed pretty puzzled but not too
unhappy about the whole thing. The boy from upstairs had
obviously decided to rejoin society and brought out a guitar.
People started singing. That worried Walter who was sure it
would cost him his licence and invited everybody inside. When
we got in, the place was so crowded that Barrow Man locked
the front door and put up a CLOSED sign. Walter pulled the
curtains shut, and I took my bottle out of its paper bag. The
deaf mute sat in the middle of the room in her flowers, apparently puzzled by what was going on, but everyone smiled
and gestured at her, and she got used to it. I offered her a
drink, but she smelled it and made a face. Walter put some
music on his record player and several people formed a circle
and danced around the girl. I didn't feel like dancing and concentrated on my whisky.

I finally drank enough to lose track of time, and from that
point on, the party was a series of moments in a sea of noise.

First moment: someone gave her a pencil and paper, and she
wrote one word. JESUS. In large scrawled capitals.

Second moment: at Jane's urging, Barrow Man publicly
announced that he would not seduce the deaf mute. He called
it a sentimental gesture.

Third moment: the unknown girl from upstairs began a
beautifully graceful and sinuous dance.

I watched her for about twenty seconds before I decided
that I couldn't take it. I went out the back door, climbed over
the fence and into my yard. I stood among the few blades of

brown grass that flourish there. The house was dark and I
didn't want to go in. Did go in. The memory of that girl
covered with flowers got to me and made me want to do something for her, not that there was anything to do.

I was making my breakfast the next morning when I heard
Olivia come in. It was quarter after eight. I couldn't really
figure out why she'd got up so early. Didn't occur to me until
she walked into the bedroom and started to undress that she
hadn't been to bed. We've only got a couple of small rooms at
the back of the shop, and from where I was standing, I could
see her undressing. I watched. I think of it as one of my con-
jugal rights, although it's not really much of a sight. Olivia is a
skinny little thing with no breasts to speak of and pathetic
little hips. She looked so pale and dragged out as she took off
her clothes that I fought off the temptation to say something
witty about the long interview.

'Do you want some food?' I said.

She shook her head and climbed into bed. One way or
another Harold must have given her a rough time. When I
walked into the bedroom, she turned her face away.

'You missed a new arrival last night,' I said. 'Barrow Man
found a strange little deaf mute somewhere. I don't know
why, but everyone got excited when she turned up and gave
her a big party. Even Barrow Man got into the act; he
promised to refrain from debauching her. At least for the
time being. It was all very strange.'

She turned over and looked at me. That's not really the
right way to describe it; she stared at my face as though something distasteful was wiggling its way out of the eyeballs.

'Don't you ever read the newspapers?' she said.

In the circumstances, that struck me as a strange question,
and I didn't answer. After all we've been married nine years
and she knows my reading habits. Pretty clearly it was a smart
crack, but its relevance escaped me.

'She's a deaf mute about seventeen wearing old clothes that
don't fit properly,' Olivia said.

I nodded.

'The police are looking for her. She stabbed her mother to death with an ice pick in some little town in Muskoka and then hitch-hiked to Toronto before anyone found the body. The story was in the paper this morning and on television last night.'

I thought for a few seconds and started out of the room.

'Are you going to phone the police?' she said.

'No. I'm going to warn Barrow Man that they're after her so he can hide her somewhere.'

'Are you out of your mind?' As she said this, she sat up in bed, the sheet falling off her and exposing her scrawny chest. For some crazy reason, I wanted her right at that moment, but I have developed a strong resistance to such impulses and I conquered this one. At least temporarily. She went on shouting at me.

'Why in the name of all that's wonderful are you going to try to keep her away from the police? Apparently her mother drank and beat her. They'll just send her to some place where she can be looked after.'

'Some nice place like the bughouse.'

'I don't know, but I know you have no business interfering. Just phone the police and tell them where she is, and they'll look after her all right. You're getting as crazy as those kids next door. Have they been giving you marijuana or something?'

'You know, Olivia,' I said in my best Cary Grant manner, 'I find your shrill grating soprano very sexy.'

She got the message and covered herself with the sheet.

'You're not really going to keep her away from the police are you?'

'Unless you distract me with your subtle feminine wiles and mysterious allure, I'm going to see Barrow Man right now.'

She flopped down in bed.

'I should have you committed,' she muttered.

'And a very Merry Christmas to you, too,' I said and walked down the hall and out. As I walked up to the door of the place next to us, Walter was putting out the tables and chairs. He said Barrow Man was still in bed, and that the girl was in Jane's room.

I went upstairs and walked into Barrow Man's room. Jane sat up bleary-eyed in the bed and said hello.

I apologized.

'All right,' Jane said. 'Nothing going on. You want Barrow Man.'

'Yeah.'

She reached out and shook him.

'Do you have a cigarette?' she said.

I shook my head, and she gave Barrow Man another poke. Jane, like Olivia, was sitting in bed naked down to where the sheet covered her. She is an ample girl, and as I stood there, I drew certain comparisons between her and my wife. Jane poked Barrow Man twice more, and he began to make noises. Another hard poke in the ribs and he turned over.

'What's the matter?' he said.

'Olivia tells me our little friend is wanted by the police. She did in her mother with an ice pick.'

'The old lady probably deserved it. Anyway, Olivia's a liar isn't she?'

'Don't really know. She says it's in the paper.'

'Everything in the paper is a lie.'

'What will they do to her if they find her?' Jane said.

'Put her on trial. Send her to some kind of institution.'

'Nasty,' Barrow Man said.

'Poor thing,' Jane said. For some reason that prompted her to cover herself with the sheet. I refrained from asking why.

'What shall we do with her?' Barrow Man said.

'Turn her in or hide her,' I said.

Barrow Man scratched his head.

'Don't suppose you have a cigarette.'

I shook my head.

'We can't just turn her in,' Jane said. 'I'd feel like a Judas if we did. After last night.'

'Of course we didn't know last night,' I said.

'Doesn't make any difference,' Barrow Man said.

'No,' I said, 'it doesn't.'

'Let's hide her somewhere,' Jane said.

'Where?' Barrow Man said. 'The fuzz will be watching the streets pretty carefully.'

'We could put her in our back shed until tonight,' I said.

'Maybe no need,' Barrow Man said. 'Just keep her in the house and if the fuzz shows up slip her out to your back shed.'

'I wonder if she knows they're after her?' Jane said.

"She can probably guess,' I said, 'if she really did go at her old lady with an ice pick.'

'Let's go and see her,' Jane said. She climbed out of bed, stood there naked without embarrassment, stretched and put on a short cotton dress that she found on the floor beside the bed. Barrow Man pulled on a pair of pants and we went down the hall to the next door. Jane lifted her hand to knock, realized there wasn't much point, and stuck her head in. She opened the door and walked in. We followed her.

The girl was sitting on the floor at the far side of the room. She looked terrified as we walked in, and I wondered why. There was an unpleasant smell in the room, but it didn't much surprise me. Jane always looks a bit dirty. The girl was staring straight ahead.

'Oh my god,' Jane said. 'She's not housebroken.'

She pointed to the other corner of the room, at a brown lump that was unmistakably the source of the smell. I looked back at the girl who was hiding her face in her skirt.

'Look,' I said. 'She's worried about it. I guess she didn't know where to go.'

Barrow Man went over to her and lifted her face. He tried to indicate to her that it was all right, that we didn't care about the mess in the corner and that Jane would clean it up right away. Jane got a little cardboard box and did. She took it away to dispose of. Meanwhile Barrow Man started another little pantomime, asking her if she had been hitch-hiking. She nodded.

'How in hell can I ask her if she knows the cops are after her?'

'Try a traffic cop,' I said, 'or a motorcycle.'

Barrow Man had a go at it, but the girl looked confused. Barrow Man patted her on the head and sat down. Jane walked into the room. I jumped from my chair and attacked her with an imaginary ice pick. She didn't look very surprised, for she has believed for some time that I am a man full of suppressed vices. She believes this because I have never tried to make her, in spite of numerous opportunities and substantial provocation. After I had finished with Jane I turned to the girl. She looked sick. I pointed to her and nodded my head. She buried her face in her skirt again.

'Oh well,' I said, 'I thought we might find out something.'

'Looks to me as though she did it,' Jane said.

'Maybe,' I said.

'I'll take her down to get some breakfast,' Jane said.

Barrow Man stood up.

'Keep her in your room today. I'm going to try and find some flowers to sell. If the cops show up, put her in that back shed.'

Jane took the girl by the arm and led her downstairs. I followed them to the bottom of the stairs, then turned down the hall toward the front door. On my way, I ran into Walter, who was looking worried as usual.

'You getting much business these days?' he said.

'The usual.'

'I don't know how long I can hold out. I've got to eat.'

'Belly god,' I said and walked back to my own house of sorrows.

It was almost nine and I left the door of the shop unlocked and walked back to the kitchen. Olivia was asleep in the bedroom, but something made me think she'd been up after I left. My sense of smell is sometimes very acute. She'd probably phoned the police.

I put the kettle to make some coffee and stood in the doorway, looking in at her. She dyes her hair a colour they call champagne and it was all wild and fluffy around the little face that looked weak and pinched like that of an undernourished child.

When I had made my coffee, I took it into the shop, closed the door to the kitchen behind me and sat down at my work table near the front door. To amuse myself, I did the week's disastrous arithmetic.

It was less than half an hour after I sat down at my work table that I looked out the window and saw a police car pull up next door. I got up and ran to the back door, climbed over the low fence that separates the yards, nipped in the kitchen door and up the back stairs. As I crossed the kitchen, I could see down the hall to where the cops were coming in the front door. There were two of them, big uniformed public servants with thick necks, and at that moment, it seemed to me that I was even crazier than Olivia gave me credit for being. But my mother had died in a particularly nasty government institution (a fact I have never told Olivia) and I didn't want to see this little girl put away under the thumb of some dykey matron or frustrated social worker. I grew up with social workers.

When I got to the upstairs hall, I ran as quickly as I could to Jane's room and opened the door. The girl stared at me, frightened as a bird. I gestured to her to come with me, but she didn't move. She probably didn't trust me since I had ice-picked Jane. I tried to take her arm. No dice. I ran next door to Barrow Man's room to see if Jane was there, but the room was empty. Downstairs I could hear the voices of Walter and the cops, and I knew that Walter would give her up as soon as sneeze if that was the way to avoid trouble. He had given a hostage to Fortune when he opened the coffee house, and Fortune was getting pretty good mileage out of it.

I went back into the room, spent three seconds trying to calm the girl, then picked her up and carried her along the hall and down the back stairs.

My physical condition is not outstanding. By the time we got to the kitchen, I was dizzy and thought I'd faint before I could get the girl out of there. She wasn't quite fighting me off, but she wasn't making it easy either. But for a change I got a lucky break. Jane came into the hall and into the kitchen.

'The cops are out there,' she whispered.

'I know. I'm trying to get her out into our back shed, but she's afraid of me.'

Jane reached out to the girl and took her hand. The girl looked a little relieved. We all slipped out the back door and over the fence. When I finally got the lock on the back shed undone, the girl refused to go in until Jane went with her. Jane took her hand and led her in among the cartons and snow shovels. She turned around and looked at me.

'Do I have to stay here?'

'She'll feel a lot better.'

'Well,' Jane said, 'I just want you to know that I wouldn't do it for anybody else but you.'

'I like you, too,' I said. Then I locked the door of the shed and went back into our shop. I sat down at the front table looking innocent. A few minutes later, I saw the cops leave and drive away. From the kitchen, I got our transistor radio and put it on in the shop to listen to the news bulletins. Within a couple of hours, they were saying that the girl had been reported seen in the Yorkville area and that the police were checking this.

I was pretty sure that they would be back soon. They knew she had been in the house last night, Walter must have told them that, and they would probably have someone watching the house in case she came back. In a couple of hours when they turned up no trace of her, they would come back and try to put more pressure on everyone in the house, threaten arrests for drugs or contributing to juvenile delinquency. Luckily no one there saw me leave with the girl, so that no amount of pressure could tip them off where she was. Which suited me fine.

At quarter to twelve I started making lunch, and made extra of everything for the girls in the shed. I took it out on tinfoil plates, feeling like part of one of Tom Sawyer's games. Jane complained of the discomfort of the shed, so I passed in a couple of folding cots so they could lie down. All this, I tried to do in such a way that it would not look suspicious from any of the upstairs windows nearby. Good old Tom Sawyer, where would I have been without him?

It was about two o'clock when Olivia got up and wandered into the front of the shop with a towel wrapped around her.

'There's nobody here but me,' I said. 'You might as well get dressed.'

'Spare me your wit until I wake up a bit. Where's that girl you were telling me about?'

'In our back shed.'

'Not really.'

'The cops came looking for her next door, so I slipped her out the back and put her in the shed.'

'They're going to put you in jail, do you know that? Or they're going to send the men in white coats for you. Either way, there's going to be nothing left of you around here except your clothes. Unless I keep a scrap-book of your newspaper clippings.' She shook her head. 'It should make quite a trial. Tell me that's why you're doing it, that it's just a publicity gimmick so the store will get mentioned in the paper. That must be it.'

'I'm doing it because I don't want her put in an institution.'

'Well, you're going to end up in one, the way you're going. I really find it all just a little bit hard to understand. Are you going to leave her in the shed forever? You could drill a hole in the wall and charge a dime to peek in. God, when the police find her, I'll be able to charge admission to see you. The man with a hole in his head.' She turned away.

'Don't phone the cops again, Olivia,' I said. 'Or I'll break your neck.'

'You're developing a taste for cheap melodrama,' she said as she disappeared.

I could hear her in the shower and moving around in the bedroom getting dressed. Half an hour later, she was headed out the front door. She'd just raised the hem on her shortest skirt another four or five inches. I hoped whatever she had on underneath looked good.

'I have to see some people downtown,' she said.

'Just don't phone the cops,' I said.

She left. I watched out the window as she walked down the street, her skinny legs very white in the sun. When she disappeared round a corner, I didn't have the energy to move away from the window, and I was still standing there when

Barrow Man appeared and began pushing his empty cart along the street toward me. As he passed the window, I tapped on it and motioned him in. He left his barrow by the side of the road and came in.

'The cops were here,' I said, as soon as he was inside the door.

'Did you get her out?'

'Just in time. She and Jane are in the back shed.'

'What's Jane doing there?'

'It was the only way I could get the girl to go in.'

Barrow Man giggled.

'I got hold of a friend of mine,' he said, 'who's got a place out in the country. It's just a beaten-up old farmhouse but she'll probably be all right there. He says he can use a house-keeper if she wants to work.'

'That sounds fine, but how are we going to get her out of here?'

'I said we'd meet him at nine-thirty tonight.'

'But they'll have cops all over.'

'Suppose so.'

'We might just sneak her past in the dark.'

'What we really need is something to attract their attention, start a riot or something.'

'We could burn a house down.'

'Wait a minute, wait a minute.'

He was thinking. I could tell by the look on his face.

'Look,' he said. 'I'll light a fire on my barrow and lead the cops away with that. It will draw a crowd for sure. Then you grab the girl and take off.'

'It'll ruin your barrow.'

'I'll get a new one. You got any old paint and turpentine?'

'In the back shed.'

I gave him the key.

'Watch for the girl,' I said. 'Don't let her out.'

It was at that moment that a customer came into the shop. I knew it must be a mistake and went to clear it up, but I ended up by selling something. I thought it must be some kind of omen. When I looked out the back I saw that Barrow Man had his little cart covered with cardboard boxes that held half the old paint from our shed. If he wasn't careful he'd burn down the whole neighbourhood. He stuck his head in the back door.

'Nine-thirty tonight, okay?'

I said it was okay.

'You meet my friend two blocks up Avenue Road. A brown station wagon.'

I nodded and he closed the door. I went back to work in the shop. For hours I sat and waited.

Finally, at suppertime, I brought Jane and the girl into the house. I couldn't see taking another meal out to the shed, and I figured they might as well be inside. After supper, I turned on the television set for them, and the three of us watched it until it started to get dark. A little bit after nine, we all went into the shop and sat by the front window waiting for Barrow Man to light his fire.

At nine-fifteen he did it. It was a dandy. He must have had about ten gallons of paint and solvents on his barrow, and when they went up, one whole area of the street was lit. We could see him grab the handles of his barrow and start down a side street with it.

'He's going to burn himself,' Jane said.

'Or get arrested for arson,' I said. 'Let's go.'

We led the girl out the front door and along the street away from the fire. All evening, she had been looking more and more withdrawn, and now she seemed completely out of touch. We led her along dark streets and she followed, but apparently with no idea of where she was going or why. I wanted badly to talk to her, just two or three words. Anything. Jane had tried to explain to her during the day what was going on, had even printed notes for her, but we didn't know if she could read, and nothing seemed to reach her.

We approached Avenue Road a block below the meeting-place we had arranged. The traffic was very heavy, and as we stood on the corner I saw something beside me move. It was the girl who suddenly ran into the road, miraculously made her way past half a dozen speeding cars and ran down the street on the other side. Jane and I stood and watched her, helpless until the traffic slowed a bit.

By the time we got across the road, she had disappeared. For perhaps half an hour, we walked along the streets, down alleys and lanes, but there was no sign of her. We went to tell the driver that she wasn't coming, but he was gone. He must have got tired of waiting. There was nothing more we could do. We walked down Avenue Road toward home.

'Well,' I said. 'That's it.'

'She must have been pretty frightened.'

'Poor little idiot. The police will find her eventually and put her in a box.'

'Maybe that's best.'

'No,' I said. 'That's not ever best for anybody.'

Jane reached out and took my hand.

'I suppose we were crazy to even try it,' I said.

'Maybe.'

'Tell Barrow Man I'll give him some money for a new cart.'

'If I'm talking to him, I'll tell him.'

We walked on down the dark streets. Jane was still holding my hand. She has big hands and feet. We didn't look at each other until we got home. Down the street where Barrow Man had lit his fire, there were still a few people hanging around.

'I wonder if the cops got Barrow Man,' I said.

'I doubt it,' she said.

I knew that now I had to look at her as we stood there in the street. Looked, knowing what I would see. She wanted to come in with me. And why not? Olivia wouldn't be home until morning, and if she was, she wasn't likely to say a hell of a lot, not in the circumstances. I looked down at Jane's face again. It was a wide face, not pretty, but warm and gentle. I wondered where Olivia was and what she was doing. Or having done to her. I kissed Jane on the forehead and turned away.

'I'll see you tomorrow,' I said.

I walked into the house. And don't start asking me why.

1968

Town
and Country

Michael Smith

IT WAS AFTER my father's sickness, when I left home to stay for a while on my grandfather's farm, that I learned I was a city boy. Until then, I had never realized that I came from anyplace strange at all. I might just as well have come from another country—or worse, another race. Suddenly, I had to bear the curse of learning what everybody else already knew. Suddenly, I was all alone, and very different from all of them.

"Got a new partner," my grandfather told his friends when he showed me around the town. "He's Jack's boy. From the city—you know." Or sometimes: "Come here, meet David. From the city."

"From the city, are ya?" Hard-eyed, deaf old men repeated it loudly, the words smug with malice—just the way I have heard my grandfather charitably gloat, "Arthritis, you say? Oh, well that's *too bad.*" Old men who had worked in the city themselves, and others who came in off the farm, haunted the steep staircases that led to their rooms above the main street stores. A lot had been my grandfather's cronies once, until his own fine luck left him sitting in a safe pew alone, a little above them somehow.

My grandfather had lived all his life on the farm, and he had a way of lumping up everything that was foreign as proof that the whole outside world had gone wrong. The milk board was in the city. The stockyards. And all the merchants—all Jewish, to his mind—who made it impossible to buy two-strand barbed wire. In his workshop he kept the radio tuned on Toronto, though of course it was useless for anything even so practical as the local weather report. The city stations reported so many more murders than he ever could have heard of in town. I think he must have listened to them because they confirmed his faith that city people were just as heathen as the victims of an African civil war.

It was never simply that crimes didn't happen in Little Falls, but they were usually much harder to find in the local weekly newspaper my grandfather bought. Mostly it reported raccoons in the garbage cans—and, once, how somebody found a dead dog on Queen Street—though on occasion it also mentioned minor arrests, omitting the names. It reported all the police calls just the same way that the constable had written them down, in the order they had happened. Sometimes this meant that an accident, say, got buried down at the bottom of a list of funeral escorts and other routine calls. But people who wrote in to renew their subscriptions found their letters printed right on the front page, beside the high school's honour roll.

The district collegiate was only a little more than a mile away, and so in good weather my grandparents let me ride my bike to school. The bus route for students from the country didn't go past my grandfather's farm. That was a difference between town kids and country kids—country kids *always* rode buses—and I think it might have been a first inkling of a subtle distinction for me. The truth was, I was a town kid like the rest. In fact, though his farm was mostly out in the township, my grandfather's house and outbuildings stood just inside the town line. He used to burn all his trash on the border because he said that he could never see the value in having to buy a fire permit. If the provincial police drove down from Brough he could always claim he was on the town side. He was over the line in the township if the constable came out from Little Falls.

Little differences like that came hard for my grandfather unless they served his own purpose well. The difference between town and country—which seemed easily blurred in my new life—seemed as clear to him as black and white. But his blind spots never let him see how city could differ from suburbs, for instance, which was just as clear and obvious to me. I had heard a rooster crow not very far from where my parents lived, but that was one of the stories that my grandfather refused to believe. My father had bought a house in the suburbs, and he had to travel nine miles into the city to get to work. Still, the once I remember my grandfather visited, he drummed his fingers on the arm of his chair as if we had locked him up in a tenement room downtown.

One of the first things I can remember about the suburbs is standing by myself in the driveway outside my parents' home. It's summer, the sun is shining, and I'm studying a row of ants as they cross a broad flat piece of rockery stone. The stone is hot. I'm wearing short pants. The year must be about 1950, and I'm nearly four years old. It's almost as if I had a photograph of that summer afternoon—although I know I don't—because it seems as if I could stand aside and look back at myself. Perhaps it was the first time I was really aware that I was the person I am.

The driveway that I remember is paved, the way the driveway is today, but at the time it must have been just dirt. Our little house—one of a dozen identical bungalows—stood in the middle of farmers' fields on a road that still has never been properly paved. It must have seemed as out of place then as the lonely knots of new houses built twenty years later on the outskirts of Little Falls. Out in the fields there were squatters' shacks, loose little shanties run up with silvering wood and tarpaper walls. I can remember poor small farms where families kept goats as well as chickens, and at one place a bull that was tethered by a ring in his nose. Some people along our street lived years in basements which had no houses on top.

To me this was scarcely the city—isn't yet, with all its changes today. The city was way downtown, where my mother's parents—my other grandparents—lived in half a house that I knew they didn't really own. Where there were horses clopping in the streets, drays that hauled delivery vans, silent on rubber wheels. And nuns—nuns!—who sometimes walked down the sidewalk right in front of my grandparents' place. Even then there were people in their neighbourhood who couldn't speak English at all.

When my father took sick I was just starting high school, and still there were cornfields between the school and home. Our suburb that many years ago seems not far different from Little Falls even now—but when I was just a fourteen-year-old boy how could I convince my grandfather of that? Young families moved out to the suburbs from the city because the land sold cheap. The old were farmers who limped in off the land to cramped apartments overtop the old houses that were lately being built into stores. The only outsider that I can remember was an Italian girl named Yolanda who turned up at our school about the time that I was in Grade 8. My parents' old neighbourhood swarms with Greeks, Italians, Poles, Finns and even a French-Canadian family now.

In the early years of our suburb we used to travel to the city by bus, and almost all the passengers knew each other, at least enough to nod. In bad weather, if we were lucky, a car would stop and my mother and I could get a lift as far as the top of the street where the buses ran. Once when I was very small I saw a black man sitting in the bus, and the utter shock drove me to asking so many questions and whining that my mother had to cut our trip short. I remember the driver gave us a transfer, so we could get on the next bus for free.

In Little Falls the only black man was a rundown old workman who swept the streets and cleaned up garbage until he got so tired and lame that he had to leave the job for a younger man.

Our suburb, much more than Little Falls, has changed. The

downtown bus is gone; one finger of the subway reaches all the way out to the corner of my parents' street today.

I remember now my first rides on the subway when it was just a short run way downtown, in an area where I hardly ever had any need to go. I remember the race to sit at the front of the train so I could see the lights changing colours like stoplights along the tunnel ahead. Little children, and adults too, still sometimes make a run for the front. Strangers to the city talk right out loud, and—very worst—sometimes they look across the aisle and catch their fellow travellers eye-to-eye. It was something that happened on the subway just lately that set me thinking about all this.

This particular day I was glad to see that the car was half empty when I got inside, because there had been a lot of shoppers waiting on the platform with me. There was space enough for three people on the seat across from me, though only an old man with a bulky leather briefcase was sitting there now. Then just before the conductor blew his whistle a black man rushed into the car and sat beside the old man, even though there were other seats.

The black man was obviously poor, and shaken, I think, by his run to catch the train. He wore a shabby blue flannel suit, no tie, and an old brown fedora hat which matched only his worn brown shoes. The old man was very neatly dressed, but also very old. He wore a fierce white military mustache, and he reminded me of my grandfather a bit, though much more stooped and tired. The old man moved his briefcase out into the aisle to give the black man room to stretch his legs. They both stared straight ahead at first, which forced me shortly to look away.

I tried to read my newspaper, but after a while I realized that the old man and the black man had started to talk, and both were looking across the aisle at me. The old man seemed upset, even angry at something. The black man was talking quietly, using words I had trouble hearing, though I have to admit that I tried to overhear.

"You should get off," the old man was saying. "Get off this

train right now!" He shook his head, as if the black man had offended him somehow. "Why couldn't you ask somebody first? You should have asked me earlier. You want the other line," he said, and I realized that the old man was waving his hand toward a map of the subway route on the wall, just above my head.

The black man mumbled something, waving his hands too, and then he held up his arms in an exaggerated shrug. The old man studied the black man's face, and cocked his ear as if he found him hard to understand.

"Islington?" the old man said at last, louder than before. "Oh, Islington! I thought you were saying Eglinton, man." He pointed again toward the map. "Look here—you go to the end of the line, then you transfer, and then you go west to the end of the line again. That's Islington—do you see?"

The black man smiled, and repeated something that sounded like *Islington* to me. Then he looked up at the map again, very seriously, and squinted as if he was looking into the sun. It embarrassed me, and I turned back to my newspaper. Islington, I recognized, was where I was going too.

The two of them didn't stir again until it was time for the old man to get off. But I was afraid at first that he wouldn't be able to get across the aisle in time. He was having trouble even standing up, and I had almost decided to offer to help him when the black man reached up timidly, then gave the old man an awkward heave by the rump.

The old man didn't say anything to the black man; he shuffled his briefcase across the aisle, growling and grumbling to himself, and stood at the doorway beside my seat until the subway train stopped.

The black man and I both used the same door when we reached the St. George station, where we would have to transfer to get on the other line. As soon as the black man got out on the platform he stopped a subway attendant, I guess to ask the way to Islington again. For all the old man's help with the map, I don't think the black man could read it for himself.

The next I noticed of the black man, he was standing studying a map on the wall and squinting, just as he had on the train, but tracing the subway line now with a stubby, dirty finger. Then a train rumbled out of the station upstairs, and suddenly the black man looked up at the ceiling, throwing back his head in a gust of hearty laughter.

When the black man turned and started to talk I could see how the old man must have found him hard to understand. There were only two or three teeth in the black man's mouth, and he spoke in some singsong kind of a dialect that I could hardly get through. It was clear that the black man was enjoying it, though, and it was clear that he recognized me from the other train, so I nodded to him. I waited until he laughed and shrugged once more, and then I raised my newspaper and pretended to read.

"Old walls, hold on!" the black man said, or something like that; I couldn't be sure. Most of what the black man said I couldn't completely understand. Just I could hear him hollering something, and the deep rich sound of his laughing there beside me.

I kept my face behind my newspaper even after the black man stopped. Somehow it made me mad that he was acting so pleased with himself. I was getting scared that the black man might want to sit beside me on the Islington train. I was afraid that he might spew his palaver at me in front of somebody else. But when the train finally tore through the tunnel toward us I pointed a finger at the sign on the front, and said very loudly: *"Islington!"*

The black man smiled, and looked very smart.

The train stopped in front of us in such a way that there were two cars to choose from, and the black man and I both started for the same door. But in the last moment I changed my mind, and turned to get on the other car. The black man seemed to hesitate too, but I could see when I got inside that he got into the car behind.

After that I began to read my newspaper again, but soon I realized that my stop was also Islington, and I would have to see the black man on the platform, getting off. I started feeling embarrassed for what I had done to the man. Now and again I looked up through the glass in the doors that con-

connected our cars, and I could see the black man sitting alone, not talking to anybody now, though once I thought I caught him looking back through the glass at me.

Then the subway train stopped at the Ossington station, neae where a lot of the black people live, and I was startled to see the black man standing among a crowd of people on the platform, looking lost again, bewildered and afraid. Get on, I thought—get on, you fool!—and I think I even started getting up to shout out the door, but the conductor blew his whistle, and I had to sit down, ashamed that any of the other passengers might have seen that I didn't know just what to do.

Then I thought: maybe Ossington really was the right station. Maybe the old man and I both had got it wrong. Maybe Ossington, near his own people, was where the black man belonged—not Islington, out in the suburbs, at all. And thinking that made it easier for me to forget about the black man.

And now I remember how a young man, walking, came up to my grandparents' porch one evening after dark to ask his way to another farm not very far along the road. When my grandfather came back into the house my grandmother asked him who it had been.

"Well, I didn't think to ask him that," said my grandfather, leaning into his chair. "All I know for sure is, it wasn't anybody that knows his way around here."

That afternoon in the subway, too, made me think about the days I had spent alone out on my grandfather's farm. I thought about my grandfather, and I wished I could be with him again. I had brushed very close to my grandfather that day in the subway, then more than ever. I moved closer to him than I had ever felt before as I sat there just reading my newspaper out to the end of the line.

1977

The Old Lady's Money

David Lewis Stein

OUT OF THE darkness of Poland, out of anger and outrage she had come and now, sitting in front of the old lady's withered body, Aaron could feel only wonder at himself. He wanted to weep for his grandmother. He wanted to show some grief for the broken dream and the sour hatreds that had ruled her life. But he had never been able to talk to her when she was alive and there was nothing to say to anyone else now that she was dead. When there had been his father, they had tried. Twice he remembered their going to one of the old lady's cluttered rooms to plead with her to come and live with them. But she refused to leave the sagging streets of the old neighbourhood. The old lady served them tea and wept bitterly. Aaron could understand just enough Yiddish to know the old lady wanted more money. She always wanted more money. Only Aaron's father gave it to her. The other boys, shcutzim, bums, gangsters, better they had never been born. When it was time to go, she pressed Aaron to her bosom and covered his head with kisses. Aaron was a good boy. Aaron would take care of her when she got old. The old lady had outlived three of her four sons. Only Jake was left to grieve for her. Jake and Aaron, the last of the Paguraks.

Jake sat beside him in the front row of the chapel, his head covered by his old grey fedora instead of a skullcap. Jake had buried his face in his hands and was sobbing loudly, "Why couldn't it be me? Why couldn't it be me?" Aaron could hear people beginning to shuffle into the rows behind them. He wanted Jake to shut up. He wanted the people to go away. He wanted to be left alone with Jake and the old lady and the old ghosts. The rabbi, very young and very pale, stepped up to the lectern beside the coffin. "My friends," he began in a reedy voice, "Gertrude—Gitl—Pagurak was an inspiration to all of us, a woman who lived according to the best of the old Jewish life and who raised her children to be the glowing jewels in her crown of womanhood. . . ."

"The funeral was bad enough," Aaron said. "But the feldt was even worse."

"The feldt?" Margaret said.

"The cemetery. Jake was supposed to say the kaddish before they lowered the coffin. But he broke down completely. I had to say it for him. We had to practically carry Jake back to the car. God he makes me sick."

"Stop it," Margaret said. "Just stop it."

She poured him more coffee and sat down on the couch, tucking her legs up under her. Even now, at one o'clock in the morning, wrapped in a faded housecoat and her face white with sleep, Margaret was still beautiful. At least to me she is, Aaron thought. It was so good to have a woman of his own, so good to have someone to wake up in the middle of the night. Margaret was another world, a million miles away from Spadina Avenue and the old people. But which world did he belong to? What would Jake say, what would his father say if they could see him now in Margaret's apartment?

"You think I'm being childish, don't you," Aaron said. "You think I ought to try and make things up with my uncle, don't you?"

"I think you ought to do whatever you think is right for you. I hate to see you all hung up like this."

"Listen," Aaron said. "When my father died, I was eleven years old. Jake was the one they sent to get me out of school. He was crying then, too. Just like today. But when my mother started asking him for some help—she wanted to open a little dress store—he didn't have any money. He could gamble away a thousand dollars a night, I know that, Margaret. My father even told me that. But he didn't have a dime to spare for me and my mother. My uncle Max and my uncle Sam were the same way. They wouldn't give you the right time. They came to my father's funeral and I never saw them again. My father was the good son. He gave money to his mother. He wanted to be a lawyer, you know. He would have been a good one, too. He had that kind of mind. You think I'm pretty smart, but it's all him. He was going to train me to be a lawyer. Everything I ever wanted to do, he gave me an argument. You know why he never made it? The old lady, my grandmother. He went to Detroit, he was going to take law at night school, and they followed him there. So help me God, the whole family moved to Detroit so my father would have to help support them. That's why they all hated my mother so much. My father was the meal ticket and she took him away."

"But your grandfather?"

"All he ever wanted to do was play cards. I don't remember him very well. He died when I was six, but that's what people tell me. He was a tailor. I probably get my good clothes sense from him. Maybe it's in the genes or something. But it was the old lady who held the family together. She wanted all the boys to get rich. They did too, at least Max and Sam did. But they never gave her a damned thing."

"Aaron, take me to London."

He stopped his pacing then and came to her on the couch. She curled up against him, burying her head in his chest.

"You're a strange creature," he said. "I don't really believe you exist."

"I want to spend six months in London, just tramping up and down the streets and going to plays and art galleries. A different pub for supper every night. Then north, all the way to Scotland. All the way out to the Isles."

"And school? You've only got a year to go; I have three. You going to give up your B.A. and everything just to go to London for six months?"

"I can always come back. Besides, what am I going to do with a degree, anyway? Teach school? Work in a publishing house? I want to go to England. I want you to take me there."

"But what if I get serious? What if I want to marry you and make it all legal and permanent?"

"I'd do it."

"You would too, wouldn't you?"

"I might," Margaret said. "But you're not going to. So let's not talk about it." She drew his head down to her.

"I wanted to talk to you after the funeral," Rabbi Leiner said. "But I didn't get a chance to."

"I went right home," Aaron said. "I didn't go for the shiva."

"I've been calling you all week," the rabbi said. "I'm glad you could come today."

"I got your message," Aaron said. "But there were exams. You know, mid-terms."

"Oh, I know," Rabbi Leiner said. "I went to M.I.T. You shouldn't be surprised. I didn't get religion, as they say, until after I'd graduated. I was going to be a marine biologist. But I decided hanging over a boat in the middle of the ocean is no place for a nice Jewish boy."

Aaron refused even to smile. He had taken an immediate and intense dislike to Rabbi Leiner. The man was too young, too small, too pale. A rabbi to a congregation of old men, as Leiner was, ought to be an old man himself, a bearded ghost floating through the downtown streets. But Leiner was young, a man of Aaron's own time who had chosen to go back into the murky roots. Aaron had met the type before. He despised them for their foolishness. They were trying to make themselves a bridge between the old times and the new Jews. He wants what the old people had, Aaron thought. And he thinks it was faith, but he's wrong. The old people were afraid of God; they hated God for His cruel laws and their own poverty. Only some of them, like my grandmother, could turn the hate outward and ride it with the dream. It wasn't God's blessing the old lady wanted, it was ease and comfort, luxury even, so much money that no one could ever hope to take it all away from her.

"Your grandfather belonged to the Ostrovtzer Society," Rabbi Leiner said. "You know what that is? Well, it's made up of men who came from the same town in the old country. It's a kind of mutual benefit society. They took care of all the funeral expenses."

"Thank you," Aaron said. "I didn't know that. I didn't even think to ask."

Behind Rabbi Leiner's head, full book shelves rose all the way to the ceiling. Beside Aaron, on the mantel over the fireplace, stood a blue Israeli Menorah, a picture of Leiner's wife and children in a leather frame and an Eskimo carving of a seal. It's too much, Aaron thought.

"I went to your grandmother's room. Someone had to see to her personal effects. I gave her clothes to the United Jewish Appeal—she didn't have very much, you know—and I also found this." He reached into his desk and took out a small metal box, painted black.

"I had to pry open the lock," Rabbi Leiner said. "Go ahead, open it."

Aaron took it and lifted the lid. The box was filled with bills in dirty, disorderly bundles.

"Eight hundred and seventy-five dollars," Rabbi Leiner said. "I suppose she was saving it for her funeral. Maybe she forgot about the Ostrovtzer Society. Or maybe she didn't trust them. Old people tend to get that way. But the president of the society is in my congregation. He made all the arrangements even before he called me."

"What are you going to do with the money?" Aaron said.

"I'm giving it to you, Mr. Pagurak."

"You're giving it to me?"

"I know it's not mine. But sometimes a rabbi has to make decisions. It's part of his job I guess, although they didn't teach me things like this at the Yeshivah. But I tried to think what your grandmother would have done with the money. I never knew her, so the best I can do is guess. But an old lady usually thinks most often of her grandson. Especially if he happens to be an only grandson. I had to choose between you and your uncle."

"But you're giving it all to me?" Aaron said.

"Your uncle is already an elderly man," Rabbi Leiner said. "He is, at least, self-supporting. And you are a young man still going to college. So I made a decision. A rabbi likes to get a little of the pleasure of giving too, you know. But on my salary, I can hardly be a philanthropist. If you were a literary man you might call this vicarious philanthropy."

It's true, Aaron thought, money really does burn a hole in your pocket. He lay on his bed, alone in his room, and the money was a fiery wad in his back pocket. No one except that little phoney Leiner knows I've got this dough. I can do anything I want with it. I can even take Margaret to England. He tried to picture them having supper in a London pub. It would somehow be all dark oak and glowing brass. He laughed at his own dreams. And yet, why not? Why indeed not?

There was nothing to hold him to Toronto any more. What did he have here? A rented room, one year at university, a couple of friends and an uncle who would never know or care if he left the city or stayed. His mother and sister had got out. They lived now with his sister's husband in Teaneck, New Jersey. Toronto for them was a place they had once lived in where bad things had happened to them. When Aaron came to visit, they asked him questions about people they had once known and clucked their tongues.

"If my father had lived longer or died when I was younger, it might have been different," Aaron said. "But he died just when I was getting to know about him and I had to stay in Toronto and find it all out. My uncle Max and my uncle Sam were just cheap rackos. They never gave a damn about anyone but themselves. But Jake and my father were close in age and there was something between them. They had it with the old lady, too. They were the ones she had real hopes for. The ones she expected money from. My father and Jake were booking together before the war and when the war started, Max and Sam wanted them to come in on the black market deals with them. My father told them to go to hell. He wouldn't join up and fight—he had a family to support but I don't think he would have joined up anyway. But he wouldn't go in for the black market stuff either. Jake did though; he was their muscle man. I've had people come up and tell me that in his day, Jake was the toughest man in Toronto. You know, he once threw a cop through a window. It was when he and my father were together. They had a store on King Street and a cop came in and tried to shake them down. They were already paying off downtown and Jake got so mad, he picked the cop up and threw him through the window of the store. Anyway, Max and Sam beat Jake out of his share and he came out of the war just as broke as when he went into it. My father never talked to them again. But Jake used to come to our house about once every six months and my father would bawl him out and tell him to get out of the rackets and buy a cigar store or a cab or something and Jake would start roaring that it was none of my father's goddamn business. But they had a bond between them; you could call it a kind of love. They understood each other. And I understood them. But my mother and sister couldn't. All they saw was the yelling and screaming. They never saw what was going on underneath it. Now everybody's gone except Jake and me."

"And me," Margaret said. "You've still got me."

Aaron rolled over in the bed and kissed her.

"You're a good man, Aaron Pagurak," she said. "You think you're crazy, but you're not. You're the sanest man I know."

Aaron reached down and pulled her nightgown up to her shoulders. "What a magnificent body you have," he said.

"It's too small. My legs are too fat."

Aaron began to nuzzle her stomach.

"You need a shave. Why don't you go home and shave?"

"It's two o'clock in the morning."

"I hate men who don't look after themselves."

Aaron rubbed his chin into her breasts.

"Stop it, stop it, stop it," she cried. Aaron lifted his head and she pulled him down to her.

In the morning, he lay on the bed with a sheet pulled across him and watched her brew coffee in the tiny alcove that served as her kitchen. She had pulled on a robe of scarlet flannel over her nightgown. She called it her "French whorehouse robe." Aaron liked to watch her face, that marvellous oval, the pale, white skin, the high cheekbones and the grey, slanted, almost Chinese eyes. Whatever Margaret did, Aaron reflected, whatever people did to her, she would always look as though she had just stepped out of the bath at a convent school.

She brought the coffee to him on a tray with two buttered rolls.

"Real croissants?" Aaron said.

"Mmmm, something like that."

"We should go to lectures," Aaron said. "It's almost eleven o'clock."

"So get dressed and go."

"What will you do?"

"I'll read. I have lots of things to read."

"Margaret, why did you pick me?"

"I told you. You were the best-looking boy at Tony's party."

"That was four months ago. We've been to a party almost every week since then. Lots of good-looking men."

"Don't I know it."

"Are you in love with me, Margaret?"

"Yes."

"But you don't want to move in with me?"

"No."

"And you don't want to marry me?"

"I didn't say that. We might get married. Who knows? I've never wanted to marry anyone else."

"You were the first for me, you know."

"I didn't. But it doesn't matter. You weren't the first for me. Does that matter to you?"

"Why should it?"

"I don't know. You can be so damn moralistic sometimes."

"I wonder what would happen if you brought me home and introduced me to your parents."

"Ah Aaron, don't ever grow up. You'll ruin us both if you

do. I haven't been home in three years. I'll probably never go back. You make such a fuss about your family and Toronto and all that. You should have grown up in a small town, like the one I came from. Then you'd really have something to cry about."

"Don't you ever want to go home?"

"It was a mess, Aaron. My parents were a mess and the whole town was a mess. When I got down here, I just made up my mind I was never going back there. I've never regretted it. Not for one minute. I write to my sister. She's starting to wake up to things, too. She's going to leave as soon as she can get some money together."

"I could send her the money."

"You're going to take me to England. Or did you forget all about that?"

"Piccadilly here I come; right back where I started from," Aaron sang.

"Aaron, do you really want to go?"

"Yes. The whole thing is crazy, me and you are crazy, but yes, I want to go. The money won't last long, maybe two or three months after we pay our boat fares and then we'll have to get jobs. But we'll make out. It's the best thing either of us has ever done."

"We'll be happy hobos," Margaret said. "No ties, no homes, no education."

"Margaret, it's time to go. All I care about now is you. I want to tear up the past, tear up the roots. The hell with them all. It's the going that counts. And this time, I'm going with you."

"Oh God, Aaron, I hope you mean it. I hope you know what you're saying."

"Put down that coffee cup and c'm'ere."

"Who do you think you're talking to?"

"C'm'ere I said, and none of your lip."

"Ah Aaron. My good, good Aaron."

Rabbi Leiner called for three days before Aaron consented to see him. The messages on the hall table in front of Aaron's room became steadily more insistent until finally there was a note pinned to his door: he must come to Rabbi Leiner's study immediately. Immediately was underlined. Aaron could just see Rabbi Leiner shouting into the telephone, "And underline that!"

"It's your uncle," Rabbi Leiner said. Aaron sat in front of the rabbi's huge oak desk while Leiner paced back and forth in his study. Every time I see him, Aaron thought, he gets smaller and paler.

"I didn't seek him out, Mr. Pagurak. You must understand that. But he went to your grandmother's room. He was going to gather up her clothes, just as I did. It seems I misjudged him, Mr. Pagurak. I hope I haven't misjudged you."

He paused in his pacing to look searchingly at Aaron. I know him now, Aaron thought. He's a nice little boy and he's frightened. He's touched something he doesn't understand. He's seen a little of how the old people really lived and it scares hell out of him.

"Call me Aaron," Aaron said.

"Your uncle knew about the money in the box. He knew about it all the time. He hasn't said anything to me directly, Mr. Pagurak. I hope you understand that. But I made the wrong decision and I hope you'll help me make the right one now."

"First commandment for rabbis," Aaron said. "Don't play God on weekdays."

"I don't think that's very funny, Mr. Pagurak."

"All right, rabbi. I'm sorry. But I'm not going to give any money to Jake. Like you told me when you gave it to me, Jake is a grown man and he can look after himself. I'm still going to school and I need every dime I can lay my hands on."

"You don't seem to understand, Mr. Pagurak. There may be a legal question."

"Boy, Jake really got to you, didn't he?"

"Please, Mr. Pagurak. I tried to do the right thing. Now it looks as if I may have made a terrible mistake."

From Rabbi Leiner's study it was only a few blocks to Ledofski's restaurant, but Aaron took a cab. He sank into the back seat, cursing Jake as he went. He found him at a back table, a bowl of sour cream and vegetables in front of him.

Jake came every day to Ledofski's and stayed until five or six when it was time to go out in his cab. He had his breakfast in Ledofski's, read the newspapers, talked to his friends and quoted the latest odds on the football and hockey games. The grey fedora was pushed back on his head and he held his spoon like a shovel.

"You finally come to see me," he said to Aaron. "I figured maybe you thought I was dead, too."

"I've just come from Rabbi Leiner's house."

"Eh?"

Aaron raised his voice. "I've been to see the rabbi. The one who buried the booba."

Jake unbuttoned his suitcoat and turned the dial on the hearing aid clipped to his shirt pocket.

"I talked to the rabbi," Aaron shouted.

"You talk good to that rabbi, eh?" Jake said. "He's your real pal, eh?"

The tough voice, the surly growl, that would never change, Aaron thought. But the face was getting old. The skin was almost colourless—Aaron could see the network of worn out veins—and the eyes behind the rimless glasses were watery and red. But he still had the Pagurak look, the humorous, wiseman wrinkles around the eyes and the thick sensual mouth that could hook downward in a con man's sardonic grin or lock tight in a madman's rage.

"What are you doin' now? You still goin' to school?"

"I was," Aaron said. "But now I'm going to England."

"England! What the hell you gonna do in England? You wanna talk to the queen. You can talk to me. I won't charge you nothin'."

"I've got the money, Uncle Jake. The old lady's money. The rabbi gave it to me."

"The last of the big spenders, that rabbi. He don't care what he does with other people's money."

"He thought he was doing the right thing. He was trying to help me."

"So why don't he help me, too? I could have the police on him you know that? What he did was worse than stealing. He took money off a dead woman."

"Cut the crap, Uncle Jake. He was just trying to do his job.
That's what rabbis get paid for."

Jake shot out his hand and dug it into Aaron's coat. "If your
father was alive, you wouldn't talk to me like that," he said.
"He'd give you what for. You lissen to me. That money don't
belong to you and it don't belong to that rabbi. You hear?"

"It doesn't belong to you either, Jake."

Jake twisted his fingers viciously into Aaron's coat. Aaron
felt himself being choked. He began to be afraid that Jake was
going to lose control. "You and that rabbi, a couple of thieves,"
Jake said. "Who gives you permission, eh? Who makes you
such big shots?"

"What do you want the money for, Uncle Jake?" Aaron said.

Jake let go of Aaron's coat and sank back into his chair.

"I'm an old man," he said. "You think it's fun to push a cab
around in the wintertime? I get stiff. Some mornings I can't
hardly get out of bed. Maybe better I should have been with
the gangsters. You live good and then they rub you out. You
don't get old like me. You don't live long enough to suffer."

"You could make book full time," Aaron said. "You should
be able to make a living at it. You know lots of people."

He watched Jake's jaw muscles wrestle with the anger and
then his mouth broke into the mocking Pagurak smile that
Aaron remembered so well from his father.

"You're a real wise guy, ain't you?" Jake said. "Who made
you so smart? When I was your age I was earning my own
living. I didn't have to ask nobody for nothing. I didn't have to
steal off a dead woman. I was eight years old, my father sent
me out to sell papers on a street corner. Look at those hands.
You got hands like that? That comes from those big pennies,
the old fashioned ones. They drop them into your fingers
in the wintertime. You get hands like mine. You don't know
what it's all about, my friend."

Aaron could feel his own anger begin to rise. I know what
you want the money for. The horses and the crap games. You
want to take my England money and piss it away. You yell
about me robbing a dead woman and you want to rob me. He

was on the edge of saying these things when Jake looked away.

"Hey Manny, how ya doin'?" Jake said. "How's things?"

"Oh I keep alive, Jake. And this is Louie's boy, eh?" Aaron felt a hand, warm and strong, grip his shoulder. "I'd know that face anywhere. He's a Pagurak, all right. The spitting image of Louie. My God."

Aaron turned. The man was tall and homely, his face all hooked nose and disorderly streaks of grey hair.

"My name's Manny Baumgartner," he said. "You don't remember me. I was a friend of your father's. In fact, we once lived together, when we were about your age, in Detroit. I was at your grandmother's funeral; you didn't see me. Mind if I join you for a cup of coffee?"

"What do you think of a kid steals money from his dead grandmother?" Jake said.

Baumgartner looked at Aaron's face and then down at his hands clenched desperately together on the table. He reached into his coat pocket and took out a cigar.

"This is where I came in," Baumgartner said. "You remember the arguments you used to have with Max and Sam and Louie. I used to walk in that house, I was sure somebody was going to get murdered. I hope I never hear arguments like that again as long as I live. And always about money. And you know something Jake? The more money each of you got, the more you fought about it."

"His grandmother," Jake said. "My own mother, you understand? She had everything she owned in that room. Him and that rabbi, they went up there and they took it all. Just like that. They took it and they split it up between them. What do you think Louie would say if he could see what his kid does?"

Aaron stood up slowly. The anger filled his throat. He couldn't find the right words. Son-of-a-bitch son-of-a-bitch son-of-a-bitch. . . .

"Don't do it," Jake growled. "I'm warning you, don't do it. You're my brother Louie's kid. I'm warning you, don't do it. You hear me?"

Aaron turned abruptly and marched out of Ledofski's. A grey February wind had begun to blow. Aaron turned up the collar of his overcoat and stood for a moment irresolute in the middle of Spadina Avenue. Then he turned north toward the campus. Oh Jake, don't lie like that. Con me if you have to, cheat me, even swing on me. But don't tell lies like those. I'm my father's son. We can fight like men.

Aaron felt again the warm hand on his shoulder and he turned around.

"I'm out of breath," Baumgartner said. "I've been running to catch up. Do you mind if I walk along with you?"

Aaron nodded. Baumgartner fell in beside him and he started up Spadina Avenue again in silence. Once the broad street had been all Jews. Now the signs in the stores read in German and Hungarian. The Jews had fled north. We're a suburban people now, Aaron thought. We listen to rabbis like Leiner, Anglo-Saxon Jews.

"You mustn't be so hard on your uncle," Baumgartner said. "You'd be a better man to try and understand him."

"I do understand," Aaron said. "That's what makes me so mad."

"Everybody in your family was always mad. I never saw a family like them."

"You knew my father well, didn't you? But we never went to your house; you never came to our house?"

"Louie and I grew up together. We went to Detroit after high school. We were going to study law. Baumgartner and Pagurak. But I came home and went to work for my father in the fur store. We drifted apart. We got married and you know how it is with wives. But every six months or so Louie would call me for lunch. He always had some new idea to tell me about. He was going to make us both rich. Louie was a pip."

"He was crazy for money, too, wasn't he? Like Jake and the rest of them."

Baumgartner clasped Aaron by the shoulders and turned him around. His face had turned red in the cold and his cigar had dwindled to a grey buff.

"You mustn't think that," he said. "You're a young man.

Too young to have such bitterness."

"I'm nineteen," Aaron said. "At nineteen my father was already a married man."

"You're just like him, it frightens me. When I was trying to catch you, I could see you from way back. You walk flat-footed, just like Louie. You're a real Pagurak."

"I didn't know my father very well," Aaron said. "I was only eleven, you know."

"Your father was afraid of Jake, too. He'd shout and scream at him, but when it came down to a real fight, he'd always back off. You never knew with Jake what he'd do next. It's true, you know, he once pushed your grandmother down a flight of stairs. I was in the house when it happened. When Jake got mad, it didn't matter who you were, man or woman, he'd just go after you. And when he got going, you couldn't pull him off."

"But my father wasn't like that."

"Your father had a temper too, let me tell you. He could give you a look, you would wish you were a thousand miles away. But where your father would give you a dirty look, Jake would tear you apart. I think maybe that was the real difference between your father and the others. Louie always tried to think about what he was doing. He wanted to be perfect; he wanted the world to be perfect. And when the world wasn't perfect, that wasn't Louie's fault, it was the world's. To be perfect, you need money. To make money you have to stay in one place and slug it out. That kind of patience Louie never had. That's why he got so bitter. That's why the whole family got so bitter. They wanted too much and they never really got anything. Well, this is College Street. I turn off here. Come and see me. I would like to talk to you again. You remind me so much of Louie. I'm just a block away from here. Royal Canadian Furs."

"Mr. Baumgartner, would you give any money to Jake?"

"Let me ask you, how much money is involved?"

"Almost nine hundred dollars."

"Your mother never said anything to you? She never mentioned anything to you?"

"About what?"

"Maybe I shouldn't tell you. I don't know. Louie was my friend and the things I did for your mother were nobody else's business. Some of the boys got together after your father died, you understand. We helped your mother get on her feet again. Louie had some insurance and there was one policy, three thousand dollars, made out to your mother and your grandmother. I pleaded with her, Lillian you need the money, but she made me give it all to your grandmother. She didn't want the old lady to have anything to say against Louie's memory. Now I don't know for sure where that nine hundred dollars came from, but I know for a fact none of the other boys left her anything. As for what to do with it, Aaron, what can I tell you?"

Margaret had fallen asleep at a table in the library. Her head lay cradled in her arms. Aaron picked up the books spread around her. *The Complete Poetry of Alfred Lord Tennyson. The Poetical Works of Robert Browning. The Complete Poetry and Prose of Matthew Arnold. Matthew Arnold* by Lionel Trilling. He sat down beside her and put his head in his arms. How many worlds can a man pass through in one day? From Margaret's bed to Rabbi Leiner's study to Ledofski's restaurant to Baumgartner and the old ghosts. Aaron felt himself a pilgrim, a part of all the people he had dealt with that day. Yet he belonged to none of them. He was always moving on to another world that they knew nothing about. As long as he kept moving, he would be all right.

"Give me some money," Margaret said. "I'll get us a steak."

Aaron opened his eyes. Margaret had turned to look at him, her chin still resting on her arms.

"Let's make love," Aaron said. "Right here. Right now."

"All right."

"Why are you reading all these books?"

"I'm doing an essay."

"I can see."

"I went to a lecture today, too."

"What in?"

"Nineteenth-century thought."

"Margaret, what do you think about nineteenth-century thought?"

"Give me some money for that steak."

"I'll walk over with you."

"Go home and get cleaned up. Shave. You look like hell. You always look like hell."

Aaron's room was a shambles. The mattress had been torn from the bed, even his pillowcase had been yanked off. His dresser had been pulled from the wall and all his drawers dumped out. His closet was open and all his clothes and papers lay in a huge, dirty pile in the centre of the room. Aaron stood beside it in silence for several minutes. Then he shoved the mattress back onto the bed and sat down on it. "Oh Jake, Jake," he said, out loud. "Oh my uncle Jake."

Jake had gone too far. It was like getting a sudden whiff of bad breath in a crowd. It was like eating food from someone else's plate, like sleeping in someone's unmade bed. It was like overhearing a stranger talk to himself in the street.

"How do you know it was Jake?" Margaret said.

"It had to be. Nothing was taken. The room was searched; that was all."

"But why didn't he find the money?"

Aaron took the roll of bills from his pocket and laid it on the kitchen table.

"Have you been carrying it around like that all this time?" Margaret said.

"If I hadn't have been, Jake would have got it."

"Ye gods," Margaret said. "I don't know which one of you is worse. Do you want some coffee?"

"Later. You cook a mean steak, woman."

"I got something today when I was shopping," Margaret said. "I stopped at the post office."

She reached into her purse and laid the forms on the table beside the money. They were passport applications.

"One for you and one for me," Margaret said. "You need them now to get into England. We can get work permits when we get over there."

Aaron picked up one of the applications and crackled it

between his fingers.

"We'll have to get our pictures taken too," he said. "I know a place over on Yonge Street, we can get them cheap. We'll go tomorrow morning."

"Oh Aaron." Margaret came around the table and sat in his lap. "It's our chance. We can get away from here, away from all these people. We can be alone. Maybe we can make something for ourselves."

"What do you want to be, Margaret?"

"I want to be free, Aaron. That's simple enough, isn't it? I don't want to have anyone ever again tell me I have to be someplace or I have to do something just because. I want all my time to belong to me."

"What about me? What if I tell you to do something?"

"Oh stop it, Aaron. I love you. I really do love you."

"So why don't you sew my name into your underpants like I asked you to?"

She turned around in his lap and kissed him.

"Why can't we be free here, Margaret? What's so special about being in England?"

"You're asking me that question?" Margaret said. "Look at you, all tied up inside because of your family. Look at the hold they've got on you! Now they've got their hooks into me, too. We can't even be in the same city with them. We can't even be in the same country. Funny, isn't it. This is the new world and already it has too much history. We have to go all the way to the old world to make a fresh start."

"You love me that much, Margaret?"

She kissed him again, thrusting her tongue into his mouth, pressing her lips against his until he could taste blood. The fear that overtook Aaron so often when he was with Margaret fluttered in him now. I am not used to being loved, he thought. I am used to being Jake: make your way alone in the world; keep your head down and bull your way through. I have to be so careful. I mustn't do anything to hurt Margaret.

Margaret kissed him on the neck and laid her cheek on his shoulder. She looks so old when she drops her guard Aaron thought. She feels so warm. Margaret ran her fingers over his chest and began to loosen his tie.

"Not now," Aaron said. "I have to go out."

"You'd rather go out in the cold than stay here with me."

"I have to go and see Jake for the last time. I'm taking Leiner with me."

"Oh stop, Aaron. Please, please stop. Let him alone, let yourself alone."

"It wasn't just me, Margaret. He was insulting my father, too. My father had a good name in this city and I won't let Jake throw dirt on it now. I'm going to take Leiner down there with me and we're going to tell Jake exactly what happened. We're going to throw his lies back in his face. That's the end of it, Margaret, I promise you. Goodbye and go to hell, Uncle Jake."

"And then Jake will come to your room again and then you'll go to see him again and the whole thing will just go on and on. Oh Aaron, can't you see what's happening to you? You have to cut the ties once and for all. You can't just talk about being free. You can't just sit here and make me talk about it. You have to do something yourself. You have to will yourself free. Oh God, Aaron. Don't go! Please, please don't go."

"I'm so glad you called, Mr. Pagurak," Rabbi Leiner said. He stood beside his car, turning up his coat collar against the bitter wind. "I think we should be able to settle this whole thing reasonably."

"I'm not going to give any money to Jake, rabbi."

"But why did you call me, Mr. Pagurak? Why did you get me way down here so late at night?"

"We're going to face Jake together, rabbi. We're going to tell him exactly what happened. We're going to shut him up. At least we're going to try. Come on, rabbi, this will only take a few minutes and then you can go home again."

Aaron led the way across Front Street to Union Station. As Aaron had known he would be, Jake was sitting in his cab in front of the station and when the last train for the night had given him his last fare, he left to play cards or shoot craps. This was part of Jake's Toronto. It had always seemed to Aaron the glamorous heart of the city, the taxis wheeling and swerving, their passengers dashing out of the windy street to catch trains for distant places or disappearing into the warmth and music of the Royal York Hotel across the street. Around here, everyone knew good old Jake, the waitresses in Murray's, the cops, the railway porters, the doormen in front of the hotel.

Jake saw them coming and climbed out of his cab. He was wearing an old brown overcoat without a scarf and had stuck his metal taxi driver's shield into the band of his fedora. He looked paler and older than Aaron had ever seen him before.

"Look who's here," Jake said. "You guys come to visit me? Wait a minute, I'll put on the coffee pot."

"Tell the rabbi what you told Baumgartner this afternoon," Aaron said. "About him taking the old lady's money."

"You want me to call a policeman?" Jake said. "What you did was worse than stealing. They put you in jail if you steal."

"I thought I was doing the best thing," Rabbi Leiner said. "Please try to understand that. I don't want to hurt you and I don't want to hurt your nephew. I am only trying to do what I think your mother would have wanted me to do."

"She told you what to do, eh? You got a special message from the other side?"

"Please, Mr. Pagurak. Let's try and talk. I'm sure we can work something out between the three of us. I was only trying to do what I thought was the best thing."

"You want to do the best thing, rabbi? You get the hell out of here. You hear me? You get your nose out of my business. You hear?"

"Please Mr. Pagurak, if I made a mistake, I'm sorry. From the bottom of my heart, I'm sorry. But what do you want me to do? What do you want me to say?"

Without warning, Jake struck. He brought his right arm around in an awkward, sweeping blow that knocked Rabbi Leiner to his knees. Aaron jumped at his uncle and caught his arm before he could swing again. Jake wrestled him trying to get past, trying to get at the rabbi. He lashed out with one foot and caught Leiner in the chest. Aaron felt hands pulling at him and saw others fighting with Jake. He relaxed and let himself be pulled away.

Jake thrashed against three taxi drivers. One held him by the waist and the other two tried to control his arms. Aaron saw that the old man's hearing aid had fallen out of his ear. Jake was locked into his own fury.

Aaron shrugged off the taxi drivers holding him and walked up to Jake. He took the wad of bills from his pocket and dropped it onto the sidewalk.

"I'll kill him," Jake screamed. "Lemme go! Lemme go! I'll kill him! I'll kill the little bastard! I'll kill him! I'll kill him!"

Aaron turned, helped Rabbi Leiner to his feet and started back across Front Street. All the passion and the grief withered in the end to this, a sick old man fighting in the street. I'm free of them now, Aaron thought. There's nothing more they can do to me. I'm out of it. From here on, it's just me and Margaret. At least I've still got Margaret.

1968

Dance of the Happy Shades

Alice Munro

MISS MARSALLES IS having another party. (Out of musical integrity, or her heart's bold yearning for festivity, she never calls it a recital.) My mother is not an inventive or convincing liar, and the excuses which occur to her are obviously second-rate. The painters are coming. Friends from Ottawa. Poor Carrie is having her tonsils out. In the end all she can say is: Oh, but won't all that be too much trouble, *now? Now* being weighted with several troublesome meanings; you may take your choice. Now that Miss Marsalles has moved from the brick and frame bungalow on Bank Street, where the last three parties have been rather squashed, to an even smaller place—if she has described it correctly—on Bala Street. (Bala Street, where is that?) Or: now that Miss Marsalles' older sister is in bed, following a stroke; now that Miss Marsalles herself—as my mother says, we must face these things—is simply getting *too old.*

Now? asks Miss Marsalles, stung, pretending mystification, or perhaps for that matter really feeling it. And she asks how her June party could ever be too much trouble, at any time, in any place? It is the only entertainment she ever gives any more (so far as my mother knows it is the only entertainment she ever has given, but Miss Marsalles' light old voice, undismayed, indefatigably social, supplies the ghosts of tea parties, private dances, At Homes, mammoth Family Dinners). She would suffer, she says, as much disappointment as the children, if she were to give it up. Considerably more, says my mother to herself, but of course she cannot say it aloud; she turns her face from the telephone with that look of irritation—as if she had seen something messy which she was unable to clean up—which is her private expression of pity. And she promises to come; weak schemes for getting out of it will occur to her during the next two weeks, but she knows she will be there.

She phones up Marg French who like herself is an old pupil of Miss Marsalles and who has been having lessons for her twins, and they commiserate for a while and promise to go together and buck each other up. They remember the year before last when it rained and the little hall was full of raincoats piled on top of each other because there was no place to hang them up, and the umbrellas dripped puddles on the dark floor. The little girls' dresses were crushed because of the way they all had to squeeze together, and the living room windows would not open. Last year a child had a nosebleed.

"Of course that was not Miss Marsalles' fault."

They giggle despairingly. "No. But things like that did not use to happen."

And that is true; that is the whole thing. There is a feeling that can hardly be put into words about Miss Marsalles' parties; things are getting out of hand, anything may happen. There is even a moment, driving in to such a party, when the question occurs: will anybody else be there? For one of the most disconcerting things about the last two or three parties has been the widening gap in the ranks of the regulars, the old pupils whose children seem to be the only new pupils Miss Marsalles ever has. Every June reveals some new and surely significant dropping-out. Mary Lambert's girl no longer takes; neither does Joan Crimble's. What does this mean?

think my mother and Marg French, women who have moved to the suburbs and are plagued sometimes by a feeling that they have fallen behind, that their instincts for doing the right thing have become confused. Piano lessons are not so important now as they once were; everybody knows that. Dancing is believed to be more favourable to the development of the whole child—and the children, at least the girls, don't seem to mind it as much. But how are you to explain that to Miss Marsalles, who says, "All children need music. All children love music in their hearts"? It is one of Miss Marsalles' indestructible beliefs that she can see into children's hearts, and she finds there a treasury of good intentions and a natural love of all good things. The deceits which her spinster's sentimentality has practised on her original good judgment are legendary and colossal; she has this way of speaking of children's hearts as if they were something holy; it is hard for a parent to know what to say.

In the old days, when my sister Winifred took lessons, the address was in Rosedale; that was where it had always been. A narrow house, built of soot-and-raspberry-coloured brick, grim little ornamental balconies curving out from the second-floor windows, no towers anywhere but somehow a turreted effect; dark, pretentious, poetically ugly—the family home. And in Rosedale the annual party did not go off too badly. There was always an awkward little space before the sandwiches, because the woman they had in the kitchen was not used to parties and rather slow, but the sandwiches when they did appear were always very good: chicken, asparagus rolls, wholesome, familiar things—dressed-up nursery food. The performances on the piano were, as usual, nervous and choppy or sullen and spiritless, with the occasional surprise and interest of a lively disaster. It will be understood that Miss Marsalles' idealistic view of children, her tender- or simple-mindedness in that regard, made her almost useless as a teacher; she was unable to criticize except in the most delicate and apologetic way and her praises were unforgivably dishonest; it took an unusually conscientious pupil to come through with anything like a creditable performance.

But on the whole the affair in those days had solidity, it had tradition, in its own serenely out-of-date way it had style. Everything was always as expected; Miss Marsalles herself, waiting in the entrance hall with the tiled floor and the dark, church-vestry smell, wearing rouge, an antique hairdo adopted only on this occasion, and a floor-length dress of plum and pinkish splotches that might have been made out of old upholstery material, startled no one but the youngest children. Even the shadow behind her of another Miss Marsalles, slightly, older, larger, grimmer, whose existence was always forgotten from one June to the next, was not discomfiting—though it was surely an arresting fact that there should be not one but two faces like that in the world, both long, gravel-coloured, kindly and grotesque, with enormous noses and tiny, red, sweet-tempered and short-sighted eyes. It must finally have come to seem like a piece of luck to them to be so ugly, a protection against life to be marked in so many ways, *impossible*, for they were gay as invulnerable and childish people are; they appeared sexless, wild and gentle creatures, bizarre yet domestic, living in their house in Rosedale outside the complications of time.

In the room where the mothers sat, some on hard sofas, some on folding chairs, to hear the children play "The Gypsy Song," "The Harmonious Blacksmith" and the "Turkish March," there was a picture of Mary, Queen of Scots, in velvet, with a silk veil, in front of Holyrood Castle. There were brown misty pictures of historical battles, also the Harvard Classics, iron firedogs and a bronze Pegasus. None of the mothers smoked, nor were ashtrays provided. It was the same room, exactly the same room, in which they had performed themselves; a room whose dim impersonal style (the flossy bunch of peonies and spirea dropping petals on the piano was Miss Marsalles' own touch and not entirely happy) was at the same time uncomfortable and reassuring. Here they found themselves year after year—a group of busy, youngish women who had eased their cars impatiently through the archaic streets of Rosedale, who had complained for a week previously about the time lost, the fuss over the children's dresses and, above all, the boredom, but who were drawn together by a rather implausible allegiance—not so much to Miss Marsalles as to the ceremonies of their childhood, to a more exacting pattern of life which had been breaking apart even then but which survived, and unaccountably still survived, in Miss Marsalles' living room. The little girls in dresses with skirts as stiff as bells moved with a natural awareness of ceremony against the dark walls of books, and their mothers' faces wore the dull, not unpleasant look of acquiescence, the touch of absurd and slightly artificial nostalgia which would carry them through any lengthy family ritual. They exchanged smiles which showed no lack of good manners, and yet expressed a familiar, humorous amazement at the sameness of things, even the selections played on the piano and the fillings of the sandwiches; so they acknowledged the incredible, the wholly unrealistic persistence of Miss Marsalles and her sister and their life.

After the piano-playing came a little ceremony which always caused some embarrassment. Before the children were allowed to escape to the garden—very narrow, a town garden, but still a garden, with hedges, shade, a border of yellow lilies—where a long table was covered with crepe paper in infants' colours of pink and blue, and the woman from the kitchen set out plates of sandwiches, ice cream, prettily tinted and tasteless sherbet, they were compelled to accept, one by one, a year's-end gift, all wrapped and tied with ribbon, from Miss Marsalles. Except among the most naive new pupils this gift caused no excitement of anticipation. It was apt to be a book, and the question was, where did she find such books? They were of the vintage found in old Sunday-school libraries, in attics and the basements of second-hand stores, but they were all stiff-backed, unread, brand new. *Northern Lakes and Rivers, Knowing the Birds, More Tales by Grey Owl, Little Mission Friends.* She also gave pictures: "Cupid Awake and Cupid Asleep," "After the Bath," "The Little Vigilantes"; most of these seemed to feature that tender childish nudity which our sophisticated prudery found most ridiculous and disgusting. Even the boxed games she gave us proved to be insipid and unplayable—full of complicated rules which allowed everybody to win.

The embarrassment the mothers felt at this time was due not so much to the presents themselves as to a strong doubt whether Miss Marsalles could afford them; it did not help to remember that her fees had gone up only once in ten years (and even when that happened, two or three mothers had quit). They always ended up by saying that she must have other resources. It was obvious—otherwise she would not be living in this house. And then her sister taught—or did not teach any more, she was retired but she gave private lessons, it was believed, in French and German. They must have enough, between them. If you are a Miss Marsalles your wants are simple and it does not cost a great deal to live.

But after the house in Rosedale was gone, after it had given way to the bungalow on Bank Street, these conversations about Miss Marsalles' means did not take place; this aspect of Miss Marsalles' life had passed into that region of painful subjects which it is crude and unmannerly to discuss.

"I will die if it rains," my mother says. "I will die of depression at this affair if it rains." But the day of the party it does not rain and in fact the weather is very hot. It is a hot gritty summer day as we drive down into the city and get lost, looking for Bala Street.

When we find it, it gives the impression of being better than we expected, but that is mostly because it has a row of trees, and the other streets we have been driving through, along the railway embankment, have been unshaded and slatternly. The houses here are of the sort that are divided in half, with a sloping wooden partition in the middle of the front porch; they have two wooden steps and a dirt yard. Apparently it is in one of these half-houses that Miss Marsalles lives. They are red brick, with the front door and the window trim and the porches painted cream, grey, oily-green and yellow. They are neat, kept-up. The front part of the house next to the one where Miss Marsalles lives has been turned into a little store; it has a sign that says: GROCERIES AND CONFECTIONERY.

The door is standing open. Miss Marsalles is wedged between the door, the coatrack and the stairs; there is barely room to get past her into the living room, and it would be impossible, the way things are now, for anyone to get from the living room upstairs. Miss Marsalles is wearing her rouge, her hairdo and her brocaded dress, which it is difficult not to tramp on. In this full light she looks like a character in a masquerade, like the feverish, fancied-up courtesan of an unpleasant Puritan imagination. But the fever is only her rouge; her eyes, when we get close enough to see them, are the same as ever, red-rimmed and merry and without apprehension. My mother and I are kissed—I am greeted, as always, as if I were around five years old—and we get past. It seemed to me that Miss Marsalles was looking beyond us as she kissed us; she was looking up the street for someone who has not yet arrived.

The house has a living room and a dining room, with the oak doors pushed back between them. They are small rooms. Mary Queen of Scots hangs tremendous on the wall. There is no fireplace so the iron firedogs are not there, but the piano is, and even a bouquet of peonies and spirea from goodness knows what garden. Since it is so small the living room looks crowded, but there are not a dozen people in it, including children. My mother speaks to people and smiles and sits down. She says to me, Marg French is not here yet, could she have got lost too?

The woman sitting beside us is not familiar. She is middle-aged and wears a dress of shot taffeta with rhinestone clips; it smells of the cleaners. She introduces herself as Mrs. Clegg, Miss Marsalles' neighbour in the other half of the house. Miss Marsalles has asked her if she would like to hear the children play, and she thought it would be a treat; she is fond of music in any form.

My mother, very pleasant but looking a little uncomfortable, asks about Miss Marsalles' sister; is she upstairs?

"Oh, yes, she's upstairs. She's not herself though, poor thing."

That is too bad, my mother says.

"Yes it's a shame. I give her something to put her to sleep for the afternoon. She lost her powers of speech, you know. Her powers of control generally, she lost." My mother is warned by a certain luxurious lowering of the voice that more lengthy and intimate details may follow and she says quickly again that it is too bad.

"I come in and look after her when the other one goes out on her lessons."

"That's very kind of you. I'm sure she appreciates it."

"Oh well I feel kind of sorry for a couple of old ladies like them. They're a couple of babies, the pair."

My mother murmurs something in reply but she is not looking at Mrs. Clegg, at her brick-red healthy face or the—to me—amazing gaps in her teeth. She is staring past her into the dining room with fairly well-controlled dismay.

What she sees there is the table spread, all ready for the party feast; nothing is lacking. The plates of sandwiches are set out, as they must have been for several hours now; you can see how the ones on top are beginning to curl very slightly at the edges. Flies buzz over the table, settle on the sandwiches and crawl comfortably across the plates of little iced cakes brought from the bakery. The cut-glass bowl, sitting as usual in the centre of the table, is full of purple punch, without ice apparently and going flat.

"I tried to tell her not to put it all out ahead of time," Mrs. Clegg whispers, smiling delightedly, as if she were talking about the whims and errors of some headstrong child. "You know she was up at five o'clock this morning making sandwiches. I don't know what things are going to taste like. Afraid she wouldn't be ready I guess. Afraid she'd forget something. They hate to forget."

"Food shouldn't be left out in the hot weather," my mother says.

"Oh, well I guess it won't poison us for once. I was only thinking what a shame to have the sandwiches dry up. And when she put the ginger-ale in the punch at noon I had to laugh. But what a waste."

My mother shifts and rearranges her voile skirt, as if she

has suddenly become aware of the impropriety, the hideousness even, of discussing a hostess's arrangements in this way in her own living room. "Marg French isn't here," she says to me in a hardening voice. "She did say she was coming."

"I am the oldest girl here," I say with disgust.

"Shh. That means you can play last. Well. It won't be a very long programme this year, will it?"

Mrs. Clegg leans across us, letting loose a cloud of warm unfresh odour from between her breasts. "I'm going to see if she's got the fridge turned up high enough for the ice cream. She'd feel awful if it was all to melt."

My mother goes across the room and speaks to a woman she knows and I can tell that she is saying, Marg French *said* she was *coming*. The women's faces in the room, made up some time before, have begun to show the effects of heat and a fairly general uneasiness. They ask each other when it will begin. Surely very soon now; nobody has arrived for at least a quarter of an hour. How mean of people not to come, they say. Yet in this heat, and the heat is particularly dreadful down here, it must be the worst place in the city—well you can almost see their point. I look around and calculate that there is no one in the room within a year of my age.

The little children begin to play. Miss Marsalles and Mrs. Clegg applaud with enthusiasm; the mothers clap two or three times each, with relief. My mother seems unable, although she makes a great effort, to take her eyes off the dining-room table and the complacent journeys of the marauding flies. Finally she achieves a dreamy, distant look, with her eyes focused somewhere above the punch-bowl, which makes it possible for her to keep her head turned in that direction and yet does not in any positive sense give her away. Miss Marsalles as well has trouble keeping her eyes on the performers; she keeps looking towards the door. Does she expect that even now some of the unexplained absentees may turn up? There are far more than half a dozen presents in the inevitable box beside the piano, wrapped in white paper and tied with silver ribbon—not real ribbon, but the cheap kind that splits and shreds.

It is while I am at the piano, playing the minuet from *Berenice*, that the final arrival, unlooked-for by anybody but Miss Marsalles, takes place. It must seem at first that there has been some mistake. Out of the corner of my eye I see a whole procession of children, eight or ten in all, with a red-haired woman in something like a uniform, mounting the front step. They look like a group of children from a private school on an excursion of some kind (there is that drabness and sameness about their clothes) but their progress is too scrambling and disorderly for that. Or this is the impression I have; I cannot really look. Is it the wrong house, are they really on their way to the doctor for shots, or to Vacation Bible Classes? No, Miss Marsalles has got up with a happy whisper of apology; she has gone to meet them. Behind my back there is a sound of people squeezing together, of folding chairs being opened, there is an inappropriate, curiously unplaceable giggle.

And above or behind all this cautious flurry of arrival there is a peculiarly concentrated silence. Something has happened, something unforeseen, perhaps something disastrous; you can feel such things behind your back. I go on playing. I fill the first harsh silence with my own particularly dogged and lumpy interpretation of Handel. When I get up off the piano bench I almost fall over some of the new children who are sitting on the floor.

One of them, a boy nine or ten years old, is going to follow me. Miss Marsalles takes his hand and smiles at him and there is no twitch of his hand, no embarrassed movement of his head to disown this smile. How peculiar; and a boy, too. He turns his head towards her as he sits down; she speaks to him encouragingly. But my attention has been caught by his profile as he looks up at her—the heavy, unfinished features, the abnormally small and slanting eyes. I look at the children seated on the floor and I see the same profile repeated two or three times; I see another boy with a very large head and fair shaved hair, fine as a baby's; there are other children whose features are regular and unexceptional, marked only by an infantile openness and calm. The boys are dressed in white shirts and short grey pants and the girls wear dresses of grey-green cotton with red buttons and sashes.

"Sometimes that kind is quite musical," says Mrs. Clegg.

"Who are they?" my mother whispers, surely not aware of how upset she sounds.

"They're from that class she has out at the Greenhill School. They're nice little things and some of them quite musical but of course they're not all there."

My mother nods distractedly; she looks around the room and meets the trapped, alerted eyes of the other women, but no decision is reached. There is nothing to be done. These children are going to play. Their playing is no worse—not much worse—than ours, but they seem to go so slowly, and then there is nowhere to look. For it is a matter of politeness surely not to look closely at such children, and yet where else can you look during a piano performance but at the performer? There is an atmosphere in the room of some freakish inescapable dream. My mother and the others are almost audible saying to themselves: *No, I know it is not right to be repelled by such children and I am not repelled, but nobody told me I was going to come here to listen to a procession of little—little idiots for that's what they are*—WHAT KIND OF A PARTY IS THIS? Their applause however has increased, becoming brisk, let-us-at-least-get-this-over-with. But the programme shows no signs of being over.

Miss Marsalles says each child's name as if it were a cause for celebration. Now she says, "Dolores Boyle!" A girl as big as I am, a long-legged, rather thin and plaintive-looking girl with blonde, almost white, hair uncoils herself and gets up off the floor. She sits down on the bench and after shifting around a bit and pushing her long hair back behind her ears she begins to play.

We are accustomed to notice performances, at Miss Marsalles' parties, but it cannot be said that anyone has ever expected music. Yet this time the music establishes itself so effortlessly, with so little demand for attention, that we are hardly even surprised. What she plays is not familiar. It is something fragile, courtly and gay, that carries with it the freedom of a great unemotional happiness. And all that this girl does—but this is something you would not think could ever be done—is to play it so that this can be felt, all this can be felt, even in Miss Marsalles' living-room on Bala Street on a preposterous afternoon. The children are all quiet, the ones from Greenhill School and the rest. The mothers sit, caught with a look of protest on their faces, a more profound anxiety than before, as if reminded of something that they had forgotten they had forgotten; the white-haired girl sits ungracefully at the piano with her head hanging down, and the music is carried through the open door and the windows to the cindery summer street.

Miss Marsalles sits beside the piano and smiles at everybody in her usual way. Her smile is not triumphant, or modest. She does not look like a magician who is watching people's faces to see the effect of a rather original revelation; nothing like that. You would think, now that at the very end of her life she has found someone whom she can teach—whom she must teach—to play the piano, she would light up with the importance of this discovery. But it seems that the girl's playing like this is something she always expected, and she finds it natural and satisfying; people who believe in miracles do not make much fuss when they actually encounter one. Nor does it seem that she regards this girl with any more wonder than the other children from Greenhill School, who love her, or the rest of us, who do not. To her no gift is unexpected, no celebration will come as a surprise.

The girl is finished. The music is in the room and then it is gone and naturally enough no one knows what to say. For the moment she is finished it is plain that she is just the same as before, a girl from Greenhill School. Yet the music was not imaginary. The facts are not to be reconciled. And so after a few minutes the performance begins to seem, in spite of its innocence, like a trick—a very successful and diverting one, of course, but perhaps—how can it be said?—perhaps not altogether *in good taste.* For the girl's ability, which is undeniable but after all useless, out-of-place, is not really something that anybody wants to talk about. To Miss Marsalles such a thing is acceptable, but to other people, people who live in the world, it is not. Never mind, they must say something and so they speak gratefully of the music itself, saying how lovely, what a beautiful piece, what is it called?

"The Dance of the Happy Shades," says Miss Marsalles. *Danse des ombres heureuses*, she says, which leaves nobody any the wiser.

But then driving home, driving out of the hot red-brick streets and out of the city and leaving Miss Marsalles and her no longer possible parties behind, quite certainly forever, why is it that we are unable to say—as we must have expected to say—*Poor Miss Marsalles?* It is the Dance of the Happy Shades that prevents us, it is that one communiqué from the other country where she lives.

1962

Notes on Contributors

Margaret Atwood (1939-   ) was born in Ottawa and lives on a farm near Albion, Ontario. She has published several volumes of poetry including the Governor General's Award winning *The Circle Game* (1966); a critical overview of Canadian literature, *Survival* (1972); and three novels—*The Edible Woman* (1969), *Surfacing* (1972), and *Lady Oracle* (1976).

Don Bailey (1942-   ) was born in Toronto and turned to writing while serving a sentence in Kingston Penitentiary. His published works include a novel and two collections of short stories, most recently *Replay* (1975).

Morley Callaghan (1903-   ) was born in Toronto, where he has lived most of his life. Since the appearance of his first novel, *Strange Fugitive* (1928), he has published numerous short stories, collected in *Morley Callaghan's Stories* (1959). His novels include *Such Is My Beloved* (1934), *More Joy in Heaven* (1937), the Governor General's Award winning *The Loved and the Lost* (1951), and *A Fine and Private Place* (1975).

Jim Christy (1945-   ) was born in Richmond, Virginia, and now makes Toronto his home when he's not wandering in places like Alaska. He has published two books—*The New Refugees* in 1972 and *Beyond the Spectacle* in 1973.

Austin Clarke (1932-   ) was born in Barbados and came to Canada in 1956. He has published several novels, including *Among Thistles and Thorns* (1965) and *The Meeting Point* (1967), and a collection of short stories, *When He Was Free and Young and He Used to Wear Silks* (1971).

Matt Cohen (1942-   ) was born in Kingston and now lives in Toronto. He has published a collection of stories, *Columbus and the Fat Lady* (1972), and several novels including *The Disinherited* (1974) and *Wooden Hunters* (1975).

Shirley Faessler (?-   ) was born in Toronto and has published a number of short stories that reflect immigrant Jewish life in Toronto. Her stories have appeared in such magazines as *Tamarack Review* and in such anthologies as *The Narrative Voice* (1972).

Raymond Fraser (1941-   ) was born in Chatham, N.B., where he still makes his home. His published works include four books of poems, a collection of short stories, *Black Horse Tavern* (1973), and a novel, *The Struggle Outside* (1975).

Irena Friedman (1944-   ) was born in Orenburg in the Urals and lived in Poland and Israel before moving to Canada in 1959. Her stories have appeared in such magazines as *Tamarack Review, Saturday Night,* and *Fiddlehead.*

Robert Fulford (1932-   ) was born in Ottawa and moved to Toronto at an early age. His publications include a collection of essays, *Crisis at the Victory Burlesk* (1968), and a collection of film criticism, *Marshall Delaney at the Movies* (1974). He is the editor of *Saturday Night.*

Hugh Garner (1913-   ) was born in England and grew up in the area of Toronto that he used as the setting for his most famous novel, *Cabbagetown* (1950). His other novels include *The Silence on the Shore* (1962), *The Sin Sniper* (1970), and *Death in Don Mills* (1975). *Hugh Garner's Best Stories* (1963) won a Governor General's Award.

Margaret Gibson (1948-   ) was born in Toronto, where she still lives. Her first collection of stories, *The Butterfly Ward*, was published in 1976.

David Helwig (1938-   ) was born in Toronto and teaches in the Department of English at Queen's University. He has published collections of short stories and poetry and two novels, *The Day Before Tomorrow* (1972) and *The Glass Knight* (1976).

Hugh Hood (1925-   ) was born in Toronto and teaches at the University of Montreal. He has published a collection of essays, *The Governor's Bridge Is Closed* (1973); several collections of short stories; and a number of novels including *White Figure, White Ground* (1964), *You Can't Get There From Here* (1972), and *The Swing in the Garden* (1975).

Gwendolyn MacEwen (1941-   ) was born in Toronto, where she still lives. She has published a collection of short stories, *Noman* (1972); two novels, *Julian, the Magician* (1963) and *King of Egypt, King of Dreams* (1971); and several volumes of poetry including *The Shadowmaker* (1969), which won the Governor General's Award.

Alice Munro (1931-   ) was born in Wingham, Ontario. Her first collection of stories, *Dance of the Happy Shades*, won the Governor General's Award for fiction in 1968; her more recent works include a novel, *Lives of Girls and Women* (1971), and a second collection of stories, *Something I've Been Meaning to Tell You* (1974).

Marilyn Powell (1939-   ) was born in Toronto, where she still lives and works as a freelance writer and broadcaster. "Home Grown in the East End" is Ms. Powell's first published story.

Patrick Slater is the pseudonym of Toronto lawyer John Mitchell (1880-1951), who in 1933 published *The Yellow Briar*, a collection of connected stories.

Michael Smith (1946-   ) was born in Toronto and now lives in St. Marys, Ontario. After a brief career as a reporter for the *Globe and Mail*, he turned to writing stories. His work has appeared in *Anthology* and in such periodicals as *Tamarack Review*, the *Journal of Canadian Fiction*, and *Canadian Fiction Magazine*.

David Lewis Stein (1937-   ) was born in Toronto, where he still lives and works as a town planner. He has published a number of short stories and two novels, *Scratch One Dreamer* (1967) and *My Sexual and Other Revolutions* (1971).